THE DOOR

Book Seven of The Circular Scrolls

PART ONE
BEYOND LIFE

Bridget Trafford

Grosvenor House
Publishing Limited

This book is published by
Grosvenor House Publishing Ltd
Link House
140 The Broadway, Tolworth, Surrey, KT6 7HT.
www.grosvenorhousepublishing.co.uk

A CIP record for this book
is available from the British Library

ISBN 978-1-80381-373-8

Dedication

For my daughter Alexandra
Who always insists on a happy ending

What is Love?

What is Love?
*

Is it a mountain?
Reach to the sky...
Too high
Too high
They cry
*

Is it a West Wind?
All turmoil and guile...
Too wild,
Fey child
They smile.
*

Is it an ocean?
Calm, storm and still...
Too deep
Too deep
They trill
*

Or is it a flower,
A bloom frail yet spry;
A many side bower,
Where a strong man may cry...

Ah yes, Ah yes, they sigh...
BT

Out of the night that covers me,
Black as the pit from pole to pole,
I thank whatever gods may be
For my unconquerable soul.

In the fell clutch of circumstance
I have not winced nor cried aloud.
Under the bludgeonings of chance
My head is bloody, but unbowed.

Beyond this place of wrath and tears
Looms but the Horror of the shade,
And yet the menace of the years
Finds and shall find me unafraid.

It matters not how strait the gate,
How charged with punishments the scroll,
I am the master of my fate,
I am the captain of my soul.

William Ernest Henley

We shall never cease from exploration
And the end of all our exploring
Will be to arrive where we started
And know the place for the first time

T S Eliot

This is a love story...or perhaps a story of love

SAMANTHA

There was no safety in familiar things, thought Sam. But familiar things felt safer. In truth they were just as potentially hazardous as any other subdivision of life but because you didn't have to get to know them, they reassured you and sometimes falsely so.

So to say that she missed parts of the old life would have been untrue but she did miss their familiarity. And she missed the level of assured acceptance that the old environment had implied. And amongst that she missed Steve's ready acquiescence of the elements that made her, Sam, what she was and his endless capacity for modifying his view to incorporate new elements. She wondered, in these new unfamiliar surroundings, what drove her to challenge herself like this. What was it that forced her to keep up rooting and why she had refused his offer, given without restraints, to accompany her. Kevin would say that whatever it was, when she found it she would know it because the light that shone on it and from it would leave her in no doubt.

Well, Steve was gone now. He had died tragically and not knowing how much she missed him; missed his tolerance, his fortitude, his faithfulness and his humour.

And now there was Luc, who was just as steadfast and just as sharp witted and who wanted her to –to what?

Sometimes she felt as if she was following something –or someone- and whatever it was, or whoever it was, held a torch in front of it. She could see the beam of light playing back and forth across the path they were following but then, way in front, there was dark, only the dark… Her only guide was the light of the torch up ahead and the outline of the object or figure which the light of the torch cast backwards, illuminating...

Maybe Kevin was right. Maybe she did not know why or what because she had not found it yet...

Kevin had taught her many things. He had taught her how to understand what truth was; to follow her path and if it feels right, to keep following it and if it is the right path, the means, the opportunity and the reason will make itself evident or, sooner or later, it will be blocked and you will be forced to change direction.

So I follow my path... But I can't seem to do it without the constant questioning of purpose and motivation. Why is that?

Because I learn more about myself and therefore more about the complexities of the human condition?

Because I can learn first-hand about fear and doing it anyway –reaffirming my faith by constantly taking the leap?

Because through it all I can reach my own place of safety and harmony?

Because by examining the process, I have carved a path through the jungle?

Because I'm a bloody writer and I can't stop thinking.

Because I can shoot at the moon and maybe fall in the stars?

It was a risk.

Kevin.

What would Kevin say about risks?

He'd say

What's a risk like this to the biggest risk taker in skinny jeans that I have ever met?

Is the woman who wears a T-shirt with –unwrap me for Christmas –going to shy away from this?

Sam bit her lip and looked around nervously.

But it's all for show, she murmured.

No it isn't! You have the scars to prove it. Besides there is a man out there waiting for you to find him.

Do you think so? Sam murmured.
Don't you?
Steve; Luc; Alex; Tom; Wanigi; brothers all.
A brother?

Still, there were things to do. A new home to establish; the script to collaborate on; and a new framework of life to create –something to live within and beyond.

What happens, thought Sam, when you run out of energy for such things? When you run out of physical, mental and emotional energy.

Well then, said Kevin in her head, then spiritually you will have metamorphosed in the present cycle as far as you can go and achieved a catharsis and the timing will be perfect!

Contingency plans aside, the new home itself was delightful. It was what in England would have been called a chalet bungalow. It was of wooden construction, single story, more or less, and painted pale blue. It was spacious without being gargantuanly overbearing or disproportionate, light and airy, accommodating and welcoming. It had wooden floors and plain walls, either soft toned polished pine or painted in warm, natural colours, which made you think of sunshine and spring flowers. Outside the building was surrounded on all sides by a deck veranda which was overhung by the roof, providing both shelter and shade, with steps down both front and rear, leading to the yard, a complete misnomer in real terms as it was a smooth garden area of grass, with shrubs and trees and flowers, of about an acre and surrounded by a high palisade fence with a carport to one side.

Inside there was a huge, in Sam's terms, living area with windows the length of one full wall giving views of the black hills and light on the darkest of days. There was a dining kitchen also of fair proportions done in light wood with table and chairs and a door leading out onto the back yard and giving easy access for animals of the small furry kind. There was a master bedroom with on suite shower of magnificent proportions and a dressing room. Yes, an actual room allotted for dressing. Go figure! Two extra bedrooms and a bathroom, that a baseball team and all their mascots could have happily cleansed themselves in. And then, for Sam, there was the most beautiful and best room in the house. Her office, study, snug, library, gallery and haven –her place of work and rest, achievement and solace; home of the homes. One wall was shelved. It held mostly books but interspersed here and there with creative memorabilia, anything from African figurines to native American carvings; from soft toys to crystals; from Greek urns to jewelled caskets; from abacus to polished wooden fruits; from Winnie the Pooh to dinosaurs and elephants.

One wall was glass, looking out across the rolling land to the horizon beyond. Sam's desk, with its classic Winnie the Pooh with bees and plains Indian with wolf, figurines, stood in front of this window.

The room also had her workstation, two armchairs, audio and video players and a bureau. The walls were pale yellow and the wood was mellow. There were several large, squashy bean bags which the furry inhabitants had a habit of commandeering. It was untidy in an uncluttered way and a quick survey of its contents revealed everything that was important to her but not in any prioritisation. It gave you the elements but not the depth. There was a theme here but it would take a very determined excavationist to uncover it. Perhaps, thought Sam, that's the way I like it.

Since Steve's death and the untangling of the web that had surrounded and linked her life with Luc's, she spent a lot of time alone in this house. The number of boxes had dwindled and the rooms had gradually taken on a personality, hers mostly, but also one of their own. She had spent a lot of time reading, writing and meditating and her dream world, which trauma and emotional challenge had inhibited, had once more come alive. And they in turn had opened the door to memories of dreams, or dreams of memories, from the past, images that she believed had significance for her now.

One in particular had repeated itself over many years. Details varied. But essentially the dream was the same. There was a long path or corridor leading to water, a pool of some kind, not tidal, safe. Sometimes it was screened with a glass door, or barrier of some kind. She was led down the path or corridor to the glass door or screen, taken by the hand and led to the waters edge. The clothes she was wearing gently removed or falling away, leaving her naked. The firm gentle hand taking hers and gradually leading her down into the water. The water rippling, soothing, accepting, removing emotional strain; all risk gone. Just acceptance and love. These elements were all the same. So was the guiding hand. Who was he? For it was a he –the man of her dreams or the dream of a man; brother, lover, guardian angel –all of them? The final frontier; the door to beyond...

Wanigi had been a brother; but there had been another brother, an older brother, who had never had chance to be an older brother because he had died in a tragic accident before her birth. She could recall what he had looked like, somehow; she could recall he had blonde hair...

She recollected a movie she had once seen about ghosts coming to terms with ghosts; acceptance as the tool for understanding, the key to the last door...

So many inner guide meditations used the 'lead down through water' method, to access the inner sanctum. She had done it many times herself. Maybe the time had come to risk the link with another soul on a path; maybe the view from a shared path, even if only for a while, would give a whole new dimension. Maybe the time had come to see what the water was like beyond the glass screen. It had after all never been a solid door. She had always been able to see through it. Maybe it wasn't a door at all, just a symbolic threshold.

Again she thought of Steve and his steadfast wall of love. That she had bulldozed down. How safe that wall had been.

Suddenly she missed him terribly. But I'd have become a monster, she whispered to him. And you'd have lived on with the monster but I couldn't have lived with myself.

Does that make me crazy?

Right from the start the door, the archway, had huge significance. She gazed out through the expanse pf glass to the rolling hills of the Buffalo Gap beyond.

I believe in circles; the end is also the beginning.

I believe I am the architect of my own fate.

I believe in rainbows...

It was clearly not time to settle down, to build a cocoon, to create a wall. No. It was time to walk through the door...

VIVIAN

When it happened, all she could remember was sitting in the favourite armchair and holding the crystal Wanigi had given her all those years ago, and gazing into its amber depths...

"I presume you know where we are" Kevin had said..

"That's not how it works !" said Sam. "You always know where we are."

She gazed around. What the hell had she been reading? India-yeah, that was it. India again...

The East...Siva...

'The East bowed low before the West
In patient, deep disdain,
She let the legions thunder past
And plunged in thought again'
A Mathew Arnold quotation in a book by...

And then the world went black... Then grey... Then white... And she was suddenly bombarded with noise; the kind of noise you get when men are destroying men... explosions, gunfire, yelling, screaming and then the smell... The smell of cordite, blood and death...And it was cold, bitterly, limb numbing cold, the coldness of the Arctic... And she was watching ... Oh God, what was she watching?

It was difficult to tell because the picture kept switching, as if an old slide projector was in operation but whoever was doing the operating was choosing what to put up on the screen randomly, to create impact whilst destroying cohesion. ..

There were lines and groups and camps of people, more than it was possible to count, spread over a wild, harsh, barren, snow covered landscape; and whoever they were, wherever they were, they were in the grip of circumstances which were destroying them, physically and metaphysically, because it was obvious, even to an inexperienced eye, that extreme physical conditions had incapacitated them to the point of immobility, so demoralised them that every movement was an act of unparalleled will and that for some the will had died somewhere back on the track.

She was watching a camp that was just starting to move at dawn and it was evident, not only that the environment in which they had spent that night had taken them to the brink of human suffering but also that there were many who would not rise from it.

There were women and children, men, young and old; Indians? Clearly from a country where such conditions did not prevail and they were just sitting, singly, in small groups, just waiting. Waiting for death...

There were soldiers, Europeans among them, walking, some on horseback; but even these, possibly more greatly inured to a climate of frost and snow, even these were disheartened, almost incapacitated beyond their ability to command or serve... beyond their capability to hold rifle or sabre.

And they were afraid; all of them were afraid, palpably so...their fear flowed over her.

There appeared to be some difficulty in organising the order and precedent of the march. The advance guard seemed to be mixed up with the baggage train and camp followers, as if the only motivation possible was to get to the front and get away at all costs.

It looked as if they had bivouacked in the open, literally, for there were few tents, but Sam could see that their next challenge was to attempt the passage of a gorge, long, narrow and shut in on either hand by cliffs so high that surely no rays of the winter sun could ever reach the valley floor. And the only sound emanating from it was that of a powerful mountain torrent racing through it, at the edge of a narrow track, sometimes on one side, sometimes on the other...

Sam cried aloud in horror and pain, every muscle braced for the impact of more and the slide changed again...

There was a new sound, felt rather than heard; the reverberation of an echo, deep through the defile, the resonance of thousands of tramping feet...

Now there was a group of soldiers in front of her; the grim jaws of the pass behind them; clearly soldiers because they wore the remnants, the battered, torn faded remnants of a uniform, a long slow line of soldiers, dejected, stumbling, some through the icy waters of the river, some through snow which came up over their boots to their knees, some clearly injured. There was little attempt by comrade to help comrade, though some tried, for all were beyond the purpose that only hope could give them... They were moving so slowly. At the front was a soldier on horseback, clearly an officer, who kept looking behind to check the troop following him and also scanning the path before him and the heights above him, calm but clearly tense. His face was thin and taut as if hunger and sleepless vigilance had become the daily trial. The pass had narrowed even more here, if that was possible, and there was another mounted officer bringing up the rear of the small, lifeless contingent, watching the men in front, also glancing nervously at the rock outcrops on both sides that hemmed them in. They were trapped in this rocky defile with no way to retreat and only this treacherous, rock strewn, narrow crevice as a means of escape. The narrow but fast flowing river surged on their right and occasionally a man stumbled and slipped with one leg into the water. Sometimes the comrade behind or in front stopped to pull him out. More often he was left to flounder until the officer at the rear caught up to him and hauled him free. These men were not captives but they were already defeated.

Sam desperately wanted to close her eyes but it was not possible.

Suddenly there was a rush of noise, loud and abrasive and terrifying and hordes of tribesmen, bearded, with wild hair and ragged garments flailing out behind them, were leaping, jumping, falling from the rocks and crevices above, like armed lemmings, waving ugly pointed knives and cutlasses and rifles. There were others above, safely positioned behind breastworks, clearly excellent marksmen, easily picking off stragglers, dealing out death with impunity.

The soldiers seemed to be shocked into rigidity by the fighting numbers of the assailants whose sum far outweighed their own, blocking their route forward and back, and forcing them to fight in what could only be described as a cleft in rock. Any order there had been disintegrated in panic, men and followers abandoning baggage, arms, ammunition in an attempt to lighten their load and gain the end of the pass.

The two officers in particular she could see quite distinctly. Both were relatively young-thirties maybe-both were dressed in red- one dark and narrow faced; one blond, gold and silver blonde; both hatless; both with rifle and sword. For a fraction of a second the troop was frozen in time, giving her a chance to see them clearly, to read their expressions. Then the men at the front, finding their way blocked by the more daring of the enemy who were riding in amongst the column, cutting down stragglers, turned and ran backwards, pushing their comrades out of the way, trampling the dead and the dying, in a desperate bid to retreat and escape the carnage. The dark headed officer at the rear tried to hold them but he stood no chance. It was a rout. Their action was so violent he was unhorsed, his mount rearing in terror and plunging away through the running foot soldiers. His blond counterpart jerked his horse around on its haunches and set it galloping back to him and bent down to drag him into the saddle. But his horse was shot from under him. He stood up and momentarily glanced at the wounded animal. Then he looked up and knew it was too late anyway. He put his revolver to the horse's head and pulled the trigger. The hordes were upon them and they were both on the ground, both fighting, standing back to back and fighting for their lives...

A bend in the track prevented Sam from seeing what was happening to the foot soldiers but she could hear them; she could hear their screams... Her vision was occupied with these two last combatants fighting for themselves and each other, because that was what they were trained to do-to the last man-even though there was no hope; none at all... Then a huge, bearded tribesman armed with a curved blade slashed forcefully at the dark haired soldier. And he went down. The blonde officer registered the attack but could not avert it. He glanced down, saw the severity of the wound and did the only thing he could. He straddled the dying man's body and fought like a demon. But what chance did one man have in this Armageddon? What chance did he stand... A sabre cut slashed into his neck and his right arm hung limp. He tossed the sword into his left hand and went on fighting. Though besmeared and bloody, the upper part of the blade shone like glass, as if in reward for its toil it had earned good care. Now there were three about him, hacking and cutting. He parried two severe blows but at the third his sword blade gave in and snapped, a portent to its master and he fell, first to his knees and then, deliberately it seemed, across the body of his friend and comrade. And the men with the wicked knives, shrieking in triumph, fell upon the two fallen men... And when they finally moved away, some scaling back up the cliffs like monkeys, some in pursuit down the defile, there was nothing of man or life remaining; just heaps of bloodied rags and some shining, faithful relics...

Her last visions were of moving along a route, where little groups of camp followers, clearly starving, frostbitten, to judge by their limbs, many gibbering like idiots in bedlam, passed by, the tribesman not bothering to kill them but only to strip them and leave the elements to do their work. Naked, they strove to hold on to each other in a bid to forestall the inevitable end...

And further forward her gaze swept... To see a pass, the narrowest yet, almost choked with corpses, evidence of unrelenting butchery meted out to the unarmed and the walking wounded...

How many have died? How many... It was thousands... Surely she had read that...

And Sam could bear it no longer and cried out in protest... And tears, a useless offering, many years too late, streamed down her cheeks and then the noise faded, moving further and further into the background and leaving the stone cold silence of the grave...

She was finally able to close her eyes, to unclench her teeth and her fists. She did not move. She simply stood where she was, drinking in the blessed silence and calm whilst the tears, the only evidence left of the debacle, dried on her cheeks, leaving them taut and sore.

Quiet normality had returned and when she finally opened her eyes the scene had changed. It was warm, with the warmth of a fading day that had known extreme heat. A small wind was blowing and in the sun's last rays she could see that there was a gathering of riders in the near distance. She shaded her eyes. They appeared to be in uniform. One of their number had peeled off and was approaching. Offering her a closer look. That would be good.

"I don't know what the hell all that was about but I think we might be in India now Kev. Maybe 19th century judging by...Kev? Kevin!! Where the..."

The distant figure that had detached from the others was no longer distant. Something in his manner alerted Sam, who was used to participants in her pageants being completely oblivious to her presence.

There had been one or two who could...some subliminal connection which had allowed them into each other/s lives... Siva... that was India too...

Surely this soldier couldn't see her? Surely he was not looking at her?

My God, he could! He was! He could see her!

Hell and damnation!

What possible connection could she have with a soldier!

Damn it, where was that rat?

The red blue and black mirage came steadily towards her. Rooted to the spot, Sam could only stare transfixed. His helmet was black, a tall, black shako, worn by officers in a British army in the 18th and 19th century, with the close fitting scarlet jacket sporting gold braid and tight, figure hugging dungarees which, if she remembered correctly, were called overalls. The overall (!) impression was one of extreme height, not only the man but the horse he rode, a black stallion with exquisite lines and a supercilious expression. The helmet largely covered his face but she could just see vivid dark blue eyes, almost black, wearing a sleepy, indolent, slightly querulous expression.

He had been absorbing her attire as much as she had his. She glanced down monetarily nonplussed that she was still wearing the denim jeans, white T-shirt and boots she had that morning.

Self-composure was quite clearly a necessary attribute of the officer class as he demonstrated by his next move. He reached up and removed the headgear and set it in front of him on the saddle and said

"Good evening, ma'am, can I be of assistance?"

He was possibly the most beautiful member of the male species that she had ever laid eyes on. His hair was blonde, streaked with sun scorched gold and silver, mismanaged straight and gently lifting in the wind and his skin was tanned a deep honey brown. His mouth was wide and sensitive, a nice balance to the thinking, blue-black eyes. But his fascinating eyebrows were hypnotic, black and slightly arched, reiterating the question he had just posed. He had the easy confidence of a man who knows his assets but has little interest in them. Maybe, in youth he had been shy…but with maturity had come an indifference, born of suffering…and perhaps loss…

\Sam surprised herself with such thoughts. And she simply stared at him unable to think of anything that could possibly explain her presence there before him. Her reaction to him must have been obvious. He must get it any time he made a new acquaintance, female or male.

So he tried again.

"I can see that you are taken aback by my sudden appearance, as am I by yours. Perhaps we should repair to a quiet corner in order to acquire a mutual understanding?"

It was like taking elocution lessons. His voice was deep, resonant yet soft, like being stroked with warm velvet. She didn't know whether he was inviting her to his lodgings, his stables or his bed and to be perfectly honest she really didn't care. He apparently could also read minds because his perfectly shaped lips curved into a dazzling smile and his eyebrows went a little higher as he said

"Nothing untoward I do assure you! You are however dressed a little –shall we say unconventionally and it might be better if we conducted our interview somewhere more private?"

Sam nodded.

"Will you allow me to escort you?"

Sam nodded again. Anywhere…

After a moment's consideration he swung one long leg over his saddle, dismounted, took the reins over his horse's head, grasped them in his right hand and offered her his left arm. Sam watched, hoping, praying that her thoughts were not written on her face. The swift Indian dusk was upon them and an enormous moon was rising, drawing ghostly silhouettes from a variety of unknown structures all around. Sam linked her arm through his and was glad of it.

"To my bungalow I think" he said conversationally. "It is quiet at that end of the cantonment and most of the officers are at a mess dinner. I am on duty so am thankfully excused."

The night was warm, his arm was firm and he smelled of warm leather and soap. There had not been a man in her ;ife since Luke; that seemed a long time ago...

They reached the end of the bungalows much too soon for Sam and the horse gave a soft whinny as they approached the last one. Clearly the stables and his companions were at the back of the building. A tall, spare man with black, streaked with grey, hair and a relatively pale complexion, penetrating hawk eyes and a hooked nose, came quickly towards them, taking the reins from his master without comment and with only the merest glint in his eyes to suggest surprise at Sam's presence, although it was obvious that he could see her. The officer looked down at her. His face was in shadow but she could tell he was smiling.

"If he says anything they won't believe him anyway! You are not in crinoline or sari and they will think he was drunk." He made to turn away and then added

"He will not talk. He does not talk. And he certainly doesn't drink. You are quite safe."

He guided her up the steps on to a veranda which appeared to lead both ways around the bungalow and then pushed open the door which led into a large, airy sparsely furnished lounge. There were two armchairs, the legs of which looked as if they had suffered from some form of non-human activity, a small table and a desk beneath the window, similarly defiled; currently the shutters were drawn. A small lamp burned on a sideboard in one corner and a partially open door on the right hand side gave a glimpse of a severe functional bed covered with a white counterpane. The room was austere in the extreme and there was an indefinable sense of loss which seemed to permeate the very air. It was at odds with the composed, smiling man whose living quarters it clearly was. Sam turned quickly and caught him studying her with something of that loss in his eyes. Then it was gone and the lazy considering expression was back.

"Would you like something to drink?"

"Yes, definitely. And food?"

He seemed surprised but clapped his hands and another man, small this time and older, with wrinkles that told their own tale, emerged from regions at the back of the bungalow to present himself before them.

"Could we have –tea?" He looked across at her, his eyebrows asking the question to which Sam nodded vigorously.

"And a whisky for me and –"

"Whatever you've got" said Sam. "I'm famished!"

His eyes were filled with amusement and fascination. The average Victorian woman did not have a recognisable healthy appetite Sam supposed. How could they in whale bone corselets. Explanations were going to be necessary and somewhat complex but like any good soldier –or rat –dealing with the essentials came first. And in this instance it meant food.

The tea and the whisky came first. It arrived in a very large pot with a very small cup and saucer. Sam looked at it dubiously.

"Do you have anything bigger? To drink out of I mean."

Bearer and soldier exchanged a glance.

"Fetch my travelling mug".

The bearer disappeared and returned some moments later carrying a respectably large tin mug.

"Perfect!" said Sam.

She hefted up the teapot with some difficulty and filled the mug to the brim whilst the bearer looked on with a bemused expression on his face, his small hands darting back and forth as if protesting the curtailment of his duties. Sam heaped five spoonfuls of sugar into the mug, it was a very small spoon, and stirred vigorously. She looked up and caught them both watching her and the spoon. She shrugged. It was a very small spoon. Only the dishonest claim to like tea with no sugar. She turned towards the bearer and asked

"What's your name?"

He looked startled and glanced appealingly at his master.

"His name is Ali and he has been with me for more than 25 years. My name is Vivian; Captain Vivian Ashley –Forbes."

"Vivian!"

"And yours?"

"Vivian. From the Latin, used by the Romans, meaning alive."

"Erudite as well as beautiful. An alluring combination! And yours?"

"Could we have the food first? The whole explanation thing could take some time."

"Of course. Please forgive me. Ali –"

Ali disappeared into the nether regions at the back of the bungalow.

"Who is Kevin?"

"Kevin!" said Sam in some alarm.

"I heard you speak the name as I approached, in some agitation if I remember correctly."

"Ah- that's going to take even longer" said Sam with a sigh. His mesmeric dark eyes were watching her intently, his eyebrows lifting and lowering as if in response to some complex and still contained emotion.

"How long have you got?"

He responded to her literally.

"I am on duty all night but do not have to go out again until dawn, providing all remains quiet."

Sam felt a small shiver run through her. Fear? Anticipation? Both and more...

"I am certain –"she stopped as the food arrived. Later. He had all night.

The food was a delight. Sweet, coconut flavoured dahl and chapatis. She piled spoonfuls of the dahl onto the bread, rolled them up and bit into them lustily. Glancing up at Ali, who was hovering, she said with her mouth full,

"'Licious! Wonnerful!" and reflected that she sounded exactly like the anonymous Kevin.

She swallowed and added,

"Did you make it yourself?"

Ali hesitated, looked at his master, who nodded and said "My wife was a good cook."

Vivian answered Sam's unspoken question.

"They have been with me for many years, Ali since I was a boy - since before, before...his wife died some ten years past..." He stopped and the look was there again in his eyes. Sam finished her last chapatti, licked her fingers and got to her feet. They had both watched her performance with a kind of fascinated suspense, as if the process was the prelude to something more and not just her normal eating practice. She went across to Ali, put her hand on his arm and kissed him on the cheek.

"Well it was wonderful. Thank you – both- and I am sorry."

She looked at his proud, well formed face, wrinkled now but once very handsome and said curiously

"Don't officers, Sahibs of any kind, tend to have armies of serving people?" She couldn't bring herself to say servants, especially as Ali seemed more like an old uncle than anyone who waited tables.

Vivian replied cautiously

"Ali has piggybacked me when I was small and fought at my side in combat. When the fighting was over I was pretty well good for nothing when I got back here and he dismissed all the servants and took care of all my needs, as he always had. He and Mohammed of course, for the horses. I believe he thought that was the best way to contain gossip."

He looked at Ali with a wry smile of affection.

"He gets in help if he needs it."

Sam glanced from one to the other.

"That was a very honest answer" she said.

Vivian smiled at her.

"You like honesty?" he said.

"Yes. And I hate gossip. Although I know it must be an occupational hazard in a place like this."

"I suppose all communities suffer from it. But here in India- well, the speed and distance at which it travels sometimes passes belief!"

"Perhaps it's as well then that only a select few can see me?"

"Perhaps. That will depend on the other restraints that situation poses."

His gaze was intent; his expression indecipherable.

Ali returned to the kitchens, the opportunistic appearance of this new mem'saab apparently meeting with his approval and Sam and Vivian were left alone. He appeared to have recovered himself for he smiled and asked

"Now do I get my story?"

"Okay. Kevin. But you must promise –"

"I promise nothing. Only to listen."

He was going to need more than listening sklls, Sam reflected.

Where to begin? At the beginning.

"When I was young I was a bit of a loner, and a bookworm–"

"A bookworm?"

"Yes –you know –someone who reads a lot of books."

"Yes I see."

"Well there was this particular book and as I read it I seemed –I fell –"

How in hell did you explain to a 19ᵗʰ century soldier of the queen that you'd fallen into a book, met a rat, who incidentally became your spirit guide, taken on a new personality and gone on a mystical journey involving a lot of other animals, a lot of dicey adventures, an uncomfortable amount of water, and a citadel full of mystery and death?

So she tried again.

"I've always had a sort of inner voice" said Sam cautiously. "When I was young I gave it a personality –well a body really –"she looked at him anxiously.

"Please do continue. I'm fascinated."

"A rather unusual personality and he became very real –"

"He?"

"He? Yes he- well after a while he became very real, so real in fact that I couldn't –I didn't –"

"You couldn't tell if he was real or not?"

"Yes" said Sam, "that's it! In fact sometimes I felt that real was with Kevin and the rest was unreal and then I began to wonder what was real anyway?"

Vivian said quietly

"Reality is a very subjective thing." It came out so calmly, so matter of fact that Sam felt her spirits rise.

"Yes exactly. And so if it's reality that is subjective then it must follow surely that the individual can change his or her own reality."

There was a pause.

"Yes" said Vivian, a little lift of surprise in his voice as if the concept was new but recognized. "But what about this He, this Kevin? Is he still around? Are we looking at the old archetypal tripart affiliation here?" The comment was teasing but oddly serious.

"The best shape to hang a drama on?" said Sam with a laugh.

"I think I may be losing some of the threads here."

"Do you like small furry things?" said Sam.

"What! I am lost again. If you ride a horse the way you think we will all need to be on the alert!"

Really! thought Sam. That was a distinctly sexist comment. Some things never change. She said fiercely

"You think that having an agile, immaginative mind necessarily precludes a logical brain which can grasp commonplace logistics and fundamentals?"

See Kevin! Wasp woman hasn't been completely overrun by Miss flopsy bunny!

Vivian's eyebrows were in his hair line and his eyes were shining with a kind of fascinated addiction. And then he laughed and said

"I wish –"he stopped. "Please go on. I did not intend to cause offence in any way."

Sam said

"OK. But it's not easy –"

Vivian said

"Please. I promise to follow your intellectual summersaults to the best of my ability, and without interruption."

Sam looked at him sharply but there was no mocking in his steady gaze so she tried and strangely enough the words flowed easily as if she was back there, walking the hills and vales, contending with the dangers and all that water, working it all out again with Kevin at her side, guiding, explaining, illustrating, hypothesizing and castigating. . When she reached the marble courtyard with the images of liquidising warriors and the doors to the citadel, she paused and looked at him.

If she was expecting derision or disbelief she saw none, only curiosity and understanding.

"Does your spirit guide have a name?"

"Kevin" said Sam.

"Ah, so this is Kevin! So he is still with you?"

"Yes" said Sam. "That is – we had lost touch –well I had lost touch. All my fault. I probably thought I could manage on my own –until recently that is –"

"A rat as a spirit guide –that is very Indian. In some parts the rat is cherished, taken care of, fed, and allowed to live in the temples and shrines."

So he was curious and considering; perhaps non-judgmental; sufficiently so to embark on an explanation of how she ended up here. Perhaps she should start with past life regression? It had, after all, motivated, coloured and enhanced her early life and determined the direction she took. Perhaps then between them they could figure out how she had ended up in 19th century India, dressed in habitual denim, being visible to one man and his two closest companions and no one else.

Okay. No time like the present.

"Kevin and I did a lot of exploring together when I was younger. We travelled to the American plains, well about this time really, and lived among the Native Americans. In fact I was a Native American, a boy, who led his mother and his sister many miles to join another tribe after his had been massacred. I made a friend there, who became my brother. He was blind but with far reaching inner vision and - that's a whole story on its own really. After that Kevin and I travelled to South Africa in the 1700s following a young boy who had escaped from the slave pens in Southern Africa and was trying to find his sister who had been abducted by slave traders and sold."

She looked at him for signs of scepticism or derision again but all she saw was a fascination with the spoken word that was painting images that it looked as if he could see.

Suddenly he said

"If my eyes were mirrors I could see my soul; but they are windows, so only other souls can see who I really am'"

Sam was catapulted out of her deliberations and into another time and just as quickly fell back again.

"What did you say?" she snapped.

He looked startled and vaguely embarrassed. He mumbled

"Oh, nothing. Just something that came into my head."

"Where did it come from?" Shock made her sharp.

Those were her words! A very long time ago now. In Africa. An image flashed into her mind; a woman, very tall and very straight, with skin like polished mahogany and eyes like peat pools. And there was another image, but this one was on the very edge of her consciousness almost beyond her grasp...time twirled...

Straight, broad shoulders, almost too broad for the small waist, as if the adult had projected them upwards in advance of the boy's torso; narrow hips. Tight muscled and flat. Nice. But a disturbingly intellectual seriousness in some way, as if the parts that fitted together so well were missing a vital element...*if my eyes were mirrors I could see my soul; but they are windows, so only others can see who I really am...*

But that wasn't true in this case. *She* couldn't see, not yet, he had shuttered the mirrors and the windows...

For Sam, the obvious intellect was entrancing in one so beautiful...

He watched her watching him, one hand on his hip, gawky, but like a colt, peering through the windswept hair, flicking it aside. He looked healthy, naïve and just a bit mysterious.

Sam gave herself a mental shrug. This was not the place and certainly not the time to be falling in love...

Somewhere in the future, or in the past, in a hot, parched alien landscape interspersed with forest, the *tuink?* the plum-headed parakeet making contact with his brothers...echoed down a lost corridor in time...

"I don't know. Is it important?" He had recovered his composure and was now blithely curious, his attention diverted from the words to Sam's reaction to them.

"It's actually very important" Sam said tightly, trying ineffectually to separate the emotional threads one from another and becoming hopelessly entangled.

"How could you possibly know about that" she said wonderingly.

Africa and the lovely Noni who had captured the heart of an American hunter and shown Sam what love looked like for the first time. A beautiful African girl ...

"For she was beautiful. Her beauty made the bright world dim'" she murmured and stopped.

"That's Shelley" Vivian said.. "The Witch of Atlas."

She was still looking at him, still saying nothing. She had been telling him about Africa, about Kevin; about Mogo and Noni... And she had been picturing Noni and how the artist's hands had shaped her with love...

He smiled then, a warm, knowledgeable smile. He said

"I believe that telepathic communication works all ways."

She stared at him and then smiled back.

"Yes. I believe it does."

Vivian said suddenly

"Yes. Do you believe it all, what's happened to you...what you've seen? Do you believe it's true?"

And Sam laughed and said

"That doesn't matter. All that matters is that it's true for whoever is doing the believing!"

He nodded in acknowledgement and said

"Will you continue then?"

She nodded. Maybe if she continued she would make some sense out of what had just happened. *Somewhere in the future, or in the past, in a hot, parched alien landscape interspersed with forest, the tuink? of the plum- headed parakeet making contact with his brothers...echoed down a lost corridor in time...*

"In my late teens I spent most of my time between out of body investigations with Kevin and personal and sexual explorations with my best friend Steve."

"How old are you?" said Vivian, startled. "Sorry! I must apologise. A gentleman doesn't ask a lady how old she is" he added.

" OK. Not a lady. 37" said Sam.

"37?"

"What's the matter? Don't tell me –I look 10 years older!"

"No. No! Absolutely not. You look like a young girl. Most women of that age look –look –well, they'd probably have had half a dozen or more children by then and are considered matrons."

"Well there you go. Let's just say things have moved on in 100 plus years!"

There was silence for a few minutes while Vivian absorbed the meaning of her last statement and Sam realized that he was grappling with the concept of being face to face with the future.

"So here and now, in 1867, you haven't been born?"

"I think he's got it!" said Sam with a smile. There was no response, just the steady navy blue stare and the flickering eyebrows. So she went on.

"In all previous instances I have either been regressed to an individual of the era in which I found myself or I have been an observer, watching events and individuals as if on a screen. This –"and she waved her hand about to indicate present circumstances, "this is completely new to me. You can apparently see me, as can your bearer and your syce but others can't. Also I have not been translated into an individual of this time but have remained exactly as I am in my own time, not to say exactly what I was standing up in this morning, but able to interact with you all instead of just watching."

She paused again, then said anxiously

"How far back did I lose you? Am I making any sense at all?"

He spent so long in answering that she thought the scenario had changed once again, the way it had when she and Kevin had dipped in and out of circumstances to discuss their implications. Then he said

"I do not fully understand the concepts you are presenting to me but I can feel a response to them; as if their teaching has come to help me understand and maybe accept something else. And I can see…"

They sat looking at each other with that understanding hovering between them like a mirage on a hot desert.

Then he said

"And I have read Indian texts like the Mahabaharata, and others, which perhaps enable me..." He paused. Then he said "What do you do in your 20 th century world?"

"I'm a writer" said Sam.

"Tell me. You write about regression obviously, but what about characters?"

"My main character, in my stories, does not usually have a description" said Sam.

"What, none? Why is that?"

"Not a physical description anyway. Nor mental. You find out about her or him from the way they behave, the way they react, their humour, their concerns, their choices and their feelings. I think my reason for writing is more about the exposition of ideas than story telling. If you talk to someone, they attach the words to you and react to you; they may lose the words, the thoughts and understandings that they represent. But if they read the words in print, each word, and each sentence will be interpreted in the light of what they already know, believe and understand. That still may mean rejection of your main ideas but that doesn't matter because even in the act of rejection there is some affirmation of something else. But whatever interpretation is placed on the words, it is theirs, to accept or not. And they might read it a bit, cover to cover, or not at all; now, or years later, in the light of new experience. In some way it has been incorporated for personal use. I like that. That's why I write."

"But your original meaning might have been lost."

"Why should that matter? There has been a change; a butterfly has opened its wings and the world has changed, albeit infinitesimally; with the very consideration of the words, change takes place and change is good. And-"

Vivian raised his eyebrows and she went on

"And I don't pad out the main characters because I want the character to be available to every reader as a sort of jug, vessel, into which they can pour their own thoughts and dreams and hopes."

"A temporary alter ego?"

"Yes. They will have thoughts and ideas but no personality traits to react against."

"Because that might cause a blockage in the transferal of ideas?"

"Yes. I want everyone to form his or her own impression of my character. I want it to be the tiny grain of sand in their oyster world, an irritant, the beginning of their pearl..."

"It's the oyster not the grain of sand that creates the pearl" said Vivian.

"Exactly!" She beamed at him. Maybe the thinking man becomes extinct later; or maybe I'm looking in the wrong places.

"If you remove the potential mirror from the individual they are forced to look at themselves?"

Sam gazed at him. He was so good looking you could be forgiven not anticipating a brain.

"Have I understood?" Vivian persisted.

Sam nodded, still staring. She shook herself and went on,

"And I try and include humour. Comic relief Shakespeare called it. The Greeks too. I think it softens the landing of the more strident ideas and if it gets a smile from the reader it may open their hearts and minds and the ideas might just slither in and settle and create their own unique significance."

He smiled and looked as if he was about to say something else and then there came a rap on the door and the moment was sliced in two. Vivian stood up abruptly and crossed the room, opened the door and went out onto the veranda. There was a muffled exchange and he returned, buttoning his jacket and reaching for his sword.

"My sergeant requires my attention to something in the troop lines. I do not think it will take very long. I will have Ali fetch water so that you might have a bath. I imagine you would care to refresh yourself. If you give him your clothes he will see to it that they are washed, dried and pressed for the morning." He paused, made to leave and then turned back

"And your name?"

"Samantha" said Sam. "Long for Sam."

"Ah." The eyebrows wiggled.

"I cannot call you Sam. I have a Sergeant called Sam." He frowned. "Indian dialects emphasise syllables. I will call you Samanthar."

With that he swung round abruptly and left the room leaving Sam wondering how she and Ali were going to cope with this new situation.

She need not have worried and as Ali busied himself with the preparations she wondered if this exercise was not new to him. Although the rooms and décor gave no sign of it perhaps there had once been a lady about the house. And didn't bachelors live in bunches?

Ali's expertise in the bathing ritual was unchallenged. The bath, in a medium sized room with a marble floor, at the back of the bungalow, was basic but adequate, the water was warm and smelled faintly of rose petals and the towels were thick and plentiful and he seemed to manage the whole operation without the slightest hint of voyeurism or servitude, although she did let him abdicate from the pouring of jug fulls of warm water over her head. Too much for both of them she thought and managed it quite nicely on her own. It was, after all, what you did with babies and puppies even now, unless you wanted to drown them.

It was indeed wonderful to feel clean and sweat free and when she had stepped out of the bath and swathed herself in towels Ali came quietly in, gathered up her clothes, including a very scanty pair of black and red knickers, without a trace of a raised eyebrow, and disappeared once more. As she had no change of garments at her disposal, Sam curled up in a nest of towels on the small sofa in the sitting room. She was just wondering whether or not to do some unobtrusive investigating when the door opened and Vivian strode back in. Tossing his forage cap on a chair and unbuckling his sword he folded himself on to the sofa facing her and stretched out his legs and sighed.

As if in answer to her unasked question he said

"Just a small matter of little importance really. A trooper with too much to drink and a wife with too much to say. Sergeant Harbour could have dealt with it easily but was reluctant to pronounce for one side or the other." He sighed. "I pronounced on both! We have 2 to 1 European against native troops, since –since the reorganisation of the army and sometimes –well let's just say it was easier in the past."

"Do you have different religions within the regiment?" Sam said.

"Yes. It wasn't always so. But now we have mixed units, the idea being we are less likely to have trouble if we have different racial groups within it. We have Rajputs, Sikhs, Punjabi Muslims from the hills; they're all different."

"Do you have favourites?"

He laughed.

"Some days, most definitely!"

He then looked straight across at her and said

"Ah, you have managed a bath I see. We do actually have a shower, of sorts. It is a bit rudimentary and sometimes malfunctions but you can at least stand under a stream of water. Gerald fixed it up for me on a sort of hand pump basis and the temperature of the water depends on the day of course but at least you get the feeling of being clean head to toe. Ali is perfectly capable of operating it; he's just a little old fashioned and I think pouring water over my head in a bath gives him a sense of past times which he enjoys. We change the water and when you've finished you just stop pulling the chain and it drains away out of a hole in the corner. Just make sure you check the bathroom before you start; there is a cover for the hole but I have known some exceptionally persistent snakes and rats!"

He had been examining her carefully arranged sari of towels and lifting his eyebrows he said

"You want for clean garments I expect."

He got to his feet and went across the room to a door on the other side, pushed it open, was gone for a few moments and then returned with a long and rather fine white silk shirt. "Will this suffice for present?"

He leaned forward and laid it across her knees.

Sam ran her fingers over the soft luxury. It was a new experience.

"Oh yes. This will do just fine."

Without thinking, she stood up, letting the towels drop to the floor and slipping her head into the shirt to let it fall to her knees. Then she looked up.

"Oh –"

His expression was somewhere between awe, delight and embarrassment. His eyes had become very large and very dark and his eyebrows were flickering uncertainly.

"I am so sorry! I had forgotten where I was and who I was with. Our behaviours are separated by 100 years or so – and I am so relaxed in your company...please forgive me."

For several moments speech evaded him; then he said shyly

"No. Please don't apologise. I am entranced."

He certainly looked entranced but perhaps something more as well. A light had come into those eyes that she hadn't seen before, as if a memory was reaching out to him and blending his present with his past.

He shook his head as if to send it away and said

"Shall you tell me more of your alternate realities?"

Alternate realities? Sam thought, did I use those words? She thought not. And suddenly without thinking she asked

"You've lost someone, someone close? A woman? Who was she?"

He stared at her with such pain in his face that her eyes filled with tears. The brows drew together and the eyes darkened to black holes and severe lines became stark around the beautiful mouth, making it tight and unforgiving.

"I need a drink" he announced, and getting up from his sofa strode across to the desk, reached for and uncorked the brandy bottle that stood there and poured a large measure into the glass standing by it. He drank it in one, the bottle still in his hand, his back turned towards her.

Sam said

"None of my business"

And he turned to look at her, and carefully put the bottle down on the desk.

"I apologise. An old habit after a frustrating encounter. Do you like brandy?"

"No" said Sam. "Not even a little bit."

He relaxed and said

"Yes. I was married once. It seems a long time ago now. She...died."

They looked at each for some moments and then Vivian said

"You must be tired. We have a spare room. I will have Ali make it comfortable for you."

He went through to the back of the bungalow and after some opening and closing of doors Ali appeared beside her.

"I have upset him?"

Ali said quietly

"He is a very private man. Always. Even when young."

He looked at her sadly.

"There have been too many losses in his life."

Sam said

"Losses?"

"His father, his mother, his sister, his wife and daughter... before them his close friend from youth" He gazed beyond her as if the past was just a little way distant near enough to see, to recognise. "I knew them all. As a young man I was his father's bearer. I married young and my wife was ...how do you call it... maid to his mother. After his father's...loss I stayed with the household, with her young son and daughter..."

He stopped abruptly as if compassion had betrayed him into divulging secrets.

But, thought Sam, it is a blessing for him to speak of it. He has shared this with no one before me...and his wife was dead too...a mother, a sister, two wives and a child...all female...... how long ago?...10 years...what happened 10 years abo...the Indian mutiny, now called the first was of indepwnce... Cawnpore...

She looked at Ali with so mucj horror and pity he knew she understood.

He said

"Your history books have told of the cruelties and betrayals inflicted on our beautiful country."

"Yes. Oh Ali..."

"We survived. But for some the survival came at a high cost."

"Too high?" said Sam, thinking of the look in Vivian's eyes.

Ali smiled at her.

"Each day is a gift to treasure."

They had moved into the other room by now. It was a pleasant room but had an air of being...what was it... stripped...as if everything that gave it personality had been removed leaving only remenants of a half forgotten dream.

She turned to Ali.

"Was she ..." she stopped. What did it matter now. She was gone.

"Yes" said Ali. "She has gone. With all the others. May their spirits rest."

Sam sat down on the bed. Firm, almost hard but somehow reassuring. She yawned.

"You must be tired. Can I get you anything more?"

"No Ali, nothing more. And yes I believe I am."

He placed his hands together, bowed his head over them and left the room, closing the door behind him. Sam swung her legs up onto the bed and lay there looking up at the ceiling.

Terrible, haunting pictures filled her mind.

A dying fire…

A lonely, troubled, disorientated Native American boy…

Afraid to lose his friend…his life…

And another boy, a boy with black hair to his shoulders, and bird- wing blue eyes, through which you could see all the bright colours of the earth; mountains and rivers and streams that separated and then joined again, flowing deep, with all the hues of the earth and the sky; of trees and flowers…

'Life takes many forms. It is the spirit that is constant… remember that. Believe.'

And she had said

'I doubt my strength! I doubt my belief!'

And the boy with the bird- wing blue eyes had said

'Belief without doubt is not belief at all. It is fear with a fence around it. Death is not the end; it is only a change of form… and a new beginning…

A new beginning…'

She woke with the dawn light. Unfamiliar noises invaded her ears.

There was a tap on the door and Ali came in carrying a tray which had on it a small terracotta cup. Sam squinted at him and sniffed. It smelt wonderful.

He brought it to her and said

"I thought you would like an Indian morning refreshment."

"What is it?"

"Chai. The English ladies do not like it so much, but I thought that you…you are very like Vivian's father's wife…"

Sam sipped it; very hot; had anything ever tasted so good.

"Thank you Ali, it is wonderful."

"The master is out all day. He told me to tell you he will be back for evening …and storytime. I have washed and pressed your clothes. I will fetch."

Vivian returned as dusk was falling.

"Are you rested? You look well rested; you shouldn't but you do!" His blue-black eyes sparkled.. "I have the whole day free tomorrow; is there anything that you would care to do?"

And Sam, gazing out of the window at the emerging stars, said

"Yes. I want to go out there!"

"It shall be done!"

Ali brought her tea at 5am and she joined Vivian, already seated at the breakfast table and reading through letters and papers.

They ate mango and drank tea, sweet and thick and delicious and Sam remembered reading someone's reminiscences of Indian breakfast and his aversion to mango because it had the taste of paraffin! She could only suppose that if lamb chops were your idea of the ideal breakfast then mango was not really going to suffice.

Vivian had Mohammed saddle his horse and for Sam, a pretty, roan mare called Tuska, with soulful eyes and eyelashes the length of her finger. They rode out down the cantonment road towards the plain and the hills beyond.

Sam had always loved wide open spaces. Concrete and crowded buildings made her feel vaguely claustrophobic. The vistas of South Dakota and Northern India and the plains of East Africa made her feel unfenced and free. But this, the India of 1867, was wild and wide and beautiful. The spiritual grey dawn mists were rising from the plain to reveal distances beyond comprehension and as the sun rose the colours of amber and apricot and pale green suffused the land, and then the dazzling blue of a sky with no boundaries. The sun, rising over the far, white tipped mountains was spilling vermillion down their flanks. Within an hour it would be furnace hot but in this entrancing early morning the air was cool and jasmine sweet and there seemed to be nothing between her and those distant hills and beyond them the Himalaya. In the hot weather there would be drought and dust devils; when the rains came there would be swollen dangerous waterways and the metal hard tracks would turn to mud. But right at this moment, bounded by mountains and irrigated by innumerable rivers and streams, it seemed like the most beautiful place on earth, the veritable garden of Eden.

"Jannah" said Vivian and then urged his horse into a gallop and her mare followed suit and with her hair streaming behind her and laughing with exultation, Sam could not remember ever being so happy.

Vivian eventually reined in and turned in his saddle and his face too was full of joy, his eyes crinkled against the rising sun, his eyebrows dancing to their own tune and his mouth wide and smiling with something more –an expression of mild surprise, as if in some way history had been forced to accept its place. He ran his hand through the crazy, buttercup hair and said

"It's getting hot. There's a place up ahead, a shooting lodge once I think, long abandoned. Completely empty now except for wildlife. Nothing too exotic!" he added as he saw her expression. "Just a quiet place for solitude and reflection."

Sam smiled.

"Oh yes?"

Vivian looked at her but said only

"I brought food" pointing to his saddlebags. "And comfort" he added indicating a rolled blanket behind his saddle.

"Well don't you think of everything!"

"Your servant, ma'am" he said with a touch to his forehead and Sam said

"Do you like it here?"

Vivian looked at her in surprise. He said

"How not? It is a cornucopia of colour, spring, summer and winter. The crops, the trees and vines along the streams, around the villages, providing shade for the holy men to sit under with their rosary beads; and there are even roses, which

I believe is fundamental to the average Englishman's idea of a perfect garden! And fruits of all kinds grow in abundance. The gardens of Eden" he said, echoing her thoughts. "Jannah. But the serpent has still found its way in…"

"Will you tell me of… the past?"

Vivian gazed at her, his eyes very bright and said slowly

"If you will finish your story."

"Mine? Surely you've had enough of past life regression and alternate realities."

"Never! But there is something more. Something nearer to you now in time. Something that hurts you. Something that has brought us together."

His eyes held things that he could not possibly know and Sam suddenly had a strange sense of destiny, serendipity, as if the past and the future were somehow conspiring to make good the present; to make amends… for both of them.

The lodge was a house of echoes. The plaster on the walls was peeling but there was still evidence of the vibrant colours that it had once celebrated. There were arches everywhere, with beautiful and intricately carved stone lattice work, leading from room to room, leading out onto wide verandas, leading the eye up to arched ceilings and balconies. The ghosts that wandered through its naked halls were quiet ghosts, maybe too old or too tired to protest… or maybe they welcomed visitors to their placid solace after so long on their own.

"Does anyone come here now, apart from you that is" asked Sam.

"I believe some of the young officers venture the occasional liaison here" said Vivian. "I discourage it because it usually involves a married woman and on occasion another man or even a boy. We are not evolved enough to handle the repercussions if such meetings became public knowledge. But the native peoples avoid it. I believe there have been tales of ghosts and wanderings. There is a tale I believe of a young native prince who fell in love with a girl not of his race and was forced from his state. He was killed in border fighting and her spirit returns here to wait for him."

"But they do not bother you?"

"No. When we returned to our station I came here many times hoping to see –hoping to see ghosts. Hoping that I could persuade her spirit to somehow reach out to me in the emptiness. But it was not to be. All she left me were pictures of the past overlaid with blood." He stopped, as if aware that his words had suddenly blocked out the light. He turned swiftly to Sam and his face was a plea for forgiveness and she reached out to take his hand.

"I am comfortable in a place where a young woman waits for her lost love. And it is pointless for you to go in search of her... it is your wife you speak of? She must find you."

"Is that why you have come?" His voice was intent. "To help her find me?"

Sam said nothing. What did she know? But his gaze would not leave her face.

"I don't know. Perhaps. Maybe she is reaching out to you through me. Maybe if I help unlock the doors between the past and present she can walk through. Maybe all we can do is wait and see."

He seemed to be grappling with concepts that were not new to him. Then he began to speak, without prelude, as if her knowledge of the circumstances was implicit.

"We all knew there was unrest. We had all heard of dissension in the ranks at some of the outlying stations, in the north and in Bengal. We had all discussed it in the mess as if it was a topic of political interest from London. We discussed it but we did nothing and we went on with our routines and our furloughs as if nothing was amiss. I trusted my men but I was not blind to the undercurrents and as I had spoken their language from being a small boy, I knew much of the dissension came from their fears that the British were trying to undermine their religion, their faith and, in the case of Hindus, destroy their caste and by doing so suborn all their people into the western way of life. Many of those at high command level believed implicitly in their men, but without listening or understanding and ignored the younger element of officers who they thought ill experienced. Small rebellions had been put down and it was given out that the trouble had been quelled and all was well. My mother and sister were in Cawnpore and were anxious to see Elizabeth, my wife, and our new baby girl. I had a furlough due and we decided that Elizabeth should go to Cawnpore and I join her after a week's hunting trip with a colleague in Kashmir. His mother, sister and two younger brothers were all in Cawnpore also. It was reckoned to be an entertaining place for the ladies in particular; lots of shows and parades, good merchants –that sort of thing. Elizabeth would have preferred to come with me to Kashmir but we believed the baby was perhaps a little too young for the rigours of camp."

He paused, his jaw was tense, as if to deflect a blow; as if the memories of those simple decisions were slashing at him with knives. Sam, who knew her history and had read the accounts of the terrible months of the 1857 Indian mutiny for both sides, found she was holding her breath, frightened to relive through his pain what she had only experienced in print.

"Kashmir is a very beautiful place. The Dal lake, the Shalimar Bagh, the Mughal garden in Srinagar, the 'abode of love' in Sanskrit that the Emperor Jahangir had redesigned for his wife; where Jahangir built a black pavilion and had on it inscribed the words of the poet Amir Kushrau 'Agar Firdaus bar r y-e zamin ast, hamin ast-o hamin ast-o hamin ast' in Persian; 'if there be paradise on earth, it is here, it is here, it is here!' It is said that on his death bed Jahangir was asked about his 'cherished desire'; he is credited to have said 'Kashmir; the rest is worthless'."

He sighed.

"It is true – and we never- she never-"

He stopped. Sam watched the struggle. What could she do? Pain is an internal barricade.

Then he continued.

"It is more than a week's' journey from here and many more from Cawnpore. Ali and Mohammed, my syce, came with us and Ali's wife and daughter went with Elizabeth as Ayah and maid. It was through Ali and his many relatives in the villages we passed through that we heard rebellion had broken out but details were scarce in that part at that time and little more than rumour.

After Srinagar we had travelled into the hills and we had been many days out of touch, living off supplies and what we had hunted. It was exhilarating and hardy toil and I am ashamed to say we slept untroubled. Imbibed by the known tranquillity of Kashmir I suppose." He sighed, as if forgiveness for this part would always elude him. Sam put her hand on his arm and said

"Go on."

He looked at her as if seeing her for the first time. His eyes travelled over her face and body in a gentle exploration which appeared to give him pleasure.

"I had not realized...you are not unalike...." His hand moved across her cheek and he bent his head and kissed her.

He moved away and said

"So you want to hear this? You must, I think, know the outcome from your history."

Sam nodded.

He turned away and began again.

"Then one morning we entered a small village and it was alive with gossip. Ali and Mohammed went into the bazaar and came back with the news that we had surely hoped to deny for the rest of our lives. Native troops had been disarmed at Lahore. At first it was difficult to attain the reason but eventually Ali found a man with some small knowledge and less hearsay. There had been an uprising at Meerut and Delhi had followed suit, along with other stations up and down the Ganges. Lahore garrison had been disarmed to prevent spread of the insurrection through the Punjab. A relief column had been organized under command of John Nicholson and was marching down the Grand Trunk Road towards Delhi but it was expected to take at least a month as it was being waylaid by the need to counter and suppress insurrection in stations on route. Information about Cawnpore was scanty though it was believed that the garrison there as well as at Lucknow was under siege. If we joined the column we would be forced to move at their pace and would still be more than 200 miles from Cawnpore. Our families were at Cawnpore! Fellow officers and men under our command would be commissioned to join the relief force and they were marching on Delhi. In that moment we were brothers and sons and husbands, and fighters. What choice did we have?"

The appeal in his eyes was heart rending. Sam just nodded. She did not need his words of explanation to justify what he did.

"We took a little time to discuss our options with Ali and Mohammed, both of whom had family in the areas through which we would pass. Both said they would ride with us, indeed Ali's wife and daughter were attendant upon my wife and daughter in Cawnpore, as maid and ayah as I have said, and his distress was real. Mohammed said he would be in charge of the acquisition of horses as we would need to change mounts regularly if we were to demand such swift passage of them. He carried a map on which he marked numerous small villages, out of the way of the centres of dissension at Lahore and Meerut and other likely sites in Oudh. We packed as much food stuff, ammunition and water as we could carry on our mounts and we set off, fired by determination and fear but not hope. Hope, the wanton temptress of fools, we left in Kashmir. We rode without rest, only stopping when overcome with the need for food or sleep. When the horses grew lame or too wearied to hold the pace we diverted to a small village to change them and gather intelligence. This was not easy. Much of what we gleaned was hearsay and rumour and indeed many of the villages were deserted, either by inhabitants joining the mutineers or fleeing the wrath of the coming British forces. I learned much later that many people of these areas had fled to islands in the Indian Ocean or to family further south of the insurrection. Rumour at this time was that British regiments, fresh from England under Havelock were on their way from Calcutta for the relief of Cawnpore but had met with rebel factions, after leaving Allahabad and were caught up in furious battles; that the Nanah Sahib had offered sanction and saviour to the besieged but had reneged on his word; that we would be too late for anything but carnal remains and retribution."

Sam took his hand and gripped it tightly. He gazed at it like a drowning man looking at a buoy he cannot reach. All the next images were of death and destruction, and with years of dogged dismissal they reigned again with all their vivid fury.

"Hope is a strange bedfellow is she not? Temptress, giving purpose and life; a dying man's last belief; a dissimulater, urging action as a resolution to an indomitable fate. I thought I had left Lady Hope behind in Kashmir but found I could not lose her. She was my lifeline. So we rode on and joined with Havelock's beleaguered forces; and pitifully small they were. An assorted collection of about a thousand British troops, from different regiments; still in winter attire and suffering abominably in the heat. A few Sikhs; a small force of volunteer cavalry, mostly officers whose regiments had mutinied. Shop keepers and indigo planters and the usual crowd of pack animals and camp followers; few guns. A motley crew indeed. We were officers and though not with our own regiments, which had marched on to Delhi, we were welcomed. The force had lost many officers in the engagements, especially the mounted ones, and Havelock deemed it a useless extravagance to dispute our coming and although not given a particular section to command we had the experience and the authority to lead. My friend, Gerald, an engineer, was welcomed and I simply joined the volunteer cavalry and offered my services where ever they were most needed, often undertaking those duties of the highest risk. What did I care?"

He looked down again at the hand that clasped his so tightly as if seeing another. He carefully opened the fingers and stroked them individually, gently caressing each tip. Sam knew that he had never told to anyone what she was about to hear. Not to a friend, a comrade in arms or even a native whore. What he had seen and felt in those days and weeks had been trapped inside for 10 years and she felt humbled and afraid. He looked away from her hand into the pale light offered up by the candle which sat on the sill at the back of the room, as if in its trifling circle there was contained a landscape of memory and she wondered how many times he had looked at such a light and snuffed it out.

"On the 16th of July a spy made his way through to our camp with news. He told Havelock that the women and children in Cawnpore were still alive. Most of the wounded and combatants had died or drowned during the massacre at the river, the Nana's promised release to safety down the river to Allallabad. Like all the others I gave thanks and bolstered up my hope. The news from Delhi was bad; Chamberlain, in charge of the Delhi Field Force, had been wounded; so too had Daly of The Guides. But my heart remained heavy and I believe that it already knew the truth. They were already dead." He stopped at the word as if speaking it had tolled Donne's bell; annunciated a reality that he had never acknowledged. It seemed to surprise him and more than anything Sam wanted to help remove its seeping poison and the compendium of guilt.

She removed her hand from his and used both to pull him towards her. For a moment he gazed at her, his wonderful talking eyebrows lifting in response. Then he bent his head to kiss her again.

Then he moved so they were sitting side by side, shoulders almost touching and without prompting continued his terrible saga.

"We passed through the gates into Cawnpore unchallenged and Havelock sent 100 men out in front of the Highlanders to assess the situation. Gerald and I were in close attendance. Their officer approached the Bibighar, the house of the women, not knowing what he would find, pushed open the door, went in and came back out. But we did not need to see the white of his face or the shaking of the shoulders to know what was there. We had all known on entering Cawnpore. It was quiet, too quiet; the quiet of the grave. I stood side by side with Gerald, my comrade, my companion and my friend and Ali, also my comrade and my friend. Mohammed held our horses. And then we all entered the rooms where our wives, children, mothers, sisters and brothers had met their end."

Sam could feel the tremor of restrained emotion across the small space between them.

"I cannot, will not describe to you what we saw. It must have been documented and it must stain the pages of history –"

"It has, I know, I have read it" said Sam quietly. He did not speak of it but she knew he saw its images nevertheless.

"Gerald broke down and I –I was turned to stone. I can still see the colours and the images of that place but I cannot recall what I did, only that Ali took my arm and guided me back out into the brazen sunlight. The courtyard around the house of women and the trees and grass were peppered with red droplets as if heaven had wept blood. Fifty feet beyond, some of the troopers had discovered a well and in its sixty foot depths were the –the –that well was the resting place of our loved ones. I, being stone, looked into its depths and was sick as if with the cholera. So were many who ventured a glance. I forbade Gerald. I restrained him. That glance would have besmeared his sacred memories forever and stripped his young life of meaning."

What of your young life, Sam protested wordlessly; who protected you?

She turned toward him and looked at his face. The eyes were closed, the lashes wet, as images pushed so far into the past were released onto the plane of his current consciousness.

You stop feeling, thought Sam. You don't actually recognise it because some things do pierce the shield. You may even shed tears. But actually you have become inured to pain. You live in an ivory tower, where all that exists is its smooth, walls and it is possible to look out over the drama of life and learn not to care. Only within these walls was there safety. This was the teaching of pain. The soft parts grow a second skin and the emotions develop an early warning system and the ears a wary radar for low frequency inference. Though not visible to the naked eye you wore a breastplate, crafted from such stern stuff it could barely be touched let alone penetrated... A natural process really. The ordinary defence, a knee jerk reaction to keep you from the edge of the abyss. It is perhaps either that or a manufactured one, using drugs or alcohol. Or work.

Now you become afraid of feeling. But you try to hide that too. And you think you've gone beyond it all. But that's not true either. You're afraid. You're afraid that if you just once allowed an emotion to gain a foothold, the resultant tidal wave would gather up the silt of all those submerged passions and hit you with the power to carry you into the void...

She waited. She had given him the opportunity to trounce his demons and waiting was all she could offer him. Eventually he seemed to become aware of her presence once more. He took her hand as if the feel of warm skin could finally erase the cold touch of the dead. It seemed as if he would leave it there but then he said

"I must finish. I have glimpsed freedom and I have waited too long to turn from it now."

He sighed. "Our force was small, too small to render much recompense for such evil doing. Havelock was diminished by our failure. We all were. He wanted to push on to Lucknow, also under siege, but we needed to await reinforcements. So wait we did, for weeks and when they did arrive the commanders squabbled, as commanders do, and there were many –reprisals, authorised and carried out.. The licking of the slaughterhouse floor to break caste, the blowing of live men from cannons – men who we had no proof were the perpetrators, were defiled; innocent as well as guilty; it did not bring back the dead and it did not ease the pain. It was barbarous and it only lowered us to the level of those who had committed the atrocities."

"But you did go to Lucknow? You didn't have to; you had done what you set out to do. Why *did* you go?"

He looked at her as if surprised by the question.

"I am a soldier. My regiment was at Delhi and there was no one waiting for me –I stayed with Havelock's men and with them set my mind to save whomsoever I could from Lucknow having none of my own for whom to perform that duty."

The desperate anguish had receded and the sadness had returned. He gazed out of the window, seeing nothing. Sometimes Sam thought, you could not spare pain or share pain. You could only watch. And she had watched many times before but it now seemed as if she had been shielded in those times by a layer of unreality or the blanching of time passed. There was no comfort armour here; there was only a damaged soul...

"Our reinforcements came; we left Cawnpore with Havelock and prepared to fight our way to Lucknow. They had been waiting many weeks and were in dire need of foodstuffs and medical supplies but our commander was staunch and determined even though we were facing an enemy many times greater in number. Havelock was facing calls for aid from all sides; from Inglis at Lucknow; from the authorities at Agra; and then we heard that the mutineers in great numbers were threatening Cawnpore again. So back we turned to face them at Bithur, under heavy fire, the like of which I have never experienced. The Highlanders, grim and fierce, charging through the swamps, facing more than 2000 rebels. We took their guns and won our victory. And for myself I did not care if death came for me. I had watched it take a man in a moment with a smile on his face and I had watched it persecute him for hours until release. I did not care. Do you think that is wrong? To be so cavalier with life?"

The question was unexpected.

"I do not think we can always govern our feelings. Sometimes we must allow them their own time in the limelight if we are to survive. There are many things that pose a threat to life; death is only one."

He said nothing. then

"Those words –it could have been Elizabeth speaking. She was wise in a way that I will never be."

"I have never been called wise; only that I think too much" said Sam with a laugh. "Why did you stay –in India I mean? You could have gone home, afterwards, to England I mean and left it all behind you."

"But if I had left India at that point the memory of all the horror would have been with me for ever, linked irredeemably to the land. I chose to continue to live in a country I love, in a country into which I was born –my father was a soldier with the East India Company–to replace those memories, those feelings, with the light and the joy and the wisdom this country has to offer. If I had left at that point I would have been a slave all my life."

"Yes, that I understand. I'd have done the same" said Sam.

"At first I had nightmares. I was afraid to sleep so I drank myself into oblivion each night, after the war was over. Then I found that I did not need to close my eyes. Some sight or sound would conjure up an image and superimpose it on my reality. Until you spoke I had seen it as a weakness."

"I do not believe that to examine the workings of the mind or to consider what it offers us through its ramblings is anything other than a gift" said Sam. "It would be unwise to ignore it. I believe that what we are offered in the way you have described is our unconscious mind attempting to guide our consciousness and therefore our actions to a safer and more wholesome place."

Vivian stared at her for some moments and then nodded. "Yes. Now in the years that have been allotted to me since those days, I can see the truth of that."

Once again his gaze drifted to the candle flame and Sam could see the memories behind his eyes as if they were her own.

"Please go on" she said softly.

He came back to her and nodded.

"The way to Lucknow was treacherous. The rebels were many times our number and villages on our way were deserted and our commissariat wagons were well in the rear. Food was in such short supply and the rains made the roads trenches of mud. We had no spare clothing and walked, rode and slept wet and chilled to the bone each night. Fever and cholera were rife. Those of us who were mounted slept with our horses, for comfort and warmth. Havelock was undaunted. He would ride to the front of the column and address the men, exhorting them to keep their spirits high and their legs strong because women and children depended upon us. I was part of the volunteer cavalry and Havelock used us to great effect. James Outram had been placed in overall command at this point but had apparently rescinded decision-making to Havelock; in reality he constantly questioned and countermanded Havelock's judgements, causing hesitation in commands and difficulties for staff officers. Nevertheless Havelock persisted. He was tireless, driven, I believe, by a powerful sense of duty and a determination to expunge past failures, though whether these were real or just in his perception I do not know. I do know that Gerald, my dear friend, was driven by a sense of failure and self-hatred for his neglect, as he saw it, of the safety of his loved ones and the desperate need to demonstrate his love through action and vengeance. And for myself I did not care whether famine, fever, bullet or shell took me if only blessed darkness would cover me and leave me in peace.

We got to within three miles of the residency and they must have been alerted to our coming because the residency flag was flying over the tower, though to be shot down many times. The difficulty was which approach to take to minimize our casualties. The streets approaching the main gate were narrow and the buildings on either side were peppered with slots for rebel rifles. The way in was defended by many guns and sharpshooters and too narrow for us to deploy our own artillery. Havelock forged on, many men falling under rapid fire. Few of us knew where we were in relation to the residency or which way to go. Every house seemed occupied with snipers; at every corner, the muzzle of a gun. These were a well-trained enemy; the irony did not escape me. General Havelock had his horse shot from under him, again; the seventh he had lost in this way. He was determined to reach the residency by nightfall and that we would push through and get it over with. The Highlanders were sent forward again, followed by the Sikhs. And were met with sheets of fire. Neill was shot through and dead; senior officers badly wounded. Those of us on horseback carried at least one wounded man across our saddles. It was a poor effort but what else could we do under such an onslaught? As we pushed onwards through the gate of the Residency the Highlanders struck up a tune to herald our coming and were answered by pipes from within the residency. Men who had seen harsh battle all their lives were in tears at the sight of women and children running out of the dilapidated, beleaguered, buildings, many now only existing in memory, the wounded labouring their way towards us, all laughing and crying and throwing themselves at us. We were filthy, exhausted with two days hunger upon us and fit for nothing but food and sleep and we had yet to learn that whilst our small force had been spared to add protective numbers to these long time besieged, we were not great enough to ensure their safe passage from Lucknow. Basic foodstuffs were still in supply but fresh fruit and vegetables were not and scurvy was rife. Those not ill or wounded suffered the palour and debilitation of the long-time incarcerated, who fight all day against the cessation of hope.

It would be another two long months of privation and suffering before that day would come and we had considerably added to the number of those already in need."

Vivian sighed.

"It is a long tale. Have you not heard enough yet?"

"I have studied the history of the mutiny" said Sam, "but I would like to see it through your eyes. I find myself here with you and those with whom you shared this terrible time and no one else but you few can see me. There must be a reason for both of us."

Vivian eaid

"When I am with you the demons are caged" and he dropped the carpet he had brought in a patch of sunlight by the window that looked out on to the distant hills, a purple smear on the horizon. He sat down on it and taking her hand, smiled up at her.

"It is enough".

The food he had brought was simple but full of flavour and Sam was hungry.

"You eat like a starving boy!" said Vivian, watching Sam chomp her way through chicken and chapatis and something that looked like a dumpling but which tasted of banana. "You should be a small elephant but you are as slender as a gazelle."

"Flattery will get you everywhere" said Sam. "I've always been the same –except it used to be peanut butter and chocolate spread on toast."

Vivian's eyebrows danced speculatively.

"It's a long story. Yes and I will tell you" she said seeing his expression. "But not now. You first."

And truth be told she was unwilling to introduce Steve into the equation. He was a considerable part of her past but the present stood before her in all its arresting beauty and she did not want anything to disturb it.

A small striped Indian squirrel leapt out of nowhere and made a bid for freedom through the arched door, chittering angrily. They both watched it for several minutes, Sam thinking, nearly as cute as Kevin but not quite.

"You have a fondness for small animals?" Vivian enquired.

Sam smiled reminiscently.

"Yeah."

"All kinds?"

"Yeah."

"But especially rats?"

"Yeah" said Sam smiling broadly. Vivian would like Kevin and Kevin would like Vivian. How inexplicably annoying the creature was! All these years, literally through hell and high water and now he leaves me to handle this. Words will be had! Vivian was studying her face.

"He must mean a lot to you. I am quite jealous."

Sam smiled ruefully. "We have –we have worked through a lot of stuff together over the years. He has never abandoned me and I suppose I am a little unsure as to why he has now and if it was part of the plan or just a careless act of self-preservation."

"Is that likely?"

Sam thought about it and said

"The jury's out."

Vivian's eyebrows lifted and crinkled ending in a small frown and then he said

"Not a phrase that I am familiar with but I think I can probably guess the meaning. Does the English language change so very much in the years ahead?"

"You have no idea! It changes so much that I doubt you would be able to understand half of what you heard. But don't worry; half of what you heard would not be worth hearing."

"Beauty and cynicism in a woman. I am both intrigued and ensnared. If truth be told I was never much in favour of the woman we Victorians placed on a pedestal, to revere, protect and dismiss as incapable of sound judgement. One of the qualities I admired so much in my wife – in Elizabeth –"

He stopped and Sam thought, now is the time to push on to the end, whatever that brings –whatever that means –for both of us.

"You can tell me about Elizabeth later. Tell me what happened to you in Lucknow."

Vivian walked away from her to perch on the window's embrasure, his back turned slightly towards her, gazing out over the still hot plain to the hills beyond, suddenly remote and inexpressibly sad.

When he started to speak it was almost as if he was reading from a manuscript penned years in the future.

"We were trapped in Lucknow, the besieged and the relief force alike, for two more months. We dug trenches, loaded and fired shot, picked off snipers, shared out the rations and buried the dead. Men died of fever, scurvy and dysentery, infected wounds and despair. Sir Henry Lawrence had already died, as he would always have wanted, dictating letters from his bed in his room when a shell burst through the ceiling and hit. I had met him once when I was a young ensign and the impression he made upon me was inspirational and I remember thinking through those god awful months, whether outcomes might have been different had there been a lot more the like of Henry Lawrence on the political scene. Delhi had been retaken and forces were on their way to the relief of Lucknow. John Nicholson was dead. Hodson of Hodson's Horse was dead, the former leading the assault with the first brigade in the breached walls, with his sword raised and shot through the right side under his arm; Hodson, we heard, shot in Lucknow, was trying to evict mutineers from a boarded house. Eventually Sir Colin Campbell battled his way through the shell raked, tortuous streets to us, following the route sent out to him by Outram with us in Lucknow. He had with him part of the force who broke the siege at Delhi, including very welcome engineers and also the Naval brigade of Peel. We heard the bombardment of Peel's guns, firing broadsides as if he were alongside an enemy frigate on the open sea. It took Campbell three days and unconscionable losses to reach us and almost immediately, under cover of darkness and with the women and children and wounded guarded at his rear, fought his way back once again to the relief of Cawnpore whose protection was only secured by a small force of 500. The rear-guard remained at the residency until the last minute, encouraging the belief, with gunfire and bonfires, that our forces were still there, guarding the empty shell and about to launch an attack. Gerald and myself went as part of the protection guard. I will never forget that night exodus ...women and children on ponies or in doolies and hackeries;; the rest on foot, on a route exposed to the fire of snipers and artillery. Many were surprisingly calm having become used, I suppose, to walking around under enemy fire and we got them all in safety to the Sikandar Bagh. For my part I will never forget the scenes of ruin and devastation of that once beautiful city; many proud and cherished buildings imprinted with vengeance and painted with blood, some as a necessary repast of warfare but much of jaundiced and pitiless destruction...

So we joined with Sir Colin to relieve Cawnpore again and drive back a very strong force of mutineers led by one of their most successful commanders, Tantri Topi."

He turned suddenly to face her.

"I can feel your thought. Did I pursue death so fervently that I must join any command open to me to fight and go on fighting?" He sighed and looked down at his hands as if he could still see the rifles, bayonets, the sword they had held and guided; could still feel in his fingers the knuckle whitening grip of passion and revenge.

"In part, yes although with the death of Sir Henry Lawrence and Henry Havelock, who died in his son's arms as we marched away from Lucknow, and so many others too numerous to remember and with the reports coming in of the reprisals and retributions on the innocent among the guilty and on both sides, I was no longer convinced of the need for victory, as a soldier must be. Others in command thought the reprisals fitting; but when the blood cools how do you face the monster you have become? That Gerald wanted to go on fighting swayed me. He was my friend and my younger by several years and seemed lost, only coming to life with a battle strategy before us. I felt a responsibility for both his care and his conduct. I felt that if I left him then he would plummet into wild savagery with something akin to morbid pleasure that would destroy him when the fever passed...

The women, children and wounded of Lucknow made their way to Allahabad, to sanctuary although I believe that for those who had lived so long with destruction and deprivation, the gift of life and peaceful quiet was enough, though they were hailed as heroines. Gerald had made the acquaintance of a young woman whose father had been part of the residency force and been killed in its defence and whose mother had simply lost the fight to live. I had hoped –but at that time the acquaintance was too brief and maybe too soon. Gerald and I stayed with Sir Colin and three months later with a force of 30,000 men including twenty eight squadrons of cavalry and one hundred and thirty four guns- indeed so large a British army had never been seen in India-and many more followers, we attacked and took Lucknow for the third time in March 1858. This time, as well as members of the force who had broken the siege at Delhi, we had British troops fresh out from England. Some of the officers who had served their time in India were a little scornful of these new arrivals and the delays in gathering the force were unconscionable. Gerald joined with the troops of engineers who had survived the Delhi campaign and spent his time fortifying or blowing up bridges, reinforcing strongholds and damaging enemy fortifications. I rode with the cavalry, reconnoitring, skirmishing and protecting the infantry on its flanks. But there were terrible tragedies and atrocities. We lost a lot of officers, from sniping and shell. One made friends of comrades in arms only to lose them in such a short space of time. Gerald was amongst a group of engineers who had been ordered to shift containers filled with powder found on the main street. Pushing his way through the congested areas alongside the others, he was forced back by a huge explosion and struggling forward found the powder blown and with it a Royal Engineer captain and a dozen of his men. I heard the explosion and galloped across to see what had happened because by this stage the city had been retaken. I found Gerald, unhurt and with him the bodies of the dead and the dying. I have seldom felt such an inextricable mix of sorrow and relief. Gerald, who was better acquainted with them, was quite bereft and that evening I went with him to attend the funeral. It was noticeable that for some, for whom the battle cry of 'avenge Cawnpore' had been a rabble rousing cheer, the lust for revenge had died with these untimely deaths. There had been indiscriminate killing of sepoys who had surrendered and also of women and children. For some at least perhaps it was a turning point. How we two survived I do not know for the fighting had been as fierce as any I had known but the outcome was never in doubt."

He stopped, his eyes seeing nothing but the past; his memories challenging the validity of his profession.

"For many the mutiny was over but there was still a large force of rebels fighting the small actions of desperate men who know that the outcome of battle or surrender will be the same. But Sir Colin and Hope Grant had forged their reputation on sparing those who surrendered and punishing their own men who pillaged and plundered. Sir Hugh Rose, a man whose reputation among his peers varied with whomsoever you spoke, commanded the force which pursued these last renegade numbers to the borders of the Himalaya and ultimately demonstrated his worth, but it was 1859 before there was any talk of a peace treaty, for the guerrilla warfare was sustained and effective.

After the retaking of Lucknow Gerald and I discussed our future. He had finally renounced his vengeful crusade and had reached a hiatus when he had received a letter from the young lady he had met when we were in the relief column. The letter said she was still in Allahabad but her only surviving relative, an ageing aunt on her father's side, was in Lahore and would he be prepared to go to her in Allahabad and escort her there. An unusual request for a single woman but then the unusual had become the commonplace during the last two years. Gerald asked my view, and also my blessing and I was very glad to support it and give it. The lady had opened the door for him; maybe between them they could make sense of their joint and separate losses. For myself and Ali and Mohammed, still with me, still loyal, bereft as was I, we thought that perhaps we should return to our hill station and see what was left of our regiment and our home; see if my actions at the beginning of the outbreak could be negated by my conduct during it. Part of me wanted to accept a commission with Sir Hugh Rose and pursue the rebels and my destiny into an unknown future. Part of me wanted to go on following my profession, taking orders, risking life and never thinking again. But Ali, who has known me all my life, child to man, said enough was enough and now was the time to let the blood settle into the dust and be blown by the winds to join the centuries of dust on the plains of Oudh and Rohikhand."

"Was he right? That calm wisdom is usually right."

Vivian sighed. Once again he looked down at his hands and then out over the legend crafting expanse of the frontier. Then he turned around and looked straight at her.

"At first I did not think so. Many, both military and civilian, thought we had been too lenient in our administration of India. Some even thought that we had suffered a punishment from god because we had not brought them to Christianity. This horrified me. But the authorities generally agreed that the army needed some serious reformation in terms of the proportion of European troops to native and the command of the artillery. In the end the spirit of reconciliation rather than retribution was sited if not embraced by all. Few princes had become involved; many had given their support to the British as had many of the talukdars. Thousands of Indian soldiers and camp followers had fought alongside and died with the British as I had good reason to know. A proclamation was read out; the British government would rule India directly; treaties made would be honoured; religious tolerance would be observed and ancient customs respected. So...John Company was no more and the army and its structure was changing. There was a lot to occupy my time and a lot of fences to be rebuilt and old connections to be healed. Many had lost much and many had lost everything- the Nicholson family alone had lost all its sons- so I could not count my losses as singular or personal. Gerald had found happiness both in his career and his personal life and I was happy for him. But for me the future stretched as a barren land and in the few moments I had for quiet reflection, I reached for the brandy bottle.... When it got out of hand it came to the notice of my commanding officer and he took me to one side and suggested that I should not risk the loss of the only thing that remained to me for the sake of a few hours of oblivion. He said that the army and its structure was under review and would change and dedicated proficient officers would be in high demand, especially in the north, and that one of my calibre and courage, love for the country and language skills, should not demonstrate lack of courage in the moral sphere. He said men like Nicholson, Hodson and others had given their lives and men like Chamberlain fought on and I should do the same- even though I might be 'sickened with myself, the world and my cruel profession'. I curbed the drinking and settled into the featureless plane of existence, with equanimity and acceptance for the most part - and thus you found me..."

And Sam, gazing at him with tears in her eyes, thought, dear lord what am I going to do now?

They spent the rest of the day in the relatively cool confines of the ancient lodge, watching the ghekko lizards and the striped squirrels running to and fro, approaching then dashing away as if daring each other to check out the humans. A small mongoose appeared in the door way, peered at the new inhabitants, considered its options and then decided against further investigation, turned its back and scurried away, chittering crossly. Nothing larger showed any interest in them. They watched in silence, as if they were offering homage to the spirits of the dead and Sam did not feel it was appropriate to tell her tale of the future and what it held; not yet. There would be time – wouldn't there?

At dusk Vivian retrieved the horses from the cool of the ruined stables at the back of the lodge and Sam took her mare to mount. But Vivian stopped her, pulled the mare's reins over her head, lifted Sam bodily onto his own saddle and mounted behind her, leading the mare at their rear. They rode in silence, Vivian holding the mare's reins in one hand with his other resting on Sam's leg and loosely clasping his own reins. Sam leaned back against him revelling in the cooling air of coming darkness and the solid warmth of his body behind her. At any moment she might find herself suddenly locked out. Returned to her room in the 20th century, alone, or with Kevin... and with only memories, the kind of memories left by a beautiful dream, a transcendental meditation or, as when she was a young girl, an absorbing and captivating book whose pages she could not bear to leave. Maybe it would be better that way because if she had to be the one to close this life, to leave Vivian, she did not believe she would have the strength. So she leant back, gazed out at the changing colours of dusk, the rising moon and her star spangled train; strained her ears to the diffident night sounds of an Indian plain, the jackals, the owls and closed down her mind. And surprisingly for Sam, and Kevin would attest to this, her mind remained unchallenging, her only thought, I will remember this night, this ride, this warmth all the days of my life.

As if he had read her thoughts Vivian bent his head close to hers and whispered

"These moments are the gifts we are given to treasure for always."

When they reached the cantonment Vivian slid from his horse and lifted Sam down and placed her upon her own.

"Just in case" he whispered. "one never knows –something might have changed."

At his bungalow Mohammed materialised from the darkness at one side of the building and took both horses. Sam smiled her thanks and the dark face under the dark brows crinkled a little in response. The oil lamps in the bungalow were all lit and Ali was at the door. It was difficult to tell in the poor lighting but Sam was sure there was approval in his eyes.

Vivian looked at his messages, yawned and went across and opened Sam's bedroom door.

"Thank you" he said "for a wonderful day. I will be away early but will see you afterwards. Ali and Mohammed will see to your needs." He paused as if he might say something more but then turned and went across to his own room, let himself in and closed the door behind him leaving Sam feeling vaguely abandoned and not a little disappointed.

Yes there was a story to be told, her story, but it could wait. Right now she needed to do some thinking ...

Sam lay down on the unforgiving bed; it did not induce sleep and yet... The night was pleasantly cool. The square of midnight velvet she could see through the window was a sky spangled with more stars than she had ever seen. She blew out the small candle and lay in the darkness watching the sky and stars and listening to the night sounds of a quiet India.

Then came the questions. ..

The usual dialogue ensued.

What are you doing here?
I don't know! Ask Kevin!
Kevin's not here.
That's stating the furry obvious. Why isn't he here?
Not exactly appropriate at the moment.

I don't know how all this has happened. In the past I've always had an element of control albeit sometimes very tenuous. And I've been an observer, or a participant, in the given time frame. But now …

Now you are an actor in someone else's play and you've fallen in love with the leading man.

She was shocked for a moment and then rebelled.

Don't be so ridiculous! You can't fall in love with someone who's been dead for over 100 years. I must be dreaming or reading or fantasising or something. I must be crazy. I have completely lost my mind and I'm rambling in and out of fantasies of my own creation and someone is standing over me in some kind of mental institution and grading my absurd ramblings with a view to pronouncing a diagnosis…

Or it might be just another exploration, slightly different admittedly but then your explorations have always had, shall we say, a tendency to the bizarre.

You think?

Exploring a fantasy land with talking animals, as another person didn't make you afraid..

No it didn't but I was a kid.

You didn't worry about meeting Kevin and in fact Kevin has been a constant for most of your life.

Yeah and speaking of –where the furry hell is he!

But you are definitely in love

No I'm …I'm afraid.

That was right, she was afraid. She ran back through all the demons over the years, how she'd run from them, disguised them as something else. But eventually, inevitably perhaps, she had turned around and faced them. The spectres of the faceless warriors…from that very first journey… the black and silver Knight, disappearing, all those years ago, a lifetime ago; several lifetimes ago.

But this… This was the arch demon, decked out in red tights, spiky ears, forked tail… with a curved sword…Milton's Lucifer –becoming the archetypal hero; the flawed diamond,

ageless, timeless, following his destiny, following his heart...
over printed with her own vision of manhood; the dark eyes,
with their remote allure; that was a key element of course;
remote, unattainable –and if something is unattainable there is
no disgrace in not attaining it. She had created something so
incomparable that nothing else could compare. Why? To
elude the greatest jeopardy of all; the risk of a relationship
with another human being which might threaten the self. The
loss of self... It had been quite a journey to find this self and
her ego would be damned before it let go.

But would it mean loss?

Could it mean gain?

Could it just mean redefine?

There was one way to find out...

She felt like a casino player who was just won back all his
losses and prepares to stake it on one final throw. Win or lose?
Make or break.

Innumerable past lives to put to bed, so to speak, in one go.

Am I so fragile, so pathetically insecure that at one flashing,
melting glance I'll turn into a heart shaped jelly baby?

The extent of risk was in direct proportion to the
perception of fear. Am I afraid? Yes! What have I to lose?
Everything...

Vivian left at dawn the next day and Sam climbed out of bed
shortly afterwards. Her clothes, her only clothes, were in a
neat folded heap on the chair by the door, newly washed,
again, and pressed to perfection.

I don't know what the hell he uses for an iron, thought
Sam, but he's doing a much better job than I ever could! And
then, a martyr to honesty, admitted that she usually didn't
bother. She pulled them on and went to find Ali.

He was preparing her breakfast and while she watched she
said

"Do you think you could find me some other clothes?"

Ali's face looked perplexed.

"No" said Sam hurriedly, "not like these- and not crinolines either! God save me from Victorian womens' clothes in these temperatures. No, something silky, soft- maybe Pakhtun trousers and top?"

Ali looked horrified and Sam gave it up. Personally she thought she'd look pretty cool in baggy pants and a leather belt, very bohemian.

After breakfast she went round to the stables to see if Mohammed knew when Vivian would be back and found out that he had taken a troop up onto the border for some manoeuvres and Mohammed did not expect him back before nightfall. So Sam offered to help him groom the horses and muck out the stables. Mohammed also looked horrified but Sam grabbed some grooming brushes and set to and Mohammed gracefully capitulated. She would have helped him exercise the horses as well but this was obviously one risk too far for the wary syce and it was, Sam supposed, sticking the fox's tail in the fire. So she went back to the bungalow to see if she could get Ali to make some of his wonderful lemonade and comb Vivian's bookshelves in the hope they would render up some absorbing reading.

Coming into the lounge she noticed a small pile of diaphanous fabrics which proved on investigation to be clothes, assorted slim ankled pantaloons and softly draping shirts in deep and beautiful colours and something that might have been a veil but would do justice as a shawl.

"Oh Ali!" she breathed. "These are wonderful!" She held them up against her cheek. "So soft."

She turned to see him standing in the doorway smiling.

"Yes?" he said.

"Oh yes. Very yes!" and she scooped them all up and ran into the bedroom.

When Vivian came home it was already dark and it had been a trying day. He walked to the sideboard, picked up the decanter and made to pour himself a large measure of brandy until a movement behind him made him turn.

Sam was standing at the bedroom door way. She had chosen a pair of white tapered pants and a dark blue silk shirt which came to just below her hips. She had knotted the silk veil around her waist and it hung in soft, arresting folds down one leg. She had wound her hair into a ball at the back of her head and loose strands trailed downwards and around her face. She had already examined herself in the looking glass and admitted approval but even with that she was not prepared for the dazed look on Vivian's face.

"Beautiful. You are beautiful!... so beautiful. Where did you –"

"Ali" said Sam.

"Who chose –"

"Ali" said Sam.

"The man has hidden depths" said Vivian. "I had no idea that he –"

"Me neither" said Sam. "I believe I terrified him into it by asking him to dress me as a Pakhtun."

Vivian laughed out loud, replaced the decanter without pouring a drink and moved across to Sam and put his hands on her shoulders.

They stood looking at each other, each assessing the other's response.

Then Vivian stepped back and said

"I am covered in grime. I must make myself clean..."

Sam went to see about food while Vivian took a bath. She felt bad about the inconvenience she had caused for Ali by disrupting the routine of his household but he did not appear to mind and in fact seemed to be enjoying himself. Sam guessed that he had had a lot more to contend with in the past.

While they ate she persuaded Vivian to talk about the days trials. He was reluctant at first but when she pointed out that he had already given her a blow by blow account of his Indian mutiny he acquiesced.

"My commander was right. The army has changed, certainly in structure, and we up on the borders have to be prepared for territorial fighting and raids across the boundaries. The Guides in particular are first line of defence and intelligence gatherers, but we further across must also be on the alert and ready. There are more British officers in a station than there were before the mutiny and they are no longer as young or as green as some of them were at that time, or as old and infirm either I might add – although I'm sure you are aware that the Punjab also had its fair share of shining stars - Hodson, Daly, Nickel Sein! But sometimes – well let us just say sometimes I would like to bang British heads together!

The tribes of the North West Frontier are a law unto themselves. They are fierce, with exceptional fighting skills and in my opinion can handle a rifle upon leaving their mother's womb! They kill hundreds of each other each year in tribal feuds. Fine looking men; look you straight in the eye; no equivocation. You can't brow beat them; you can only defeat them –temporarily. And they like you if you can. We are really just here to make sure the tribes don't make a nuisance of themselves in India or Afghanistan. Periodically they raid the Peshawar Vale, instigating the long established custom of raiding for cattle, women and guns. The politicals usually try and sort it out by holding a large tribal durbar sort of arrangement. It must be tough on them, surrounded by that many men and having to know their dialects and their proverbs! But sometimes outside intervention becomes necessary and by force; punitive forays by several brigades. But the place and the people encapture your soul! Like the landscape; sometimes gloriously beautiful, sometimes dust and dead. Magnificent and harsh, like the peoples themselves and in the end you feel a kind of love. I know my father did. I do too."

A kind of love, thought Sam, the only transcendental emotion a human being is capable of...

It was, she thought, a long time since Vivian had expressed himself to anyone on a personal level.

"The native commanders are now allowed responsibility for the training and behaviour of their own men and decision making regarding them and that in itself provides a more responsive troop. They are fiercely loyal. I like it this way; it should have been done years ago. But we now have the makings of a fine army not restricted by the infirmities and failings of an ageing command. We do quite a lot of reconnoitring and training across the border because the greatest political fear seems to be Russia coming in through Afghanistan. And of course the Afghans themselves, though I do not believe their end game is anything other than independence and protecting their own lands. The Afghans are a law unto themselves and have always excited different responses from different people. Some of those in charge on the frontier before the mutiny tried hard to work with them, after Dost Mohammed Khan was restored to Kabul and indeed had success, for during the mutiny Afghanistan stayed quiet and did not offer sanctuary to mutineers. But others have long memories and saw them as a faithless people, even among themselves. Did not see how we could trust a country where son betrays father and brother betrays brother and whose winning ways and delightful frankness seemed to dupe the most agile of minds."

"And you? What do you believe?"

Vivian looked beyond her and saw annals of history and rivers of blood. He said

"I am a product of my time and trust does not come easily."

"Mmm" pondered Sam. "Afghanistan."

Vivian looked at her sharply. "What do you know of Afghanistan?"

Sam sighed. "I know that the western world has never been able to resist an opportunity to try and impose on others its way of life. And that politicians inevitably think they know what's best. I also know that fear is the main cause of aggression against those who would choose a different way of life."

"I can see that despite the years, in some respects things have not changed" said Vivian.

Sam said nothing.

And knowing as she did about the abortive second Afghan war in 1879 and what preceded it in Kabul, was glad to leave the matter there.

Ali came to take the dishes and handed Vivian his mail. He discarded all but one which he opened and read with interest. He turned to Sam and said

"Gerald is proposing to come and visit, bringing Henrietta with him –the young lady I told you about who he escorted to Lahore –well he married her and they have three children and another on the way according to this! You will like her and it will be interesting, will it not, to see who sees whom."

They went out on the veranda and stood together looking at the galaxy

"Gas, dust and billions of stars, the Milkjy way" said Vivian.

"I know what the constellations are but I'm not good at making them out" said Sam.

Vivian pointed.

"We are near enough to the Himalaya to make viewing good. That's The Great Bear."

Sam peered and shook her head.

"Don't know what I'm looking for" she said ruefully.

Vivian stood behind her, placed his arm over hers, took her index finger between his finger and thumb and traced a silhouette.

"Oh" said Sam. "Oh, yes…"

She turned to look at him and he smiled down at her. Then his mouth became serious and he bent his head and kissed her.

Sam had never been kissed like that before. He kissed her as if he was tasting fine wine, savouring every sip, every flavour. It was intoxicating and full of desire…

A little shiver ran through her, her body responding in anticipation. Years in the future her son would react in the same way to the embrace of a lover…

Without warning he lifted her into his atms and carried her inside towards the open door at the opposite side to the one she used. Pushing the door open wider revealed another stark room.

There was a table, a chair, both utilitarian plajn, and a bed. With its white coverlet and harsh lines, it showed no signs of either its purpose or its use. If it had witnessed passion or pain it was keeping its secrets

Her put her down, but did not release her. The kisses were gentle at first, tentative, as if he was unsure what he was touching. Then they became desperate and demanding and his hands gripped her shoulders.

. He laid her on the bed and stood over her, looking down, his mouth, so gentle and urgent moments before, now a forbidding line. Sam raised herself and lifted the silk shirt over her head, casting the veil cummerbund to one side. His gaze did not move from her face. His hands had fallen to his sides. Gently she reached out and took one and held it between her two for a few moments. He did absolutely nothing except stare intently into her eyes . Then suddenly he flung himself out of his jacket, pulled the shirt over his head and the belt from his breeches.

Sam smiled up at him and said

"Those will have to come off" and pointed at the long black riding boots.

He glanced at her, then down at his booted feet and then sat beside her on the bed to pull them off, followed quickly by the breeches. Sam lay back and watched.

It was not lovemaking. It was sex. Actually, Sam thought afterwards, it was consensual rape. It was brutal and short lived but cathartic. He orgasmed twice in succession and then laid against her shoulder and it grew wet as the dam broke and he wept for everything he had lost and denied. Then slowly his breathing steadied.

"I am sorry" he mumbled into her hair.

Sam stroked his wet face.

They lay like that for some time.

Then he turned to her again and this time his hands and lips were not harsh or urgent. Instead it was a gentle yet demanding lovemaking that had her responding with passion and delight. He touched every part of her body with tender, caressing fingers; her neck and shoulder arches; the curve between her breasts; her navel; her inner thighs. He turned her towards him and did the same to her back, her waist and her buttocks until she was quivering like a moth by a candle flame. It was long and unhurried and agonizingly tender and something more. It was healing, as if both their spirits needed solace and reconciliation and each reached out to the other and adjoined.

Sam thought, I have experienced passion and lust and a kind of love, but I have never felt like this before. I have watched it in others but I was a bystander, looking at an image on painted glass.

She recalled reading in the historical novels, amongst many other genres, that she had read in her youth, tales of men and women, men and men, who had fallen in love at first glance and had gone on to be lovers and partners for life. She remembered dismissing it as pure romantic fiction possible only between the pages of a book. But now...

Vivian said in a whisper

"I have missed her touch like the loss of a limb, waking in the night in physical anguish-until now-"

"And now?"

"Now? Now I have touched and tasted redemption, and something I had thought never to feel again... joy..."

Sam awoke just before dawn, her body relaxed and her mind tranquil with a discreet sense of fulfilment. She did not know how long this recklessness could last but she had made up her mind to enjoy it for as long as it was available.

Vivian was awake beside her, lying propped on one elbow and watching her.

His eyes were very bright...he looked down at her and then bent his head and kissed her with gentle desire. Sam moved into his embrace and then there was a sharp rap on the door. Vivian sighed and kissed her once more, lingeringly but then drew away. It was all Sam could do to not to pull him back.

"I am needed."

He slid away from her to the edge of the bed, Sam watching, transfixed by the

Michaeloangelic lines of his body. He pulled on his breeches and boots and stood up casting about for his shirt and quickly dropping it over his head. Picking up his jacket and helmet he strode to the door and turned.

His smile was wide and warm and his eyes danced with life as he said

"I shall return." And then he was gone.

She lay back down against the pillowDefinitely in love.

Okay. Maybe you're right...

If she was truthful Sam was a little anxious about the impending meeting. Would she be spending her time loitering in one corner like a misplaced ghost whilst Vivian conversed with his friends and tried not to look at her. Would Ali bring in drinks for them all and hand one to an empty space or would he just ignore her altogether. Would the meeting throw some kind of switch and catapult her away from them all...away from Vivian... What actually happened was quite different.

Gerald arrived in an explosion of sound. He was tall, thin and dark, with laughing eyes and charmijng manners. He greeted Ali with respectful familiarity, handed his wife to Vivian to kiss and threw himself down on to one of the sofas with a

"Viv! How's it going?" and proceeded to regale Vivian with military news both actual and rumoured. Henrietta was pretty, calm and very petite, so much so that Sam wondered how she managed to have children at all with a diaphragm that small. But clearly she did as Gerald informed Vivian that they had left the other three at home with the ayah in order to give Henrietta a break. Henrietta did not actually look at her but Sam felt some kind of telepathy pass between them and was not surprised when Henrietta asked if she might have her lemonade out on the veranda in order to catch a cool breeze that had arisen. Vivian glanced quickly across at Sam and raised a querulous eyebrow which she met with an equally querulous shrug but Gerald was already in full swing and Ali obliged.

Henrietta went out through the open door and Sam followed her leaving Vivian to close it behind them. Henrietta settled herself in one of the more comfortable chairs and gazed out across the open plain towards the hills until Ali reappeared with a small tray on which he carried two glasses of lemonade. Henrietta looked carefully at the tray and then at Ali and then straight at Sam and said

"So I was right! But please tell me –can Gerald not see you or is he just behaving in the most abominably rude fashion towards someone whom he assumes is a native girl?"

Sam was unprepared for such an opening and it took her some moments to recover before replying.

"I don't think he sees me" said Sam. "Most people don't. Vivian does and Ali and Mohammed."

"That does make a kind of sense" said Henrietta. "Ali and Mohammed are devoted to Vivian and have been with him so long and their minds are more –how shall I say –open, accepting, than that of your average Englishman! And I can see the effect you have had upon Vivian. When last I saw him the raw pain was gone but had been replaced with a kind of indifference which was foreign to his nature and even more troubling. But now! But now there is life. He looks as he must have looked when Elizabeth was alive."

Sam looked at her with respect. This woman might be operating as a typical Victorian baby machine but her whole persona was much broader than that. She was curious, so she asked

"So why you? Why can you see me? Is it through Vivian? Do you have a connection to Vivian?"

She was horrified at the way that came out and apologised hastily

"I am so sorry! I did not mean to sound so –possessive."

Henrietta smiled. "The possessive instincts of one who is in love I believe?"

Sam hesitated and felt herself flush. Yes actually flush! Oh, wouldn't Kevin make a meal out of that!. Was she actually going to tell a complete stranger the startling fact that she had only just realized for herself? But some form of insanity had clearly overtaken her so she said

"What I really meant to say was, do you think your ability to see me comes through Vivian or yourself? And yes, I am – very much."

"Through me I think" said Henrietta. "I was in the siege of Lucknow, Vivian has probably told you; my father was an artillery officer and they all died during the course of the siege; and I watched him die in defence of his country, not heroically or even cleanly, shot through the groin and taking forty eight hours to die; I counted them... and my younger brother die of cholera, in terrible pain and distress, the flesh stripped from his body; and I watched my mother give up hope of relief or rescue and lose the will to live. I watched the buildings disintegrate with shell and round shot to be further destroyed by the rains so that nowhere was safe for man, woman or child to rest... I believe those sort of experiences either close you down or open you up. They closed Vivian down. Gerald, when I met him, was hovering on the brink of something that may well have destroyed him and we reached out to each other and stepped back from the edge. But in Lucknow, after my mother's death, something inside me parted and opened doors. I was desperate I suppose to find some kind of meaning in it all, some reason in everything I had seen, so that I did not lose my own. I helped with the sick and injured; I cared for the children; I focussed on the native troops, who refused all temptations from their mutinous comrades to join them and desert us, who stepped in and took over wherever it was needed; gave their food and their lives... I did whatever I could to bring me meaning to life; I listened and thought upon different approaches and attitudes to life and death; I considered who in this life is ever completely wrong and who ever completely right; and let beliefs other than my own move in to share the space in my heart and in my head. And it was from that space that I was able to reach out to Gerald and ask for his assistance in a way that I would once have considered unbecoming and impossible for a young woman of my station and my time. I have not returned to what I was before the mutiny and I still pursue the knowledge that other cultures and religions have to offer us in an attempt to stay far away from the bleak despair of that terrible time in my life."

She smiled, shyly and warmly and added

"Perhaps it is that which allows me to consider the possibility of some kind of –alternative –I do not know what to call it –which I have before me today. And the complete transformation of Vivian only adds weight to my conclusions. What do you think?"

"I think you are a remarkable woman, with enormous compassion and a mind frame well beyond your time!" said Sam.

"So if I were to guess that you were not of this time, that you were born – possibly some-time in the future –I would be nearer to the mark than if I supposed you were an intelligent but eccentric Victorian lady?"

"120 years, give or take, in the future" said Sam.

"And if his change in demeanour is anything to go by then Vivian is also in love with you?"

"I haven't asked him and he hasn't said anything" said Sam warily.

"Oh there is no doubt!" said Henrietta. "The only question is what will happen if and when you have to return to your time in the future."

And Sam, hearing her fears spoken out loud in the warm calm tones of this amazing young woman, sat down suddenly and put her head in her hands.

Henrietta sipped her lemonade and watched for a while. Then she said

"You have considered it but you do not know the answer. And I believe you are afraid to face what it might mean; what it might mean to live without Vivian...and what it might do to him."

"Yes" said Sam quietly. "I am afraid."

"You must have experienced this kind of travelling, for want of a better word, before, surely? The circumstances themselves do not appear to distress you, only what has happened within them."

"You are much too perceptive for comfort" said Sam. "Also telepathic. I feel as if I am being read from the inside."

Henrietta laughed.

"Have you not found that if we allow circumstances a little freedom, resist the urge to curtail or hide bound them, then they do, over time, unravel themselves into strands that we may grasp with safety and re-plait?"

"Yes" said Sam. "Yes I believe that completely and have attempted to practice the creed but this –this thing –has left me more vulnerable than I have ever felt before. I cannot bear the thought of being, of living without –"

She stopped.

Henrietta said

"Without Vivian. I understand. How could I not understand? I am a soldier's wife. Gerald was young and passionate and damaged when I met him but a soldier nonetheless. He spends his working life fighting in, or making provision for, dangerous interactions on the borders between the Punjab and Afghanistan and he wouldn't do anything else if he could. Apart from me it is the love of his life and if I love him I must love that also. So I try not to look into the future but to enhance the present with the understandings of the past. I am sure that you know your history just as I am sure that you could tell me of the perils and the tragedies that await us."

She looked at Sam keenly and Sam, vividly remembering the accounts she had read of the 2nd Afghan War and the conflicts leading up to it, nodded but said nothing. There were, after all, many survivors and Gerald did not belong to The Guides. There was a better than even chance he would survive, even if he was amongst those who fought their way back to Kabul with General Roberts to retake the city after the 1879 Mission was annihilated. Survive that war at least. And by the time of The Boer Wars he would be 57. With a bit of luck he might have retired.

"Our fates are written?" said Henrietta, watching her face.

"Yeah."

And instead she said

"They plan on changing the British uniform shortly- to khaki, like the Guides."

Henrietta clapped her hands in delight.

"Finally! Finally clothes suited to the purpose. There have been rumours and some opposition but it is only sensible surely?"

"It has always seemed to me utterly ridiculous that men should be expected to go into battle in clothes so tight that they restrict breathing; but in India. Madness. Have no fear; the army of the future will be dressed as appropriate to combat and not parade ground!"

"It is a pity that I cannot tell Gerald. He has always envied the Guides their uniforms but I think if I try and explain how I acquired the information he will think I am suffering from some pre-birth indisposition and fetch the doctor to me!"

"You and he do not discuss your open minded views and alternative thinking then? Does that not put a restraint in your relationship?" said Sam curiously.

Henrietta looked down at her lap and laid a hand on the small rounded lump just above it.

"We will in time. In the meantime my children speak the languages of this country as well as their own and I am sure they ply our servants with all the questions that children do and through those responses they get a much wider perception of life than I could ever give them. And eventually through us all Gerald will reach a point where he can let the past recede, become dust and let it blow away on the wings of the plain winds."

Sam said "Ali said something very similar to Vivian when he was considering joining the forces who pursued the rebels into the hills."

Henrietta smiled. "Ali is and always has been a very wise man. As a young man he was Vivian's father's bearer, did you know?"

Sam nodded her head. "From Ali. But Vivian has not told me about his early life, only that he was born in India and his father was a soldier."

"Ask him about it. It explains something of his attachment to Gerald and his sense of responsibility for him."

Sam looked at Henrietta speculatively for a few moments and then she said

"I do not in general find women a particularly attractive species. I generally prefer the company of men."

Henrietta laughed. "I could see why your particular brand of honesty might not be approved or well liked in female circles! Certainly not in my time."

"But you're different. I could certainly have made a friend of you. But you obviously survive amongst the female population of the station. How do you do it?"

"I am a married woman so I smile pleasantly in female company and if at all possible make a point of engaging the gentlemen in conversation. Both sexes may think I'm a little eccentric but the gentlemen forgive it because I am attractive and the women forgive it because I am married, well known happily married."

"You are a very rare commodity" said Sam. "A thinking woman with a tolerance of the boundaries of her current life and situation. Does your Gerald know what a lucky man he is?"

"Possibly! He is an attractive sociable man much in demand at any entertainment, and pursued by both sexes I am told, but he only has eyes for his wife where many stray. I believe I am the lucky one."

They talked on, of many things. Sam plied Henrietta for details of the station at Lahore, of their life and what it entailed and Henrietta asked Sam about the changes the future would bring for women and finally they talked of alternate realities, Sam's experiences and Henrietta's cultural explorations. Then they heard movements from within, smiled at each other warmly, and Sam moved to the other side of the veranda and Henrietta closed her eyes as if she was taking a small nap. Vivian came out through the door first with a slightly anxious look on his face and Gerald followed him. Completely ignoring Sam and smiling down at his sleeping wife, he touched her gently on her cheek and said

"So you did need a rest!"

Henrietta opened her eyes and stretched out her hands to him.

"It has been wonderful. I have really enjoyed myself." And she looked across at Vivian and smiled broadly. "You are a lucky man, Vivian, to be here with –this" and she waved a vague hand which took in Sam and the beautiful vista at her back. Vivian's eyebrows shot up into his hair line and Gerald said

"She loves open spaces Viv. Not surprising really when you consider-" he didn't finish the sentence but pulled Henrietta to her feet and put his arm about her.

"We must be going my love. I am on duty tomorrow."

"We must come again Gerald, before too long. I like it here very much!"

Mohammed brought the small trap round to the front of the bungalow and Gerald lifted Henrietta into it and climbed in himself, took the reins and set off down the cantonment road with one hand held high in the air in a farewell salute. Henrietta, turning slightly in her seat, put the fingertips of both hands to her lips and blew a soft kiss.

When they were out of sight Vivian put his arm around Sam's shoulders and kissed the top of her head.

"I assume that small gesture was for you."

Sam just smiled.

Vivian also had duties which took him to beyond sunset but when he returned and they were sitting on the veranda luxuriating in the cool breeze coming in from the distant hills, he asked her about Henrietta.

"What she went through during the siege changed her, and she feels, for the better" said Sam. "It taught her to listen, to explore her feelings and those of others, to appreciate that what an individual believes is his own choice, and cannot be forced on him by others, and it taught her acceptance even though throughout that time acceptance involved pain. She allowed it to change her and welcomed the change. She embraced change as a route to development and growth, and that as a route to potential peace, personal peace. Metamorphosis. Even though the last metamorphosis, in this life, is death, she accepted that death was only a change as well and that a life of change prepared us for it and she welcomed that too. It gave her strength and helped her make sense of everything that was happening. It brought her Gerald's love and an ability to consider the possibility of the existence of things beyond her comprehension."

Vivian looked at her appraisingly.

"So much understanding gained in so little time- and you liked her."

"Yes. Very much."

"I am getting the distinct impression that liking a woman is an unusual occurrence" said Vivian.

"Let's just say I am particular about those whom I would choose as friends" said Sam.

He was smiling and then his expression suddenly changed and Sam was sure that he was going to ask her about her most recent experiences, about Steve and about Luc and suddenly she really didn't want to talk about either, so she said quickly

"Henrietta said something about Ali being your father's bearer when he was young. You haven't told me about your father. Will you now?"

Vivian was quiet for a long time. Sam gazed out at the huge expanse of the starlit night and reflected on the countless novels and movies that had featured a sky such as this. And then Vivian broke into her thoughts.

"I was seven when my father went with the forces who were sent to reinstate and protect the replacement Amir in Afghanistan, in Kabul. The Army of the Indus they called it. Gerald's father, an engineer, was also part of the contingent and they were close friends although their wives only acquaintances. And they had some success at first, defeating the Afghans and forcing Dost Mohammed, the current Amir, into exile. Macnaughton, the Envoy, and the politicians were sure of their actions and the sovereignty of their diplomacy and confidence was high. Macnaughton was paying huge yearly amounts to the tribes who guarded the Kyber pass and others, and the troops passed through the defiles with little difficulty, while the monies were paid. They made themselves at home, like soldiers always do, and built cantonments with parade grounds and racetracks and after the camp had been settled the women were invited to join their husbands in the new cantonments. We had letters from my father at that time, as did Gerald's family and our mothers compared them. Both shared the same views and reservations. The people of Kabul had no liking for our new Amir; the means to support him and our troops were inadequately thought through, especially in such a poor, cold, remote strong country; we had close ties to the Sikh Emperor, Runjeet, which made the Afghans detest us; the army commanders and the political wallahs could not agree amongst themselves; the new Amir had objected to the

Balla Hissar where his palace was, in Kabul, being made into a stronghold for the British troops and our envoy had capitulated. Both my father and Gerald's father strongly condemned the newly built cantonments, sited on a plain outside the city walls. He said they made 'every conceivable mistake', including poor judgement and false economy. The ground was swampy, bounded by river and canal and overlooked by forts, not one of which was occupied by the British. The whole area was hopeless for the quick movement of cavalry or artillery and as a cavalry officer he felt keenly this inability to defend. He could not understand how anyone with experience in the field could possibly have squadroned their forces in such a ludicrous military position.

So he wrote, and many times, and from this point I believe my mother knew what the outcome would be. There was more, much more, to do with the size, shape, low walls; but I have forgotten. The commissariat was sited outside the walls, some quarter mile away; I remember that. There was apparently an outcry about this from junior officers, Gerald's father among them, but no one in authority listened...

Anyway as it happened, at the time of the call to families to join with their spouses I was ill and my mother was unable to go. There was a fever going round that had affected some of the children and Gerald was another and because of that and the fact that their husbands were in Kabul, our mothers became friends. They both planned to travel to Kabul under a separate escort once we were well but in the meantime my father had written to say that he was even more uneasy about some of the things that were happening in the outlying forts. That whilst cantonment life continued much as always, it was not safe to go shooting in the surrounding countryside and that effectively they were 'confined'. He wrote also that some of the tribes on the outlying hills were already challenging the cantonment area, and that they were better armed and sadly, better led. Also some of their British confederates were arousing the enmity of the male population of Kabul by consorting with the women of the town and hostility was growing. In addition, there was an appalling; decrease in morale and with it, discipline and he was concerned about the competency of the command. Both he and Gerald's father had agreed that their wives should delay the journey until more was known. Others had received similar reports in letters from their relatives also in Kabul and there were rumours that the cost of the whole operation was becoming embarrassing and Macnaughton's payment to the three tribes guarding the passes was being curtailed. Though both women were anxious to be with their husbands my mother felt that my father would not have taken such a decision lightly. They were very close and she felt his fears were grounded. As I am sure you know he was right to be concerned and that the fate of that doomed contingent was never in any doubt. There was only one survivor who made it to the walls of the fort at Jalalabad from that fateful retreat of 1842 although some of the captive women and children and wounded officers were later released and others, Indians, survived and made it back to Kabul. My father was not among them. Nor Gerald's... More than sixteen thousand died in that retreat, including camp followers and soldiers' wives and families.

In later years I read accounts of those who were part of the ensuing retributive campaign and their fight to finally leave Afghanistan in the footprints of those who had gone before them. I know that their trail was littered with the corpses of thousands of men and animals, scattered, and in states of defilement and decomposition. I know that in parts the passes were so narrow that it was impossible not to tread on them. I know also that the tribesman had sometimes arranged the corpses, lying one in another's dead arms and that the troops were appalled by such flagrant sullying of the dead. I know that some balked at the acts they were given to perform in the city of Kabul; were disgusted with themselves and the profession which made them licensed assassins.

We abandoned the country to the Afghans, succeeding only in rescuing the captives. We had attempted to place the yoke about their necks and they had thrown it off and retrieved their fierce independence at a brutal cost to us...

And in England, as in India, there were families who wept for those whose bones lay in the passes of Afghanistan only too aware that as a general once said 'war cannot be made without loss...'

I always imagined that my father died fighting in one of those terrible ice ridden passes... But only his killers and the carrion birds know where. I do not remember if I suffered a boy's rage and desire for vengeance. Later, after I read the accounts I hoped that he and Gerald's father were two of those they joined in the embrace of the dead..."

He bit his lip hard to restrain the flow of words. This too had not been shared until now. He was not looking at her; he was not with her at all.

"I was seven and saw it as my duty to look after my mother and my siblings but Gerald was only four and devoted to his father. I suppose I became an elder brother and someone on whom he could rely."

Henrietta was right, thought Sam. That did explain a lot.

"Many women in that situation would have returned to England. Why did your mother and Gerald's mother not do that?"

"I was too young for such considerations and so I never asked her. I was born in India so it was my home and at the time it made perfect sense. When I was older I came to realise that everything she held dear and all her most beloved memories were here and to leave it would be akin to leaving my father. I think Gerald's mother felt much the same. Both men came from wealthy backgrounds and our mothers were well provided for and they were not reliant on the army for support. So Gerald and I grew up together and lived quite close for most of our youth."

"And Ali? Why was he not with your father?" said Sam.

Vivian laughed mirthlessly.

"He was conjoined by my father to stay with us. I believe he protested strongly but my father would not be moved."

The moonlight enhanced the small frown that had appeared between his brows and Sam lifted a fingertip to smooth it out carefully.

She said "Do you think he knew?"

"When I was 17 I read John Kaye's History of the War in Afghanistan and as his material was taken from letters and diaries of those with first-hand experience I felt very close to my father in its pages. But I had no reason to think that he might have had foreknowledge until- until I started to consider that there were more things in heaven and earth…" He looked at her. "I don't know. But I think Ali believed he did because from that point he saw us as his life's work!"

"Yes" said Sam and was humbled by the thought. Then she said

"Try not to let history repeat itself."

"What do you mean?"

What could she say? It was an impossible conjecture.

"Nothing. It will repeat regardless."

"Yes" said Vivian soberly.

They said nothing for a while, each occupied with their own thoughts and then Sam said

"And was he drop dead gorgeous like you? Your father I mean."

Vivian laughed and moved closer to her and put his arm about her shoulders.

"You have a wonderful way with words!"

"You have no idea!"

"I can see that in some ways the English language has become more –picturesque" said Vivian.

"You have no idea!" said Sam again.

"I do not remember the way he looked very well. Only an impression" said Vivian, in reply to her question. "But I am told that I am a lot like him and in looks."

Sam sat up and pulled away from him.

"What's wrong?" said Vivian, concerned.

Sam closed her eyes and saw again that devastating, heart rending, grotesque scene of mayhem and butchery.

"I know what he looks like, looked like; your father; I have seen him."

Vivian stood up and stared down at her.

"How could you?" he demanded.

Sam opened her eyes and looked up at him. They were so alike, they could be one and the same. The same hair, the same eyes, the same build and the same loyalty to others. Vivian knew how and where his father had died, knew it as a boy; had read about it as a man. What purpose could all this congenital detail serve?

But his eyes locked her in and his mouth was a determined straight line. She wished she could take him by the hand and lead him back over the line, to see it all for himself and decide what he would choose to remember and what he would allow to rest, out there in a rock and bone strewn pass across the border in Afghanistan, so short a distance from Kabul.

But she had no possible means of doing that.

And so it would have to be words, her words and it would punish them both but she had no choice. It had not been presented to her for her own inner guidance. It was for him. It would open another door...

So she began and after watching her intently for a few moments he turned away and leaned on the veranda rail and watched the moon fade to a silver curve and then disappear.

She left nothing out; not the noise or the smell; not the savagery of climate and condition and brutality; or any little detail of the horror and valour of his father's end and she lived through every moment of it again.

When she reached that final scene she became suddenly aware of Vivian again and she looked across at him. He was still standing as he had at the onset, staring out into the night but some of the tautness had gone from those straight, broad shoulders and there was an indefinable aura of tranquillity about him. She continued to watch him for a long time but he did not move or turn.

Then she said quietly

"What was his name?"

He turned then as if surprised he was not alone and stared down at her, puzzled.

"Your father-what was his name?"

He looked away again, into the distance, into the past and said

"Vivian Montgomery Ashley-Forbes. Captain Ashley-Forbes."

"And that was Gerald's father wasn't it? The dark haired officer whose body he was standing over to-at the last?"

"Yes. That was Gerald's father, and his friend."

"So alike" murmured Sam.

Vivian smiled then.

"Yes" he said. "My mother was dark and so was my sister. But I take, took after my father. Gerald's mother was blonde as were his sisters and brother but he is like his father too. I met him once, before they left for Afghanistan. I had forgotten. Gerald was pink and round at the time. I had not thought to compare them..."

He looked at her, his dark eyes questioning and then he said

"Strange how life gives us back what we have lost, in ways we could not conceive."

Sam stared at him. He had lost a father at a young age and then a close friend before he reached puberty; as a young man he had witnessed the terrible carnage that took the life of a mother, sister, wife and daughter; he had seen his best friend suffer agonies at the same loss; and he was counting his blessings! Truly the man was a paradigm among men. She said

"I expect you would like Gerald to know too, wouldn't you?-but that's not possible is it?"

"No" said Vivian thoughtfully. "But maybe one day..."

And Sam unwittingly found herself thinking that perhaps there was a debt to be repaid and could not control the shiver that ran through her.

The days merged into weeks. Sam lost track of time. Army life had patterns and proceedures, not normally to her liking. But now they gave her a framework into which to slot Vivian and herself, and in that, a kind of comfort.

Then there came the morning when Vivian arrived back for chota hazri, little breakfast, (which Sam thought Kevin would approve; another meal added to the standard list) after morning stables and parade, as he usually did if things had gone according to plan. One look at his face told Sam to expect some change to the routine. Although anxious to have the details she didn't push him, knowing that when he had arranged it in his own mind he would share it with her. Two coffees later he said

"Orders have just come down. The regiment is going to prepare to leave for a bout of insurgent quelling. We get a lot of these campaigns these days. It will be good for the men; we have been training hard in the new ways and it will give the daffadars a chance to work their men and I have a couple of young subalterns who need blooding." He talked himself through the positive justifications and then. looked at her anxiously.

"It's what you do" said Sam. "I know that. It wouldn't be my choice of profession for you. But that's not my call and –"she thought carefully; what she was about to say was almost unprecedented; "and I love you just the way you are!" It sounded, she reflected, a lot lighter than it felt and appallingly reminiscent of a chorus line in a musical.

Vivian breathed out. As if he suddenly felt the freedom to talk about his profession he said

"We've had to change, stationed up here. It's no longer-stand in line; fire, reload, fire; volley after volley; fix bayonets; charge. The terrain does not permit it. The warfare does not support it. We have all had to become snipers, trackers, skirmishers and spies. Move under cover of darkness and be ready to attack and defend at a moment's notice. The tribes we fight up here are the best at what they do. It's their land and they know it intimately. They appear out of nowhere and disappear into dust. Every rock has a marksman; every vale hides a hoard waiting to pour down on us and attack and kill for the faith." He sighed. "Sometimes it just feels like a game. Fighting for the honour of winning; shake hands with the losers and no hard feelings- anyway it's not actually that far away. Just over the border. One of the border tribes has been doing some pretty resourceful and effective raiding amongst the villages, stealing everything from livestock to women. It's the only way they have of supplementing their living, in their perception anyway, and I will admit to a certain sympathy for them. Their land is little more than grass covered rock. Anything more than the odd rangy goat and some poor crops and they have to come down from the hills to find it. It is an unforgiving land. Besides which the damn tribes love fighting! It's just a great game!"

"I'm sure it is" said Sam. "Especially as they all believe they have a fast ticket to paradise if they kill an infidel. That must do a lot towards allaying any fear of dying."

Vivian looked at her curiously.

"Do you believe in paradise? In God?"

"I believe that if there is a God, he's got one hell of a job on when some of us get up there" said Sam. "Either way he's got to be partisan and take sides or the best adjudicator ever. And he's going to upset a lot of people. Have you read Milton?"

Vivian laughed out loud.

"Yes I have actually. I always felt the best arguments were on Lucifer's side!"

"There you are then" said Sam.

"Do all 20th century women have your sense of satire?"

"No" said Sam.

"Ah" said Vivian perceptively.

"When do you leave?" said Sam.

"Two days' time" said Vivian. "But I do have some good news" he added, seeing her face. "Gerald's troop of engineers are ordered to join us. We're not given a choice in how we deal with these insurgents; if we don't punish them they just do it again and more and worse. And sometimes it means the destruction of a lot of villages. So we take the sappers along to repair and make good where possible for those caught in the crossfire. And as it happens engineers are amongst the best fighters; Gerald is no exception. He'll be in his element! I suggested he brought Henrietta here and I will leave Ali with the both of you. Mohammed will come with me and Gerald's bearer and syce. He agreed. He knows Henrietta likes it here although she hasn't told him, I don't think, just how much and why. I also think he feels she would be better off, in her present condition, with Ali and away from the small cricket team she is amassing. Ali agrees."

"You could point out to Gerald that the cricket team, as you call it, has more than a little to do with him!" said Sam sardonically. "But yes, that will be good although she must be quite far on by now. I hope I won't be required to play midwife. What I know about babies would go on the back of a postage stamp!"

"About seven months I believe" said Vivian. "And I doubt it. I'm sure if it came to that Henrietta and Ali would manage."

It was somewhat prophetic, if misaligned.

And he reached down and pulled Sam to her feet and said

"I think I need more practice at taking off those beautiful garments you are wearing.Let's make the most of what's left of this wonderous night."

Midway across the living room he suddenly stopped as if something had just occurred to him.

"Babies ..."

"Babies? What about them?"

"I never asked –I suppose I assumed – I am sorry – it never occurred to me –"

He stopped, embarrassed and lost for words.

"Don't worry" said Sam, trying not to laugh. "I've got that covered. Other things –as it happens –have moved on quite a long way although I do believe that you Victorians have your own varied methods of contraception."

Vivian smiled sheepishly.

"Although" Sam went on, "judging by the size of some of your families most of you didn't bother."

Vivian was watching her with an obvious expectation of some kind of explanation so she said

"At some point between now and the 20th century women decided, well some of them anyway, that they wanted more from life than running a baby production line. Over the years various forms of research were conducted, not all of them welcome in the early days, and ended in the production of the contraceptive pill available to all who want it, to allow sex without pregnancy. I have a small capsule inserted in my arm which does the same thing and lasts about three years. I have been living in the USA" she added.

She looked at Vivian.

"The monthly cycle is still a pain but not as much as it was. God is definitely a man!"

As there was no real corollary to a statement of this kind, Vivian smiled in a bemused fashion and said

"Shall we continue then?"

24 hours later Gerald came bursting in like a whirling dervish as usual, deposited Henrietta and a significant amount of baggage, kissed his wife passionately, thanked Ali for his services and crashed out again shouting to Vivian as he went, that he would see him at the assembly point in a day's time.

Sam watched Gerald leap on to his horse and gallop furiously up the cantonment road and turned to Henrietta.

"Does he do everything like that?"

Henrietta smiled shyly.

"Almost."

"Hell!" said Sam.

Ali moved Henrietta's baggage into the spare bedroom and went off to make tea whilst Henrietta unpacked some of her luggage and changed her travelling dress for something more comfortable. Whilst they were alone Sam quizzed Vivian about the campaign and what he expected.

"They are typically short and swift. Tribal attack is usually violent, often unexpected and habitually vociferous; they believe in killing; they believe in killing the wounded and mutilating the dead –"

"Well that's okay then" said Sam faintly. "I like a man who doesn't deem it necessary to spare a woman the bald facts of the matter."

Vivian smiled at her boyishly.

"That's what you lead me to believe!"

"Now I'm regretting it."

"The advantage is they don't stay around to prolong battle. If they can't kill and win they charge off back into the hills."

He looked at her carefully and then said

"It is a no man's land. Some tribes show allegiance to the Amir. Many do not. The only rule is knife and bullet. But it is curious; many of their traits strike a chord –they love shikar, hunting, they will often combine the pleasures of hawking or hunting with dogs with the more exciting business of highway robbery, cattle stealing and burglary - and their ability to entertain themselves and be entertained is quite extraordinary!"

Sam digested this. He actually liked them. He was going out with the express intention of killing those for whom he had both respect and liking! How did that work?

"What do you do then? When they are chasing back into the hills" she asked.

"If the ground's good enough we might get in a cavalry charge just to keep them running, set up a couple of piquets outside the camp to make sure they've left no snipers behind and keep an eye out for the engineers whilst they finish off whatever it is they're doing."

"The only rule is knife and bullet" Sam quoted.

"Yes" said Vivian.

"You make it all sound so very mundane" said Sam, "and" she added resentfully, "enjoyable!"

"If you are trying to ask me whether there will be any action –the answer is yes. If you are asking me –will it be fierce? The answer is yes. We will be in the unknown white the men of the tribes know the hills and the passes like they know their own families. I have seen us start to remove the piquets from the hilltops, where they have watched over our camp; watched them flee down the hills in a hail of rifle fire, as the local men, boys many of them, take their places, only the fastest making it back to their troop. I have seen a soldier have to fight for his life against a young man with a curved knife, trying to prevent the theft of his rifle, have his flesh slashed to ribbons. I have known the commanding officer have dinner with the Khan of a local tribe the night before and that same man set out to kill him the next day by sniper fire. So If you're asking me if I will get hurt, the answer is –I don't know." He paused. "And yes, it is enjoyable, although the word is too narrow to convey the meaning; the challenge; the fighting; the pursuit, riding side by side with men you trust and would give your life for-"

"Semper Fidelis" murmured Sam soberly.

"What?"

"The motto of the marines" said Sam.

"Ah yes" said Vivian. "And others."

He said almost as an afterthought,

"They have their own rules, you know, their own laws that they live by. And one of them, as you obviously know, is vengeance; retaliation for every slight, personal injury, insult or damage to property. But there are others. Feed and shelter any traveller arriving at their house; grant asylum to anyone seeking protection at his home, even if that is an enemy. You probably would not approve of their treatment of women for most are considered just property and very tightly reined. It is largely a male dominated society but then so is our own, in army life. But they can be most jovial and cordial in entertainment and relaxation..."

He stopped, as if his own words had somehow made a nonsense of his profession.

Sam wondered how much difference there was, if you took away the jezails and tulwars, between tribal life and English village life. She said

"Will you be frightened?"

Vivian looked at her strangely. He said

"Before we go into attack, yes. Very few are not. You just have to put it away somewhere and go ahead."

"Especially the man out in front" said Sam.

He came across to her and put his arms around her.

"I am a soldier" he said against her hair.

"I know; I know; its what you do" said Sam. "It doesn't mean I have to like it."

He took her face in his hands and kissed her.

He leaned back to look into her face. Sam thought for a moment and then said

"Part of the reason for my" she chose the word carefully, "disparagement of your profession is that I know what the future holds."

"More weapons? Better weapons?"

"Yes" said Sam, "and slaughter the like of which you cannot imagine; slaughter that makes the Mutiny and the debacle of the retreat from Kabul seem like pricking your finger. Youth poured down a pitiless drain."

She thought about what she had read of what was now laughingly called The Great War, where the machines gobbled up young lives like demons from hell, desecrating their bodies, destroying their lungs; violating their minds, their beliefs, their hopes. And the crushing of the spirit, where men came to realise what they thought was an honourable profession in the defence of the realm was nothing more than a sacrificial offering to the gods of war.

Suddenly the lines of a poem by Sylvia Plath came to her.

"The prince leans to the girl in scarlet heels,
Her green eyes slant, hair flaring in a fan
Of silver, as the rondo slows, now reels
Begin on tilted violins to span...

Until near twelve the strange girl all at once
Guilt stricken halts, pales, clings to the prince
As amid the hectic music and cocktail talk
She hears the caustic ticking of the clock"

Cinderella. It had always haunted her...with its strange girl and the prince..Was *she* Cinderella, just waiting for the clock to strike? To signify that she must leave; she must return...

Then Henrietta came out from her room and her prince let her go and walked out through the front door to go round to the stables and supervise the preparation of the horses and tackle.

Sam looked across at Henrietta and said, with a slight shrug of her shoulders

"Soldiers!"

And Henrietta nodded and they smiled at each other, and then Ali came in with the tea.

Twelve hours later he was gone.

It was a pleasant sojourn for the two women. Henrietta was in her element because she got to talk about subjects other than babies and children and Sam because Henrietta was her idea of an intelligent woman, spiritually motivated, with a sense of humour *and* a soldier's wife.

Henrietta, brought up in a military family, could explain to Sam how their chosen career effected such men, what was expected of them and what it drove them to do.

"They walk a thin line sometimes" she told Sam. "They are expected to be brave and courageous, confident but never overly so. They are expected to put honour and loyalty before all else and courage before both. It is taken for granted that they show no fear nor any aversion to killing. They are expected to put their regiment and their men before their family and all before themselves. A good officer, they are told, will never ask a member of his troop to do anything he would not do himself."

"All that could be very difficult to achieve in some circumstances" said Sam. "The pressure would be tremendous on some men. Hell! Some of them are only boys when they first come out here."

"That is very true" said Henrietta. "As young officers they must find their place, with their regiment, with their men and amongst their peer group. The standards of the officer's mess can be truly demanding! They are also expected to excel at sports and horsemanship. And to drink, but be able to hold their liquor! To be manly at all times but never lascivious. To play like boys and fight like men!"

"And dance. And be polite in mixed company" said Sam. "Is the suicide rate high?" She'd meant it flippantly but Henrietta answered soberly.

"It is not unknown. But they are very close, all of them; it is a family."

"Vivian does not appear to follow the mess procedures; he eats at home and does not take part in any kind of social activity which does not involve sport. How does he manage that?"

"I think perhaps the circumstances surrounding his return from the campaigns suppressing the mutiny may have had something to do with it. He was obviously not alone in his losses but I believe his commanding officer may have made allowances in order to ensure his fitness for duty and his continued contribution to the regiment."

Henrietta watched Sam's face and added kindly

"It is not an easy life up here on the frontier. Some transfer; some sell out; some meet their death, willingly or unwittingly. What we are left with up here is the best. Vivian is one of the best. And I know what you are thinking. A good wife does not ask her husband to make a choice between her and his regiment because she knows what his answer will be."

Sam thought grimly, living in another century has its advantages then.

She said

"Do you go up to the hills, during the hot weather?"

"We do not suffer the extremes that they do further down on the plains but many of the wives do go to the hills for the hotter months; for diversion, for entertainment. I stay with Gerald but not just because of him. If the weather is hot I just ignore it. It is a challenge and I apparently still like challenge. I tell people I am staying to be with my husband but the truth is when all the women and children leave, India breathes a sigh of relief and goes back to being herself and you stand a chance of getting to know the real culture and its people away from the superficiality of cantonment life."

"I would do the same" said Sam and then suddenly realised that was never going to happen and hurried on. "Things do change you know" she added, thinking about the advent of electricity and fridges and air conditioning...and weaponry. "In the wars to come... 50 years from now" she paused considering her words, "50 years from now there is a war which dramatically changes people's perceptions of fighting, even those of the dedicated soldier... Which in some way levels the playing field... Prioritises the priorities..."

Henrietta's said

"I am glad to hear it. Does it mean that there are less wars?"

"No" said Sam. "Only different ones. It goes against any political or governmental edict, but sometimes I believe the world would be a better place without border lines."

The days were pleasant. Sam persuaded Ali to take them out in the small trap so that she could show Henrietta the old ruined lodge where Vivian had finished his story of the siege of Lucknow. Even in this short space of time jungle creepers had slipped further sinuous fingers into the cracks of the walls. Nature was reclaiming its own. She asked Henrietta about her first meeting with Gerald and what had made her hold onto his memory and then ask for his help.

"My first sight of him was a thin, ragged skeleton of a boy with a face nearly as black as his hair!" Henrietta smiled at the memory. "He had been in the rear-guard, firing guns, lighting fires, to cover our night-time retreat. One of the women travelling in the same cart was suffering from fever and at my request he rode off and came back with water and cloths. He had cuts and abrasions all over his face and was clearly bone tired but his smile was like a beacon of hope and I believe I fell in love with him at that moment. He stayed close, riding beside the carts and carriages until we reached the Alam Bagh just outside the city which the rest of the relief troops were holding. We stayed there a short time. He came by often in those days, to make sure we had what we needed, to provide, if at all possible, what we had not. He brought news of the planned retreat to Cawnpore and our proposed journey to Allahabad. I met Vivian on one of those occasions. I remember thinking how polite he was, and young too, and how his face looked as if it had been carved from stone."

"What happened when you were in Allahabad?" asked Sam.

"This will sound very strange" said Henrietta "but it seemed too clean, almost too civilised. It was the contrast I suppose. And there was so much talking! Women talking and gossiping endlessly. They were glad to be alive I suppose but I couldn't wait to get away. So I wrote to Gerald, not really knowing if my letter would reach him or not. But it did as you know and I believe at an opportune moment. He wrote back, the briefest of missives, simply stating that he would be with me shortly and would take me wherever I wished! I hardly had time to get myself ready before he was at my door."

"Like a whirling dervish?" said Sam.

"Yes! Exactly like that."

"Well," said Sam, "you were either going to love him or hate him!"

"I loved him" said Henrietta simply.

"Do you know what he felt about you?"

"Not at the time. Much later he told me he had fallen in love with me from the minute I poked my head out of the curtained cart."

"And he took you to Lahore? What happened then? Did he court you?"

Henrietta laughed.

"No. He passed me in the street when I was out with my aunt and saluted me very prettily but he didn't call. Then there was a military review and my aunt said that we should attend. I thought it was an unusual suggestion coming from her but the weather was pleasant and they are always entertaining. And somehow, and even now I really don't know how she managed to contrive it, we were at the same refreshment table as a group of officers and my aunt introduced us both as relations of veterans of Lucknow and Gerald was among them. My aunt found someone within the group who had known my father, her brother and engaged him in conversation, whilst making sure I was left with Gerald. He stayed with me all afternoon and by the end of it I at least was very sure of what I wanted. After that he came most days, when duty permitted and my aunt was the most discreet and complicit hostess!"

"Wonderful woman. It must run in your family. How long was it before he asked you to marry him?"

"Two weeks. It took two months more to persuade his commanding officer to allow it. He was very young. I believe my aunt might have had a hand in that also though she refused to admit to it."

"Is she still up there with you?" asked Sam.

"Oh yes. She lives quite near and visits the children daily when I am away. She is my father's sister and the military tradition runs in her veins. I think she would have preferred to be born a man though such things are never directly alluded to. For myself I am glad she was not. I might have lost them both in the fighting."

They drove home as the sun was setting and after the evening meal, sat together on the veranda looking out towards the low foothills and the cragged peaks beyond, both preoccupied with the same thoughts.

Sam suddenly turned towards Henrietta and said

"Do you ever get a sense of what is happening to him when he is away from you?"

Henrietta looked at her sharply.

"I have. Yes. Why do you ask?"

"Do you feel anything now?"

Henrietta didn't reply for a moment. Then she said carefully

"I feel a little anxious but I assumed I was picking up your concern for Vivian."

Sam stood up and went to stand with her hands on the balustrade surrounding the veranda. She told herself she was being foolish, that she was allowing foreknowledge to cast a shadow on present time, allowing anxiety for Vivian to conjure up doubt over his safety. But why now? She had not felt it earlier... The last days had been unclouded. In the end she could contain it no longer and turning to Henrietta she said

"I am afraid."

And Henrietta said

"I also."

They stayed there on the veranda until past midnight and then decided that at present there was nothing to be done and retired to their separate rooms. Before she did so Sam went and found Ali and told him of her concerns. He looked at her inscrutably and then nodded once and settled himself by the front door. It was enough to know he was there.

Sam was awakened by Ali some-time in the hours before dawn. He told her there were riders coming down the cantonment road and the Memsahib should be ready. Sam had not undressed. She went directly to the guest room and woke Henrietta.

Seconds later the door burst open to admit Gerald, wild haired and eyed but whole and in complete command of himself.

"It is Vivian and he is hurt." He turned as he heard the sound of an approaching vehicle. Then he looked back at Ali and his wife.

"Mohammed is with him. He said we must bring him here and he was right. He said something strange –he said –never mind that now - There are many injured and the surgeon and his orderlies are overwhelmed. Mohammed rode with him and I came on ahead to warn you. It was – I have not the time to explain it now –Mohammed will tell you –I must go back. My troop I have left with my lieutenant –he will be all right but I am in dereliction of duty –and Vivian's men are without him and his daffadar –and his subaltern –well I am sure he'll manage –but I must return –"

He turned quickly as Mohammed, followed by two men carrying a stretcher came in through the front door. Gerald glanced at Ali who nodded and lead the men into the bedroom and then looked at his wife and then back at Ali who was standing in the door frame.

"You will manage? I could not leave him there – not after –"

"Go! We will manage" said Henrietta firmly.

"I am so sorry!" Gerald looked at Ali desperately and then to his wife

"I will return as soon as I am able."

Sam was standing in the middle of the room and Gerald, striding past, suddenly stopped and turned and seemed to look right at her

"Tell him", he paused as if surprised by what he was saying, "tell him that the daffadar and I live and he is duty bound to do the same!"

And then he was out of the door, onto his horse and the deadening dust and the darkness ate up his departure.

In the bedroom Sam saw that Ali and Mohammed had already stripped Vivian of his clothes. Hastily she looked him over but even to an unprofessional eye the damage was obvious. Whilst his face and arms were covered in slashes and cuts, and his right wrist had suffered trauma of some kind, it was the wound at the top of his left thigh where the serious damage was done. It had been bleeding profusely; it still was. Mohammed had affected a rudimentary tourniquet to staunch the bleeding and it seemed to be working. The wound was torn wide and so straight it was easy to imagine what kind of weapon had inflicted it. But there was no sign of damage to the bone and therefore no reason to think, provided the wound could be adequately cleaned and closed up, there would be any problem with long-term healing.

Sam said to Mohammed

Do you have any idea how we could close such a wound and what with?"

Mohammed nodded and left the room. Sam looked at Ali.

"Go and boil water, lots of water and tear up two or three sheets and immerse them in the boiling water. We will use them to clean up all this mess and to use as bandages. I don't know what Mohammed will come back with but it must be boiled too. Everything! The water he drinks; and the bowls and cups he eats from. Everything!"

Ali nodded. Sam nodded too. Of course, he had been there when Elizabeth had tended Vivian through the cholera. He remembered and approved.

Mohammed was back. In his hands he had something which looked like a needle and thick thread from the land of the giants.

"What in god's name is that?" said Sam. "No! I don't want to know. I presume you are going to try and sew up the gash?"

Mohammed nodded solemnly.

Ali said "it is what he uses when a horse sustains an injury. He is very good."

A poor man's suture and needle kit! Let's hope so, thought Sam.

"Boil it!"

Mohammed handed the two items to Ali and then showed Sam what he had in his other hand.

"The surgeon gave it to me. He said it might help and would do no harm."

He handed her a small bottle with cloudy liquid in it and a pile of what looked like lint. The bottle's label proclaimed it to be Carbolic Acid and so the small heap of material was probably surgical gauze.

Sam and Mohammed looked at each other and then Sam said OK. Let's get started."

Ali was returning carrying a pile of steaming, molten cloths and a newly scrubbed basin of cooling water. They all turned to the bed. Sam looked down at the comatose man, seeing the slightly greenish pallor of the skin under the tan. She suppressed a shudder of fear and asked

"Have you given him anything or is he still unconscious from the wound?"

"He became un calm during the journey because of the jolting. I gave him brandy and opium" said Mohammed efficaciously.

Sam smiled.

"That will probably keep him quiet for a while then."

Mohammed, who had administered both in generous doses, nodded sagely.

They all, Henrietta included, immersed their hands and washed them vigorously in the cooling, boiled water and Ali whisked it away and went to fetch more. All that Sam could remember of the dangers for wounded men in the 19th century seemed to amount to one thing. Lack of hygene in the cleaning and treatment of wounds externally and drinks and foods, either contaminated or in dirty receptacles, internally.

He was not going to die and he was especially not going to die from that if she had anything to do with it! In the past she had dealt with a fair number of minor calamities and also illnesses ranging from bee stings to dysentery. But nothing like this. Nothing remotely like this. No time now for feminine reticence.

Sam and Ali washed all the open wounds on Vivian's face and arms and then turned to the slash on his leg. Sam saw with relief that the blood was beginning to congeal and Ali cut away the tourniquet.

"Has he lost a lot of blood?" Sam asked Mohammed.

Mohammed nodded.

"He is young and fit" said Sam. "His body should take care of that." It was a defiant proclamation to the universe as much as a voiced opinion to the others.

Very carefully and slowly she removed the clotted blood from around the terrible hole and then said to Mohammed

"OK. Over to you" and nodded at the needle like implement and sutures lying on a clean square of cloth.

"Please hold together" requested Mohammed. Sam gaped at him, then took a deep breath, bit her bottom lip between her teeth and, as gently as she could, forced the two skin edges together. She watched the first insertion of the needle and then closed her eyes, fighting a wave of nausea at the reflex pain that the undertaking gave her. Then she opened them and looked at Vivian's face. He was still completely out of it and she gave herself an angry shake.

It took quite a long time and it seemed to Sam that none of them drew breath because when Mohammed finished there was a gusty and universal sound of expelled air. Ali fetched another dish of boiled water to which Sam added some of the carbolic acid and then soaked squares of the gauze and laid them carefully over Mohammed's, it had to be said, fine needlework. Ali had torn one sheet into long strips and Sam bound these cautiously over the gauze and around the leg which Mohammed held slightly raised.

It was over. Henrietta and Ali gathered up all the bloody utensils and cloths and took them for washing and Sam looked at Mohammed and wondered if he ever drank alcohol and if he would like a brandy. The question didn't arise because she went and fetched the bottle, poured brandy into a glass and held it up to him with raised eyebrows. He smiled his quiet smile and took it from her and her eyes told him, I won't tell if you don't! Then she poured herself one, sat down on a chair next to the bed and put her head in her hands. If she could just sit like that for a little while there was every chance she would not throw up.

Ali and Henrietta returned with more boiled cloths, boiled water and tea and they all partook. Two brandies and two mugs of tea later and Sam thought she was ready to hear what had happened. Mohammed, clearly a practical man, was also reticent in speech. At some points his English failed him and he reverted to Pashtu but Sam got the gist.

All had gone reasonably smoothly; the regiments had met up at the appointed place and there had been a night march to the boundaries of the village where the insurgents were causing havoc. At dawn they had been found with their booty about to make off with camels, horses, a good deal of grain and number of rifles and women belonging to the headman. They were just in the process of setting fire to some of the habitats when the army appeared. They were in large numbers, more than anticipated, but they were already in disarray and it seemed an easy task. The troop skirmishers went out to their left and their right and the infantry followed up firing as they came. But the insurgents got up onto the hills above them and things started to go wrong. They drove them to a mile beyond the village, where the cavalry took over with intent to drive them back up into the hills. But now senior men were being picked off by sniper fire and whilst the charge was pursuant there was a river to ford and heavy rains had damaged the bridge and made it impassable. Some of the rebels attempted to cross the water on horseback but some turned to face the pursuers. Vivian was up in front with daffadar Razi Khan and Mohammed was just behind to his left.

"The fight was ours" said Mohammed in disgust. "And then some fool of a dog sowar sees his brother among the fleeing scum and goes yelling after him!"

Then all hell had broken loose. The fleeing rebels turned and charged back shrieking and slashing, into the infantry and the cavalry had gone at them hard. Gerald and his troop, on way to the damaged bridge got caught on the flank and Gerald had his horse shot from under him. There was a tribesman making straight for him, standing in his stirrups, teeth bared, and Vivian had spurred forward, knocked Gerald to one side with his horse and lashed out at the tribesman with his sword and caught him across the face, receiving a severe cut to the shoulder as he did so. The man wheeled away but another came at him with a lance, almost reaching his chest but Vivian parried it away with his sword. Vivian had then turned back to Gerald when the same man had changed his mind and swung back in for the kill. Daffadar Razi Khan had seen the move and tried to block it and been cut across the face and then the sword arm and had gone down through lack of vision but not before Vivian had seen the danger. With Gerald on the ground and stunned he had half turned his horse and parried the slashing blade with his sword in his left hand and deflected it, (his blade will carry the mark of that cut forever! Mohammed had added gleefully) but the tribesman's charge had been so fierce that the blade came down on his thigh and onto his horse's flank. The horse reared and Vivian was unseated. Mohammed, by this time clearly done with sword play, pulled up his carbine and shot the man.

Vivian was on the ground but still enough in charge of his faculties to command his subaltern to give chase, and reassured by Mohammed that Gerald was only stunned, passed out.

Gerald was now on his feet, with just a sprained shoulder and a bang on the head and he and Mohammed summoned help for Vivian and Daffadar Razi Khan but the field hospital was under pressure to get the wounded from the field and into shelter before the night temperatures froze them all to death or the insurgents got chance to return and inflict the kind of obscene mutilation which constituted their method of the dispatching of their enemies and when Mohammed suggested he had help at home the surgeon didn't argue. A few elemental warnings, a few surgical aids and Mohammed had commandeered a small wagon and departed. Gerald had issued orders to his men, told them he would soon return and departed with Mohammed. The Commander had been badly wounded and was undergoing treatment so for the moment there was no one to gainsay his actions.

There'll be hell to pay thought Sam.

"He was insistent to know what help I had so I told him" said Mohammed.

"What! What did you tell him?" squeaked Sam.

"I told him Ali had training and that the lady sahib had new ways" said Mohammed apologetically.

Sam stared at him.

Henrietta sat down abruptly and said

"We can deal with that later" and smiled wanly. "He is unharmed. Vivian is safe. What else matters?"

No one said anything for a few moments and then there was a groan from the bed and regimental consequences were dismissed.

Vivian had his eyes open and was frowning.

"Where am I? What the hell's happened. Why are there-"

He tried to sit up but with a scream of pain fell back down again.

"Lie still!" Sam commanded;

She bent over him. He looked flushed and underneath it, a peculiar colour. She placed a hand on his forehead. It was hot and he was shivering. She turned to Ali.

"Fetch a covering and get me some boiled water!" then she added, "Please" and smiled at him apologetically.

Sam went to the far side of the room and rummaged among the clothes and the few items she had with her when she first arrived. Yes! Quite why she had Brufen capsules with her she was at a loss to remember. But there they were, a full packet of extra strength. She pulled three from the foil and went back to the bedside where Ali was waiting with a small dish of boiled water. Sam broke open the capsules and emptied their contents into the water and swirled it around until dissolved while the others looked on, the expressions on their joint faces as those who have just watched a magician perform an amazing trick. She then picked up the brandy decanter and poured a generous measure into the dish and swirled it again. Then she asked Mohammed if he had any opium left and he produced a small tin. She took two, glanced at him, took another two and crushed them between two spoons and added it to the mixture and stirred. Then she bent over Vivian.

"Vivian!"

He opened his eyes. They were clouded with pain but still lucid.

"I want you to drink this!" Her voice brooked no discussion.

Vivian looked at her through half closed lids. She lifted his head, placed the dish to his lips and gently tipped it. Amazingly he drank. He was probably very thirsty thought Sam and the brandy helped. He choked once but she held his head and the liquid found its way down his throat. She laid his head back on the pillow and took the warm, damp cloth that Ali gave her and placed it on his brow. He opened his eyes one last time and looked at her with a puzzled frown and then closed them again. After fifteen endless minutes his breathing relaxed, became deeper and Sam stood back and turned to the little rapt audience about her.

"He should sleep now."

"What was that you gave him?" asked Henrietta.

"A 20th century pain killer" said Sam. "Nothing fancy. Just a non-prescription pain relief. Designed for headaches and muscle aches really. But mixed with opium and brandy I'm hoping it will give him the rest he needs. It will help bring down the fever although it must be done slowly because the fever is the body's way of boosting the immune system and fighting infection."

She looked at their ambivalent but respectful faces. There was little in the way of understanding but there was, she thought with some surprise, there was trust.

"We'd better go easy on the opium though otherwise we'll have him addicted before the wound heals!"

Nobody said anything.

Now there was just the waiting. Sam said

"And now if you will excuse me I will just go outside for a while" and she left the room quickly, went out of the door, down the veranda, across the garden to the stables and then into the bushes, beyond which she was violently sick. Note to self, she thought sardonically, keep off the brandy.

A few moments later Henrietta was by her side.

"Better?"

"Yes. Thank you" said Sam.

"I have never been convinced on the efficacy of brandy for quelling anxiety" said Henrietta thoughtfully.

"You took my thought" said Sam and they returned to the bungalow.

Vivian was sleeping. He had not moved. Sam changed the cloth on his forehead and then looked at the three confederates.

Henrietta looked exhausted and Mohammed was asleep on his feet. Only Ali seemed the same calm, untroubled soul. She thanked Mohammed for everything he had done that day and told him to go to his own quarters and sleep. He went.

"You too" Sam said to Henrietta who said

"If you are sure-"

"Oh yes I'm sure. If Gerald sees you looking like that neither Vivian nor I will ever see you again."

And Henrietta went without further demur.

Sam looked at Ali.

"I am going to sleep by his bed, in case he wakes. Will you sleep?"

For an answer Ali fetched his bed roll and laid it by the bedroom door.

Sam said "Thank you Ali, That will be good" and she went and sat down on the charpoy that Ali had already placed by the bed. Actually she thought, in the absence of Kevin the man was a more than adequate substitute and in some ways a lot more useful. Everyone should have one of each. And she laid down, as she was and was asleep.

She was awakened in the early hours by restless movement from the bed. She stood up quickly and reeled. Damn that brandy! Ali was at her side. Vivian was on his back but tossing and turning from side to side, muttering and sometimes calling out. Sam put her hand on his forehead and said to Ali

"He's burning up. Hold him still while I take off the dressing and see if there's any sign of infection."

She carefully unbound the leg and cautiously lifted the lint. It was bloody but not dramatically so and the wound itself, whilst ragged, looked clean and calm. Between them they replaced the gauze with new and bound it with clean strips of sheet.

It's probably just a reaction to shock and trauma thought Sam. Ali nodded. Damn it, could he read minds as well? She went and got three more Brufen, broke them open as before and mixed it into the small cup of water that Ali brought her.

Between them they raised his head and poured the liquid down his throat. He struggled and clenched his jaw but most of it went down.

"OK let's try that" and she took the damp cloth handed to her by Ali and laid it across Vivian's forehead and held her hand there. She sat on the side of the bed beside him with her hand on the cool cloth on his forehead and gradually he seemed to relax and finally his arms became still at his sides.

"I will stay here Ali. Will you be close?"

"Very close sahiba."

Sam smiled at him warmly. She had never been called a lady before.

For two days and nights this was the routine. Vivian slept for much of the time but there were periods when his face and body burned with an unrelenting heat and others when he shivered convulsively and talked incessantly. Sam racked her brains but could think of nothing other than what they were doing already to assuage the fever. It would have to run its course. When he came out of the drugged sleep he seemed unaware of where he was or who she was and Sam found she was trying to convince herself that memory loss was not a side effect of fever. In the short interludes of consciousness she got him to drink as much boiled water as she could and then took his hand and just sat by him.

On the third day after another distressing night, he seemed to be resting peacefully. Sam, who had sat at his bedside for most of the previous 48 hours had now climbed onto the bed and was resting propped up behind him, to one side. Everything was calm and her eyelids were drooping. One hand was resting on his shoulder and suddenly she was aware of another hand covering it. She sat bolt upright and looked down at Vivian's eyes looking up at her, clear, bright, lucid.

"Samanthar?"

Sam slid off the bed and sat down beside him immediately putting her hand on his forehead. But she could tell from the touch of his hand that the fever had broken.

"You've been out of it for a bit. But I think you're OK now."

He looked puzzled.

"Out of it?"

"Unconscious."

"How did I get here?"

"Mohammed" said Sam.

"How did I get off the battlefield?"

He remembered that then.

"Mohammed and Gerald" said Sam.

"Gerald! Gerald was hurt –I –"

"Gerald said I have to tell you that he and Daffadar Razi Khan live and you are duty bound to do the same" said Sam, "although I think I was meant to tell you as a spur to recovery but-well lets just say we had a lot on our plate and the conditions were not conducive to motivational speeches."

Vivian gave a small forced laugh and winced. He looked down at himself.

"Something hurts like the devil!"

"That will be the enormous gash in your left leg" said Sam laconically.

"Did you do all this?"

"Me and a small private army" said Sam. "And before you ask, the stitching is down to Mohammed as well. Apparently he does it with horses."

Vivian laid back down on the pillows and took Sam's hand.

"I'm glad you are here and that you were not a dream. I thought when I woke that I might have imagined- everything-"

And Sam looking down at him, knew that memory loss was not a side effect of fever.

Later Ali came in with a cup of something which he said was a herbal remedy that he used to give Vivian when he was a boy. Vivian squinted at it suspiciously and Sam sniffed it. It smelt of ginger and something else, possibly camomile and possibly cardomon, or coriander and honey. Vivian, after a little persuasion and the promise of a full debriefing later, drank it down and with Sam still holding his hand drifted into a deep and natural sleep and Sam, exhausted beyond endurance, slept too.

The next two days followed the same pattern with Sam, good to her promise, giving Vivian Mohammed's summary of the action on the frontier, in excerpts. When he was told about Gerald's actions he groaned. When he was told about Mohammed's comments to Gerald, he groaned.

On the third day the surgeon arrived unannounced. He ignored Sam, that she had expected, greeted Henrietta with surprise and pleasure and Ali with respect. He went through into the bedroom to find Vivian propped up on pillows and feeding himself from a bowl of chicken soup. He unwrapped all the bandages and carefully removed the lint, squinting down at the wound, nodded in satisfaction and turned to Ali.

"Nice job. Your work I assume?"

Ali nodded, glancing at Sam, adding "and Mohammed."

"Ah yes! Mohammed Khan, your syce. The man is getting himself quite a reputation!" said Surgeon Major Collier. "Well there's nothing wrong with his needlework here. If he ever wants a job –"

"I think that unlikely sir" said Vivian. "He is much fonder of horses then he is of men."

"Yes. Well. Can't blame the man really can we? Feel the same myself on a lot of days. Anyway. You'll do."

"How is Daffadar Razi Khan?"

"Mending. Mending. Took a nasty slash. But he's past the worst."

"What about the commander?"

"He was pretty banged up; unconscious for two days; possibly just as well for some people's reputations as I understand it. I sent him home and suggested he might like to take some leave."

He watched as Ali carefully replaced the lint and the bandages and said to Vivian

"The last of the wounded came in today. The engineers lost a man who fell into the river at the broken bridge I understand. Gerald Madeley is pretty cut up about it. But from what I've been told there wasn't much he could have done. I think he may be on his way down here. Collect his wife and all."

Major Collier picked up his bag and made for the door.

"Take it easy for a while. I know what you young fellows are like. And no riding until that wound is fully closed up. That's an order."

"Yes sir" said Vivian meekly, looking at Sam.

Moments later the door burst open and Gerald came striding in. He took one look at Vivian, passed a tired hand over his face and sat down in a chair next to the bed.

"Viv! It's good to see you. The last time I saw, you were unconscious, green and very bloody. Mohammed was right then."

"Right about what?" said Vivian with a trace of anxiety.

"Oh I can't really remember now. Something about help; having help here. To be honest I didn't have a lot of choice. I couldn't have left you in the surgeon's den so it was either here or the battlefield!" He tried to make light of something that had clearly caused him a lot of anxiety. Vivian said

"I'm all right Gerald and thank you."

For a moment the two men shared a long look. Sam thought, he *was* repaying a debt; he doesn't know it but he was. Dear man. They are joined by something stronger than childhood friendship. Whether they realised it or not, that was love... There was a noise behind them and Sam and Vivian looked up to see Henrietta standing in the door way. Gerald turned around and leapt to his feet guiltily as if he had forgotten that he had a wife.

Sam and Henrietta exchanged glances.

Soldiers!

Gerald might have seen Henrietta's glance. If he did he wasn't in the mood for surrealism. He put his arms round her and kissed her so hard she squeaked. Sam suppressed a giggle. She didn't know if the whole invisible thing included sound.

"We must be gone my dear. One breach of protocol is enough for one week I think. I'll go and see if Mohammed has fetched the ghari. Will you be ready?"

Henrietta smiled and nodded. Gerald left with a rush of cold air and Sam said

"He's exhausting!"

She went to Henrietta and put her arms around her.

"Thank you for all your help."

"I did not do very much" said Henrietta.

"You washed, you boiled, you fetched and carried and the moral support was priceless."

Vivian reached out and took her hand.

"Thank you Henrietta."

"And my thanks to you Vivian, for saving my whirling dervish's life. He is a dust devil I know but he would be sorely missed would he not?" and there were tears in her eyes.

She went to the door and with Ali following with her baggage, went down to the waiting trap.

Sam sat down on the bed next to Vivian and he turned to her and said

"I have not really thanked you" and his eyes burned. Sam moved away and said lightly

"I'll have to get in line."

"What do you mean?"

"Well lets see. First there's Daffadar Razi Khan, then Mohammed; then there's Gerald and Mohammed again; then there's Ali and Henrietta and then did I mention Mohammed?"

Vivian laughed. It was very good to hear that laugh and see that look in his eyes again.

"Why did you move away?" he asked quietly.

"You know damn well why!" said Sam in exasperation. "You heard what the surgeon said."

"He was talking about horses."

"He was talking about any kind of strenuous exercise!"

"It doesn't need to be strenuous" said Vivian cajolingly.

"That'll be a first then will it?" snapped Sam.

He took her hand and gently kissed the palm.

Sam sighed. He was obviously not going to make a good patient. The upside was he

would probably make a speedy convalescence.

"Does it still hurt a lot?" she asked him.

"Like the devil!"

"Good!" And then seeing his expression, "Ha! Not the ministering angel you thought I was."

"I never said I wanted a replica" said Vivian with quiet perception. "It's not a competition."

Sam burst into tears. Vivian gently put his hands on either side of her head and laid it down on his shoulder. He kissed her forehead and laid his cheek on her hair.

"Its all right now" he murmured and Sam, exhausted with worry and lack of sleep, cried as she had never before cried in her life.

The tears slowly diminished to leave the pregnant silence of the unspoken thought.

Finally she said "I have always believed that falling in love was falling in lust. An immediate and strong physical attraction."

"Ah" said Vivian. "So you have never been in love?"

"Possibly not" said Sam.

She thought, I'm afraid of falling in love. Afraid of how vulnerable it would make me; afraid that I would lose a friend, a brother, a guide, a companion…

Aloud she said

"This is not the way it should be. For one thing people in love have arguments!"

"I'm sure I can accommodate if that's what you wish" said Vivian smoothly.

She looked at him, her eyes filling with tears again.

Vivian sighed. He said

"We are not children Samanthar. The years have to count for something."

He pushed aside the sodden hair and looked into her face.

"You look very beautiful when you cry. Not crumpled and red nosed; just clear eyed –and wet."

He took her face in his hands and spoke softly looking into her eyes.

"Main tumse pyar karti hoon"

"What language was that" said Sam.

"Urdu" said Vivian.

"What did you say?"

"I told you how much I loved you" said Vivian.

"All that to say I love you?"

"The English language is a poor creature against the Asian when it comes to speaking of love."

"Even Shakespeare?" said Sam.

"Even the most beautiful of the sonnets" said Vivian."Aap ki bahut yaad aa rahihai. I miss you" and he pulled her close to him and she could feel his heart beat through her hand on his chest."Aap khubsurat hain. You are beautiful."

Sam sighed. "How many dialects do you know?"

"Dozens" said Vivian.

Sam sighed again. She managed French and a bit of German and a smattering of Greek and Latin but as the rest of the world appeared, embarrassingly, to be fluent in English her attempts to learn the language of the countries she'd travelled had been half-hearted.

"What language do you think in?"

Vivian laughed.

"It depends on who I'm with and what I'm doing! A lot of the time I think in Urdu and speak it."

"Do you sometimes think in Urdu and translate it into English?"

"Oh yes, quite often, for the benefit of English speaking colleagues; although many of them have been trained to speak and write in the native languages."

Sam sighed.

"It's intoxicating."

"What is?"

"Thinking in the vernacular and then speaking in a different tongue. It's really sexy!"

Vivian laughed out loud.

"I assume that means you find it –attractive?"

"You bet I do!"

He seemed to be considering it for a moment.

"I wonder why that is" he said.

"I don't know."

"People all over India can do it; both Indians and Europeans. Are you going to fall in love with them all?"

"Who said anything about falling in love" said Sam. "Say something else. How about in Pashtu?"

"Za ta sara meena kwam. I love you,"

"Za ta sara meena kwam" Sam repeated, looking up at him and felt his body respond. She struggled to sit upright. This was not going to happen. But Vivian held her close, his arms around her body now, one hand stroking her thigh. She leaned back against him and gave herself to the pleasure of his touch. It had been a while...He was kissing her now and she was kissing him back and then simultaneously they both pulled away and Vivian whispered, his mouth against her hair

"Marry me."

Sam jerked upright and almost fell off the bed.

"What?"

"Marry me."

"What, now?"

"Well maybe not right-"

"Are you completely out of your mind?"

"Is it not what people do 120 years from now? Is marriage no longer an accepted custom?"

Where to begin! Mixed marriages of all kinds; eventually she supposed women would marry women and men would marry men. It was moving that way now. That wasn't the point.

"That's not the point! You're in the 19th century, I'm in the 20th. How do you think that's going to work out? And while we're on the subject- who are we going to use for the ceremony? A deaf, dumb and blind priest? Better make sure we get one who believes in reincarnation!"

"That's not going to be difficult" said Vivian placidly.

Sam was standing now, quivering with – with what?

"Don't you want to marry me?"

"Don't change the subject."

"I thought this was the subject."

"I can't marry you."

"Why not?"

"Because I'm, because you're...because..."

"Because you don't love me?"

"I didn't say that."

"So you do?"

114

"Do what?"

"Love me."

"Is this really the time to-"

"It's the only time there is."

"I don't need your fucking sophistry! I need to think."

"Then think."

"I'm confused."

"You're confused! Sometimes talking with you is like walking through mud with a bag on my head."

Sam stood in front of him, shaking with fury and completely speechless. Those were Kevin's words! All those years ago. Kevin's words. How did he know?

"Well at least we're having the prerequisite argument" said Vivian.

And Sam, for the second time in her life and the second time that day, sat down on the floor where she was and cried.

Vivian tried to move, bit his lip to muffle a scream of agony and leaned back, resigned. There might have been a better moment he thought reflectively.

After a little persuasion, well quite a lot really, he was amazingly patient, Sam came back to the bed and stood before him in mutinous silence.

"What's this all about?" said Vivian quietly.

No answer. He tried again.

"You love me, don't you? I know you do."

No answer.

"It can't be the age difference surely? What can that matter when there is a century between us!"

No answer.

Vivian sighed. Was it supposed to be this difficult?

"Will you marry me?"

His voice held the promise of a love for all time. A, once in a lifetime love, that you might get offered once, if you were lucky and most were not. The love she had always promised herself; romantic, spiritual and physical love combined, and across lifetimes; for ever...

How could she explain; how could she tell him that she saw no way out of the inevitable; that even if they assembled a little band of loyal people who could see her and know her, they were still in a dream world and they would have to wake up. This was not Primeval; there was no gateway in time where people could slip through and stay or go back as they chose.

She looked at him, into those beautiful fathomless eyes that were watching her and reading her soul. He understood what they faced. He was prepared to take the risk.

What difference did it make if she said yes?

And she wanted to, so much.

She sat down on the bed.

"Yes." It was a snuffle.

"Yes?"

"Yes. I do. I will. Whatever."

Nothing had changed and everything was about to.

Vivian said

"I sometimes believe that our souls cannot see reality in itself until they are liberated from the distortions and inaccuracies of the physical senses. I sometimes believe it is birth which is the sleeping, the forgetting, the soul going from a state of great awareness to one of clouded consciousness. Words cannot capture that which is beyond the physical realm. Words conceal rather than reveal; and now they are inadequate to express what I feel, how I feel…"

Sam stared him. She said

"Are we sleeping or waking?"

"It doesn't matter does it? If all this is the trappings of unreality." He waved his arm. "If you can't take it with you across the line it's not real in its most meaningful sense."

Sam had heard those words before. Kevin had used just those words explaining the intersections of life to her. The points of light at each intersection; always there; not always visible. That something or someone you had lost might just be at another intersection. She remembered. She had made him cross with her lack of understanding and he had gone back to washing, as rats do.

Vivian leaned forward and with some difficulty, pulled her towards him, turned her face and kissed her slowly and deeply and then said

"Do men still propose to women? Have you ever been asked before? I'm sure you have."

"Yes" said Sam.

"How many times?"

"Three" said Sam.

"And what did you say to these poor, love-struck creatures?"

Sam thought back and said

"You must be joking! NO. If you like."

Vivian thought about this for a moment and then said

"So I'm definitely out in front."

Yes thought Sam. It was the mud that did it. The mud and the paper bag and dear Kevin!

Later, Vivian had fallen into a deep sleep, clearly exhausted, thought Sam, by the effort of proposing to me and she had gone to find Ali and tell him.

"And I said yes" she said. She watched him anxiously.

"Yes. The Sahib has spoken to me of his love." And he smiled.

"What do you think?"

Ali shrugged his narrow shoulders expressively.

"What can it matter? Things are written for us."

Ce sera sera thought Sam. What will be, will be.

But spoken with certainty and assurance.

By the end of the week Vivian, at his insistence was sitting in a chair for part of each day giving Sam a panic attack every time he eased himself from the bed into it. He wore baggy pakhtun trousers which she and Ali managed to pull on over the bandaged leg and tied round his middle, a process which took at least five minutes every time and which he seemed to enjoy far too much, Sam thought, for a man supposedly in recuperation.

He finally agreed that if Sam would sit behind him on the bed and he could put his head in her lap he would forgo the chair every day and just use it once in every three. Sam agreed and caught Ali smiling to himself as he went about his tasks.

They were sitting thus one afternoon when Sam said

"When are we going to do this thing?"

"You mean the ceremony? I thought we might leave it a few weeks" said Vivian.

"Really?" said Sam in surprise. All that insistence and he was putting it off!

Vivian looked down at himself.

"Well it's not going to be much of a wedding night like this."

"Your second in a state of physical debility" said Sam with asperity.

Vivian raised his eyebrows and said something in Urdu.

Sam, who had persuaded Ali to give her lessons in the language and was actually getting on quite well said

"So I have a tongue like a sword do I?"

"Like an assassins dagger actually" said Vivian smoothly.

And Sam who could remember more than one occasion being told that she was so sharp she would cut herself, had the grace to look abashed.

"I had hoped to give you a night you would never forget" Vivian went on, his eyes flashing.

"I've already had a few of those" said Sam and they looked at each other with conspiratorial acquiescence. Then Vivian said

"And there's Gerald."

"Gerald? Is there something I should know?"

"No. Yes. Henrietta I'm sure will want to be there and it would be good-" he stopped.

Of course. Of course he wanted Gerald there.

"Do you think he might be- that there's a chance-"

"He's been through a bad couple of months, what with the fighting and losing one of his men-"

"And nearly his own life and yours" said Sam.

"Yes. And then getting me off the battlefield and then Mohammed's comments and breaking protocol- it changes a man, to be brought face to face with mortality."

"Well Henrietta thought that there was every chance his mind would become more- eclectic- open to the unorthodox patterns of life" said Sam, remembering Henrietta's optimistic view of Gerald's mind set.

"So we wait?" said Vivian, his eyes dancing.

Sam stretched an arm across his chest and moved her fingers gently up and down.

"We wait."

"I like that you are learning Urdu. How-"

"Ali" they said in unison.

"It helps if you speak it to me" said Sam.

Vivian looked up at her. Then in that wonderful, deep, velvet voice he began to speak. Sam listened to the mellifluous words, passing over her like a warm breeze, caressing her senses. It was seduction in its purest form, light, uplifting, and deeply satisfying. When he finished speaking she sighed and asked

"What did you say?"

"I told you that your beauty has engaged my soul in rapture and desire. Your mind reaches out and touches mine to create certainty and belonging. Your body, your parts, invites my worship. Your feet and your hands are the slender carven images of a goddess that I long to caress with my eyes and my lips. The touch of your hair against my cheek transports my senses to the marble terraces and pavilions of love as it drifts across your face under my touch. I am yours in body, mind, soul and heart for all time."

Sam was silent for some minutes, looking down into eyes which held her in a gaze she could not break. Then she looked down at her feet and said

"My feet? I've always thought that I had nice hands –"

And Vivian, his eyes full of laughter now, raised his arms and pulled her down to meet his kiss. When he released her he said gruffly

"God damn this leg!"

But Sam wasn't thinking about his leg. She was thinking about the future and what it held.

Once a week Sam fetched Mohammed and got him to examine Vivian's leg. To her untrained eyes it seemed to be healing well and the man himself was ridiculously robust. But she wasn't sure. In the early days Mohammed would just nod as if all that could be said was that it was not getting any worse. With Vivian becoming increasingly irritable with the inactivity, Sam went and fetched him again. She un-bandaged the leg and watched Mohammed, thinking how curious it was that she called for him and not the surgeon at the hospital. I suppose, she reflected, it's all about trust. Mohammed was a man of few words so she didn't expect a lot. She was not disappointed for the few words he said were outweighed by their significance.

"It is good. I have seen this in horses. The difficult part comes now. The horse must learn to stand on the leg without damage. This requires much care by the handler" and the amusement she heard in his voice was reflected in his eyes. OK. So that's how they see me!

Vivian threw several rapid sentences in Pushto at Mohammed who answered likewise. Sam only understood the odd word but the gist was clear. How long before I can get on a damned horse! Sam also knew enough to interpret the timescale. Two weeks maybe three. Now, would the sahib be happy with that?

Vivian was not altogether pleased but when Sam pointed out that it was probably time to start with a little movement and asked Ali to procure a walking stick of some kind, he cheered up. The wound itself was still very ugly and wrinkled and the scar he would be left with would be quite dramatic, but it no longer looked as if it would part at the seams. As to other forms of physical exercise –she really wasn't very sure. Mohammed insisted that a horse could make a full recovery over time but the horse had four legs not two and Vivian was a cavalry officer.

From that point Vivian spent a short time each day walking around the bungalow with a stick. It made him cranky but it also tired him out so there were pluses and minuses. The wound was now bandaged very lightly and it was easy to check for signs of damage. It was in fact much more obliging than Vivian. Sam asked Mohammed if it was advisable to apply any kind of cream or unguent to soften the scarring. Mohammed said yes, once the scar tissue was less prominent and Sam asked Ali to procure something suitable. She was fairly sure that Vivian would enjoy the process.

A stream of officers in the station and the men in Vivian's command now came to visit including daffadar Razi Khan, newly recovered and promoted to Risaldar. He was a pleasant young man with grey eyes and quite a dazzling smile who managed to be both respectful and humorous. Vivian obviously liked him a lot and spent some time with him listening to a blow by blow account of the action he had missed. He still had a bandage around his shoulder and walked with a stick but assured Vivian that when he returned from leave, he was going the next day, he would be back in the saddle and ready for action. And Vivian assured him likewise. And Sam thought, god give me strength –they're like boys with a Nintendo! It's just a game.

One morning Ali brought in the mail and Vivian picked up one letter, scrutinised it and then said

"I think this one is for you."

Sam went across to him to peer over his shoulder. Surely the wonders of 20th century technology could not extend this far. She looked at the envelope.

"It's addressed to you."

Vivian read from a sheet he held in his hand.

"Dear Vivian, please excuse this unorthodox method of communication but I could think of no other way of getting in touch with Samanthar. Could I ask you to pass on to her the enclosed letter. Kindest regards and wishes for your renewing strength and my dearest affection. Henrietta."

Sam took the letter he handed to her and unfolded the single sheet carefully. She read it over warily and then said

"I'll read it out loud. It concerns us both."

She pulled up a chair next to him and read.

"My dear Samanthar, I lost the baby. Do not be alarmed. I am well recovered now although still a little weak. Gerald was distraught. He blamed himself for the loss. He said he had cared so much for Vivian he had no thought for me, leaving me as he did to care for his friend. He was beside himself and would not accept my refutation of his claims. I became very concerned for his state of mind, so I told him. I told him everything. He thought I was losing my mind after the loss of the child and became even more distraught and then he remembered something from the night he had brought Vivian back. And then something that Mohammed had said on their journey. And then he said –is she tall and fair?

So I ask you please can we visit? Gerald has refused to ask anything of Vivian but he will come if Vivian sends. Your loving friend, Henrietta."

Sam and Vivian looked at each other.

Sam said "universal timing. You've got to love it."

And Vivian said

"Kismet" and they smiled at each other.

Vivian wrote to Gerald asking when he would be able to come over for several days.

"We might as well do the whole thing at once" he said.

"You mean Gerald's baptism of fire and the marriage?" said Sam. "Are you up to it?"

"It won't be for a few weeks yet; he'll have to request permission. So yes, I damn well will be!"

A week later a letter arrived from Gerald, brief and succinct.

"Be there on the 27th. Have the drinks ready!"

Two days after English Christmas, thought Sam. They had three and a half weeks to wait.

The week before Gerald's arrival Vivian insisted on getting on a horse. Sam was against it but Mohammed was unconcerned although he insisted upon the use of the quietest mount in the stables and accompanying Vivian. Sam went too. It was glorious to be out on horseback again, with the wind in her face, its cool strength blowing her hair out behind her. Vivian found his snail's pace irksome but took pleasure from watching Sam canter on in front and then back to him at a faster pace, laughing, eyes bright. The days were calm and filled with light, the sun warm, the snow topped peaks in the distance, alluring and Sam felt she had survived a nightmare and woken in a dream.

They went riding each day, Vivian gaining confidence and suffering the consequences of forgotten muscles and Sam treating the shrinking, jagged scarring wound each night with Ali's cream and massaging his stiffened leg and thigh muscles with scented oil. Vivian clearly enjoyed the whole process but now, just three days before the proposed ceremony, they planned to marry the day after Gerald's arrival, he seemed to be shy of any prolonged physical contact.

The night before Gerald's arrival Sam sat down on his bed and looked at him.

"Is something wrong?"

He took her face in his hands and kissed her with so much desire that she could hardly breath.

"No. nothing."

"Then why aren't we-"

He looked away and Sam sat up and pulled away from him, rigid with shock.

She stared at him, biting her lip, fighting back tears, then she got slowly to her feet, left the room and went out through the front door into the night. She followed the veranda around the bungalow and made for the stables, nearly falling down the steps blinded by tears. Mohammed had retired to his quarters and the stables were dark but her favourite mare, Tuska, whinnied a welcome and Sam went to her stall. Sam opened the gate and went in and put her arms round the mare's neck and buried her face in soft mane and cried.

She heard no sound; she did not hear Vivian come into the stable. She didn't know anything but the warmth of the equine love until his arms went about her.

He turned her towards him and began to kiss the tears.

"My love-"

"Love! You don't love me!"

Vivian took her face in his hands and he was smiling. He was smiling!

She pulled away in a fury. He was smiling! She tried to walk away but Tuska blocked her path. So she turned furiously on Vivian and hissed,

"All that talk of love; all those preparations and now you can't bear to make love to me? What the fuck-"

"Ah, the little wild cat again. .A 20th century wildcat at that!"

"You're laughing at me" Sam expostulated.

"No. No I am not. Well perhaps just a little" said Vivian. "I am sorry. I should have explained. I did not realise how important to me it was until- I am sorry. It's just- I am marrying you the day after tomorrow and I want our wedding night to be- to be – special-"

"Special? And what were the other nights? Practice runs?"

"I am so sorry."

"So you said."

"Samanthar, please –"

"Who said you could use my Sunday name? Basterdised! I don't understand. I –"

But suddenly she did understand. She understood so clearly she felt a fool. He had been married before and the circumstances of that marriage almost mirrored this.

He wanted to expunge that previous night and what it had led to; he wanted to replace it with something he had now, something real, something that would create a new memory. So he was human. She sighed. Vivian looked at her helplessly. She said

"It's OK. I do understand."

"It was foolish. Stupid of me. What difference could it make?"

"It makes a difference to you and that's enough."

"Can you forgive me?"

Sam looked into his deep, almost black, serious eyes and smiled.

"Forgive you for being human? I think I can manage that."

He took a step forward and put his arms around her and held her so close that it was a few minutes before she realised he had come out without the stick.

He murmured into her hair

"I don't think I want to wait."

"Well you're bloody well going to wait" said Sam fiercely.

He kissed her then and she almost weakened. Da do ron ron...

Gerald arrived, with Henrietta, late the following day, bursting in, whirlwind style as he always did and then stopped abruptly, perplexed, and stared at Sam. She had taken a lot of care with her appearance, choosing fine woollen trousers and matching long sleeved top in rich dark green, which Ali assured her came from Kashmir and it certainly felt like it. She had left her hair down to soften the haughty look and judging by Vivian's face she had achieved the desired result. Respectful approval, with just a hint of desire.

Gerald, though clearly able to see her, seemed completely at a loss. Vivian pushed himself up from his seat and went to stand next to Sam. Vivian said

"Gerald, this is Samanthar - soon to be my wife."

And Sam stepped forward and held out her hand.

Gerald stared at her, his thin dark face a picture of incredulity. He didn't take her hand and after a moment Sam let it fall to her side. The moments passed and nobody moved or spoke. Then Gerald ran a hand through his already untidy hair and then his face broke into a grin, a boyish mischievous grin and Sam saw the Gerald that Henrietta loved and Henrietta saw it too and burst into tears. Gerald looked from one woman to the other and said

" My love? It's all right. Really, it is!"

And he turned to Sam, scooped her up in his arms and twirled her around and around saying joyously

"I have a sister. I have a sister!"

And then he put her down again and took his wife in his arms. Vivian said

"It's alright Gerald. Tears seem to be the order of the day at present."

Sam whirled on him furiously but stopped when she saw his eyes, full of love and happiness and something else- something she had once read- something called –the serenity of knowledge- of one who is in harmony with the stream of life, no longer fighting his destiny-and she was humbled.

Gerald insisted on the whole story and Vivian complied, leaving out some of the more sensational parts. Gerald listened without interruption, his eyes growing large and moving from Vivian to Sam and back again. Finally he said, turning to Henrietta

"And you knew all this? From that first time?" And when she nodded he said

"What have you brought me to woman! I used to be such a straight thinking Englishman."

Vivian handed him a large drink and said

"You still are. Still straight, just more thinking."

Gerald turned to him and the look that passed between them, Sam thought, disclosed a love as deep as the ocean and inscrutable as Buddha himself and as everlasting.

The marriage ceremony was to take place the following morning. Ali seemed to have done most of the arrangements and Sam was happy for it to be so. When she went into the spare room that night she found a set of clothes lying on the bed. They were of the same pushmina fabric as the ones she had worn that day, only finer if that was possible. Soft and flowing and more beautiful than anything she had ever seen, let alone worn, cream in colour with cream embroidery at the neck and sleeves. Laying with them was a scarlet silk scarf, as fine as a cobweb. Red for the celebration of marriage. Vivian came to the door and saw her expression.

"Do you like them? I had Ali get them from –it doesn't matter –do you like them?"

"I have never seen anything quite so beautiful in my life. I will feel like a princess soon to become a rani… . I think I will try them on."

"Then I will leave you to it" said Vivian. "I do not trust myself to watch you-I will go!"

He smiled, his eyes full of mischief and pleasure and Sam watched him go with reluctance. It was going to be a long night. Then she called him back.

"Are we having rings? Do they have rings in Indian ceremonies?"

They had discussed the form the ceremony would take shortly after Sam had accepted. Vivian had decided that a Christian ceremony would be impossible and Sam had agreed. The result of such an attempt would be to send a clear message round the station that Vivian had completely lost his mind. After some discussion with Ali Vivian had suggested that they made up their own ceremony, very loosely based around the seven step Hindu rite and including the speaking of the mantra with clasped hands. Sam had searched Vivian's bookshelves and read all she could about Hinduism, its lore and its practices.

She had always liked the number seven. It was said to be a holy number believed to connect the rational to the irrational;

the masculine to the feminine. This appealed to her. There were seven archangels and seven celestial halls. There were seven planets, although they kept messing with them and seven days of the week. There were seven colours in the rainbow and seven chakras and she had read somewhere that seven characterised time. That seemed singularly appropriate.

She had studied various chakra balancing systems. The seventh chakra was the crown chakra. It symbolised thought, purpose and understanding. There were a whole load of issues associated with it if she remembered rightly. Amongst them, belief systems, divinity, vision, self-knowledge, development of wisdom, ability to perceive and analyse and assimilate information. And union. A sense of spiritual connection. The world as my teacher. In this here and now with Vivian she was facing all of these. Beliefs are built from interpretations of experience but then subsequent interpretation becomes based on those beliefs, sometimes erroneously. The thought surprised her as did its recognition. To go beyond all that, to realise our universal identity is to recognise our many personalities as costumes...Kevin again; Kevin would approve.

But in Hinduism there were even more sevens. In the Vedic times there were three planes, the top being the domain of the gods, ruled by Indra but later in the Puranas there were four more above the heavenly plane of Indra, corresponding to the sheathes, planes, of consciousness of the body with the higher seven planes also corresponding to the chakras. There were lots of sevens in the Hindu scriptures, including the seven energies that are achieved during spiritual practices. Seven sages were said to have played a role in the bringing of the Vedas and other texts to earthly consciousness. There were seven sacred places, seven holy cities and seven sacred rivers. And of course the seven steps around the fire at the end of the ceremony to consecrate the marriage. In tradition the bond thus sanctified lasted through seven lives. That should cover it she thought!

She found a natural predisposition towards Hindu beliefs which soothed her anxieties about her current circumstances, but left her worrying about causing offence to Ali or Mohammed or any of the Gods who might be party to the proceedings. Vivian had reasoned that anything so based upon love could hardly offend anyone who was worth worrying about and Ali had agreed.

Ali had said

"It is for you who love; each man to his own belief" which Sam interpreted as –live by your own beliefs; don't force them on others, a sentiment with which she fully concurred. And Mohammed apparently was a Muslim. But they had not discussed rings and she could not remember any reference to rings other than entwined threads of some kind linking the bride and groom.

"I have dealt with the rings" said Vivian now.

"You have?"

"Yes."

"Can I see?"

"No."

"How do you know mine will fit?"

"I just know."

Sam thought about this for a few moments.

"Did you exchange rings – the last time?"

"Yes."

"What happened to them?"

Vivian sighed and looked away.

"Elizabeth's ring was on her finger when they threw her into that-pit- and when I saw it-" he struggled with himself briefly

"When I saw it I removed mine and threw it into the pit with her."

There was a crushing finality to his words but it did not disguise the pain. Sam went to him and placed her hands on his chest, looking up at him. She didn't say anything. What could be said?

Vivian came back from that place in the past where a life had ended and looked down at her, his eyes clear once more.

"At the time, it seemed the right thing to do. Now I know it was."

He studied her face.

"You are beautiful" he said. His eyes travelled down her body and back to her face. "So beautiful."

"No I'm not" said Sam. "I'm attractive to some men, those that like boy looks rather than girl curves."

Vivian laughed.

"You are slender as a nymph and I am transfixed by your straight lines and smooth planes."

"You make me sound like a racehorse" said Sam, not sure what she felt about it.

"Horses are my second love! Do you ever wear a dress?" Vivian asked.

"Not if I can help it. Would you like it if I did?"

"I like you in as few clothes as possible."

"I had a rather nice black dress once" said Sam considering. "It had a high neck line at the front and cut down to below the waist at the back, and those long, straight pointed sleeves of Queen Guinevere's time and it fitted where it touched so to speak." She paused seeing it again and the impact it had had on Steve when she wore it.

Vivian was mesmerized, seeing it too.

"And I once wore a black leather all in one jumpsuit" said Sam, remembering that too. That was some night.

"Leather? All over? I do not think I have any experience of such a garment" said Vivian, trying to come to terms with something that was about 100 years beyond his grasp, and failing.

"No I don't suppose you have." Sam thought about the effect that outfit had created and said

"I think you might have liked it."

"I'd still be removing it" Vivian said quietly.

He put his arms around her and they stood like that for maybe five minutes and then he released her and said

"I will leave you to try on your clothes and I will see you in the morning."

He bent his head and kissed her lingeringly and then left and Sam turned back to the bed and her own thoughts. It was going to be a long night.

She sat down on the bed next to the wedding garments and reached for a sheet of coarse Indian paper on which the mantra was written. Vivian had told her that these words were spoken by both the groom and the bride after the seven steps. He had given her two copies, one in English and one in Urdu. She had been practicing the Urdu as it was beautifully eloquent but she wasn't at all sure that she could remember it all. Vivian had promised to prompt her if she forgot. In English the words were:

"We have taken the Seven Steps. You have become mine forever. Yes, we have become partners. I have become yours. Hereafter, I cannot live without you. Do not live without me. Let us share the joys. We are word and meaning, united. You are thought and I am sound. May the night be honey-sweet for us. May the morning be honey-sweet for us. May the earth be honey-sweet for us. May the heavens be honey-sweet for us. May the plants be honey-sweet for us. May the sun be all honey for us. May the cows yield us honey-sweet milk. As the heavens are stable, as the earth is stable, as the mountains are stable, as the whole universe is stable, so may our union be permanently settled."

She loved the part about *word and meaning united*. And *–you are thought and I am sound*. And especially *–I have become yours. Hereafter I cannot live without you*. She wasn't so sure about the bit with the cows but reasoned that one had to see it in context.

Reading it through again now it seemed so perfectly natural in the small dream world, with its four people, so dear to

Vivian and now to herself, who saw her and accepted her without compunction as if she had always been part of their lives. And it suddenly occurred to her that perhaps this was why Kevin was not there with her. He wanted her, for a short time at least, to accept what was happening without his spiritual guidance. (Not to mention his caustic wit!) He wanted her to interact with this life and give it substance; for the future? So she accepted the gift and for once in her life embraced the present.

She took off the beautiful green Kashmir trousers and shirt and laid them over a chair. Then she lay down on the bed next to the cream wedding robes. She didn't need to try them on.

Sam awoke just before dawn, with her dreams fading in the strengthening light and a sense of unreality. She realised that she had no idea what to do. Did she stay there? Did she get up and have breakfast? Did she have to hide from Vivian? From all of them?

Then there was a tap on the door and Henrietta came in, with a smile of complete competency and tea. Sam, realising she was stark naked, leapt up, grabbed the green over-shirt from the chair and sat down on the floor. Henrietta regarded her for a moment and then said

"Shower before or after breakfast?"

Sam relaxed a little. Vivian had created a tiled bathroom at the back of the bungalow. The room had been there and he had installed a pipe from which flowed tepid water which then drained away through a hole at skirting level and if you put aside your remembrance of a power shower and skated over the fact that it was possible for a snake to enter through the sluice hole, it was a pleasant experience. It was certainly more manageable than the one in the main bathroom which Vivian used.

"When is the ceremony?" she asked Henrietta.

"Whenever you are ready" replied Henrietta. "Have you been married before?"

"No" said Sam.

Henrietta raised surprised eyebrows.

"Really! I had thought-"

Sam smiled.

"I've had lots of attempts and I lived with someone for quite a long time but we were never married. I've been to a few ceremonies as a guest but I've never actually-"

"Ah" said Henrietta.

"Yes" said Sam.

"Yes?"

"Yes to your unspoken question. I am as terrified as a virgin bride without the virgin bit!"

Henrietta laughed and blushed at the same time. It was very becoming.

"Were you afraid?" Sam asked.

Henrietta said

"I was anxious about the wedding night part- I was a virgin- but marrying Gerald was like a homecoming."

A homecoming. How perfectly expressed Sam thought. That was exactly what it was.

Henrietta remained in attendance like a loyal serving woman. She helped Sam with a shower, she guided her back to her bedroom, she towelled her hair and combed it out. Then she went away and returned with breakfast but for probably the first time in her life Sam found herself unable to eat. She managed a peach and more tea. From the bed she looked up at Henrietta and said

"What now?"

"Now? Now we dress you!"

Sam looked at the cream robes that Henrietta held across her arms. This could not be happening.

"Stand up" said Henrietta.

Sam stood up and Henrietta dropped the soft silken folds of the cream tunic over her head and then held the slim trousers out for her to step into. They were bounded by a silken cord which she tied around her waist. There were no words to describe the feeling of the fabric against her skin.

No adequate words. Henrietta produced a pair of very soft leather ankle boots which she pulled on over bare feet and then she moved over to the glass and examined her reflection. She scrutinized her face. It did not look as she had expected. But then what had she expected? Did what you had learned, what you had experienced, show in your face? Was there a wrinkle or a furrow for each piece of knowledge or each traumatic experience? If that was the case she'd be looking at Tutankaprune now! If there had been no Owl, no Wanigi, no Mogo, no Steve, no Kevin... Would that face look different now? Or was it not the face at all? Was it the way you looked at the face? Was that what made the difference? Or indeed the way you looked at anything? Was observance simply part of perception and perception was a feature of the mind and not the eyes?

She'd never had much time for mirrors!

The woman who looked back at her now seemed a stranger. A beautiful stranger...was this the one that Vivian saw... Henrietta broke into her thoughts.

"We haven't finished yet."

She made Sam sit down again and brushed out her hair, now dry in the warmth of the new day. She coiled it loosely into a knot at the back of Sam's head and pulled out tendrils to hang either side of her face and across her forehead. They had been so bleached by the sun that they hung like threads of gold about her. Henrietta took the scarlet silk scarf and draped it loosely around her neck and then stood back and said

"Perfection! Just one more thing."

She went across the room and took from the table a small box which Sam had not noticed before.

"What's that?"

"This as a gift from Vivian. He would I think like you to wear them today."

She handed Sam the box and took off the lid. It was a beautiful box and its contents were even more so. Sam lifted from the silken cushion a pair of gold earrings. They were long and dangling like threads of the sun. They were created so that one long stem pierced the ear and pulled through to dangle with the second strand just below the chin. When she moved her head they caught the light and created a myriad patterns all around her like crystals hanging in a window full of sunshine.

"Oh" said Sam in a whisper. She loved earrings but hated studs. They hurt the back of her ears. She liked plain and not gaudy. And she liked them long so that they moved when her hair moved, when she moved. How could the mere male of the species know all that?

"Oh" she said again.

"I told him that you would like them. He was unsure but only because of the occasion I think. It is nice to be loved and known is it not?"

Sam bit her lip and nodded.

"You look so very beautiful" said Henrietta quietly.

"I'm not beautiful" said Sam stubbornly.

"Does Vivian not tell you, you are beautiful?"

"Yes, but-"

"He is right and does anything else matter?"

Sam smiled at her then.

"No" she said.

"Are you ready?"

Ready, meaning prepared, equipped, complete. Ready? She stood up and went across to the mirror again. The stranger looked back at her. The stranger was ready. Henrietta went across the room and opened the door and stood back to let the stranger walk through it...

The first thing Sam saw was a small group of people and a lot of smiling faces. The second thing she saw was Vivian.

He was standing a little apart from the others and he was dressed as she had never seen him before. He was wearing a long, cream belted tunic, almost the same shade as her own and cream pants tucked into long, tan leather boots. The tunic was heavily embroidered down the front and around the collar, in what looked like gold and silver thread. His sword hung at his right side, its hilt protruding from the scabbard, and was polished to an eye aching shine. His beautiful, wind tossed gold hair hung across his brow almost hiding the querulous black eyebrows which were lifted to her approach. He looked like a prince from a fairy tale and she stood where she was, gazing at him, unable to make her legs move. He stretched out a hand and she glided forward to take it. As she stepped to his side he bent his head and whispered

"I thought I had better wear the sword. I am, after all, a soldier!"

His eyes embraced her dress, her hair, her face and then he reached out across her body and took her right hand in his.

The next half hour passed by in a dream for Sam. They went through the modified rituals, the steps; they spoke the beautiful words of the mantra, Vivian first and then Sam, who only forgot one small part of a sentence and was quietly prompted by Ali who seemed to have taken up position as her surrogate father. A curious position, she reflected, because she had always seen him as Vivian's surrogate father. Vivian then took her left hand in his and slid a slender gold band upon the second finger from the left and handed an almost identical one to her which she put onto the same finger on his left hand. At the very end the small quiet figure of the priest came forward and gave his blessing and Vivian gave him a small bag. Sam looking at the wizened face was fairly sure that he was blind but nevertheless he looked supremely content. Henrietta then produced garlands of flowers, gold and yellow and hung them about their necks. And Sam, lost in her dream world, felt as if she had been turned inside out and every thought, belief and desire she had ever harboured had been revealed to all eyes.

Afterwards there was champagne and food and talk and Vivian's eyes following her every move, her every thought with love and admiration and desire. Finally Gerald stood to one side and said

"I think it's time that the happy couple left for their honeymoon! Mohammed Khan can you fetch the carriage?"

This was apparently the totality of his best man's speech.

Sam looked at him horror struck. It was almost dusk. The cantonment would be alive with people, most of whom knew Vivian. She could not begin to imagine what would happen when they saw him outfitted like an Asian prince, in a carriage with a strange woman dressed like a Begum from the north!

Vivian saw her face and came close.

"Do not worry. Ali has it all in hand."

Of course he has thought Sam. Silly me! Carriage?

Vivian said

"Only in its dreams. Just a small trap really. Gerald's idea, Ali's adaptation. Do not worry. It will simply be seen as my bearer taking me out for fresh air in the cool of the evening to aid my recovery and Mohammed taking the opportunity to exercise my favourite horses under my watchful eye. What could be more natural?"

"And the clothes?"

"Mine? I am wearing comfortable attire as befits a convalescent. And you my goddess they will not see, had you forgotten? Though how your beauty could fail to arrest even the most turgid of minds I do not know."

"And the embroidery, on the tunic?"

"I know I am a prince among men but really no one is going to study me that closely! You need not concern yourself. What can go wrong?"

What a time to make a statement like that thought Sam.

"Where are we going?" she said, anxiety not quite suppressed.

"To our lodge, our very own ruin. That is all I know. Mohammed will leave the horses with us and return with Ali in the ghari. I know no more so I can tell you nothing further. We must wait."

"But people will notice their return. And see that there are no horses and you are not there!"

"They will return circuitously and enter the stables from behind the bungalow. If anyone sees, and I am certain they will not, it will be assumed that I am already within. The only people likely to be about at that hour will be the young ensigns and they, if they see anything, will not be believed on account of strong liquor on active imaginations! Now my beautiful inquisitor, have I succeeded in answering all your questions and may we leave?"

Sam allowed herself to be reassured. After all it was Ali and Mohammed. They had not been found wanting thus far.

Gerald and Henrietta were returning home the following morning so they said their goodbyes.

Sam hugged Henrietta and thanked her again but words seemed inadequate. So she handed her a small piece of paper on which she had written the last verse of a poem.

She whispered

"I wrote it a long time ago. I think it fits you."

Henrietta unfolded the paper and read

What is love

Or is it a flower,
A bloom frail yet spry;
A many side bower,
Where a strong man may cry...

Ah yes, Ah yes, they sigh...

And looked at Sam with tears in her eyes. Then she looked across at Gerald who was standing with Vivian by the door; they were smiling at one another, their faces mirroring the same look. And then he turned and saw his wife and came to her.

He put his arm about Henrietta's shoulders and looked at Sam. He said

"Whatever life gives us or takes from us, we will remember this day."

And he looked across at Vivian and then down at his wife and then back at Sam.

"It is lovely to know you Mrs Ashley Forbes!"

So they left, down the long cantonment road, leaving the lights and sounds of station life behind them, Ali in front keeping the horses to a brisk walk and Mohammed alongside riding one horse and leading another, Sam's mare. Vivian had been right; they attracted no attention, caused no surprise beyond the salutation from a few acquaintances. The night was dark and spangled with stars, the far hills and mountain ridges hidden, waiting in the wings on the moonrise. The air was cold, with a sharp tang that promised early frost and Sam leaned against Vivian, his arm tight about her, tingling with anticipation.

She had expected to come upon the old lodge, looming out of the darkness like a shrouded apparition. Instead what faced her was a castle of light, every window ablaze, every arch and door way festooned with light and colour. The small buggy was halted before the veranda and Ali climbed down and with Mohammed unloaded a considerable number of packages and carried them up the steps and through the front arch. Vivian jumped down and then leaned, took Sam in his arms, lifted her down, paused at the foot of the steps and then carried her up and through the archway into the large, white walled room, last seen in its faded colours and shared with assorted small rodents and lizards. He placed her down gently on her feet and they stood side by side and gazed around them. The floor had been swept and polished, the walls were hung with beautiful tapestries in rich deep colours, lined chicks, the cane screens of the east, hung down over each window embrasure and each arched doorway and vases of yellow marigolds ornamented surfaces and sills. Beautiful brass and silver lamps filled the rooms with light that spilled out onto the veranda, each creating a aureole around it like a blessing made manifest. A low couch had been placed against the far wall and carpets and quilts surrounded it, all scattered with cushions.

Ali and Mohammed had finished unpacking and in the corner was a small charcoal stove, newly lit and surrounding the couch low tables with dishes of delectable looking foods and wine ready to open, next to tall silver goblets.

Sam stood with one hand pressed up against her mouth and her eyes wide with astonished delight and Vivian turned to Ali who was now standing by the door arch, preparing to leave, and said

"Kakaji, I am humbled to be so honoured with such devoted care." He spoke in Urdu and Sam understood most and guessed the rest.

"It has been many years since thou used those words to me, Huzoor" Ali replied, also in Urdu.

"And thou to me" said Vivian, and Sam saw the small boy, losing his father at a tragically early age and turning to this man, then young and also bereft, forging a relationship which would take them beyond death.

Vivian turned to Mohammed and spoke some words of Pustu, which Sam did not understand and Mohammed bowed his head in thanks and then said

"The horses are fed and watered, Huzoor, with plenty for two days, maybe three. May Allah watch over your dreams" and he bowed to Sam and turned to follow Ali out onto the veranda. Sam rushed forward and stopped each as they left and said in halting Urdu and then in Pustu

"I am blessed" and kissed each man on the cheek. And then they left and Sam turned to find Vivian gazing at her. She walked slowly over to him and he led her to the couch and sat her down and went and fetched the wine, and poured it, red like ripened plums, into the gleaming silver goblets. He sat beside her, his damaged leg stretched out, the other folded under him and she moved into the circle of his arm. They did not speak. After a while he took the glass from her hand and placed it with his on the table beside them and then he bent his head and kissed her, slowly and deliberately. Then he moved his head back to look at her. He murmured

"I have become yours. Hereafter, I cannot live without you. Let us share the joys."

And Sam whispered back

"We are word and meaning, united. You are thought and I am sound. May the night be honey-sweet for us"

And she stood up from him and with infinite care removed the soft leather boots from her feet. Then she unbound the red silk scarf from her throat and dropped it on the floor beside the boots. Carefully she lifted the soft folds of the kashmir tunic and untied the plaited silk rope that held the trousers and let them fall to the floor and gracefully stepped away from them. All this time Vivian held her eyes and she did not release them. She lifted her hands and removed the pins from her hair and let it fall, gently tossing her head so the strands fell about her shoulders, streaked winter gold sunshine through trees, in the lamplight. Finally she raised her arms and lifted the tunic over her head and let it fall. Wearing only the gold ear strands, flashing in the lamplight and the plain gold band on her left hand she moved towards Vivian and reached out that hand and released his eyes. Then she knelt down on the cushions below the couch and Vivian, his eyes moving over her like a warm breeze, looked back into her eyes and slid from the couch to beside her and took her in his arms…

Their passion was fierce and demanding and their mutual response as fundamental and expressive and as old as time.

Only the moving shadows on the walls watched them; only the quiet ghosts approved them; many spirits who had loved and lost, and now all united in blessing.

During the night Sam awoke and Vivian stirred beside her, pulling her close.

"I remember reading once about a girl who was a devotee of Kali. The goddess told her that there was no bridge that love could not cross; no door through which love could not pass; that love was more powerful than death and that in your lives to come you could meet again those you have loved –"

Vivian, his lips pressed close to her temple whispered

"Hinduism believes in reincarnation of souls. That souls are immortal and death is but a resting place, where the soul assembles its resources and adjusts its course. That through death and life we achieve a state of equanimity and finally completeness."

"Make a wholeof me" murmured Sam.

"What did you say?"

"'That from the pieces we might make a wholeof me'- it's a poem, from a long time ago- are you a Hindu Vivian?"

"I only know that I am a man in love and for me that is all that matters right now."

"Hindus believe that all living things have a soul don't they?"

"Yes."

"If everything has a soul why are the dogs treated so badly?" Sam persisted.

"You ask me questions to which I have no answers. So many questions. Too many questions. Answer me this instead."

He looked into her eyes and Sam turned to him and surrendered to a passion that matched her own.

The next time she woke the light of the new day was forcing its way through the hung chicks and Vivian was propped on one elbow and looking at her.

"You sleep like one at peace" said Vivian.

"That must be your influence. I used to sleep like a snuggled embryo, my feet and hands all tucked in. And I have also been referred to as a dormouse!"

She smiled up at him, examining the shadowed contours of his face, the tumbled hair, the querulous eyebrows and the fathoms deep, dark eyes.

"Why don't you have a moustache? Everybody in these times has a moustache."

"Because I look ridiculous."

Sam frowned and then her brow cleared.

"It grows black, like your eyebrows!"

"It looks like someone has drawn a khol line across my top lip."

"But your beard is gold, like your hair. I saw it when you were ill before Ali shaved you."

"Like I said, ridiculous! Do you think we could have some breakfast before I get so distracted that I lose my appetite for food – again!"

Sam slipped out from under the quilt, turned to look at him, standing quite as naked as the embryo to which she had just referred, saw the expression in his eyes and then hastily slipped on the robe that someone had placed conveniently on a table on the other side of the room. But it was too late and breakfast was delayed.

They stayed for four days. They opened the chicks; they closed the chicks; they drank wine, red wine and lemon tea and strong dark coffee. Ali had left an amazing variety of what might be called in later years, convenience foods. These included chappatis, lentils, dried meats, fruit and vegetables and the soured milk drink called lassi. He had managed with the use of lined boxes and cold places to keep everything fresh. Each day they rode out into the foothills and Vivian shot game and showed Sam how to prepare and cook it. They went out just before dawn and Vivian took them to different places where they could watch the sun rise up over the mountain tops and its early rays cascade from the snow tipped peaks down the dramatic chasms, painting cadaverous ranges so dramatic they imparted terror as well as radiant beauty. They rode until they were tired and then found some shade under which to tether the horses and sat side by side watching the birds and the wildlife and the changing patterns of the clouds and colours of the sky. Then they went back to their private ruin and made love. Vivian's leg was stiff at times but it didn't seem to trouble him much. It certainly didn't impede any of his activities. Sam found that Ali had left her a pot of his wonderful green unguent and she massaged it on the healing wound and watched it shrink into an ugly puckered line, as scars do. Vivian's body, stripped thin by the fever, was gaining strength and elasticity once more and Sam watched him and fell in love all over again.

Watching him she thought, Why have I waited this long to experience love... It makes no sense whatsoever. And from somewhere way back in her existence a smallish but very resolute voice said- love comes when you have pulled down the barriers you have erected within against it...the clever want to change the world; the wise change themselves...

He looked over at her and she felt ridiculously embarrassed, like a fifteen year old caught in an act of voyeurism. She was stark naked and suddenly very glad of her own slender form. Vivian's eyes swept over her and then held her gaze. She could think of nothing but the feel of his hands on her body, the touch of his lips on hers and she saw the reflection of her own desire in his eyes. He dropped the towel he was holding to dry his hair and came across to her and took her face in his hands and kissed her slowly, taking his time. His body was cool and barely dry and his hair was wet and disordered, and more so as she ran her hands through it. And then he picked her up and carried her bsck to the couch...

Undeniably in love, was her last conscious thought.

In the four days they did not explore the past or the future, past relationships or events; future possibilities or exigencies. They learned about each other; every nuance, every thought, every feeling, every belief, every doubt. And were happy.

On the third morning Sam awoke very early while Vivian still slept. He had left one of the upper arches open to the sky and the moon threw its beamed torch onto the carpeted floor creating a small pool of iridescent colour. She closed her eyes again but the patterns fashioned a kaleidoscope of thoughts in her mind that she could not ignore.

What is love? The question plagued her. She and Vivian loved and were in love. But what was this love?

'My life for yours' – she had read that phrase given one to another in declaration of fealty. Was that love? Where one person would lay down their life to save another? And was it the same love that bound a mother to a child, a brother to a brother, a man to a woman, a woman to a woman, a man to a man? And sex? Did it enhance love or just complicate it?

Once she had seen sex in a very hands-on way. Good exercise; very powerful, if transitory, sensations, for some anyway; a good relaxant. But love? Well it was supposed to enhance the sex, in the sense that it made the partners more attuned to each other's desires and sensitivities, areas of pleasure etc. Perhaps it could even prolong the activity, although this could be achieved by an experienced, conscientious and considerate lover. But did it change the quality of the act? Was it after all just an act, part of a time honoured reproductive system for mammals and being mammals was it not also part of the system for the male of the species to walk away? Was it not also true that in the human species sometimes the act threw out tentacles that ensnared unwary emotions which could then weave a treacherous web of expectancy and co-dependency and in worst case scenarios even erode any love, had there been any in the first place. If one of the parties was vulnerable in some way, physically or emotionally, might this destabilise the relationship? If through sex an attachment formed with all its ownership attributes it could become a destructive force which might ultimately destroy. Could love survive all this? For those immune to the demons of insecurity and attachment it would not be an issue. But for others, for me for instance, thought Sam, might it not turn you back into a self-doubting, self-critical analyst, prone to interpreting every casual word and glance in a negative manner and fighting a losing battle with self-doubt. How wearisome was that! Just when you thought you had reached the plain of equanimity, you found yourself coming unglued and about as complete as a polystyrene Pinocchio with no strings. No wonder Hindus thought it best to go through many lifetimes to reach completeness and divorce from attachment. Smart.

All her life Sam had taken risks; was it just cowardice to run from this, the biggest risk of all? Luc would have settled for a platonic relationship; so would Steve; with reluctance. Not his first choice but he would have accepted it. Was that love?

And then she heard those words again: love comes when you have pulled down the barriers you have erected against it; love is stronger than death; there is no bridge that love cannot cross and no door through which love cannot pass. Then she looked down at Vivian and was overwhelmed by a sense of rightness, of destiny and completion. Was that love?

If he opened his eyes now and looked at her, before he focused on her, before his eyes sent the image to his brain, before any interpretation took place, what would he see? He slept on.

If only...

If only we'd met in some other time-

In his time-

In my time-

There was no answer was there? What was it Ali believed? Our paths are written...

What if

What if, one day we say,

Let's play the game the universal way;

What if,,,

"What if you come here" and Sam jumped.

Vivian was awake and looking at her, his eyes hooded and sleepy.

"Ah love! Could thou and I with fate conspire

To grasp this sorry scheme of things entire
Would not we shatter it to bits- and then
Re-mould it nearer to the heart's desire!"
His voice, despite the early hour and the sudden awakening,
was the usual warm velvet.

Sam stared at him.
"You know The Rubaiyat of Omar Khayyam?"
"Contrary to popular thought the average soldier can read!"
"I didn't mean that. I just didn't know-"
"It was published in 1859, translated from the Persian and
I was curious on that account, although I believe the translation
takes some liberties with the original."
Sam stared at him.
Vivian looked back at her calmly.
"Are you convinced, my 20th century wildcat, that I am a
worthy subject for your love? Do you need more proof? What
if you come here and I show you-"
What if...
Sam said
"I seem to remember that the next verse goes something
like –
'But see! The rising Moon of heaven again
Looks for us, sweetheart, through the quivering plane,
How oft hereafter rising will she look
Among those leaves,, for one of us in vain?'"
"Something like that, yes."
"What's your version?"
"Ah, Moon of my delight who know'st
No wane
The Moon of heav'n is rising once again:
How oft hereafter rising shall she look
Through this same garden after me –in vain!"
Sam thought for a moment.
"I like yours better; it must be the first version. But it's
sadder..."

"Do you know the work of John Donne?"

"No man is an island –ask not for whom the bell tolls, it tolls for thee?"

"Yes. But not that line. 'If our two loves be one, or, thou and I love so alike, that non do slacken, non can die'."

Sam gazed at him, deeply moved. Vivian said again

"Now, what if you come over here and I show you?"

What if...

In the very early morning of the fifth day, as the moon slid from the sky, before the fingers of the dawn hooked over the edge of the mountains, they returned to the cantonment. They went circuitously, as had Ali and Mohammed previously, and entered the stables from the rear. They rode side by side, their horses flanks almost touching and so slowly, as if each knew that every step took them nearer to a conclusion that neither wanted to face. Mohammed was waiting by the stable entrance, his face inscrutable, his eyes warm. What did he think, Sam wondered, a Muslim, a believer in the one God, of this masquerade? She knew he approved of the liaison, if only for Vivian's sake. But with a woman from the future? What did his religion tell him about that? Maybe he was one of life's true believers for whom God was literally the all-powerful and therefore all capable, making all things possible. He was a soldier as well as a syce; he must have seen much that challenged his beliefs. Maybe he just left things to his God and did not question the wherefore. How smart.

Vivian was watching her as he lifted her down from the saddle.

"You're thinking again!"

"I know. My gift and my curse." Sam smiled at him.

"Maybe life has taught Mohammed Khan that there is only one goal but many paths and he does not have your need to question the path and its validity?" Vivian spoke quietly as they left Mohammed with his precious horses and went into the bungalow.

"Have you always been able to read minds?"

"No. But there are many things I have not done until I met you."

His look was so intense that she wished they were back on the rugs of the old lodge and time had been arrested for the foreseeable future and she need never think again. As Ali came forward to greet them and take their wraps Vivian whispered

"We will go again tomorrow and the next day and for as long as my 'convalescence' lasts."

They had six weeks. The surgeon came to see Vivian and proclaimed that whilst the wound was troubling him less and less, it was hardly practicable for a cavalry officer in charge of men to go back on duty with a limp and a tendency to wince if undue pressure was applied! Once Vivian would have rebelled, protesting his fitness, but the borders were quiet and for the first time in a long time he had something that occupied him to a greater extent than soldiering. Sam had expected rebellion and frustration but he demonstrated neither. She spoke to Ali, wonderingly and he had replied

"He has happiness, what more could a man ask?"

And Sam found herself pondering how she, of all people, could have ever been a contributory factor in someone's happiness.

Vivian was determined to show her as much of his environment as he possibly could without arousing comment or suspicion.

He spoke of his love for the country of his birth.

"India is a land of variety and contrasts. If you have an artist's soul you see the country stretching into eternity, with its immense sky and its always distant horizons. When I go out into it, when I take the trouble to look around me, I feel very, very small and being so small has the effect of intensifying my awareness of everything around me. Sometimes it's just a beige flat landscape, on and on, and then you see flashes of flame, a gold mohur tree! And then the mountains, the

Himalaya; the gateway to the gods! Some young subalterns come up here and find it barren and unproductive. They dislike the rocky hills and the prickly, unforgiving thorn and long for the green pastures of home. But here is just one aspect. Some of the landscapes are rich with fields of yellow mustard and acres of sugar cane. Some are tropical jungles. Some are water and ice; mystic, opulent beauty; tragic poverty. I love them all! The horizontal lines of blue smoke denoting a village; pale dust hanging over slowly returning cows; the scents and the sunsets give me a sense of affinity, of kinship. I belonged here from the moment I was born."

He turned to Sam, his eyes glowing; seeing it again, she thought, through the boy's eyes.

"That must be a wonderful feeling" Sam said. "That discomfort and struggle are subordinate to a greater feeling of belonging." And she thought, I would like to have that...

They rode daily; they went regularly to the ruined lodge. He took her to many places where there were small ruins of temples and shrines, some long lost and neglected, gradually being drawn once more to nature's bosom; others clearly still used and accepting offerings from the villagers in the nearby communities. The gods and goddesses were many and varied and Sam was fascinated. The creeds of karma and reincarnation and learning, moving you toward a plateau of equanimity she could easily embrace. But all this lot? How did you choose? Why did you choose a particular god to worship? Was there a handbook? Although Ali was a Hindu and Mohammed Khan a Muslim, they both seemed to espouse Kismet.

When she asked Vivian he was very matter of fact.

"They were both young men when they joined my father's household, teenage boys really. They had their separate religions and their different cultures and families. My mother was a Christian but my father had been brought up among men of the north, of the hill states and I believe his religion was an amalgamation of everything he thought good about those disparate beliefs. Mohammed believes in the one god;

Ali is free to believe in whomsoever he wishes. But above all that I think they came to believe in a code of love and loyalty that somehow took precedence in their life. In battle, Mohammed would kill an infidel without compunction; in famine, Ali would make offering to the appropriate god. They would both give their lives to save me as I would for them. Does anything else matter?"

Sam listened to his words and thought, if all men could reach that plateau surely there could be a world without strife.

One particular shrine seemed to have great significance for him. Before they took their leave, he went to his saddlebags and removed a small wreath of marigolds, somewhat crushed after their journey, and placed it carefully at the foot of the effigy. And Sam wondered if now, in this situation he currently found himself, the creed which incorporated reincarnation and many lives had suddenly increased in appeal or whether he was just covering all bases.

They made their way home via the ruined lodge, as they often did and Vivian produced wine and chapatis from his saddlebags and a rug for them to sit on. The sun was still high in the sky but the large room with its arched windows and doorways was cool and surprisingly still clean. They sat together leaning against the far wall in complicit and restful silence.

"I want to take you somewhere" said Sam.

Vivian raised his eyebrows.

"Where? Now?"

"Yes. An old memory."

"Whose?"

"Mine."

"Where?"

"When I was young I can remember standing in front of a painting by Cezanne. It was a painting of a bridge in a forest and I simply can't remember its name. I remember thinking quite clearly 'that's what I want!' I want to be able to stand in a place like that, completely alone and be content. I remember the word. Content not happy. Content with me. Needing nothing; desiring nothing; just me; me OK with me. All this time and I can still remember it so clearly."

"So important to you" said Vivian

"Yes. But I don't think I recognised how important; not then. Or the lengths that I would go to or all the safety I would turn my back on to achieve it. Just to say 'I am' and for it to be enough."

"I suppose you are talking about inner peace" said Vivian.

"I suppose I am."

"Did you forget it along the way?"

"Yes. Every day. And remembered it, weeks, months, and years later."

"But you never forgot it completely?"

"No."

"All those bridges crossed to find the one you recognised at the start."

"Do you know that a bridge crossing in dream terminology represents moving forward and changing?"

"I do actually, yes. When I was young I had a close Hindu friend, who died-I told you, remember? He was six years older than me and my father was friends with his and we used to visit his hill state, where his father ruled. I used to have a lot of vivid dreams and he had studied dream interpretation. He taught me a lot."

He smiled at Sam in a boyish way.

"I think I may have had a crush on him. He was tall and very good looking; dark hair; flashing dark eyes!"

"And you so sweet and Sabrina fair!. Does he have something to do with that shrine where you left the garland?" said Sam.

"In a way. He died of the cholera just before his fifteenth birthday. I was heartbroken. I had lost my father and now Dayaal was taken from me. I took to visiting all the Hindu shrines to see if I could get through to him there. To see if I could reach his spirit. My father had once told me, when

I was small, that was what he did when he was young and lost someone or something dear. I attended his cremation and at the place where they put his ashes into the water I planted a small flowering bush, a jasmine. Surprisingly, or maybe not, it still grows. I think I believe now that he will always be with me. I think I believe that each time it flowers, he lives. When we were together down here we used to visit that small shrine." He paused for a moment, considering something. Then he said

"I wrote a poem, after he died. I tried to put down what he meant to me and what I felt…"

"You wrote a poem!"

"Yes. Is that so surprising?"

"No! Yes –well maybe."

"Because I am a soldier by profession? I wasn't then. And there are many writers and artists among us."

"Yes. I know that. And good ones. I was just –surprised. You were very young; do you still have the poem? Can I see it?"

"I kept it with me. It seemed important to do so."

"What? Here? You came here with him?"

"Yes."

He was over at the small desk, hardly more than an occasional table, opening its one insignificant drawer. He brought out a sheet of yellowed, coarse Indian paper and brought it over to her.

"It's a bit faded I'm afraid but still legible I think. "

The handwriting was rounded and childish and the punctuation sporadic but it was beautifully presented with little hieroglyphics at the top and the bottom as if its author had wanted to make it special. She balanced it carefully on her two palms and read:

The dead are cold, soon rotten, buried deep, forgotten.
burned to dust, scattered wide,
framed in marble; tarnished pride.

Trapped forever, drowned by tears,
sightless
soundless.
formless fears.
A smear upon a time now past, a guilty dent that did not last.
The dead are cold..
*

Life and death are one, then and now are one
Future past and present, together,
side by side
a mere stride
between..
*

With death a step away, and thence to life,
what need for strife
or pain, despair
or blame.
For as we came, so will we go
our lives, a snail trail, glistening, show
a progression, nothing more
a game of one with zero score.
To end is but to start, explore
another realm, dimension, perennial flaw.
The only thing we have or are,
and cannot lose is love,
our keeper, guide and mentor,
and our right to choose.

Those last lines were Kevin's words.
Underneath the childish hand had inscribed:

For Dayaal, who I loved and who went before me.
I miss you.
V A-F

Sam couldn't speak for a few moments. Vivian watched her face and said nothing. She looked up from the paper with tears in her eyes. Then she said

"You wrote it for your friend. But you could have been writing it for your mother; and your father and you could have been writing it for the older Vivian who was going to have to suffer so much more and for his friend Gerald…"

Vivian smiled a sad acknowledgement.

"Did he know how much you cared?"

Vivian nodded. "He knew. He once…it doesn't matter…he knew." Then he said

"So are you going to show me this bridge?"

"Yes."

"Can we do that? I mean can I go to your old memory?"

"Yes. I think we've been doing it already. Do you trust me?"

"Yes. Implicitly."

"Then it will work. Give me your hand."

"You've done this before, haven't you?"

"Be quiet. You don't need to hold it quite so tightly!"

"I'm anxious."

"I'd never have guessed! Close your eyes, make your mind blank –and concentrate."

So many old memories… So many…

"Now… I'm going to talk you there… Listen… See what I see… Nothing else… Just what I see…

It's dark, but not black, it's green, deep forest green, deep and alive; as you walk it separates into particles of many greens like fragments of a stained glass window; there is no sky, there is no natural light; it is an inner world; it represents inner and outer peace; the inner peace as it would be reflected outwards; the understanding that that was the objective; it is filled with murmurs; it is breathing, growing, expanding. But you are safe, completely totally safe. Everything is still; the stillness is absolute. You look down to one side and there is a stream, the sleeping stream, no breeze disturbs it. You look up but there is no sky to reflect in the stream. The trees above you stand tall; they are breathing; they are protecting you, guiding you, whispering the ancient wisdom to you… You become aware that there is a bridge spanning the stream; its ancient moss covered stones merge so well into the trees it was completely hidden from you until now... You approach. It frames a gentle arch over the stream. The trees step back to allow it to stretch across. You place your foot on the worn warm stone. It welcomes you. You move up the gentle incline until you are standing next to the parapet. You lean on it and look down into the still, serene water whose surface mirrors the emeralds in the trees above. You stay there some moments in contemplation, attuning to your inner most feelings. Then you look up and forward. Through the leaves of the trees at the far side you see a patch of golden light. You move across the bridge to the other side, towards the light..."

Sam let go of his hand and laid it gently, palm upwards on his knee. She felt very calm. With her eyes still closed and the trees all around her she said

"What did you see?"

Vivian sighed deeply, leaned back and opened his eyes.

"Everything. Everything, just as you described it."

"Where were you?"

"I was there. But it was strange. It was as if I was watching pictures of me there. As if I was creating the pictures as well as being in them."

Sam waited a moment then she said very quietly

"Where was I?"

He took so long to answer Sam thought he had fallen asleep. When he finally responded he spoke slowly, as if he was considering every word.

"I didn't *see* you exactly. But I knew you were there."

"On the bridge?" Sam fought to keep the anxiety out of her voice.

"No. Not on the bridge. You were beyond the bridge. In the light. I was walking towards you. Towards the light."

They sat together for ten minutes or more, not speaking, not touching, as if each was unwilling to ask the question to which both wanted the answer.

It was Vivian who broke through the fragile shell of no words which was all that stood between them and the uncertainty.

"What does it mean?"

Sam sighed. Her words were as big a disappointment to her as they would be to him.

"I really don't know."

But deep within there was a very small corner of relief. *He was not there on the bridge, with me.*

"Why are you so relieved that I was not there on the bridge with you?" asked Vivian.

Sam jerked out of her reverie.

He was looking at her very intently. She sighed again.

"Because if we are separate, and know each other, we can find each other again."

"No bridge that love cannot cross" murmured Vivian. "If we had been together on the bridge we would be trapped? Trapped in time?"

Sam turned to him. She looked at his face, the sharp lines and hollows accentuated through fever, the black querulous eyebrows puzzling, demanding, the deep dark blue eyes, black with anxiety and hope. Would it be so very bad to be trapped in time? She turned her head away and leaned up against him and he put his arms around her.

"Why did you take me there?"

"I have been there before, looking for answers. I have a gift of being able to see spirit, sometimes; clairvoyance in its truest sense, able to connect to and see through to the heart. I thought I might be able to see us both but I could only see you, on the bridge, and the light…"

"I have no experience of this" said Vivian quietly, "but it seemed to me as I watched myself, that it was a place of journeying and of hope."

Hope…

Vivian regained his health and strength and was back on active duty. And so their lives went on in a simple routine bounded by the hot sun, the winds which could spring from nowhere and then die just as quickly and then the rain. For Sam, not a great patron of rain at the best of times, the mind numbing battering of its onslaught was beyond belief. Indoors you were deafened by it; outdoors within seconds you were soaked to the skin, to return home leaving a trail of water in your wake and extract yourself from your clothes like unpeeling a banana. On one occasion they had been out riding and Vivian had headed for the ruined palace and once inside, had done the unpeeling for her with such obvious delight and sensual expertise that it had temporarily changed Sam's views on torrential rain, at least in present company.

But whether by some unspoken agreement or some shared but hidden knowledge, they did not talk of the future.

Until the night she dreamed about Kevin

Vivian had come in late and wet and frustrated over some orders that had come from central command which he would have liked to vehemently contest. Ali had provided the water for his bath but Sam had fetched the towels and rubbed him all over until he was not only dry but laughing and considerably aroused. They had made love and Vivian had fallen asleep almost immediately and Sam had dosed, drifting in and out of consciousness.

And then suddenly there was Kevin. He was standing halfway up a short flight of steps and he was on his back feet with his front paws held out in front of him, like Caesar addressing the senate.

And he was speaking in one of those long, involved monologues he had been so fond of when she was young. And she could hear every word.

Imagine a grid he had said.

And she had had to ask him to explain.

Like a spider's web but square not round with the lines criss-crossing. And at each intersection, cross over of lines, there is a point of light, and each point of light is a something.

And she had asked if he could be more specific.

The lines of the grid go backwards and forwards and sideways in time. Each of us can only see those points around us –but they are all there and sometimes we can sort of see them all, not with our eyes but with our minds and our hearts.

And she had not understood his words but they had painted a picture in her mind and she could see *that* and she could feel what he meant. And she had asked him if he was a light spot and he had said

No. *I'm different. You and I, we are part of a whole, the same light spot if you like.*

And she had said that she did not understand and Kevin had said

No, but you will. You don't ever need to lose me. I am part of you.

And then he had said

This is your movie. You are producer, director and principal actor.

And just as in the past she asked him, in her dream, well what now Kevin? And Kevin, being Kevin, dear boy, had disappeared and Sam woke up.

She thought about the dream a lot during the ensuing days. It gave her no real explicit understanding of her present situation but it did give something else, something that was perhaps more valuable. It reminded her that she had chosen to be here, in this time, with this man. She had chosen –and whilst pain might be involved she would not have chosen that as the end game.

At first she thought to discuss the dream with Vivian and to see if their shared understanding of its meaning might bring comfort to both. But the man was plainly happy and she was unwilling to take even the smallest particle of that happiness from him. So she reined in her incessant need for answers and understandings on the basis that if it was meant to come up for discussion the universe would provide the opportunity.

And the dream had provided comfort, the same comfort it had given the young Sam back then who was afraid of losing her guide. He had said that with our hearts and our minds we can see all the points of light, even if vision denies them, and –"you don't ever need to lose me. I am part of you." Surely that was the best definition of love there could ever be.

But as the weeks went on Sam began to realise, to acknowledge, that something might have to be lost in order for something to be gained and equally to acknowledge that she could not remain, in any real sense, in his time but he could, if she was prepared to take the risk, come into hers. She did not know how it could be done but she did know that it could. There were many accounts of people who have experienced and remembered past lives. She was one herself. And if there was anything on the planet that could forge a bridge between lives, it was love. So she allowed the thought to plant a seed and she encouraged it to grow in the hopes that the courage to pick the plant would grow with it.

Vivian was out for long hours these days. Sam read a lot, worked hard at learning Urdu and Pushto and expanding her vocabulary. Most days Vivian left Mohammed with her so she could go out riding until his return but occasionally Mohammed went with him and Sam was left to amuse herself.

It was on one of these occasions that Sam decided that she was a big girl now and what possible harm could come to her just riding a horse she knew in an area with which she was well acquainted? It was a beautiful morning, sunny but with a fresh breeze from the hills. What could go wrong? Ali had gone to the bazaar early and Vivian had said they were going too far out for him to return for breakfast as he often did. So. And if she heard the small coercive voice that insisted this really, *really* wasn't a good idea, she completely ignored it.

Tuska was fresh, tossing her head, impatient to be given full rein. Sam held her in until they were passed all the cantonment buildings and the horse lines and then gave her head. There was no one about; indeed there did not seem to be anything, in any direction, as far as the hills. Just grass tracks and undulating slopes; a keen wind and sunshine. She was wearing warm woollen robes and her hair fought its way free of restraint and streamed out behind her. To a girl brought up to ride in tight jodhpurs and a hard hat this was freedom to die for!

Eventually their pace slowed and Sam pulled the mare to a walk and looked about. She and Vivian had been this way before. Up ahead there was a small bank of trees, peripheral to deeper jungle beyond. They walked on, the mare easy now, Sam relaxed in the saddle. She would get to the fringe of the trees and then turn back. Judging by the sun she had been out for 3 hours or more. No sense in causing Ali unnecessary concern.

There was a stream up ahead if she remembered rightly. The land was criss-crossed with such waterways, falling down as they did from the mountains, allowing the villagers to grow small patches of crops and graze their cattle. She would go as far as that, they could both have a drink and then return. No anxiety assailed her. Predators of the region seemed to do their drinking at the approach of sunset. She was assured in her safety and therefore totally unprepared for the corpulent, red firebrand that charged out of the trees beyond the stream and splashed straight into the water where Tuska had just lowered her head to drink, trailing squeaking piglets on both sides. The horse flung up her head and half reared and with a violent jerk turned on her hindquarters and bolted. Sam had lost both the reins and one stirrup and was flung sideways but she was a good rider and kept her seat until Tuska, in her frantic haste, stumbled badly over an anthill and Sam pitched forward over her head and the ground came up to meet her with considerable force. And Sam thought as the blackness descended upon her

"Now I know how it's going to end. I fall; I fall, round and round, like a feather loosed from the wing of a bird... and then I'm back. It's going to happen like this again..."

But she was wrong.

She was in a dark space but not totally dark. Somewhere just in front of her eyes was a pinprick of light. It sparkled slightly. She moved towards the sparkling light expecting it to travel away from her as she moved forward. But it stayed where it was and sparkled a little more keenly. She reached out her left hand to touch it and as she did so another hand came out of the shadows to her left and grasped the pin prick of light. The left hand, not her own, was identical in shape and form and size to her own and as it grasped the light she could see that it was not a light at all but a beautiful piece of golden thread whose end was shredded into filaments. It shimmered in its own radiance across the palm of the strange, familiar, other hand. The strange, familiar fingers closed over it. The hand moved towards her own, still slightly extended in the attitude of reaching. The hand, with its folded fingers lightly touched her fingertips, moved down into the centre of her hand and laid the thread of gold there, released it and moved away. She looked down at her palm as the other hand gently closed her fingers over the gold thread. She looked up to see her own eyes and heard in her head the words

"Where I have been before you, so can you follow."

And the light from the golden thread seemed to expand and fill up all the space around her and inside her and just for a moment she and the light became one and she was filled with an intense and complete understanding that went far beyond any knowledge.

And then it was gone and the golden thread too, leaving only darkness...

There were shadows and movement and pain and she opened her eyes, not knowing, and there was Vivian.

I am not dead; I have not gone back, Sam thought and she closed her eyes again.

The next time she opened them it was clearly night for all the lamps were lit. She turned her head slightly and winced.

That hurt! Vivian was there beside her, his face bleached with anxiety and his mouth a very tight line. A very angry line Sam reflected. She smiled vaguely and lifted up a hand to try and erase the line and winced again and let it drop.

"Shit and damnation. That bloody hurts!"

Vivian's face relaxed.

"My 20th century girl has not lost her wonderful linguistic talent. Now all is well."

Sam scowled at him.

"What happened? How long have I been unconscious? Where am I?"

Vivian said

"I don't know. 36 hours. Here with me in my bungalow."

He smoothed her hair from her forehead and then said

"I should be very angry with you."

Sam frowned at him.

"You should be getting me something to get rid of this bloody awful headache!"

Ali was standing on the other side of the bed and Vivian looked across at him.

Ali nodded and said

"I believe the memsaab has suffered no permanent ill and will be better with rest. I will bring a sleeping draught." He spoke in Urdu but Sam got most of it.

She snapped

"I don't want to go to sleep again. I just want rid of this headache. God it hurts. Did I fall on my head?"

"I believe so" said Vivian calmly. "What about those things that you gave me when I had the fever?"

"Yes! Those! They're over there somewhere!" She waved a recalcitrant hand in the direction of a corner cupboard and winced again.

Vivian went and sought them out and Ali fetched tea, laced with, Sam reflected later, more than a drop of brandy. She laid back then, drowsily listening to Vivian's deep velvet tones as he told her what had happened from his end.

Ali had come back to find her absent and her horse gone. The young syce left in the stable had said he had returned to his duty to find the mare Tuska gone but had thought perhaps the Captain had leant her out to someone who had collected her in his absence.

Sam by this time had been gone more than three hours and Ali, concerned, had sent the young man to find Vivian and his troop, with an inexplicable message, so the young man thought, that the mare had been taken out and had likely gone to places known by the Sahib. Vivian, gleaning Ali's covert meaning had left his troop in charge of Risaldar Razi Khan and with Mohammed, headed down from the borderlands and across to where he and Sam rode most often. He considered the old lodge and dismissed it on the grounds that it would not be Sam's first choice without him.

He had chosen the undulating plain before the belt of trees backed by the jungle and had seen Tuska through his field glasses some distance from the stream. Sam he found near the horse, who had stayed beside her and who seemed a little jumpy but steadfast and unhurt. He had carried her back across the front of his saddle leaned up against him, Mohammed taking the mare on ahead to warn Ali of their approach.

"Mmm" murmured Sam sleepily, "What happened then?"

"You were unconscious, with a bad gash to the head. We could find no broken bones nor sign of internal damage. You stayed that way for the rest of the day and the next-"

"Mmm" murmured Sam. "Were you worried?"

She didn't hear his answer.

When she next opened her eyes Vivian was still sitting by her on the edge of the bed. Sam studied him for a moment and then said

"Come here" and reached out her arms, biting back a squeak of pain. Vivian stayed where he was looking at her critically.

"Come here!" Sam demanded. "Into the bed!"

"That's not a good-"

"Dammit! Just get in and hold me or I'll climb out now and seduce you!"

She was not at all sure she could fulfil the threat but Vivian was convinced. He removed his boots quickly and climbed into the bed and took her in his arms. Sam sighed with satisfaction and fell asleep again and Vivian laid awake and watched the moon rise and fall and eventually the dawn break...

Vivian appeared to have rearranged his work schedule. Sam didn't know how he had managed it but was fairly sure that it was on her account. Possibly Risaldar Razi Khan was filling the breach, he seemed to come around a lot, but Vivian hardly left her side. It was very pleasant; it was a little disturbing. Finally she tackled him.

"I'm OK really now. No headache, just a few pretty bruises and a sore shoulder. I really am quite safe to be left alone."

"You want to be left alone?"

"No! No. But I'm sure it's going to cause comment if you keep bending rules."

Vivian seemed unwilling to discuss the matter.

"I thought we might take a ride out to the lodge –if you think you could manage it?"

"Of course I can manage it! But I'll only go if you tell me what's wrong."

"Nothing's wrong."

"I didn't realise it was that bad" said Sam. And when Vivian started to protest she added

"No one says *nothing's wrong* when nothing is wrong!"

She looked at him closely. Some of the anxiety she had first seen when she regained consciousness had gone but there was a shadow across his eyes and they had stopped dancing.

"You thought I had gone. Then you thought I was dead and then when I recovered you started thinking about how it might happen; how you might lose me; how I might leave –"

Vivian didn't respond. So Sam went on.

"I thought that too. Not that I was dead but that I was leaving; I've experienced that kind of falling into darkness before-"

The image was so sharp it hurt.

And she was falling, floating, round and round in circles, gently, like a feather loosed from the wing of a bird... And a voice, a quiet young voice that said –life takes many forms; it is the spirit that is constant...

Vivian was watching her. His voice was harsh and only just under control as he said,

"I know it has to happen. I know! But not yet. Please god not yet."

Sam said

"I will tell you something I was once told a long time ago when I was full of fear."

She closed her eyes for a moment. She could see Wanigi, his calm face, his long, black hair, his bird-wing blue eyes...and she could hear his voice as if he were there before her.

"I told him that I was afraid; that I doubted my strength and also my belief as I looked towards tomorrow and he said 'there is no need. Belief without doubt is not belief at all; it is fear with a fence around it. Only the mountains last and death is not the end. It is only change of form and a new beginning.' I have never forgotten his words."

Vivian looked at her, searching her face as if he was trying to see the same images and hear the same voice. Then he moved to take her in his arms and whispered into her hair

"I *am* afraid."

And Sam said

"Me too."

These days Sam found Vivian far more willing to talk of his first wife, Elizabeth. Her impending departure and the similarities between herself and Elizabeth seemed to encourage him to speak of her and Sam asked him questions about her and their marriage.

"How did you meet?" asked Sam. "At a ball? No. You were excelling on the sports field on the back of a horse and she fell hopelessly in love!"

"No and no!" said Vivian laughing. "Nothing nearly so romantically traditional."

"Well go on then. Don't keep me guessing!"

"It was 1854 and my regiment was due to ship out to the Crimea. The losses had been heavy and they were dying like flies of disease and cold. A number of Indian regiments were cited to travel overland via Alexandria to reinforce. But we were hit by an epidemic of cholera. Two of my havildars and a dozen of the men came down with it and I was among them."

Sam, whose knowledge of warfare in the Crimea was quite extensive, closed her eyes for a moment. Vivian saw the look and reached out a hand, saying

"Yes, in all likelihood I would have been in that charge."

Sam opened her eyes and smiled.

"It's what's known in current jargon as being between 'a rock and a hard place'! I am so glad you chose cholera!"

"You would have known no different" said Vivian.

"No" said Sam, biting her lip. "I would not have known of you...Go on, please."

Vivian studied her face for a minute and then continued.

"I was shipped to the hospital instead and Elizabeth was working there, doing her best to help out the surgeon and the orderlies, who were pretty well overwhelmed. Ali came with me and when he found out that there was nothing to be done, other than clean me up and administer fluids, he had me brought back to the bungalow. It was, as I am sure you know, no job for the faint hearted. Elizabeth came with him. She told him that I was young and strong and as long as all cooking utensils and fluids were boiled to help prevent contamination, I would survive. She came three times a day, when she had finished her work at the hospital, to make sure I had not taken a turn for the worse and to give Ali a break from changing the bed and cleaning me up and getting me to drink. I believe

I was determined to get well if only to refute the necessity of being nursed like a sick baby! She gave me laudanum to make me drowsy and then poured as much cooled boiled water down my throat as she could get me to swallow without choking. In my lucid moments she told me that dehydration was the killer and that the diarrhoea and vomiting stripped the body of fluids and they must be replaced. That the disease came from water or wells, food or cooking utensils that had been contaminated and the operative word was clean. I don't think I cared a damn at the time but Ali took her at her word and followed it to the letter. It took a while and I was ridiculously weak for weeks afterwards, but I survived. I learned a lot about cholera and even more about Elizabeth. She was always calm and clean and fresh, always competent, never doubting. And the things she did for me –even now I shudder to remember-"

"I was aware that Ali had some experience of the importance of cleanliness when we were treating your leg wound. He told me you had survived cholera... I have read that bearers did not always transfer well into the household after their master's got married. Obviously Ali was not one of these."

"Oh no. He got to know Elizabeth very well whilst I was ill and admired her and came to love her..."

"You can only have been 20 then; you were only 22 during the mutiny, weren't you? How long had you been married then?"

"Two years" said Vivian.

"How did you manage that?" said Sam in surprise. "From what I have read young officers were actively discouraged, not to say forbidden, to get married at that age!"

Vivian smiled wryly.

"Yes. One needed the permission of one's commanding officer. Elizabeth was five years older than me and a colonel's daughter. He did not approve of her hospital work but she did it anyway. I had missed my chance to fight in the Crimea and during my convalescence Elizabeth kept up the visiting. I found that I looked forward more and more to her calls. She brought me news of the conflict and the battles they fought. News of my own regiment. Gerald had gone out with the engineers and I was desperate for news of him. He was too young to be in battle but I did not trust him not to find a way of getting amongst the fray. She had an active mind given to pursuing any new ideas, theories and remedies that she could get her hands on. She was a lady but had no fear or horror of the ugliness in the world, or of hard work. I fell hopelessly in love and I think everyone thought me a fool but when the colonel's daughter, the beautiful colonel's daughter, returned my feelings –well let's just say the passage of matrimony was made smoother. I believe her father was well aware that she knew her own mind and if she had chosen me I must be something above your average 20 year old British officer. We were married as soon as I was fit enough to stand upright!" He paused and smiled at the memory.

The full tale of the circumstances of his first 'disabled' marriage gave Sam new insight.

"Maybe even in love the colonel knew that you were a soldier first" she said quietly.

Vivian looked at her sharply, then said lightly

"You have uncovered my secret."

Sam watched him, wondering if he would talk about Elizabeth's death and what it had done to him. The thought clearly transferred for he looked at her solemnly and said

"When she died, something in me died. It sounds melodramatic to say it out loud but it is the only way I can explain what happened to me. I had fallen in love and I had risked loving. From the moment of her death, the moment I realized and accepted that I would never see her again, the part of me that was willing to take risks, emotional risks that is, closed down. The process that had started with my father had been furthered by the loss of Dayaal. Elizabeth's death completed it. I never wanted to feel like that again; like something I'd done or not done had been the cause of an ending like that. Oh yes I still took risks, riding and fighting recklessly, in war, in sport; playing too hard; drinking too much. Then one morning I woke up to the sheer pointlessness of my existence. That was the turning point. It could have gone either way. That was the day my commanding officer sent for me. Kismet? Maybe. So I chose my profession. I put my competition pistol away in its proper place. I accepted everything, every challenge, every task which came my way. Everything I had ever felt or experienced on a personal level got projected outwards. And I committed myself to staying safe on the inside."

Sam looked at him with compassion. He would not have been the only one to be damaged in this way.

She said

"No diversions?"

"No. Nothing. There was no link between what I was doing or saying on the outside and what I was on the inside. I had become an actor in my own play. The performance was exemplary but there was no interface, outer with inner. A woman would know that. I expect they did..."

"What about-" Sam broke off. She wasn't at all sure she wanted to know.

"You are referring to sex? No. There were courtesans available-and willing-some very beautiful- but the drive for pure physical satisfaction seemed to have died too and to begin over again with a new relationship-well the risk was too great. And to start to create a need in someone that couldn't and wouldn't exist for me –that seemed immoral."

"That was very considerate" said Sam.

"No I don't think so" said Vivian. "Just practical."

"Were you not pursued? A single man, wealthy, young; very eligible – and gorgeous. The mamas at least must have had their eye on you."

"Perhaps. I didn't really notice. I had men to take charge of, to train and horses. Warfare was changing and we were obliged to learn new methods and new skills; all of us. I had fellow officers who like me were forced to embrace new challenges and I still had a dear and close friend in Gerald. Some of my young subalterns showed an interest but I couldn't engender any mutual feeling for them either. No I didn't really notice anything until I met you..."

He was studying her intently, examining the woman who had made it worthwhile to take risks again.

"You said she was five years older? That would make her 37 now. Mmmm."

"I can see that you are drawing conclusions" said Vivian wryly.

"And she was beautiful?" said Sam.

"Yes. Very."

Sam laughed.

"I thought you were going to tell me that you loved her for her mind!"

"That too."

"And me?" She really hadn't meant to say that, to ask that.

Vivian looked at her for so long that she thought he would not answer. What did she expect him to say? His eyes looked so dark they were almost black and there was a small frown between his brows as if he was giving the question serious consideration. Then he stood up, came to stand in front of her, took her hands, and raised her to her feet.

"I love you beyond life."

He looked down at her seriously as if he'd just realized what he said and what it meant. And then his brow cleared, he lifted the hand that bore his ring to his lips and he repeated

"Beyond life."

She had not said anything in response and he did not seem to need one. It was as if his declaration stood alone and needed no reciprocal pledge, to confirm, to enhance or to qualify. And it lay between them like a thread of gold, an insoluble, binding connection untouched by time. He only said it once and Sam didn't need him to repeat it. His behaviour demonstrated it every hour, every day, every time they were together. And the desperate need to qualify or define love merged into the present joy. It was like all the experiences she'd ever had through all the lives she had ever lived, had fused. That was how she felt with Vivian. He didn't make her complete in the missing part sense, but through him she became complete. This is my love story, she thought, with my past and with my future, in my present. A love story with myself, my inner being and my God. The entirety was love but then she had known that for some time and she knew the time was rapidly approaching when she needed to take that step that would sever their happiness; the only thing that was in her power to do, to try and shape the future. She did not talk to him about Steve or Luc or Wanigi, or any of the others because somehow it no longer seemed relevant. What purpose did it serve to speak of past relationships and how they had changed and shaped her, to make her what she was today, when what she was today was the woman he loved.

Laying beside him that night she had a feeling of being part of something... something that was too big, far too big for comprehension or comfort. She closed her eyes fully committed to spending the night hours trailing over fences after sheep and focusing on wavering black squares of velvet but she simply passed out; one moment she was awake, thinking, I'll never sleep and then there was nothing...

And then she was aware of the light; not daylight, nor the light of the moon. This light danced like firelight dances once it is gone beyond the struggling, smoking stage and the vision of it enticed a memory that was at once sweet and full of bitterness...

He was sitting in the entrance of the tepee, silhouetted by the flames beyond him, for now she could see it was a fire and around the fire there were figures dancing, clad in native dress, stepping purposefully, tossing their heads so that the headdresses and decorations they wore in their hair glinted like so many eyes.

He was sitting absolutely still, his legs crossed, his back straight as an arrow. He appeared to watch the dancers and his gaze was intent but of course he could not see them, only in his mind, from the sounds and the aroma of wood smoke and the movement of the air...

They danced; he watched; Sam watched, remembering another fire, remembering watching this same figure from behind, sitting just as this one sat, statue like in his stillness...

Somewhere in the night hours she received an understanding that had eluded her all her life because its form had always moved out of reach in advance of the morning light and re-joined the shadows.

And she dreamed again and she awoke just before dawn, the grey mist ridden, blue grey dawn of Indian magic and far away like the remanents of a fading memory, she heard a tiny tinkling sound, like silver bells being rung in crystal water and she heard again Kevin's voice:

It's only a line; you can't see me and you can't see the line but it's there and all you have to do is step over it.

So.

So whatever this was, wherever she was, it had the approval of the boy with the bird-wing blue eyes and Kevin; the approval of her more than brother, her kola, and her mentor and guide...

And then there were more words. Not Kevin this time but the words of a long forgotten poem.

If all unknown tomorrows
Were really with us here...

What if all our yesterdays
Came suddenly into view;
Our future, past, and present
As one composite hue;
Only a line between...
Across the line
Your life and mine...

There was more but next to her Vivian rolled over and put his arm across her and she moved her head so that her mouth was very close to his ear and whispered

"I love you Vivian Ashley Forbes and it's only a line."

And Vivian, feeling the warmth and the soft breath against his cheek, sighed and went on sleeping.

She slept late, not in real terms but late enough for Vivian to have left for morning duties and returned for little breakfast. He smiled happily and sat down with her to eat .Ali produced something in small bowls and Vivian watched while Sam took her first spoonful. It looked a little strange but it was absolutely delightful.

Vivian, already halfway down his bowl, raised a speculative eyebrow.

"It's wonderful" said Sam. "What is it?"

"Daliya, a kind of Indian porridge made from cracked wheat with the Ali ingredient!" said Vivian.

"I love it" said Sam and then paused between mouthfuls and said

"I don't think I've ever seen you eat breakfast before."

Vivian grinned.

"It must be you. You've given me an appetite!"

"I've accelerated your metabolic rate?"

He laughed.

"I relax with you and when I'm relaxed I eat more."

Sam did not reply. She had been called a lot of things in her time but relaxing was not one of them. Before she could pursue it Vivian said

"What's your favourite food, breakfast food?"

"Egg and bacon sandwiches with mayo" said Sam without hesitation.

"Egg and bacon –yes – bacon more difficult here; bread – yes. mayo?"

"Mayonnaise, made from raw eggs and olive oil, a kind of fat whipped saurce."

Vivian looked at Ali, who shrugged. He said

"If the memsaab will show me I will try."

Sam grinned. The food was awesome anyway but mayonnaise, well it just- every woman had her weaknesses...

The frontiers were calm, there were few tribal skirmishes and Vivian and the troop under his command spent most of their time doing training exercises in the field, with sporting events on the parade ground and the occasional ball constituting recreational activity. The sporting occasions were relatively easy for Sam to watch and enjoy. Ali was amazingly proficient at conducting her to some unobtrusive position where she could watch Vivian perform on the back of a horse. His skill was renowned and appreciated, not only by Sam but also by a significant number of daintily dressed young women who clapped in delight and blushed when he rode past them. The green finger of jealousy touched Sam briefly but was soon pushed away by the dazzling smile he gave his old and very dear retainer, Ali, standing beside her invisible form, and which Ali graciously shared with herself. Seemingly it was common knowledge that Ali and Mohammed, his syce, through their love of him and their shared experiences, were Vivian's dearest companions and if it caused comment it remained behind the closed doors of the female gossips. The most interesting thing for Sam was to see how Vivian's performance was monitored by the young officers in the station. Some of them looked positively lovesick. When questioned Vivian shrugged and said "They'll get over it."

Where at all possible Vivian excused himself from any social activity that involved the women and dancing, pleading work, duty, or fatigue but once in a while he was formally requested to attend by a senior officer and usually came back hot, tired and cross. And Ali told Sam that as a young married man with a wife, the couple had preferred their own company and entertainment and he said it with such a twinkle in his eye that Sam had gone to him and kissed him on the cheek. And

Ali had looked at her very seriously and some understanding had passed between them and it had made them both sad.

So Sam procrastinated and excused herself with the old adage, if it ain't broke don't fix it, until the day that Vivian walked through the door with a face like thunder and made straight for the brandy bottle.

So it had happened. Ali had prepared her.

He had heard talk in the bazaars that the regiment was to be posted out into the hills for a six month training camp and it would be before the hot weather came again. Sam had braced herself but now the news had finally been confirmed to Vivian she was at a loss. So she stood and watched him and waited for the storm to break. He turned around, glass in hand and saw her face.

"So you know!"

He was standing by the window, the glass in his hand held up to the light and gently swirling the amber liquid so that it rolled and eddied like molten metal in an alchemist's phial. He studied the glass intently as if in removing his gaze he would lose his hold on his small, perfect reality. The knuckles of his hand stood out like the bones of a carcass, bleached white by the sun on the Indian plains. His left hand was held out, twisted slightly to the left as if he had forgotten its existence. As if it should be holding something... Or offering something ...Sam stood quite still. His pain was so intense that she thought her heart would actually break. And then came the despair; the hopelessness of one who has reached the place where light and dark have fled, leaving only grey. In that moment he became fully aware and looked into her eyes. She held his gaze but said nothing.

"What am I to do?"

If there was an answer she would have offered it to him in exchange for her life at that moment.

Was that love?

He swallowed the drink in one and made to pour another, and she walked across the distance between them and took the hand that held the glass. It was cold as if the life had already left it. His fingers twined around hers in a fierce grip and then he pulled away and turned back to the brandy bottle, just for a moment and then decided against and placed the glass down, with the care of a man who has known the solace of alcohol, still standing with his back towards her. Then he swung round and said fiercely

"You could come with me! Who would know? It is possible. It is possible." He trailed off.

"No Vivian, it's not." She stood there with tears in her eyes. Then she took a deep breath, forcing her mind outside the situation, releasing tension, inviting calm. It took several minutes before she was able to speak again.

"This is the only way Vivian, the only way that leaves us any hope of any kind of future. I do not belong here. Only you and Ali and Mohammed can see me, so clearly I don't belong. Yes I know Henrietta can too but that comes directly from her belief and her love for you, and Gerald, because he loves you both, has also opened the door. I can't stay here because – because it doesn't matter what creed you buy into, I believe reincarnation is a forward move. This had to happen because –because" she looked desperately at Ali who was standing just behind her at the open door way. He looked at her for a moment and then at Vivian and then he said

"You cannot change the past or the future. The only power is through the present."

Sam sighed and suddenly became the 20th century woman she was and said

"What he said" and sat down abruptly. Vivian looked at Ali and then back at Sam. In some infinitesimal way the joint belief of the old man who had served him for so long and this woman he loved stilled the vengeful impotency which had been tearing him apart since he had received his orders, and when he spoke his voice was almost calm.

"Are you saying that if we make, if we accept, this change, this –parting, now, it may somehow change the future –change the future for both of us? Are you saying that is something that I could believe in –that I could –hold on to?"

Sam could not look up and see the desperation in his eyes so she spoke to the clenched fists resting on her knees..

"I have studied, and practised past life regression. In my experience regression is temporary but I have read accounts written by people who believe they have lived before their current time, people who have investigated and verified that earlier life and have met others who they believe have shared that earlier life. I also believe that love is the strongest binding connection that there can be."

He had not moved and she could feel his eyes boring down on her but she could not meet them, could not face being the instigator of the renewed pain.

Finally he said in a voice querulous with hope,

"Are you saying that we might meet again in your time and recognise what we had?"

"Yes. I believe that there are only three things that can never be taken from us. Our capability to change or embrace change; our right to choose; our capacity to love."

He did not speak for so long that she finally had to look up and meet his eyes. The severe lines around his mouth, that had softened and almost been erased in their time together, had reappeared and the pain in the beautiful eyes also, but there was something else as well. Hesitant, wavering, but clear.

There was hope.

The training camp was planned for the beginning of the following month and Vivian requested two weeks leave, to enjoy some recreational hunting, he told his commander. It was willingly granted. The man had barely taken any time for private use since the doomed furlough in Kashmir the year of the Great Mutiny and must be owed months.

Ali and Mohammed packed tents, cooking equipment, blankets, foodstuffs and guns into a small ghari and Ali drove the cart while Vivian, Sam and Mohammed rode, the latter leading two spare horses.

"Guns!" exclaimed Sam. "You're not actually going to shoot anything are you?"

"It had crossed my mind" said Vivian with an amused smile. "It's what one would normally do on a shooting trip."

"What-what are you going to shoot?" demanded Sam.

"Well there's all sorts" said Vivian. "Wild goat, chikara, duck, red bear-"

"Bear! Absolutely not!"

"I see" said Vivian carefully. "Duck and goat and antelope are acceptable as targets but not bear –is that right?"

Sam, who could see she had hedged herself into a small hypocritical corner said defensively

"By my time your lot have done so much indiscriminate hunting of large mammals that many of them are now protected species, because their numbers are so small. And I absolutely refuse to allow circumstances to put me in a position where I am part of it!"

Vivian studied her for a few moments and then said consideringly

"Are you saying that hunting for sport has put some animals in danger of extinction?"

"That's exactly what I'm saying!"

Vivian turned to look at Ali and Mohammed both of whose faces expressed a certain scepticism and then he said

"That is a very sobering thought. Very well then, shooting for the pot alone?"

"OK" said Sam uncertainly. When in Rome –then she added

"We can just watch can't we? That's what people do now, go on safaris and just watch the wildlife."

Vivian smiled at her.

"If that's what you would like to do, that's what we will do." And Sam felt like a small child who had just been bribed with an ice cream.

But it was wonderful. The foothills were beautiful, with a dramatic backdrop of snow topped mountain peaks and fresh running streams. There was tangled jungle and scrub, bamboo and thorn trees, every kind of terrain you could imagine. There were patches of cultivation alongside the rivers, and a lot of those had scatterings of habitation nearby. There were bright hot days and cool temperate nights. They saw antelope, wild pig, adorable when not coming straight at you, wild goat, red bear and on one occasion, whilst at a small pool, waiting an opportunity to shoot duck for the pot, a tiger, slaking its thirst before retiring to sleep away the day. And of course monkeys!

Descendants or not, thought Sam, we do have a lot in common with monkeys...

The early morning light was intoxicating as it dribbled like lemon icing down the mountain peaks before turning to a band of scarlet orange and Sam became obsessed with getting up in time to see the tableau each morning. Vivian, yawning hugely, always came with her. On one such occasion they saw a tiger again. Vivian said it was the same one, (how could he tell?), a huge male, carrying a buffalo in its mouth. Sam stared. It was so close she hardly dared breathe and Vivian's firm grip on her arm bade her be silent. Did the beast glance their way? She wasn't sure. It clasped its prospective meal in its jaws which seemed to meet around the animal's chest leaving legs dangling at one side and head on the other. One assumed this was the night's catch being carried off for a quiet undisturbed meal somewhere. It was so very large! And so beautiful, it's bright, vibrant colouring quickly absorbed into the shadows, soon to become indistinguishable from the dappled light through the trees. It left Sam with an extraordinary sense of unreality...and priviledge...a sense that there had been a purpose in her seeing it...

The days were tiring, the tents were small and the ground was hard. But the nights were perfect. As the sun began to dip below the horizon coating the trees and waterways with gold, the birds, so many birds, began their evening serenade. Finally they ceased their incessant chattering and prepared to roost, and the creatures who had slept away the hot daylight made their alternative preparations. The surrounding forest began to creak awake.to the new life of the darkness. Colours became patterns and soft and warm became hard and cold. The wind changed direction and bats swept down the jungle tunnels, jackals cackled and a lonely leopard coughed. Ali set to and prepared food for them all. They all sat around the fire after the meal, talking and sharing and watching shooting stars cross the heavens above them leaving gorgeous, spangled tails. Ali regaled them with the more dubious tales of Vivian's childhood, although Sam suspected that some of his dicier exploits lost something in the telling, due to the difficulties of the translation. Ali's English lacked the colloquial touch. And then Ali built up the fire to last the night and they all retired. Sam and Vivian spent most of the night making love, talking, and making love again as if each were creating a scrapbook of words and images to last them a lifetime. And Sam finally told Vivian about Steve and Wanigi and Luc.

She told him about Wanigi and how he had been the brother she had lost and how he had become so close that he was on her inside as well as her kola companion; about Luc and his link to Wanigi through the female bloodline and how she had left it, with the door partly open, a door which it would now be necessary to close; and Steve... The best friend ever... To whom she had said as she left him, that she had tried to find on her inside what he gave her on the outside; that he was the only one in her external reality who had ever truly believed in her, supported her and if she had wanted someone to be her hero, the 'wind beneath her wings', he would have been the one. But that wasn't what she wanted; she wanted to be the wind...

"I know I've jumped about a bit" said Sam apologetically, "but we do don't we? Some of us. In our lives. We start out on one track, believing we know exactly what we want, but then the picture keeps changing as we get more bits of the puzzle and so we revise our ideas and our plans –and sometimes there are casualties…" She looked at him hesitantly, awaiting a response.

Vivian thought for a while.

"Casualties, yes." He looked at her keenly as if trying to assess the impact of her words on their current situation. Finally he said

"I can live alongside the wind; I do not need to restrain it."

"I know you don't" said Sam smiling at him. "You are the open sky!"

They looked at each other. Then Vivian said

"You see life as a puzzle then?"

Sam also thought for a while.

"Not in the sense of an enigma, or riddle but in the sense of a lot of pieces making up a whole."

"Yes, I can see that," said Vivian, "although for some of us it is more like a long track, with rocks and ruts and a lot of bad weather!"

They both laughed and Sam thought, how good it is that he can laugh; that I can laugh…

"I'm sure some people manage to set their sights on a goal and go for it. But I've never done that. I've always changed – things, places –"

"People too" said Vivian lazily.

"Yes. People as well. I expect it makes me seem very irresponsible –even callous –"

She looked at him anxiously.

"I'm also well known for being very faithful" she said hopefully.

Vivian laughed, his eyes dancing.

"Like a hound?" he teased her.

"I've been called worse" said Sam truthfully, remembering some of her more acrimonious linguistic skirmishes with Steve.

"Maybe you were a gypsy in one of your lives."

"Or a native American" said Sam.

And then, because it seemed really important to do so at that moment, she told him about a girl called Noni and a man called Hunter who she had watched fall in love, far away and long ago, and how she had known that she might have to wait a long time but she would find that love and recognise it because she had seen it before. And she said to him

"I recognise it now" and he had taken her in his arms and kissed her passionately and held her until the dawn.

They managed to fit a lifetime into those days; a lifetime of sunrise and sunset, of moon and stars, of hot sun, cool showers and hill breezes. A lifetime of companionship, pleasure and excitement, new experiences and challenges, new understandings and new possibilities. Between four people of different creeds and backgrounds grew a bond that maybe could transcend and yet amalgamate the beliefs of all.

Neither Mohammed nor Ali seemed to question the love or relationship that she and Vivian shared. Sam thought maybe it was just the way of the East, whose mystical culture was formed over thousands of years. Or maybe it was simply, in their devotion to the man they had known so long, and with whom they had shared so much, that this new affiliation made Vivian once more alive...

So they had returned to the bungalow that had witnessed so much and Sam had helped Ali and Mohammed with the preparations for Vivian's camp. They were to leave at dawn on the following day and they retired early but did not sleep. In the cold, comfortless hour that precedes the dawn, Vivian got up and dressed and Sam, for the first time in months, pulled on her jeans and T shirt. She looked down at herself in dismay, stripped them off again and put on the dark green kashmir robes. Vivian smiled faintly. She went to stand in front of him whilst he buckled his belt and attached his sword. He put his arms around her and held her close for a full 5 minutes and then released her, and when he did so she reached for his hand, and placed a small scrap of paper in his palm and closed the fingers over it.

"For later" she said

And he looked down at his hand and then at her and nodded. Then he turned and walked out through the door, down the steps and mounted his horse that Mohammed was holding for him. As they moved away, all three of them, Sam followed and went to stand at the edge of the parade ground where Vivian had first come over to her. When he reached the line of troops who were all waiting, ready assembled, at the far side, he turned once in his saddle. Then he faced forward, moved to the front of the column and they all rode away and Sam watched until the grey mist and the dust created by their departure, almost blocked them from sight. Almost but not quite. It did not seem right that she watched them disappear completely. She was not sure why. Something she had read...

She turned her back and for a long time she simply stood where she was, watching the mist submit to the pressure of the dawn, watching it rise in a swirling red tinged haze, watching the hills and the far peaks rebirth a new day and running over in her mind the words she had written on a scrap of paper. Words written by a woman called Lauren who had died in a horrific car crash years ago and who had bequeathed to her abandoned lover a box of hand scrawled poems to which Sam had found herself an unwilling party. One written on the face of the small scrap of 20th century paper torn from the notebook she always carried, and one on the reverse.

Evolution

Many mountains seas, stars
And scars;
Many trials, hurts, breaths,
Yes and deaths,
Brought me here:
Trust in me,
For I see the whole.
Leave the mind, leave the heart,
Embrace the soul.
As the dandelion,
Our seed wings its way
Where evolutionary paths inter-stray;
Let us all lift our eyes from the fray
To watch the dust motes play

The Chosen Path

An accumulation of memories, a host of loves,
a feast of stars,
These were ours.

We have stripped us bare,
Laid waste with care,
Now each touch jars.

So, now let us face what we have,
What we are;
Let us now understand that our journey so far
Was chosen with care, to bring us to here.

So, now you in your world
And me in mine,
Unravel the skeins that
Have held us in time,
And learning, and teaching
And growing to be,
And as spirits rise,
Dis-united, and free

Why those poems, why those words? She didn't know. But
they had come into her mind as if she had learned them by
heart and she trusted that when he read them that they would
reach out and touch his. As Lauren's words had touched Peter
back then.

She walked slowly back to the bungalow, her mind filled
with that tragic interplay of personalities reflected in those
poems, which she had watched as a spectator but not shared,
reflecting upon the ironic hue it now shed on her own condition
and pushed open the door, walked through the living room
and into the bedroom they had shared for a temporal eternity.

Her discarded Indian coloured silks and the cream Kashmir
wedding outfit lay across the bed, a forlorn aide-mémoire and
oppressively sad. She stood for a while gazing down at them,
her hands playing with the silk tassels on the bonded, plaited
waist rope. She picked up her jeans. Out of habit, she felt in
the pockets. Her fingers touched something in the right hand
pocket and she placed her fingertips around it and pulled it
out. There were three small squares of Indian paper, neatly
folded twice. They seemed a little fragile. She opened the first
very carefully.

It was the same poem Vivian had shown her in the lodge,
the one that he had written for his dead Hindu friend Dayaal.
She bit her lip. He trusted her that much.

She unfolded the second sheet, less fragile, more recent.
This too was a poem but this one was written by an adult
hand.

<u>Column of Love</u>

Here am I

Just Me;
Bare walls,
And she?

And the love that I feel brims over,
and reaffirms its power,
flows from my roots to your strong stem,
our own, twice nurtured flower.

*

If loving was understanding,
all knowledge would be mine,
And this path I chose to travel,
would transcend the bands of time.

*

This life is one of many,
that you and I have shared;
That you and I have loved and fought
and laughed and cried and cared.
And if I have one single thought,
One unbowed, unquenched cry,
It is that I will " build a column of love", or in
the process die

Almost blinded by tears Sam unfolded the last sheet. There
were just three lines and his name, written in clear sloping
script.

I love you
Hereafter, I cannot live without you. Do not live without me
I will always love you, beyond life
Vivian

She stared down at it, the comfort it brought mingling with the pain. Tears ran down her cheeks.

She dropped the jeans on the floor and lay down on the bed, her fingers still closed around the small scraps of paper. She closed her eyes, turning the pages of the newly created montage of their time together on the back of her closed lids. The words of the poem to Dayaal from twenty years in the past cut across the images:

For as we came, so will we go
Our lives, a snail trail, glistening, show
A progression, nothing more,
A game of one, with zero score.
To end is but to start, explore
Another realm, dimension, perennial flaw.
The only thing we have or are, and cannot lose,
Is love,
Our keeper, guide and mentor,
And our right to choose.

Our right to choose...
Where was she?

And slowly the images were receding, or was she drawing away... until there was only one image left... the expression in the eyes of a girl with mahogany skin, as she looked into the eyes of a man whose culture was as far from hers as the savannah of Africa was from the arctic tundra in the north of his country. Or maybe not.

She had identified that expression, recognition more than knowledge, for she had yet to know it. It was not within the parameters of her experience. But she would recognise it when she saw it again and oddly enough it would have lost much of its mystique, if not its mystery and it would no longer frighten her. Yes, when she saw love again she would recognise it.

And she had known something else. Precognition?

One day I will find that love. I don't know when and I don't know what it will look like and maybe I'll think I've found it a few times but I'll have got it wrong and maybe I'll have to wait an awful long time but I will know it because I have known it before...

I know it now...

She had a deep feeling of peace, as if she were lying in a huge nest made of the softest feathers which breathed around her in whispers. She was moving across a vast expanse of water whose incandescent blue was mirrored by a sky above. She was looking out and across to a line of indigo which separated the two blues. And the calm and serenity and unfathomable depth of the water and her own inner being were one and though she could see nothing but blue she could sense the light and she knew where she was going. And although she did not know when she would arrive, she knew she was going back and it was where she was meant to be. And she knew that even if the waking hours took away the image and the knowledge, it was lodged safe within... Waiting...

The Line of Hope...

SAMANTHAR

In the weeks, the months, that followed Sam tried very hard to hold on to that feeling of peace, to the hope that the pictures had created and that the words she had left Vivian would weave a bond so strong that time would be unable to damage it. But she was unable to resist glancing through the memory scrapbook and despair came very easily…

She tried writing verse..

"As the days, to weeks, to months
Conspire to curtain pain,
I remain.
You and I
We,
In that other realm.
I need not to die,
Nor you to resurrect
To cross that line.
Nor alter time.
Our oneness is an open door
And more…
A vow, a kiss, a sacred lore.

It was pretty bloody awful as poetry went and did not meet her usual expectations. But at that moment it expressed what she felt, both positive and negative and in that way it served its purpose.

Then one day when she was all out of ideas, strategies, Hope left the stage and she gave up. She went into the study snug and sat down on one of the armchairs and gazed out of the window. It was early evening and already the sun was at the horizon and dusk was blotting out the trees and the low hills beyond. It grew dark but she made no attempt to put on any lights, or indeed to move at all. She simply closed her eyes and gave in.

"Kevin" she whispered into the darkness. "Kevin where are you? I need help. I am so alone and there is no one to help. You said you'd always be there."

Tears were leaking out now, running down the sides of her cheeks, into her ears and soaking into the squashy cushions behind her head. The room was the grey of despair and the darkness crowded in.

Help me Kevin!

There was silence and then –

I'm here.

Kevin?

I'm here.

Where? Sam searched the blackness, the utter void in front of her. It hurt to look so hard.

Close your eyes.

It was a command.

She did as she was told. And then there was light. Like an old fashioned projector on a wall. A screen. And in the beam of light she saw him and she saw herself and she reached out her hands and touched him and he raised one small paw and put it on the back of her hand. And the strain and the anxiety and the despair seeped away and mingled with the tears and ran down into the sodden cushion.

He was speaking now.

Did you think that because you were a *grown up* you were too old for small furry things? Did you think you had to do it all by yourself? Did you think a lonely seeker has to be endlessly alone? Did you think I'd desert you?

"No. Yes. I don't know." She was speaking aloud now.

Everything that happens, all experiences, have different facets. See experience as spherical. Let's move the sphere. Turn it around a bit shall we? So the light falls on a different side. On something else.

"There is no light."

There is always light. You either have to flick the switch yourself or wait for dawn.

"It's not the same as before" whispered Sam to the image of Kevin behind her eyes.

Nothing stays the same Sam. What would be the point of that? You'd still be back there with Steve arguing about Meat Loaf and the meaning of freedom.

Steve! Tears began to roll again.

Did you know that while the adult range of passions may appear at a relatively early stage in an individual, the prefrontal cortex which allows them to make social judgments and weigh alternatives does not mature until the age of 25?

"Excuse me?"

While a range of feelings is possible much earlier, the mechanism to cope with and control them doesn't develop in the brain until much later.

"In rats?" Sam sat up. She felt she had lost the plot.

Oh yeah! (can spirits be sardonic?) On the eighth or ninth reincarnation.

"You're joking?" said Sam.

Yes. (can spirits sound weary?)

There was some silence during which time Sam opened her eyes and gazed into the blackness. Then she shut them again and said

"I'm 37!"

Maybe you're emotionally retarded. Anyway, now you know why Chaucer calls it 'the slough of despond.'

Kevin disappeared, the light on the screen went out and Sam opened her eyes. A moon had arisen and was filling the lawns with light, and the fields beyond. Sam pushed herself forward and straightened her shoulders.

"I've always hated mud" she said to the walls.

It only took a day. And then there was Kevin.

Kevin who had absconded! Kevin who had picked that moment to abandon her. Kevin who could be relied upon to leave just at the moment when advice and answers were most needed! Words will be had! And they were.

But afterwards, when Sam had told him what had happened, and he had got over the fact that she had fallen in love –yes actually fallen in love –with a man called Vivian – seriously! Vivian! It had taken him some moments to get over that. But then he had made quite a useful contribution.

"I have finally faced up to the fact that I cannot coerce fate or the universe to open up the right doors for me" said Sam despondently. "I had convinced myself that if I went to enough different places and put myself in the way of enough different people and situations that eventually –" she didn't finish.

Kevin had studied her for some moments in silence. This being a very foreign mode of behaviour for Kevin under any circumstances, gave Sam pause. Kevin did not do silence. He was never unforthcoming. Even if he wasn't talking, he was eating. She waited and then said,

"What!, Come on. Out with it."

"Well" said Kevin, "you don't seem to have considered the obvious."

"Yes? And what –obvious –would that be?"

"Travel. Go back to all the places that you have experienced in your pasts, through regression, with Steve, on your own, with me. If this is that important to you revisit them all and give the universe chance, a real chance. Go back to Greece and Africa; go back to India. Go back to the places that people like you go to, to try and find answers. If what you shared is as strong as you believe it to be, maybe he will be doing the same and maybe, maybe there's just a chance that you can meet at an –"

"Intersection?" supplied Sam.

That night she dreamed, cohesively and with unbelievable clarity. Not of Kevin and intersections, nor, surprisingly, of Vivian. Halfway through the night something had disturbed her and she had lifted her head, listened, then laid it back down again, sleep tugging gently at the curtain of her mind. Then she saw the doorway. It was just as she remembered it from all those years ago except some of the images on the arch were clearer now, more distinct. And then she saw that it was not one doorway, but several, three to be exact, each placed symmetrically behind the one in front. She studied them and then suddenly saw that a door blocked the entrance through the last archway. That was different. That was new. And as she watched the door opened slowly, very slowly, and as if on an invisible walkway they came. In the lead was Wanigi, tall, straight limbed, black hair flowing out behind him on an undetectable wind; then Steve, dark eyes shining, crazy dark hair ruffled by an invisible hand; then a jumble of small creatures, too small to individually identify and then Luc, also dark haired, also smiling. And others, whose interludes had been short but memorable... Siva; Tom... And finally there was Kevin. They glided towards her and then there was a pause. Then she saw Wanigi again; only this time his long dark hair was streaked with grey and his eyes were fixed upon her; his birdwing blue eyes. He stood by the door way and as if at his behest the creatures and the other figures went back through and melted into nothingness. All except Kevin. For a single moment Wanigi paused by the door frame, his hand resting gently on the door. He was looking straight at her and as she watched he lifted his right hand and sketched the native American gesture of farewell. Then he moved through it and was gone and the door swung gently to, behind him. And then there were just the three archways, the last with a closed door, and Kevin. Kevin...gesticulating... And in her dream she moved her head to look to Kevin's left.

And Vivian appeared before her, looking directly at her as he always did, his eyes dark and querulous, his black eyebrows questioning. Vivian...

Sam sat bolt upright. Dawn was just breaking and beginning to enunciate the outlines of the near trees and the hills beyond. It suddenly seemed so obvious. The past was the past and she knew what she had to do.

*

So she started planning an itinerary, listing the countries and then breaking them down into areas and from those areas selecting places and sites she might want to visit. Kevin had decided to stay, for his own reasons or on her behalf, it was difficult to ascertain. The Food Supply was outstanding and for Kevin that was always a major consideration. And when not distracted by food his suggestions, Sam was forced to admit, were excellent. When she confessed that her writing was suffering a block at the present time and that she was concerned that many of the places she wanted to visit would have changed beyond recognition since she had last seen them, he suggested interspersing searches on flights, travel, individual locations and accommodation, with old fashioned reading, the latest travelogues; the most up to date research. After all, he pointed out, it had all started with a book.

So that's what she did. She reread all the various volumes she had on past historic events in the United States, Africa, Greece and the Greek Islands and of course India. She combed her bookshelves and pulled out MM Kaye's Shadow of the Moon, Tolstoy's War and Peace, Herman Hesse's Siddhartha, Mary Renault's The Persian Boy and Milton's Paradise Lost. Coming to the end of the latter, she found herself wondering, as she had when first she read it, what Milton had thought when he read his final draft and realized that Lucifer was the only substantial and appealing character amongst a bunch of insubstancials comprising God, Jesus and a horde of flabby angels. Vivian had said Lucifer had all the best arguments and he was right. She had always wanted to ask him if it turned out the way he had intended or whether Lucifer had simply climbed onto the page and done his own thing. Characters did sometimes do that to you. Perhaps his religious beliefs had been forced to bow to his writer's convictions.

Kevin's reaction to her selected material was typical. He announced that for his part he liked a book that he could get his teeth into and in this case it was most emphatically Siddhartha.

And thinking about Kevin chewing at the leaves of Siddhartha, she remembered the words of the holy books:

'Your soul is the whole world.' That when a man is asleep he penetrates his innermost being and dwells in Atman, the essence of the individual, the one true self...

Was her dream-world guiding her now?

Another consideration was the length of time she should spend in each place, in each country and whether she should return home between visits. Kevin said no. Plan what she could from here with a starting point, a rough draft, and finishing point and move from one to the next. Well the finishing point was easy. She would end up in India.

"And if all else fails, you can write it all down and sell it as a travel monologue."

Sometimes he was just irrepressible thought Sam, with irrational if forgivable annoyance.

"Are you going to come?" she asked him.

"Of course! Wouldn't miss it for the world."

"Well that's what you said the last time!"

"That was different" said Kevin.

"It was different all right! I looked around and you'd gone –gone without a trace!"

Kevin looked smug.

"It's an art" he said. "Anyway you'd hardly have wanted me there when you were –"

"That's not the point. Anyway you had no idea that I was –that I would –"

"No idea? It was written all over your face!"

Sam left it at that. Sometimes there was just no arguing with Kevin and besides he was probably right.

She spent some time acquainting herself with India again. Leaving aside the regression into Vivian's time, her first visit some years ago had only covered Delhi and Agra, Rajasthan and the Jim Corbett Tiger Reserve up on the foothills of the Himalaya. Buddhist monks and tigers were not top priorities this time. It didn't help that Partition had considerably changed the India of the Raj and the accessibility of the Punjab.

If she was honest, apart from Lahore being within reasonable travelling distance by horse, she had no real idea where she had spent all those months with Vivian. So she would go to North India and visit Delhi again, but also the Punjab and Lucknow and Cawnpore, which she was sure now began with a K and Himachal Pradesh and possibly Uttanchal, now Uttarakhand.

The question was- should she, as Kevin had suggested, go to 'all the places that people like you go to try and find answers.'

All of them?

"All of them?" Sam said to Kevin later.

"Why not?"

"But *all* of them? I'll be travelling for the next 15 years! I had planned on about six months. If I travel everywhere that I've been in this life, in other lives and regressions, I won't have a minute to draw breath. I'll be joining the rat race again!"

Kevin was immediately interested and diverted. He said "What's the rat race?"

Sam thought, how did we get here?

"Well, it's a term we use to describe a lifestyle –"

"You mean a sport?"

"No. It means the sort of life pattern that is just getting up, working to make money and going to bed; a pointless lifestyle."

"But why is it a *rat* race? I could understand if it was a lemming race –careering off the top of the cliff –that's pretty pointless –they're obviously related to guinea pigs."

"That's unkind Kevin. And very prejudicial!"

"Or a greyhound race" Kevin persisted, "chasing round and round the track after a plastic –plastic mind you – mechanical rabbit. It doesn't come much more mindless than that! Of course there is always the West Highland terrier race –"

"I think you've aired your views on Westies before Kevin."

"But why *rat*? Let me tell you a rat never does *anything* without a point!"

"No Kevin" Sam sighed. Whatever the point was they had left it about five junctions back.

"I suppose we do eat and sleep a lot" said Kevin considering.

"There is that, yes"

"Are you being sarcastic?" said Kevin suspiciously.

"Who me?"

"Were you in the rat race?" said Kevin.

"Me? No. Not really. I dabbled but I never made it past first base. I probably have you to thank for that."

"Could that be a compliment?"

"I'm not sure. What I am sure of is that somehow we got completely derailed. I was trying to sort out the details of my itinerary with you –and-"

"You were saying that you didn't want to spend 15 years on your travels" said Kevin. "Well don't then. Just go to India."

"OK. It's a big place. I think I should start with Northern India, but everything will have changed and-"

"Why don't you get a guide?"

"A guide?"

"Yes Parrot! A guide- like me."

"A rat?"

"Well yes if you like. But I meant a places guide- someone who knows places-"

"A tour guide?"

"That's the fella!"

"Kevin you're a genius!"

"It has been remarked upon before" said Kevin complacently.

"Tell him what historic places I'm trying to research and let him advise. Yes!"

"As you say, it's big enough and in amongst all those people and cultures and history you should be able to find something."

But will I be able to find Vivian?

So that's what she did. It was remarkably easy really. Most of it she did on the phone, specifying various places she wished to visit and the sites of historical events. She followed this up with several more phone calls to the chosen operator outlining her ideal guide, requesting someone with historical knowledge of both India and the British Raj and preferably linguistically able. She left the travel arrangements, where she should go by car or plane, up to the operator. He suggested that he send her a proposed itinerary as a basis for amendment and that the driver and car would be waiting for her at her hotel in Delhi on the arranged date. They agreed the price and also that subsequent alterations or diversions would be met on an individual basis and billed as appropriate. This so simplified all her original concerns that Sam felt immediately unburdened and free to give her attention to the other aspects of the journey. She applied her age old packing techniques of little and less, at the last minute including the green kashmir outfit which had made its way back with her, as a kind of good luck charm. If she had any concerns about the individual whose task it was to become her guide on this expedition, she put them to the back of her mind on the basis of –what will be will be - and as it happened her trust was rewarded.

KAAMAL

The flight to Delhi was long, but pleasant and otherwise uneventful. The transfer to the hotel was straightforward and quite civilised considering the volume of traffic and Sam found herself remembering, with a mixture of nostalgia and relief, the old way in which she and Steve used to travel, live and eat on a shoestring. But that was 15 years ago and the journey had been part of the living. This time it was a means to an end; getting to this point in any case. She ate in the hotel restaurant that evening, a delightful array of things in small dishes with wonderful unleavened breads. She walked several times round the beautiful, paved gardens with their statuesque fountains dropping gems of water on to lily pads, that caught the last rays of the sun, like jewels from a broken chain and under its framed archways covered in creepers of exotic colours and perfume. And then she went to her room and slept the sleep of the dead.

The morning brought breakfast with scrambled-eggs the colour of canaries and coffee, requested with hot milk and akin to perfection; and it brought Kaamal.

He was waiting at the reception desk at 7:30 am when she came down from her room with a small travel bag and a pair of sunglasses perched on the top of her head.

"You travel light!" he said with a disarming smile. His English was perfect, his voice deep but with melodic undertones.

"Always" said Sam, smiling back. If he guided as good as he looked there weren't going to be any criticisms from her side.

He told her his name was Kaamal, that he was a student of Indian history, literature, Indian and English, spoke several languages including Hindi, Urdu, French and obviously English and quite a few dialects and should they sit down with her itinerary, he waved his copy, and discuss her ideas and requirements and the best way to achieve them?

Sam, who had expected questions and difficulties regarding her intentions, was delightedly surprised. When she had finished her explanations of where she wanted to go and what she wanted to see, leaving out for the moment, the why, he looked up from the notes he had been making and said

"Lucknow is a little more than 300 miles from Delhi and Cawnpore is 57 miles from Lucknow. We are in Delhi so these we can do by car. Haryana we can also travel to by road from Delhi. We can take a flight from Delhi to Himachal Pradesh and also Uttarakhand or we can drive. There is some very nice scenery. I am from Lucknow and I know also these other places. Between us I am sure we can discover the things you wish to learn."

Sam gazed at him, her eyes obviously expressing a whole range of emotions that she was finding it difficult to put into words. Kaamal said smoothly

"Shall I order some more coffee and perhaps tell you a little about myself so that I do not appear such a stranger. And then if you feel able to do the same we could decide between us in what order to execute this magnificent plan."

"Yes and yes" said Sam. And then she asked the question that was uppermost in her mind at that time

"Is this what you do for a living?"

Kaamal laughed.

"Yes and no. I teach history and literature at the University of Delhi but I also love history in its physical form and have friends in the tour operator that you contacted. When they have clients who have a genuine interest in the history of this land they ask me if I am free to act guide. They asked and I was free."

"The advantages of both worlds" said Sam.

"Just as you say."

"When we're driving will you tell me about your life so far?"

"Of course, if that's what you'd like."

"I'd like that very much" said Sam.

An hour and two pots of coffee later they had a plan.

They decided to go to Himachal Pradesh after first visiting Lucknow and Cawnpore. With Kashmir to the north and the Punjab to the west, Sam had decided that this would be a good place to start. Kaamal painted pictures. It was a land of many peaks and river valleys and interlocking mountain chains, every pass crossing into a new valley with its own culture and deities, with villages on slopes and fairy tale architecture. Most areas could be reached by jeep with some on foot. Kaamal told her that the Buddhist monastery of Tabo Gompa, the temple carvings of Lakshmi Narayan and the glacial lake of Chandratal where they could take a hike of about five kilometres around the lake, were all a seeker of beauty and fulfilment and answers could desire. Its capital was Shimla and Sam felt sure that something of Vivian's life and time must surely filter down to her.

To the southeast of Himachal was Uttrakhand, with Tibet to the north and Nepal to the east, which had many Hindu temples and pilgrimage sites. Kaamal called it, the place of myth and mountains, Dev Bhoomi, in Hindu, the land of gods, with its holy peaks, lakes and rivers. He said there the British had left their imprint with holiday towns, once Raj hill stations and the Beatles. There were many places they could visit including the Jim Corbett tiger reserve, which Sam remembered quite vividly from her first trip to India.

He told her of the Har-Ki-Pairi Ghat, the footprint of god, where Vishnu dropped divine nectar and left the imprint; where pilgrims came to worship and floated baskets of flowers; the forests, meadows and peaks of the Govind wildlife sanctuary; the Valley of Flowers, framed by glaciers and mountains with snow on the surrounding peaks and 300 species of wild flora.

"They flower in the monsoon but it is still ridiculously beautiful outside of that" Kaamal told her, when Sam had expressed her opinion of heavy rainfall.

There was also the Swarg Niwase Shri Trayanbakshwar temple, with its magnificent thirteen stories and its dozens of shrines to Hindu deities.

These two destinations could be reached by flights from Delhi and Kaamal said that he could arrange these flights for ten days' time and in the interim they explore Delhi or they could drive to Lucknow first and make the travel decisions there.

Sam opted for the drive option. She knew the country would have changed dramatically. How not in 120 years? But nevertheless she would be travelling *through* it, as Vivian had done and there was more chance ... more chance of finding memory doors...

"Delhi is time travel" Kaamal told her. "You can see labourers hauling sacks and jewellers weighing gold. Old men threading marigolds for temple wreaths and kites flown from roof tops. It has been ravaged and reborn many times and vestiges of lost empires are everywhere. And then Gurgaon, with its sky scrapers and malls...I think Delhi is unique..."

Kaamal caught the look on Sam's face and laughed.

"We don't need to go to see skyscrapers and malls! We can remain as close to the past as you wish."

And Sam, who had read somewhere that the population of Delhi was greater than Australia, nodded her assent.

When saturated with Delhi, the plan was to visit Lucknow and Cawnpore by car. The 300 miles to Lucknow, Kaamal said, would give them lots of time to talk. He was born in Lucknow and knew the city and its environs well and it was only a short drive from there to Cawnpore. He finished by assuring her that nothing was cast in stone and could be changed with very little effort.

Sam looked into his smiling face with its black, untidy hair and challenging gray eyes and chiselled jaw; she looked at his lean well shaped limbs and tall and vaguely androgynous frame, and wondered how she had managed to acquire such an erudite guide who was so mouth-wateringly appealing and speculated if there was a woman somewhere wondering what the hell he was doing. Or if it didn't work like that in India. Maybe marriage was still based on the old ways of the princely state; womens' quarters and fretted screens. Was the independent woman traveller a thing of the future here? Was that why Kaamal looked at her so speculatively. Had no one heard of Freya Stark?

Kaamal interrupted her thoughts by asking if she would enjoy lunch and when she would like to have it and where. Sam, who felt she had been sitting for an eternity asked if they could get food to go and was whisked off to a delightful bazaar with stalls and street vendors that sold absolutely anything you could wish for or imagine. Between them they chose a variety of savoury snacks and parcels and lemon tea and sat on a bench to eat and watch the world.

That afternoon Kaamal took her to the Mehrauli archaeological park where there were more than 400 monuments dotting a forest and village and the time ravaged tombs of Balban and his son and the Rajon ki Baoli, Delhi's most ancient stepped well. Sam was entranced by the unkempt monuments, carelessly accepted and ignored by the expanded population around them, and the determination that growing things have to incorporate and obliterate creations of man. It reminded her of parts of Greece that she had visited with Steve. The step well she found quite horrific.

The Mughal palace remains, the Zafar Mahal, once in the heart of the jungle, , made her feel small and insignificsnt. The structured memorials to men and women long dead, were like fragments of burning timber that has just been blown from a huge bonfire and is waning on the grass, too far from the blaze to be reincorporated.

Then Kaamal said

"There is a special place here, a favourite of mine. Would you like to see it?"

"What makes it special for you?" Sam asked with interest.

"Come and see and perhaps I will tell you."

Not knowing what to expect in this ruin of ruins, Sam followed. What she saw defied all expectations.

It was a Ladu era burial ground for Hijras, transvestites and eunuchs, the Hijran ka Khanqar and it was beautiful. The identities of its inhabitants were unknown but it was well kept and tended and very peaceful. Sam looked at Kaamal but the sun was behind him and his face was in shadow.

"Do you think they would mind if we sat down with them for a while?"

He looked up then and smiled.

"No, I don't think they'd mind at all."

They sat side by side beneath a large spreading tree and shared lemon tea in bottles and small almond cakes. Kaamal did not venture the reasons for his fondness for this small oasis of calm and so Sam asked him about his work, the work that occupied his time when he wasn't trailing about the country with tourists. He told her that languages, history and literature had always been his passion and he had trained and was qualified to teach all. Archaeology, myth and legend were obsessive hobbies.

"There are over 1600 dialects in this country! There is an old proverb –every 2 miles the water doth change and every four the dialect!" he told her.

She then asked him about his family.

"My mother and father and one of my sisters live in Lucknow. I have two more sisters, both married."

It was a perfunctory explanation so Sam tried again.

"And you? Are you married?"

He took so long to answer that Sam wished she hadn't asked such a direct question. Finally he said

"No. I am not married although it would please my parents if I was."

"Yeah. Is it still very traditional here? What would they feel if you just lived with someone?"

"Oh I think they might put up with that" said Kaamal vaguely.

There was obviously some kind of dissention thought Sam. In some way the life he had chosen had disappointed them. She looked at him. Intelligent, qualified, working and very pleasing in manner and on the eye –how could anybody be disappointed with that?

"I'm gay." It was just a statement of fact.

Sam gaped at him, her eyes travelling over the dark ruffled hair, the carved bones which shaped his face, the laughing gray eyes. It was not possible!

"You can't be!"

"Oh? Why is that then?"

"Because –because –you're so –good to look at!"

"Some would consider that an advantage" said Kaamal smoothly.

His smile was dazzling. Sam sighed.

"What's wrong? You mind so much?"

"No! I can live a whole lifetime without the macho thing. I don't like bulges or biceps on men or women. I like flat and tight! I was just reflecting upon the loss to womankind and thinking –so that's where all the good looking men have gone –to bat for the other side –it's outrageous!"

He laughed.

"I like women."

"Yeah" said Sam. "I looked up the meaning of your name. It means perfect! Much good it's going to do me."

"You never know" said Kaamal lazily.

They looked at each other and smiled. They liked each other and, Sam reflected, I've always been good with brothers.

There was not an awful lot left of the afternoon but Sam asked if there was time to go and see the Raj Ghat and Kaamal assured her that there was. It was the end of the day and the sun was dipping and the tourists were leaving and making their way to baths and showers and food. The gardens and the walkways were quiet. Sam had been to this place before and she went and stood by the black marble platform and column that marked Gandhi's cremation and gazed up the slope at the conical trees and listened. Very softly, somewhere in her head or outside on the breeze, she heard gentle weeping, as she had on that first occasion and remembered the last words he was supposed to have said. Hai Ram –Oh God! A benediction? A plea? A prayer? The fast dusk was descending and she took Kaamal's arm and moved away. She looked up at him as they walked and she thought how suddenly sad he seemed, as if some passing ghost had reached out a hand. Then he looked down at her and smiled and the impression was gone. Almost. It was still there in his eyes.

He took her back to her hotel and she asked him to stay for dinner. He thanked her, but declined gracefully, saying that he had some work to catch up on at the university and that he had planned an early start for the following morning. They were visiting the Qutb Minar complex and it was, he assured her, best seen at dawn.

"What time is dawn?" Sam asked.

"I will be here at five am" said Kaamal.

He left her at the reception desk and with one last heart melting smile, turned and walked out of the door. Sam watched him go, a tall striding figure and felt unnecessarily and quite ridiculously bereft. Rajesh, at the reception desk, asked her if she would be having dinner and then, with surprising perception thought Sam, suggested she might prefer to take it in her room and he could arrange? Sam smiled grateful thanks and went to the lift. The room was cool and pleasant and she stripped and climbed into a shower. Wash away the disappointment. Tomorrow was another day...

She had not expected to sleep let alone to dream but she did both. It was the old repetitive dream of the long corridor leading to the glass door at the edge of the calm water; and the waiting figure with the outstretched hand which grasped hers... It was the same as it always was except... This time the door was open and she was led right up to the water's edge and this time she walked in, still holding his hand...

Vivian? And she awoke seconds before the phone rang with the early morning call, with the remembrance of the dream and Vivian so intensely in her mind that looking at the bed beside her she was surprised to find herself alone. There was a tap on the door and reality cut back in but as the young man brought in her tea, placed it on the table, smiled and left, the thought remained with her. He is here...

She dressed quickly in khaki cargos and a white T-shirt, finished her tea and went down to reception. Kaamal was waiting by the desk, also in cargoes, wide awake and good enough to eat.

They arrived at the Qutab Minar complex just as the fingers of dawn crept over the tops of the buildings and found themselves almost completely alone apart from one or two other intrepid crowd beaters. Kaamal was in fine tour guide mode and Sam relaxed, and looked and listened and enjoyed.

The first monuments had been erected by the sultans of Mehrauli, he told her, and subsequent rulers had expanded on their work, hiring the finest craftsmen and artisans to set in stone the triumph of Muslim rule. Apparently The Qutb Festival of Indian classical music and dance took place there every October/November. The complex was studded with ruined tombs and monuments. He led Sam to the ruins of Ala-ud-din's sprawling madrasa -Islamic school and tomb at the rear of the complex, and then to the magnificence of Altamish, entombed in a splendid sandstone and marble mausoleum almost completely covered in Islamic calligraphy. Sam was absorbed and entranced. The artistic endeavour and commitment of the instigators, designers and the artisans whose toil had resulted in testimonials that had left such a mark on history, was difficult to grasp. How had mankind moved from such works to fast, cheap and easy? What had made hours and days so valuable that there were none left for this kind of artistic enterprise?

She glanced at Kaamal's rapt face and could see the pleasure he got from sharing his history and knowledge, and thought, not for the first time, how much better the world would be if everyone could have something that brought that kind of light to their eyes. He felt her gaze and turned to her, smiling

"Am I becoming a bore? I forget that not everyone can share my passion."

Sam said

"I could watch you and listen to you if you were reading shopping lists! But no-I'm fascinated-I want to know everything you know- I can feel the history of these buildings and tombs and ruins weaving a tapestry in front of me that I can step on and touch. Thanks to you. Your words are creating archways and doors that I can walk through and-" she stopped.

"And what?"

Sam didn't answer.

"What are you looking for?" said Kaamal. "It must be important for you to make this kind of investigative trip- not many show such involvement in our history. Or is it who?"

He glanced down at her left hand which was half in her trouser pocket. Sam said

"When do we go to Lucknow?"

"The day after tomorrow."

"Maybe I'll tell you then" said Sam.

He studied her for a few short moments and then said

"Breakfast?"

They took a long time over breakfast and because the coffee and the food was especially good, ordered more and made it brunch.

Kaamal said

"So you're not one of the –I couldn't possibly eat more than one –brigade?"

"Not me. Finish the dish, lick it out – got any biscuits? -that's me!" said Sam. "Men seem to like it and I've never cared what women think."

Kaamal smiled and nodded and Sam felt encouraged to ask him about his background.

"My immediate family are quite ordinary" he said. "Educated but ordinary."

"And you're not so immediate family?" asked Sam.

"Well they are more interesting. My great-great grandfather was in service as a syce for an officer in the British army and his father had married an English girl. My family also have lots of romantic notions about our ancestors which are very difficult for historians to prove or disprove but it is said that on my father's side, albeit on the wrong side of the blanket, there are Kashmir princes!"

Sam took time to study his face with its lighter colouring and gray eyes.

"You shouldn't be so dismissive you know. I have read somewhere that the best looking men are born from a mix of Indian and European. You could easily have all that in your ancestry. Your great, great, great grandmother had English and princely bloodlines. Awesome!"

Kaamal laughed out loud and several people at adjacent tables turned round and looked at them.

"So you can see me on an Arab stallion with a green turban and a flashing sword?"

"You bet I can. Have you looked in the mirror lately?"

"I have never had much time for mirrors" he said quietly. "They don't always show you what you want to see –"

Too bloody true thought Sam. She remembered looking at herself in the mirror on the morning that she married Vivian and seeing a complete stranger; a beautiful stranger but a stranger nevertheless.

She murmured quietly

"When you get what you want in your struggle for self, and the world makes you King for the day, just go to a mirror and look at yourself, and see what that man has to say."

Kaamal looked a question at her and Sam shrugged and said

"I've always believed it was safer to look inside and hope that the outside reflects it."

"As it sometimes does" said Kaamal , looking beyond her.

Sam raised her eyebrows but he didn't notice.

She said

"On the other hand for those of us in the audience it is always pleasant to look at nice scenery!"

"You are wonderfully direct" he said, turning back to her.

"Is that a criticism or a compliment?"

"Oh, most definitely a compliment. Not so much now, of course, with education and career women, but customarily Indian women can be much more-"

"Coy?" said Sam.

"Yes" said Kaamal. "That's one word, although traditionally Indian women have no problem in getting their men to do what they want. As my mother can attest. Just in less direct ways."

"I've always thought coy was for flirts and reeks of dishonesty" said Sam. "Lowered glances and fluttering eyelashes. I don't do any of those."

"No you don't do you" said Kaamal looking directly at her. "I'm glad. It would be a pity to miss those beautiful, big dark eyes."

His tone was light; his gaze was intense. Then he said

"You wear a kind of invisible T-shirt."

"I sincerely hope not" said Sam.

"I will rephrase. A T-shirt with invisible writing on it. 'You can look. But if you touch without the owner's permission you'll wish you had had that operation.'"

Sam frowned.

"That's a bit obscure."

"All right then. I'll spell it out. You'll get your –"

"OK. I think I've grasped your meaning" said Sam. "Is it that obvious?"

"It is."

"Because I –"

"It is."

"Because if you're right-"

"I am."

"Oh" said Sam. "Shall I take it off?"

If she'd been younger Sam was fairly sure she would have blushed. So much for not being coy!

The sun was hot when they left the café and Kaamal suggested that they visit India's largest mosque, the JamaMasjid.

It was a good choice. It was cool, tranquil and very quiet despite the relatively large crowd of people within its confines. Kaamal had told her that it could hold 25,000 and it was clear that it barely noticed this drop of tourist impermanence.

"It was Shah Jehan's last triumph" said Kaamal. "You have seen the Taj Mahal? What did you think?"

Sam thought about the question. Her memory reproduced the Taj Mahal in all its dazzling white beauty.

"I think I was overawed. I went to see it at dawn and it was spectacular but as the morning wore on and it became increasingly international, so many people, so many different races, I remember thinking, is this what he set out to achieve? And would something smaller and more private have been just as memorable and more fitting."

Kaamal said thoughtfully "I think I feel much the same. But he was an emperor and the consensus opinion is that it was built as a monument to love. That I can understand; that I can relate to. Although it isn't so obvious today, I believe the gardens were an important part of the setting; a sort of paradise on earth."

"You mean a Muslim version of the Garden of Eden?"

"Yes. Maybe he was elucidating the place where he and his beloved would finally meet…"

"*I* can relate to that" said Sam.

He thought for a moment then said

"I like his grandfather, Akbar; he advocated religious tolerance, communal harmony between Hindus, Muslims, Sikhs, everyone, as many saints and poets before him had.

He was educated without sectarian prejudice; it didn't happen immediately but his early learning prevailed during the second half of his reign and religious toleration grew. He was interested enough to try and understand others' viewpoints and courageous enough to adjust his own accordingly. I think he must have enjoyed philosophical and religious debate but of course he was smart enough to know that toleration lead to peace and peace to productivity and then a short step to prosperity."

"What happened?"

"Oh, the usual. It lasted maybe three generations and then his great grandson set about reintroducing oppressive policies and destruction of Hindu temples."

He sighed deeply

Same old, same old, thought Sam. The dream of an earthly utopia gusted away on the breath of a tyrant.

Kaamal caught her drift.

"It was perhaps absurd to think that a country as diverse as India, with so many religions, languages and customs could ever be ruled as a united body. After all no ruler, nor maharaja, nor Moghul emperor, nor sterling invader, had ever done it in three thousand years…"

They spent another half hour within the mosque and then decided that it was enough for the day. When Sam asked what they were doing on their last day in Delhi Kaamal said

"Tombs, cemeteries and the Kashmir gate –a quiet day in preparation for leaving for Lucknow the following morning – is that alright?"

"Perfect" said Sam. "I love cemeteries –and tombs."

"Of course you do!" Kaamal said with his eyes sparkling.

She thought for a minute and posed her next question carefully.

"What are you doing for dinner? Will you have dinner with me at the hotel?"

"I have booked a room for myself for the next two nights at your hotel and so yes I had hoped you would join me for dinner."

He drove them back to the hotel and Sam went up to her room while Kaamal did something with the car although she wasn't exactly sure what. There didn't seem to be anywhere to put it. She went across to the wardrobe and glanced through her relatively small selection of clothes, trying to decide what to wear that evening and then wondering why she was giving it so much consideration. She pulled out some very slim, white cotton trousers and a silk shirt in olive green. She wore a lot of green these days she reflected.

And suddenly she was back, standing beside a tall slender man, with sun streaked gold, mismanaged straight hair and querulous black eyebrows who looked down at her with love written on every feature as he whispered 'I love you-beyond life'.

She pulled wide the wardrobe door and looked into the mirror on the back and saw a woman in dark green robes with her hair wound at the back of her head and willowy, dazzling gold thread earrings and a radiant smile.

She thought 'just as I said Kaamal, better to see inside reflected on the outside'.

She glanced over to where her suitcase lay on the chest in the corner, paused and then changed her mind. She swapped the silk shirt for a black T-shirt and put them on the bed and went to take a shower.

When she went down to the dining room an hour later Kaamal was already there and he stood up as she approached. He was dressed in slim black jeans and a white T-shirt. They looked at each other and laughed.

"We look like a pair of dominoes!" said Sam.

"This is true" said Kaamal casually, but his eyes said something different. "Up for a game?"

Sam said "Always" and wondered if she meant it.

The dinner menu was written in English but some of the explanations for the dishes were in Hindi so Sam asked

Kaamal to translate and ordered herself a whole range of miniature portions which paid tribute to some very nice Indian spices and a lot of creamed coconut. They had stuffed parathas and chapatis and a red wine that tasted of sun and fruit and not vinegar. They talked about food and tried each other's dishes and Sam asked Kaamal if he had been to England or the United States. He told her he had relatives in London and Burnley and he had visited both places and that he had been to California and The Great Lakes and Canada when he was in his early twenties.

"Did you feel at home in either of them, any of them?"

"Parts of England are very beautiful I think but there is such a lot of cold and damp. We have monsoon and heat here in Northern India and extreme cold if you climb up through Himachal Pradesh, and if the monsoons fail we have drought and famine. And in the south it is very hot and humid and can be unpleasant. I am a man of the north and in the places where we shall go after Lucknow and Cawnpore, there is beauty and emptiness so extraordinary it is impossible to imagine. I like to have that even if I do not visit it very often. I know England has the Scottish Highlands and the south has its moorland but –"

"But there is always a very high risk of cold and wet?"

"No offense intended."

"Non taken. I don't live in England; I live in South Dakota."

"And is that beautiful and empty?"

"Yes. In many parts though the buffalo no longer roam very much" said Sam.

They took what was left of the wine up to Sam's room and turned on the enormous television and watched Indian soaps while Sam practised trying to understand what was being said. After half an hour and with some correction and encouragement from Kaamal, she came to the conclusion that fundamentally the storylines and dialogue of soaps the world over shared the same level of banality.

"When I was younger I used to sneer at people who watched soaps. I labelled soaps as intellectual suicide. But since I've climbed down from that particular snobbish pedestal I can finally see how soothing and rebalancing they could be."

Kaamal raised his eyebrows so she went on.

"Mostly, good, in its own way, prevails. Although possibly these days you might need to take a universal view. Balance, within its own parameters, is restored. Lessons are learned and put in the past and life resumes a modicum of stability. Until the next trauma of course! And all without the voyeur having to operate more than the TV remote. A sort of mental ironing without effort. The day might have been shit and have fallen apart and you with it but hey! Look! Stuff happens –get over it –we survive. It all comes out in the wash."

"Possibly all shades of grey and blue to judge by most of them" said Kaamal sarcastically. "I can't ever see you using that form of therapy. I see you favouring the, turn up the heat, method."

"Probably. Their jigsaw pieces never fitted well enough together for me. But I look for other things in a similar way. I was always looking for circles. If I could find a circle in the drama, that was enough. Evidence of perpetuity."

"The end is also the beginning?" Kaamal said.

"Yes."

"That sounds like a very positive way to live."

"I,t can be" said Sam. "if you don't let the ending overwhelm you. Sometimes if you can't see where a beginning could start you might struggle…"

She was sitting on the couch amongst cushions and Kaamal sat cross legged on the floor at her feet. He lifted the bottle of wine to refill her glass and she slid down from the cushions on to the floor beside him, glass in hand. He filled it, then his own, placed the bottle to one side and put his arm about her shoulders and she leaned back against him. It was a comfortable and comforting gesture. They finished their wine and Kaamal made to get up, turning towards her as he did so. Sam smiled and he seemed to hesitate for a moment and then he bent his head and kissed her. It was a very nice kiss, gentle and undemanding, the kiss of someone as interested to give pleasure as to take it. Sam wondered vaguely if it was a feature of gay men or whether he was just by nature a considerate lover and his proclivities were incidental.

She pulled back from him a little and he looked surprised.

"Why wouldn't you want me to make love to you?"

Sam found that she was completely out of inoffensive light repartee and didn't answer.

"Because I'm gay?"

Sam shook her head.

"Because I'm not good looking enough?" He was laughing.

Sam bit her lip.

"Because of all the women or men I could choose why choose you?"

Sam just looked at him.

"All of the above? None of them?"

Sam blinked.

"Well OK, we'll just have some really friendly brother bear hugs?"

Sam looked down at her hands in her lap.

"And you've got to participate."

He held her closely so that their bodies were touching from shoulder to thigh.

"I'm sure bears don't do this" said Sam.

"More fool them!" he murmured in her ear.

"So what happens now?"

"That depends on you."

"I thought it might" said Sam with a sigh.

"We could play chess" said Kaamal.

"Chess! You want to play chess?"

"Or strip poker?"

Sam smiled lopsidedly. She said

"I've never played strip poker."

He looked at her speculatively.

"It would only take me minutes, seconds to teach you…" and he smiled a really big smile, a smile so wide you could hang sails on it and cross the Indian Ocean.

And Sam smiled back.

When she looked back on it she was still at a loss to understand exactly how it happened. The wine, their natural empathy, laughter and companionship; maybe a searching, on both their parts, for something from the past. He was an accomplished lover, unhurried and considerate and she was a willing if disturbed collaborator. If he preferred men it didn't show. Afterwards she lay in the crook of his arm in complete comfort wondering if in the half light she looked more like a man than a woman. So she asked him.

"Did that happen because figuratively speaking my body is more inclined towards the male than the female of the species?"

"That –as you put it –happened because I like you a lot and because you are uncommonly beautiful. Your body is slender and lithe and a delight to touch. And your eyes- I have already told you about your eyes."

"But you told me you were gay."

"I also told you I liked women."

"So do you do both?" Sam persisted.

" I don't DO anything. So many questions. I like you and it seemed-natural."

"Sorry" said Sam. "It can be a really bad habit-needing to understand-it has been remarked on before-by many" she added apologetically.

"Many? I see- and did I meet with your approval?"

"I thought you were-" she stopped.

Kaamal raised his eyebrows.

"I was just wondering if you'd had-tuition" mummbled Sam.

"Tuition?"

"Yes. You know, a woman to teach you how to-"

"How to please a woman? You mean a Tawaif; a courtesan?"

He was laughing at her. "Maybe. If I'd been born a prince about a hundred years ago!"

"So just a natural talent then?"

He grinned.

"There was a girl, well a woman, when I was twenty who was very, shall we say, educational."

"She should make a living of it, preferably in the US and bring down the divorce rate" said Sam.

"Oh ho!! A woman with attitude."

"Is it the same with a man? I mean the love making?"

"If you are asking me if gay men are capable of expressing themselves in a passionate, tender way, the answer is yes. Like everything else, if the basis is love, care and consideration is part of it. A gay man can commit to a man just as a straight man will commit to a woman. In some ways there are more binding ties."

"Yes" said Sam thoughtfully.

He stopped. He was looking at her with a slightly interrogative expression.

"What's the look?" said Sam.

"I was just wondering who you were making love to-"

Sam stared at him.

"Who? What do you mean who?"

"I mean whilst I could feel your enjoyment it seemed that your heart-shall we call it-might be elsewhere?"

Sam had the grace to blush.

"I-"

"It doesn't matter. Tomorrow we have graveyards and the day after, the journey to Lucknow?"

His smile was angelic. Could anyone actually be that nice. He dressed quickly, picked up their glasses and the empty wine bottle and placed them on a table and went to the door where he turned and said

"See you at breakfast? About 8?"

Sam nodded and said

"You'll have gathered I've taken off the Tshirt."

The smile broadened and he left the room quietly closing the door behind him. She stayed where she was for some time trying to understand what had just happened. She wished Kevin was there although she wasn't entirely sure that he was the most fitting individual to ask questions about love. He could have a very acrimonious attitude towards bi-peds sometimes.

Followers of Buddha believed that love and compassion were the ultimate source of human happiness and the need for them lay at the centre of the being. That real love was not based on attachment. Well, she wasn't attached to Kaamal so maybe she was just fulfilling that need? Then she thought

What am I doing? I'm 37 years old and I'm trying on men like G strings when I should be wearing vests.

Crap! said the voice of Kevin.

Crap is it? You probably think monogamous is a prehistoric member of the hippopotamus family.

No said the voice of Kevin. It's a badge you put on the front of a T-shirt.

He was on form.

Do you have anything sensible to say Ratboy?

Ok. Let's run through them then. Most recently there was Luc with the birdwing blue eyes and the Native American ancestory said the voice of Kevin.

So have swordfish and he's blind, said Sam, somewhat irrelevantly.

That makes two of you said the voice of Kevin.

You think I fell for a blind man so I wouldn't have to worry about the onset of wrinkledom as long as I could still perform in bed? That's just insulting.

I would not have put it so crudely said the voice of Kevin primly, but it would eliminate one or two of your minor squeamishes.

Squeamishes?

Troublesome details that make you shudder said the voice of Kevin.

But –

Steve is dead said the voice of Kevin. But even if he wasn't he was just a very good friend. And Wanigi –he was the brother of your heart.

So what was the point? Who were they all? *What* were they all?

Aspects of you said the voice of Kevin. All the best and all the worst, partially recognised.

What I *am*? Sam said.

Yes said the voice of Kevin.

And Vivian?

Vivian...

A couple of lines from a poem came into her head:

'I shut my eyes and all the world drops dead,
    I lift my lids and all is born again.
    (I think I made you inside my head)'

Sylvia Plath –dear girl - Mad girl's love song – how appropriate.

Vivian... He is *who* you are said the voice of Kevin. Vivian. A man of depth and compassion, a wordsmith, a troubled soul; a kindred spirit and an accomplished lover and –

Drop dead gorgeous?

Ah yes said the voice of Kevin. There is that. The question is, are you ready to love who you are?

Am I ready to stop shadow dancing and embrace the shadow? said Sam.

Just so said the voice of Kevin. Our souls cannot see reality in itself until they are liberated from the distractions and inaccuracies of the physical senses. It is birth which is the sleeping and the forgetting, the soul going from a state of great awareness to one of clouded consciousness. Words cannot capture that which lies beyond the physical realm. They conceal rather than reveal.

Vivian said the same to me. I think it's Plato? Sam said.

Probably said the voice of Kevin.

But –

A but is something that most creatures have to enable them to assume a seated position said the voice of Kevin.

But-but is he-do I – can we- Sam floundered.

And serves no other useful purpose said the voice of Kevin.

I'm not sure-

Once upon a time there was a very fine friendship between two young boys. When it came to the parting of their ways Wanigi, the Ghost Water boy, said-*look for me my brother, my friend, my sister-I will be there*- it was not about the colour of his eyes; it was about the colour of his heart said the voice of Kevin.

He was blind too.

No said the voice of Kevin. He had vision that sees mens' souls and spans lifetimes. You know this. In Vivian you have met spirit. The physical has stepped back to allow you to embrace it and feel.

Sam pondered.

She thought, so that first time, when I initially met Kevin and we went on the journey with Fox and everyone and all that stuff about crossing rivers and mountains and storms and the bridge across the ravine and the dragon and the citadel and the faceless warriors and the two Knights, all that was a portent, a sampler, a sneak preview of what was to come, a glimpse into my future. So I have worked through it all step by step and here I am looking back and I can see I've played out all the elements. I had it all then, everything I needed, just like Kevin said. I just didn't know what I had. I had to take it all to pieces and put it back together again ...

Just so said the voice of Kevin again. Because you are you and that's what you do...

Is this where the journey, the search ends then?

And where it begins said the voice of Kevin.

Vivian. It began with Vivian. And she heard quite clearly his voice speaking the mantra on the day they made their commitment.

You have become mine forever. Yes, we have become partners. I have become yours. Hereafter, I cannot live without you. Do not live without me. Let us share the joys. We are word and meaning, united. You are thought and I am sound.

That only happened once in a lifetime and she wasn't ready to give up on it yet and she turned her face into the pillow and river images cast her adrift on sleep.

Kaamal was in the dining room waiting for her. He'd ordered scrambled eggs and coffee and at Sam's nod summoned the waiter for another of the same.

His first words spoke volumes.

"Are we good?"

"You mean have I fallen hopelessly in love with you?" Sam asked.

"Direct as ever. It has happened" said Kaamal ruefully. "But not with you I think. Your heart is otherwise engaged."

Sam smiled radiantly.

"I have added you to my ever growing list of male friends."

"Good. I'd like that. I look forward to hearing about the one who holds your heart." He said the last part in Urdu and Sam grinned and said

"And I about yours" and addressed herself to scrambled eggs that looked like they'd been made from cream and sunshine.

He observed her for a few moments and then said

"You eat like a ravenous wolf and look like a bird."

"Or words to that effect."

"Excuse me?"

Sam smiled at him, remembering.

"It has been commented upon before" she said. Then she added

"That makes you at about number four."

"Number four?"

"On my compliments scale" said Sam.

"Ah, I see. What happens if I hit ten?"

"I throw you out, for insincerity, or insanity. Valid either way."

They went first to the Nicholson cemetery, close to the Kashmir Gate. It was a sad , quiet place, overgrown and tragically beautiful, the last resting place of hundreds of colonial residents and their children and Indian Christians. Most of them had died tragically young. Even John Nicholson was only 34 when he died of his injuries at the siege of Delhi in 1857. Sam remembered Vivian speaking of him. Revered by his troops; contemptuous of his enemies. Not especially tolerant of anyone, whether they served him well or not, but a great leader of men. Lord Roberts, later of the second Afghan war and Commander in Chief, had been a twenty five year old lieutenant at the time he/ had found him within the walls of Delhi, shot through and dying. She'd read his memoirs.

The gothic and Victorian setting had its own peaceful beauty, despite originally being a battle zone; four acres of overgrown shrubs and white peacocks. The headstones, many half obliterated with moss and lichen and creepers, recorded short life and the fragility of it.

Kaamal saw her face and said

"It was very difficult in the years of the Raj for European women to bring their children to adulthood. The climate itself, the travelling many were forced to do with their husbands, disease, lack of sanitation-"

"And war."

"As you say- and war. It was not an easy life. Some loved it and their adopted country; others must have longed for their native land."

"Some were born here and never wanted to be anywhere else" said Sam.

"Yes. And their bearers and syces and ayahs became their uncles and mothers and friends. It is something that an historian must learn to accept. That history has a way of repeating itself and many people suffer each time it does."

"Have you accepted it?"

"Sometimes I think I have-" He paused and then said

"Graveyards are not such a common sight in India because the usual ritual of death for Hindus is cremation. This graveyard is believed to be haunted by bhuts, ghosts. Burning frees the soul and allows it to move to the next incarnation. Burial traps it and it must wander..."

He stopped and Sam shivered, suddenly aware of the 120 years that separated her from Vivian now and what might have become of him.

Kaamal said

"And what is important to you Samanthar, in your wanderings?"

Sam thought about the question.

"Freedom. Lack of freedom would be death to me."

"And what would constitute lack of freedom?"

"To take away my ability to do what I want when I want to do it."

"And what do you ever imagine could do that to you?" Kaamal said with a grin.

"I don't know. But there are subversive ways."

"You mean you are persuaded to do something for your own good or someone else's?"

"Yes. But as with all things the greatest risk of sabotage comes from within."

"You don't seem the kind to self destruct."

"No. But all my life I have striven for balance and the way that I need to struggle implies that I am always in danger of choosing too much or too little, one way or the other."

"Man is made or unmade by himself?"

"Yes I believe so. A long time ago a friend got me to understand that whatever is happening in my life, in my outside life, it first begins on the inside, as a thought, a belief, however challenging or unpleasant that might be to accept."

"That could be very difficult to face."

"Yes it is. But it is also very liberating. Because all I need then is honesty and courage. Honesty to face what I am and what I think and courage to do whatever is necessary to change, if change is needed."

"And the reward?"

"The reward is peace of mind, calm if you like. Because it means that I am the one in charge of my life and I want to be the best I can be."

"You cannot travel anywhere and stand still..." murmured Kaamal.

"Just so" said Sam.

They stood side by side and gazed out over the tangled, tortured peaceful intertwining lines of the gravestones with their broken canopies of branches and bushes, each with their own thoughts.

"Do you believe in god?" Kaamal asked.

"Right now I'd believe in anything that would allow me –" She stopped. "I'm not sure that's what's important. Sometimes I think believing in god is part of our security, culture, being obsessed by what comes next. A god, a heaven, a someplace better, a reason to do whatever we're doing and justify it with a belief that beyond this world there is another –"

" And our god says it's the right thing to do and therefore we will achieve paradise?

How about–" and he quoted

"'My brother kneels (so

Says Kabir)

To stone and brass in

Heathen-wise,

But in my brother's voice I

Hear

My own unanswered

Agonies.

His God is as his Fates
Assign-
His prayer is all the world's
-and mine.'"

"Oh yes" said Sam. "Who wrote that?"

"It was written by Kabir, a 15ᵗʰ century mystic, poet and saint. He was brought up in a Muslim family but was strongly influenced by the Hindu teacher Ramananda. He was known for being critical of both faiths and was threatened by followers of both in his lifetime. His teaching was to consider all creatures as oneself and be detached from the affairs of the world."

"Does he still have a following?" Sam asked.

"Oh yes. There are two temples in Benares dedicated to him. One maintained by Muslims, one by Hindus."

"That would have amused him" said Sam.

"How about- the only time is now and the only true living is in the now?"

"Yes" said Sam. "I'm a writer. Sylvia Plath once inscribed that writing is a religious act, a reforming and a relearning of the world and it does not pass away, like the activity. It exists on its own in the world. I write to find my freedom."

Kaamal nodded. "Go on."

"Between the pages of a book I can say what I want, do what I want, be who I want to be. The only rules are those of my making and even those I can choose whether to obey or not. If my writing strikes a chord in the hearts of others they may be motivated to pursue their own beliefs in their own way, conventionally or not. It seems to me that western society has become a dinosaur, a sauropod, a long neck, with lumbering strides that tramples everything small enough to crush; which rubbernecks everything it comes across, with a brain much too small to assimilate the complexity and variations of humankind, or to contemplate anything which does not fit its accepted ways or further its own material growth and perpetuation. I can't fight it. I have always been a closet revolutionary but I lack the single minded focus and unassailable belief in the rightness of one cause, to be able to handle the fight head on. Once you start fighting you lose sight of the original issues and become embroiled in the struggle and it then becomes a a fight of principle and survival and not truth. And truth is a much maligned word. So is belief. Belief without questioning is not belief at all; it is fear with a fence around it. Truth is only valuable when it's true for whoever is doing the believing. I would run out of steam long before that. So I believe in following your own truths, against the ebb tide if necessary, to get where you want to be. Sometimes you may have to follow a prescribed path, say the education system for instance, so far, because to opt out would be pitting yourself against an established adversary which could steamroller you into submission, wasting a lot of time and resources. So for a time you might need to follow their path but you still don't need to believe in it or in the reasons you are given for its existence. You can keep your own counsel and when the opportunity presents itself –and that will be when you are ready –you can climb off their path and find your own."

Kaamal was looking at her, his expression complex.

"So I suppose you could say I write to support my cause and put across the message –you are in control of your own life; you have a choice; each moment, each situation –you have a choice and by making those choices you change your self and the face of your world. Your universe will support your choice for good or evil. If you say you have no choice, that too is a choice and that is what you will experience."

Kaamal watched her as if he knew behind the declaration there was a struggle. He said

"'It matters not how strait the gate, how charged with punishments the scroll, I am the master of my fate, I am the captain of my soul'?"

"Yes! That was my father's belief and his favourite poem."

"But sometimes you want to believe in fundamentals; our paths are written; love is stronger than death; we live and live again and meet again those we have lost. You would perhaps like to embrace the Hindu way, and follow and accept one or all of their pathways."

Sam smiled at him.

"You are an historian but you would make a wonderful counsellor and prophet. You are a Muslim, yes?"

"Yes. But I grew up with many Hindu friends and we all shared- our beliefs as well as our games. I learned a lot. So, I am an Indian before I am a Muslim. Then I met – someone special and learned more, how to love and what it demands of you. And then I studied, history and literature, of all kinds and-"

"And?"

"And I suppose I am now where you are. Doubting; just wanting to believe, without the need for justification and conflict, that the heart can find its peace."

Sam said

"I do believe in the stream of consciousness; knowledge outside of self; unthought of routes and possibilities. Something you can step into and ask your questions. And the universe will provide the answers."

"Yes" said Kaamal. "but you have to ask and you have to be prepared for the answer."

They sat down together, shoulders touching, on a half hidden block of stone and Kaamal said

"You smell wonderful."

"I do?"

"Yes. You smell of fresh air and soap. Easy on the senses. Some women smell like a scented bath of sheep dip mixed with sulphuric acid. Some men too."

Wow! Whatever this man's proclivities he'd had some unfortunate encounters.

"You seem more concerned with what you're thinking than how you're looking, more concerned that what you put on the in the morning doesn't give cause for thought until you remove it at night. And I like that you are aware that what comes out of your mouth can be as destructive as what goes in."

"Oh" said Sam. "Does that mean you like me?"

Kaamal laughed.

She wasn't entirely convinced that it was true. The last bit anyway. Sure, she knew words could be destructive; it didn't always stop her, as Kevin and Vivian, come to think of it, not to mention Steve, could corroborate.

Kaamal's open regard forced her to be honest.

She said

"I once told some woman that she was the worst planetary curse since the Ice Age and I hoped she'd go the same way."

Kaamal laughed even more.

"I'm guessing you didn't like her."

"She'd pissed me off" said Sam. "Does that change your opinion?"

"No. It just makes you honest. I like that too."

"You don't find me boring then?"

"Boring? No! Why would I?"

"Oh I don't know. I don't have any normal leisure pursuits, like sport or an interest in social gatherings. I don't have a huge range of conversational topics and couldn't be bothered anyway. I like reading, thinking, writing and exploring the inner and outer worlds. I like wide open spaces with as few human beings as possible, and animals. Those don't seem the optimum components in the building of a relationship. So apart from sex, which is obviously less fulfilling on one's own, what do I bring to the game?"

He studied her for a while, choosing his words.

"You are like the ocean, with diverse things at different levels, shooting here and there, in its depths. A man could get totally lost down there."

"A man might hit his head on the rocky bottom and come up with sand in his ears and a headache" said Sam, somewhat disconcerted.

Kaamal ignored the remark.

"Not all people are conversationalists. How can the imagination be fertile if the mouth is saturated with syllables. Your mind has veins and arteries just like anything else. They need to be clear of gunk to create, otherwise all you get is wall to wall ear wax chatter."

Sam blinked. What did you say to that?

Kaamal took her hand in his and looked down at it thoughtfully.

"True attraction takes place at a spirit level you know. It invites investigation. It survives debauchery. It's transformational."

He seemed to be speaking to himself. He turned to her and smiled suddenly.

"I am rambling. It is a failing. But you seem to accept the shortcomings of others with equanimity."

"Oh not always, believe me! Not always."

"I suspect that you are fairly intolerant of your own failings?"

Sam thought.

"I can be, yes."

"Is that because you see –'they know not what they do' –as a defence? But for those who are fully aware –there can be no excuse?"

"Maybe."

"Aren't we all responsible to the same degree? Can some be more responsible than others?"

Sam said

"If you believe that what you think affects the world around you - if that is your actual belief –then yes –your responsibility to make those thoughts the best they can possibly be is greater than for someone who believes in an anonymous, arbitrary power over which they have no control."

"That's almost as biased as a belief in the chosen few."

"I suppose it does sound that way but it's more about living in tune with your feelings, being your own counsel and your own judge. Your own devils advocate."

"But no one else's?"

"Yes that's right."

Kaamal said quietly

"If I had believed that strongly enough things might have turned out differently for me..."

After lunch they went to Humayun's garden tomb, thought to have inspired the Taj Mahal and predating it by sixty years. Kaamal told her it was constructed by his Persian born wife, Haji Begum and had both Persian and Mughal elements. The architectural design was quite restrained with bands of white marble which apparently followed the rules of Islamic geometry, with its emphasis on the number eight.

Kaamal was obviously passionate about the complex.

"It is also called the '*dormitory of the Mughals*' as in the cells there are over 150 Mughal family members buried. The tomb stands in an extremely significant archaeological setting, centred at the shrine of the 14th century Sufi saint, Hazrat Nizamuddin Auliya. It is considered auspicious to be buried near a saint's grave and seven centuries of tomb building has led to the area becoming the densest ensemble of medieval Islamic buildings in India."

Sam listened to his enthusiastic explanations and was once again awed by the passion that could be aroused by knowledge and appreciation that had notrhing to do with gratification. Maybe that was why he was such a good lover.

Even her unpractised eye could see that it was built on a monumental scale.

"It has no precedent in the Islamic world for a mausoleum. Here for the first time, architectural innovations were made including creating a char-bagh – a garden setting inspired by the description of paradise in the Holy Quran. The monumental scale achieved here was to become the characteristic of Mughal imperial projects, culminating in the construction of the Taj Mahal."

He stopped and turned to Sam.

"Am I becoming a total bore? Are you falling asleep on your feet? You should have stopped me."

"No! No! And why? I'm sure I've said this before but I could listen to you all day."

"You have" said Kaamal apologetically.

"I was just remembering the Humayun I knew from Barbur's Journal who seemed to be constantly in trouble! I especially like the bit where he gets a lecture from his father on how to write a grammatically correct letter."

"I suppose" said Kaamal, somewhat ruefully, " parents are parents no matter what the era or station in life."

"If the ghost of Humayun is anything like the man in his youth and with all those Mughal family members on the loose, how does anyone round here get any peace at night?"

"Hopefully they're confined in the mausoleum. Shall we go?"

"What are we doing tonight?" Sam asked.

"Going to bed early" he caught her look and added "separately, regretfully. We have an early start."

"That's a shame" said Sam lightly.

As she got ready for bed that night she thought about the next day. Lucknow and then Cawnpore – Kanpur now-Vivian, always hovering, would come right to the fore tomorrow and she and Kaamal had kind of agreed to share stories. Anticipation warred with anxiety. If she told him her story, if she told him about Vivian, would he think she was completely out of her mind and if he did, that would put considerable strain on their subsequent explorations. She could not bear to lose the opportunity to go to the places he had described to her. Should she pervert the truth?

Lying, even bending the truth always got you into difficulties. It wasn't worth it. He was a broad minded, intelligent man with strong historical and religious convictions. He would not judge. On that thought she fell into bed and was just drifting off when she heard a quiet tap on the door.

She climbed out of bed, pulled a long T-shirt over her head and went to the door.

"Who is it?"

"It's me." It was Kaamal's voice.

Sam opened the door. He was standing there in jeans and a T-shirt, with tousled hair and bare feet.

"Sod sleep! I can sleep when I'm dead. Can I come in?"

Sam stepped aside and he came in.

"I thought we were going to bed early, separately?"

"Yes. That was the plan.. I did." He ran a hand through his hair and then said

"It didn't work." He sighed and looked, Sam thought, vaguely uncomfortable.

"It's been a long time since- since I met -"

"You really don't have to explain" said Sam. "The only time is now and the only true living is in the now -isn't that what we said this afternoon? Why don't we just make the most of it?"

She took him by the hand and went back to the bed.

" Beds can seem very empty sometimes can't they?"

He watched her pull the long T-shirt up over her head and climb back into the bed and then stripped off his clothes and climbed in after her. For a few minutes they lay there side by side and then Kaamal turned towards her and propped himself on one elbow.

"I don't want to confuse or disturb anything for you. I know this isn't just a complicated holiday trip. I know it's a quest. I won't do anything that might jeopardise or distract you from that path."

"You won't" said Sam and leaned towards him and kissed him.

He pulled her into his arms and returned the kiss, slowly and deliberately with extraordinary care and expertise. Her last coherent thought was

If this is what you're like when you're out of practice you must have been a batcha in a previous life.

It was a long and extraordinarily pleasurable night. For Sam, Kaamal's lovemaking reminded her of Vivian. She did not think Kaamal would mind the comparison and Vivian? Well he could hardly have expected her to be celibate for 120 years.

They both awoke early with a sort of conspiratorial satisfaction and then Kaamal went off to pack his bag and take a shower and Sam ordered coffee to the room -for two and was rewarded with a shy smile from the boy who had fulfilled Rajesh's order. Rajesh took his reception duties very seriously.

While Sam showered Kaamal ordered breakfast to be brought to the room.

"We may as well. Everyone in the hotel will know by now."

"They might expect you to do this every time you have a client here."

Kaamal regarded her with a strange look in his eyes.

"It could never happen" he said briefly and Sam thought, no, it couldn't but did not know why.

An hour later they were on the road.

Once they finally got out of the city and were on the open road Sam settled back to watch the countryside flow past and asked Kaamal about Lucknow.

"You have never visited it before?" he asked.

"No. I have read a lot of history about it, but really any knowledge I have of it comes from the 19th century. What's it like today? And is it still possible to gain an inkling of its past from the ruins that remain?"

"I was born there as I told you. It was and still is a multicultural centre. A commercial, cultural and artistic hub for all religions. It still is an important centre of commerce, enterprise and governance as well as art and design. You will find the people polite and welcoming and its food has a reputation for excellence and variety throughout India."

"The city was fabled for is beauty was it not?"

"Yes and it still is. I will take you to the old and new. It will be delightful at this time of year and some of the places we will go do not attract the tourist numbers that we have seen in Delhi. The climate is tropical savannah with cool dry winters and hot summers with thunderstorms. Average temperatures are around 75°in the summers and 50°in the winters, with extremes of course. It lies on the northwest shore of the Gomti river in the middle of the Indo-Gangetic plain and is surrounded by rural towns and villages which you will see as we approach."

"What is the main language?"

"Hindi. Urdu is also spoken and of course English."

"I should be okay then."

"You will indeed. You will love the food and the people. We grow mangoes and sugar cane, wonderful vegetables and flowers; roses, marigolds and sunflowers. There are monkeys in the city forests and iconic buildings from the British and Mughal eras in the old part of the city. You will love it."

"*You* love it" said Sam.

"I love it. I would have stayed, I think if –"

He stopped. There was a frown between his eyes. He felt her look and glanced at her. He shrugged.

"Things happen. Things change."

"Tell me what happened. Tell me what changed" said Sam quietly.

Kaamal carried on driving. He seemed not to have heard. Then he said

"Why on earth would you want to hear about my disreputable past?"

"So when I tell you about mine I won't feel so singular."

He relaxed then and the frown disappeared.

"Before I went to college I was living with my parents. They had many friends and I was introduced to the daughter of one pair, I think with a view to a possible marriage. She was a nice girl but like me was more focused on getting an education and doing what she wanted with her life rather than marriage. It was fortunate.

I was relatively innocent and inexperienced in real terms, though outwardly quite confident I think, and struggling to come to terms with my own sexual preferences in any case. But she had a brother, two years her junior and as at our parents encouragement, we continued to visit, he and I became friends. He was a beautiful boy, fine boned and slender, quiet and intense; impossibly shy... Far more attractive to my eyes than his sister, who was vivacious and opulently curvaceous. I think he was a throwback; wherever he got his looks and his personality from, it wasn't his immediate family. I don't know why it happened; I don't know how it happened. There was a marriage of minds and spirits and something in both of us reacted to the physical attraction of the other. We fell in love on first meeting and it intensified as time went on. No one noticed. Two teenage boys enjoying each other's company, sharing each other's interests. His parents were pleased, even after they realized that nothing was going to happen between myself and his sister. He was shy and did not mix easily and they thought I was good for him. His sister realised early on I think but was neither shocked nor condemning. But we were in love and lovers are renowned for their blindness and lack of attention. We had a little over a year together and then we were discovered and then –I think the common term is –the shit hit the fan. I was shipped off to start my college education in Delhi and he was sent to England to live with an uncle in London. He wanted to train as a doctor and applied for and got a place in a London college. He qualified there, and there he remains..."

"Oh Kaamal!" Sam reached out a hand. "Can we pull off the road? Can we go and get a drink somewhere?"

Kaamal took the next exit off the main road and drove into the first village that they came to. He pulled up outside a small café and they got out and went and sat at one of the tables in the garden to one side and ordered sweet chai.

They sat in silence until the tea arrived, Kaamal gazing into the middle distance, his face without expression.

Sam reached out and took his hand.

"How long ago was all that?" she asked.

"Twelve years now" said Kaamal.

"Twelve years! Have you been with anyone else?"

"A few. Women. Nothing serious."

"Women! Not men? No men at all?"

"I started a few relationships but when it came to any kind of –intimacy–I backed out..."

Sam digested this. She said

"I bet that didn't earn you any brownie points."

Kaamal smiled ruefully.

"No. I just found it impossible, when it came to the moment... I found it impossible to make love with any man who wasn't –"

"What is his name?"

"Ata. His name is Ata. It means gift. And he was."

"Do you keep in touch? Do you have a photo?"

"We exchange letters. He is a qualified cardiologist now-how ironic is that! And very busy. But he makes time – I could not bear to speak to him on the phone, even now – hear his voice... I have wished, often, especially in the early months, that I had done things differently; been braver -but I have handwritten letters ...they seem like a part of him...they are very honest... And photographs ..."

He took a small, leather wallet from the backpack in which he carried travel documents and maps. He pulled out a sheaf of photographs and sifted through them, looking at each for several moments, a half smile twitching his mouth.

He murmured

"'Now was Salaman in his prime of growth,

His cypress stature risen to high top,

And the new blooming garden of his beauty

Began to bear'"

Then he handed one of them to Sam.

She was looking at a dark haired young man of maybe twenty five or so. He had an elfin face with fine bones, a wide mouth and dark soulful eyes. He looked serene but there was a small, puzzled frown between his brows that seemed to imply a mind given to introspection and he was extraordinarily good looking. If I'd fallen for him, Sam reflected, I don't think I'd ever look at anyone else either.

She studied the symmetry of form and beauty and then gave the picture back and Kaamal did some more flicking and handed her three older photographs, taken with a different camera. She now saw a new portrayal; a teenage version of the same man, shyer; less assured. The hair was just as untidy and a little longer, but the soulful eyes and the beautiful mouth were smiling with something akin to adoration. There was no frown.

Kaamal said

"He was six months short of 18; the last I took of him before... While we were still happy."

Sam thought, his love shines like a beacon in a storm.

She said

"He is so beautiful."

"Yes. His beauty comes from the inside and shines out."

Yes, thought Sam. She wondered if anything had changed for him.

As if Kaamal read her thought he said

"He is not wedded except to his work."

"Would he tell you if he was?"

"Oh yes. He would tell me. They severed the relationship. Not the love."

"Why don't you go and visit? Stay with him?"

But she knew the answer before he said it and her heart contracted with empathy and with fear.

"You cannot recreate the past" said Kaamal. "You must know the penalty for looking back? Genesis? Lot's wife turning to stone. Maybe when we are old we can meet again."

Sam squeezed his hand.

"What was the quotation?"

"Salaman and Absal" said Kaamal. "The Persian allegory."

"Happy ending or sad ending?"

"Depends on your point of view" said Kaamal noncommittally.

"There is no bridge that love cannot cross; no door through which love cannot pass" she said.

"That sounds like a quote too."

"Yes. It is. And I believe it with all my heart."

I have to.

They got back in the car and drove on.

"What were the women like?" Sam asked.

"Oh, various. Mostly slender; mostly independent; I didn't get involved in any match making. No one like you."

"And how did they take the breakup –when it came?"

"Again, various. There was, I seem to remember, a lot of slamming the doors, recriminations and tears. The odd glass of wine in the face. In the end I adopted a –pleasant smile but no thank you – policy. It seemed preferable."

But lonely, thought Sam.

They drove on.

"You like music, yes?" Kaamal said.

"Oh yes. What have you got?"

"Queen?"

"Queen! You have Queen?"

"Yes. 'News of the World'"

"Best ever! We are the Champions."

Kaamal laughed out loud.

"We are the Champions it is."

Sam leaned back, occasionally glancing at Kaamal whilst the music blasted out:

"And we'll keep on fighting to the end..."

Then it switched to 'Live Killers'

And when they got to

" Don't stop me now!" Sam sang along with it at full volume and Kaamal laughed so much he nearly drove off the road. But the mood was lighter and as they continued Kaamal said

"I will take you to the place we used to meet. The Sikandah Bagh. You will like it. It does not get many visitors."

"Alexaner's Gardens? After Alexander the Great?"

"Some believe so, yes."

Another beautiful, driven soul, so the writings had it. She wondered if Ata was driven.

She had been thinking about the relationship that was growing between them. She said

"In some way I remind you of him don't I? Please tell me it's not my body."

"I appreciate the lack of voluptuous curves" Kaamal said flippantly.

"Flat and straight, yes? It's more than that."

He seemed about to deny it.

She thought for a moment.

"It's the eyes isn't it? My eyes remind you of his."

Kaamal glanced across at her and smiled.

"Yes. Brown eyes, with tiny light flecks in them; honest eyes. And the small frown between your brows when your mind is troubled."

Sam thought about this. She decided she quite liked it. When she was with Steve and wearing a baseball cap, she had once been mistaken for a boy. It hadn't bothered her and it certainly never seemed to bother Steve. She was thinking of Kaamal and his relationship with the beautiful Ata when Kaamal suddenly said

"And the listening. The ability to focus and hear and feel what another is saying. That too is like Ata. Do you know your name, Samanthar, means listener?"

", No, I didn't know."

They were silent for a while and then Kaamal said

"More music?"

"Yes. What else have you got?"

"What do you feel about this?"

He pressed play and unambiguous, pounding rock filled the car with the help of the quadrophonic stereo.

"I'm gonna hit the highway like a battering ram on a silver black Phantom bike,..."

"Yes, yes!!" said Sam. "All time favourite."

They both sang at the top of their voices and laughed. Kaamal said

"One of my tutors introduced me to American rock music when I first went to college. He'd spent some time in the US. Big Springsteen fan. I think he worked out I'd been in a relationship that had come to an abrupt end and thought it might help."

"Did it?"

"Yes, it did actually. I used to blast it out. 'You're the only thing that's pure and good and right...wherever you go there's always gonna be some light'..."

"Me too. The volume can be very therapeutic can't it?" said Sam. " Dylan's Forever Young has a special place for me."

"Good choice. I've got that here too. Why that one?"

"A good friend wrote a couple of lines in a card for me- before he died" said Sam, remembering.

"Let me guess. 'May you build a ladder to the stars ... and may you stay forever young' ?"

"Yeah" said Sam, remembering.

"Well you look like you've achieved that" said Kaamal.

"What?"

"Forever young."

The music played on.

"When it's over you know we'll both be so alone..." Sam sang, while Kaamal did the background instrumentals.

They drove on for a while and then Kaamal said

"What do you feel about Indian music? Classical I mean, not film music."

"No idea" said Sam. "I've never listened to any."

"This is Hindustani classical" said Kaamal.

It wasn't melodic. It was more like how one would imagine it would sound if the trees and grasses and earth and rivers were to communicate orchestrally with each other. It demanded a response from more than just the ears. It demanded the same sort of consideration as did some jazz. It opened up the mind rather than engrossing it.

When Sam expressed this to him Kaamal agreed.

"Hindustani music from the north and Carnatic music from the south share the same origins but can sound very different. The former has more theme and harmony; the latter is more mathematical and intellectual. Vocals are employed similarly. Both demand a lot from the Western ear."

Sam nodded. It was a curious sensation. She thought she quite liked it. It was meditationally absorbing.

After a while Kaamal said

"Tell me about Vivian. I assume it is Vivian and not Vivienne?"

Sam shivered all over, as if something had reached out and touched her. Before he had played her the Hindustani music the last track had taken her right back to Vivian and the Indian music had opened her mind but...

"How –"

"You spoke his name in your sleep."

"Last night?"

"No. The first night."

"Shit!"

"Yes, apparently you are that obsessed."

Sam was reluctant now. Part of her wanted to tell this man about her love, valued his understanding and his perception; part of her was just desperate to talk about Vivian, have him made flesh by the focus of their combined thoughts. But if Kaamal thought she was a misguided fantasist, or worse, a nutcase, she would see it in his eyes and she would lose something she had come to value highly. She said slowly

"I feel as if we have come to a comfortable, mutual understanding and I am very loathe to damage it."

"Why should telling me about an important relationship, one that I had already divined incidentally, be damaging to our mutual understanding as you call it?"

"Have I been so transparent?" said Sam, distracted.

"My dear girl! You have planned the most intricate and detailed of itineraries, which take you halfway across Northern India and which any fool could have seen was intended to achieve a result. And you wear a gold band, a very fine and antique gold band if I am not mistaken, on the second finger of your left hand. And then there are the earings, in the same exquisite gold, that you never take off. You are not transparent, you are in love and cannot hide it. What is wrong with that?"

"How long have you got?" said Sam sardonically.

"Well let's see –we have about 3 hours before we reach Lucknow and then we have all night. That should at least give you time to give me a bare outline!"

He glanced quickly at her.

"You must surely know from my attitudes to the past and present that I am not given to making judgements however extreme you believe your circumstances to be."

When she still did not speak he said

"I have after all shared with you the single most important thing in my life and that is something I have done with no one else."

"No one?"

"No one. Until you there was no one with whom I dared bring him alive."

Where to begin?

So she started, as she had done with Vivian, with her history of past life regression through her childhood and teens, her explorations with a spirit guide called Kevin, who was incidentally, a rat. Glancing at Kaamal's face as she talked she saw his eyebrows lift and his mouth twitch and smile, but he made no comment.

When she had completed the introduction she looked at him. Kaamal said

"None of this is untoward in a country that has many beliefs and religions and many roads down which one may travel to attain spiritual enlightenment."

This was true. She plunged on.

"I met Vivian in a past life regression. Sort of. It was different because I neither regressed nor was I just an observer. I was just there. Hell! I was there dressed almost exactly as I am today but he could see me. Vivian saw me as soon as I turned up, but apart from him and his bearer and syce and his best friend's wife and ultimately his best friend, no one else could! And if that wasn't bad enough, complicated enough-"

"You fell in love with him."

Sam nodded. Even telling this man, with his background and his experience, it sounded utterly fantastical. Kaamal glanced across at her. He said

"And he fell in love with you. Of course he did. How not?" He said the last part of the sentence in Urdu. Sam sighed.

"I'm sure you can finish the story now" she said.

"Would you like me to?"

Sam nodded.

"OK" said Kaamal, "but first tell me what you felt about him, to make him so important that you search through history to find him."

"My first impression of him, the first time we met, was a combination of danger and safety. I felt that if I touched him I would be electrocuted but if I could bear to hold my hand there and push it through to the centre it would be the safest place on earth. And he had a kind of vulnerability which made the safety unrestricted."

"What do you mean by safe?"

"I mean I would trust him with my life; with the life of all I loved; with the universe."

She paused, then added,

"And it was mutual."

Kaamal said "Was that what you wanted?"

"I think I wanted to go on learning and growing; I think I wanted to be able to share on a level and without being in front or behind, without being in the role of teacher or pupil, but moving naturally between the two. Someone once told me, the fountain of youth is your consciousness; the psyche develops in response to the decision to grow, a feature of choice not age; growth is life and stagnation is death and that taking risks and choosing new experiences is the best way to grow. Vivian gave me life…"

"And this you shared with Vivian was a new experience?" Kaamal asked.

"Oh yes! Absolutely, brand, spanking, squeaky new" said Sam vehemently. "'And though the soul sail leagues beyond, still leagues beyond those leagues there is more sea'" she quoted.

Kaamal sighed.

"So. You stayed –months, years and life was good if tricky at times. You were heart, mind, body and soul to each other. He asked you to marry him; you argued, because that's who you are, and then said yes. You stayed and it was wonderful. But you knew that it could not last because you did not belong there –"

"You are very good" said Sam.

"I have experience in these things remember? Whose decision was it for you to return?"

"Mine" said Sam. "He would have had me stay and risk the consequences. I chose a different risk, gambled that it was just possible –"

"You couldn't stay there because you couldn't stay in the past but it was just possible that he could come to the future?"

"Yes."

"There are documented accounts of people who believe that has happened to them are there not? That they have met people they have known in a previous life?"

"Yes."

"Are you given to this kind of risk?"

"I suppose so, the bungee jump risk. I always believed that sometimes you have to trust before you can believe."

"Has the rope ever snapped?"

"No. I've stood on the edge a long time, sometimes, looking down, longer than was constructive, but in the end the timing was always perfect because the ending was always perfectly timed-"

"But now you are wondering if this time it was one bungee jump too far?"

" With Vivian it didn't seem like a bungee jump. It seemed like gliding through dream landscapes and I wanted to realise the dream; I wanted to have it all. Maybe I should have just accepted what I'd been given and left it at that?"

"And not have come here looking for answers? Oh no! I don't think so. You had to try."

Sam smiled at him.

"I did didn't I?"

"And perhaps if it doesn't work out we could-"

He stopped and Sam looked at him in amazement.

"We could what?"

"We get on very well; we have shared interests- I'm sure two of your prerequisites for an ideal man are parking the car and great sex. I qualify don't I?""

Sam looked at him blankly.

She could almost hear Kevin saying, "The triangle. The perfect shape to hang a plot on!" How very apt of Kevin to send her that thought now. How very reassuring to think she had the opportunity to create the perfect basis for a melodrama.

Melodrama. The word echoed down the corridors, in the hallways, through the tunnels, under the archways of all the memories...

She burst into tears.

Kaamal was shocked. He said

"Yah Ali, what's wrong? Why are you crying? I did not intend -"

"I'm not" said Sam.

What was it Wanigi Mini had said? 'Life takes many forms. It is the spirit that is constant. Be led by your heart, not your eyes.'

Be led by your heart...

Her thoughts were screaming - never mind the small print! Grasp the opportunity that's in front of you now. A brother, a companion, a friend. It doesn't need to be a soul mate. Look at him. Look at him! He's gorgeous! But... But... her second thoughts broke into the fray again and yelled –a lover. A lover! Why not! Why not?

Sam elbowed into the skirmish.

Because...

Because you know your path.

Kevin.

"Kevin?" Kaamal was now seriously concerned.

She had spoken aloud.

"Who's Kevin again?"

"Kevin? Kevin is just –Kevin" said Sam.

"That clears that up then!"

She shook her head to dispel the warring thoughts and said

"But I'm not in love with you and you sure as hell are not in love with me."

"Despite our mutual admiration for flat and straight beauty?"

"Despite that" said Sam.

"Alright then. But I like you a lot. And you like me, yes? I am sure there are worse relationships."

Sam leaned back and closed her eyes. She hadn't expected this. What had she expected? Scepticism? Derision? Concern? All of those. But acceptance and compromise? He seemed to read her thoughts.

"You see compromise as such a negative thing? Is it though, when the alternative is to live alone?"

Sam frowned and he chose that moment to glance at her and saw the frown and laughed.

"You choose as Ata would choose" he said in Urdu. "All or nothing. Never mind. We will be friends. Good friends?"

Sam said waspishly

"If you keep scrutinising my expressions while you're driving we're going to be very close. We're going to drive into a truck or a ditch."

They drove on for another twenty or so kilometres, Sam gazing out of the window and seeing nothing until Kaamal said

"Are you a perfectionist in all things?"

Sam looked at him sharply.

"I have never thought of myself as a perfectionist. I've never been obsessed with perfect creases in trousers or no scratches on cars; perfect settings or surroundings. If the object or setting suited me it *was* perfect. Its objective perfection did not concern me, but..." she stopped unable to take the thought further.

"What about in men?" said Kaamal casually.

"The same applies really. It was my notion of beauty, of suitability that was important. Fashion trends or social acceptability never interested me."

"Did this apply to the inside as well as the outside?" Kaamal persisted.

"Did I go seeking beautiful souls? Not consciously. But yes, I suppose it must have..."

"And if the outer world is a mirror of the inner –let's put it this way –it was always going to take a long time to find your ideal man!"

He was laughing. Sam said

"Yeah."

"And would probably be a blend of the Dalai Lama, Robin Hood and William Blake. Freedom fighters with attitude, long legs, dark eyes, a ferris wheel for a mind and a soul the depth of a 20 fathom well. Your very own personal Lord Krishna."

Sam laughed. Kaamal said

"Was he close? Vivian?"

"Yes."

"If he ticks all those boxes I think you have to try to find him again" said Kaamal.

"Yes."

"How much does it matter?"

"That he comes back into my life? I don't know. I have not really got that far. I haven't really considered just how evolved I am yet. I suppose I will have to."

"Interesting choice of words. I suppose we all have to."

Sam looked at him. He was looking straight ahead, his mouth and jaw rigid. He felt the scrutiny, turned and his expression relaxed.

"I think we will pull off the expressway here and stay the night. We are a little over halfway and if we get up early we will be to Lucknow during the morning. I would like to take you to the Sikundar Bagh first."

"That's where you and Ata used to meet" said Sam.

"Yes. I would like to show you the place where- never mind. Tomorrow I will tell you! It is a nice story and I know you will like the gardens, unkempt as they are. It is on the outskirts of Lucknow so it will be easy. There are a lot of roads around it so it is noisy but once you are in it you will forget the noise."

"I'm sure I shall and I like unkempt. What about some food?"

"Food. How did we get on to food?"

"It's a knack I have" Sam said airily. "It is important to punctuate reality with meal breaks. A very wise –individual – taught me that."

"What did you have in mind?"

"Lots of bits; lots of breads, lots of nuts" said Sam.

"Ah, the height of culinary excellence. Bread and nuts- the food of –"

"Rodents?" Sam said helpfully.

"I was going to say – the gods."

"Exactly."

"We'll add lassi, just to lift the tone."

Sam smiled radiantly. She said thoughtfully,

"Would you have asked me to marry you?"

Kaamal looked at her in astonishment. He said

"But of course!"

They had passed Agra on the expressway and they pulled off at a place called Shikohabad which was apparently a Hindu pilgrimage centre. It was unprepossessing but, Sam reasoned, more in tune with their needs than Agra, which she had visited before. The Taj Mahal was epic of course but the crowds had been tumultuous and she had spent a lot of her time buying sundry gifts from and giving money to street vendors and beggars and abhorring the eternal difference between the haves and the have-nots.

Kaamal quickly found a small pleasant hotel in a street in a quiet area and they went out and bought breads and kebabs and lassi and tea from street vendors and ate it in what appeared to be some kind of municipal park.

Sam wanted to hear about Lucknow and the places they were to visit but then decided she would get there before she learned anything.

Vivian had been there. She didn't know what that would mean or how she would feel, seeing the ruins of the places he had described and the events that had happened through his eyes again. But she was quite sure that Kaamal's historical and cultural memorabilia spoken in his usual pervasive enthusiastic tones would exemplify the whole experience. And Kaamal? This was his home and the scene of his first love. She was happy to wait...

They set off early, after a very pleasant and copious breakfast and were on the outskirts of Lucknow by 10:30 a.m. Kaamal eased back on the accelerator, leaned back in his seat and sighed.

"How long since you have been here?" Sam asked.

"A while" he said briefly.

Sam waited. He seemed to be debating with himself. Finally he said

"Lucknow lives in my heart. I will never call anywhere else home I think. It is rest; it is soul; it is home. Culture and grace are part of everyday life. 'There is no city more beautiful in her garish style than Lucknow… Kings have adorned her with fantastic buildings, endowed her with charities, crammed her with pensioners, and drenched her with blood. She is the centre of all idleness, intrigue, and luxury, and shares with Delhi the claim to talk the only pure Urdu.' I will enjoy showing her to you."

"I recognise the quote" said Sam. "It's from Kim isn't it?"

"Yes. Kipling. Another lover of the land. But now we will go to the Sikundar Bagh."

Sikundar Bagh, the garden of Alexander, or named after the Nawab's wife, depending which school of thought you belonged to, was a villa and garden surrounded by a fortified wall. The gateway was imposing and the main entrance barred but a small gate allowed admission. It was built on a traffic island, almost encircled by roads and the noise was punishing. But once you got inside, as Kaamal had said, it seemed to die away. There was no explanation for this other than the atmosphere of the place itself. There were, as Kaamal had said, few other visitors so clearly the ambience worked for some and not others. In 1857 it had been forcibly seized on the orders of Colin Campbell and was the centre for British military activity and over 2000 insurgents had been slaughtered. There had been heavy shelling, Sam knew this from Vivian's descriptions and the site had been irrevocably damaged but, Kaamal said, some historians thought that the worst of the destruction had occurred later. There were corner bastions and a rather nice pavilion in the centre of the grounds which Kaamal said had been used in its day for music and the performing arts. He led her to the fringes of the grounds where there were trees and a lot of tangled bushes, the arms of both intertwined so as to provide secret pockets of shade and privacy.

"We used to meet here. He came from his home and I came from mine. Ata loved wildlife, especially small things, and there were bugs and beetles and birds in profusion here. I underwent many unsolicited lectures on flora and fauna.

The first time we met here I was late and after hunting around for him I found him here. He was sitting on the ground with his hands cupped around a small bird. He told me it was a red whiskered bulbul and that he had found it squatting in the grass. He was just sitting there stroking its head. I think if there was a moment when I knew –when I felt –" he stopped.

"When you knew you'd fallen in love?" said Sam.

"Yes. That was the moment. I think it happened the first time I saw him but this was the moment I acknowledged it. We sat together with that small bird and just waited. I knew nothing about birds but Ata had a love of all living things and a fierce desire to heal where he could. He told me the bird was stunned but uninjured and if we were patient it would recover. I think he said more to me in those few minutes than he'd said in our entire acquaintance so far. He was painfully shy. So we waited and when it started to flutter he stretched up and put it on the highest branch he could reach. And then he turned to me and said

"Look! It's alright! It's washing!"

And it was true. It was preening its feathers without a care in the world. And he came close to me and I put my arms around him and he did the same to me and he kissed me. I remember that kiss... I remember asking him how he had learned to kiss like that and he put his finger tips on my lips and said 'from these' and then we lay down in the grass and- well from that day we were lovers; we were as one."

Kaamal sighed. "I remember thinking, if I could see through his eyes, if I could see through to the heart of everything, of everyone, I would never see spite or unkindness; I would never see death or destruction, only spirit and that is a gift indeed. Ata, my gift... I still love this place but it brings it all back to me..."

Sam said

"'Once I believed that when love came to me it would come with rockets, bells and poetry;

But with me and you, it just started quietly and grew'..."

"What's that?"

"It's a very old song... flower power era. And for years I believed the last line. Then I met Vivian and I knew I was wrong..."

"Love *was*, 'rockets, bells and poetry'?"

"Yes. For you too."

"For me too."

Kaamal laughed and took her hand and put it to his lips.

"What desperadoes it makes of us all – this love."

"Yeah."

"And it took you all that time to know?"

"Yeah" said Sam. "'You better let somebody love you before it's too late...'" she sang.

They walked on together through the trees trying to avoid getting entangled in the omnivorous, intertwined vegetation.

Sam said

"You came here often?"

"Whenever we could. No one was concerned or even interested."

"What went wrong?"

"Nothing; for eighteen months. We spent many hours each week together. We went to different places. When I passed my driving test I borrowed a car and we drove all over. We flew to Goa for his 17th birthday. In love... I look back and it seems like a dream... we talked together, shared views and dreams; we cycled to places outside the city and explored ruins- and each other...but at least once a week we would meet here. Because it was special...We had arranged to meet as usual but it was a terrible day, the rain coming down in rods. He rang me from his home to say he was alone; everyone had gone out and he did not expect them back for some hours. So I went there."

He paused. You didn't need any imagination to guess what happened.

"We went up to his room and there was the bed, a huge double bed –we'd never laid in a bed together – bushes, sand, sleeping bags, camp beds, the floor! But never a bed...I remember we looked at each other, almost as if we knew there was an inherent risk but it was intoxicating and Ata just took off his clothes and stood there and then climbed in and I was lost; we made love, deaf to the world –"

"And they found you." It wasn't a question.

"Yes. They found us."

"So you were both sent away?"

"Yes. Me first and then Ata, to relatives in London."

"Was that the last time you saw each other?"

""We never came to the Sikundar Bagh again. We were policed. I was in Delhi and his sister kept in touch with me and told me when his flight to London was booked. She was to take him to the airport and she arranged it so we could meet one last time. She said we were men not children and it was not right that we should live by the rules of others..."

He said nothing for a few moments, looking back over the years to that last time. Sam saw herself at the edge of the cantonments, watching Vivian and his troop disappear into a cloud of dust and the grey new morning, turning away just before the last glimpse, and felt his pain like a band around her heart. She reached out and took his hand and they sat down under the trees and watched the birds preening and hopping from branch to branch, with no care for the trials of humankind.

Good for them! thought Sam.

A veil of parakeets suddenly embraced the trees behind them and Sam was aware that the sun was going down. They must have been there for hours. She shivered and Kaamal put his arm about her shoulders.

"If we'd been older- if we'd had money-maybe we'd have defied them-"

His thoughts had never left the memory.

What if- thought Sam.

"Suni- his sister gave us about an hour. It was very early and we were alone. I remember we just stood together very close and watched the sun rise over the buildings; then we walked around the garden and sat on the walls; and finally we held each other one last time and kissed and then Suni came and I watched him walk away…" He gave a short, harsh laugh and added "and that was twelve years ago and I remember it, the sun through the trees, the awakening birds, the colours; every curve and hollow of his beautiful face, as if it was yesterday. I remember thinking 'the light has gone out of my life and there is darkness everywhere'"

"That is Nehru after Ghandi died" said Sam.

"Oho! So the girl knows her Indian history."

Kaamal got to his feet and pulled Sam to hers.

"Come on. Lets go. I have booked us into a nice place and when we're sorted I thought we could go into the old city and I will introduce you to food the like of which you have never experienced. And we'll visit the perfume stores and come out smelling like houris! And then I'll bring you back to the hotel and make love to you so very expertly that you will forget, just for a little while, everything. And so will I."

And he laughed at Sam's startled expression and said

"And why not? And tomorrow we will visit all the places that you put on your list and I will do my best to fill in any gaps in your knowledge and we will look at the past but remember just how much we have enjoyed the present."

What could she say?

He was right about the food. He took her to the old city, the chowk, and they dodged from street vendor to small window and bought – bought heaven on a plate, or in a parcel, or in a tray.

"You can't buy food like this in the elegant restaurants" said Kaamal with his mouth full.

Sam was taking large bites of thick, slightly sweet, flaky bread and was unable to respond for a moment. She swallowed and said

"What's this?"

"Kulcha" said Kaamal briefly and handed her a spectacularly arranged kebab as an accompaniment.

"Do you want rice and or curry?" he asked.

"Hell no! I'll burst."

"Okay then. Try this."

"What's this?"

"Andarse. It's made from rice flour and milk and freshly fried and rolled in sesame."

Sam took one of the small dumplings and put in her mouth whole.

"Oh! That is wonderful. Absolutely 'licious!"

Kaamal grinned at her.

"You're leaking bits."

Sam finished the mouthful and said

"You're the one who suggested we eat on the go. These are the consequences."

"There is no criticism I assure you. You are a delight to feed as well as to look at."

Sam looked at him carefully trying to detect any insincerity. One never knew with men just how they would react to one's eating habits. She had known some –but all she could see in Kaamal's eyes was pleasure and just a touch, maybe, of anticipation? His eyes were very bright.

"How about a drink? Lassi? Can we get lassi? And jellalabies?"

"You like lassi? That is good. We can get both just down here."

It was a wonderful evening. There were smells and light and sound; music and bells; an aroma of beauty and pleasure; Lucknow wearing its multip'licit culture and history like a temple dancer; the whole place was surrounded by old buildings and mosques and temples. It stirred the heart and the body and Sam felt alive. It got cooler and Kaamal stopped at a small shop and came out with a beautiful scarf in greens and golds which she draped around her neck and shoulders and put his arm around her, breathed in deeply of the attar of roses she had dabbed behind her ears and they strolled back to the hotel.

They went to their separate rooms and Sam didn't really know what to expect or even what she wanted to happen. But 5 minutes later Kaamal knocked on the door and came in with a bottle of red wine and a wide smile. So he hadn't forgotten his earlier declaration.

They sat on the couch amongst a huge pile of cushions and Kaamal opened the wine and poured them a glass each. Then he laid back on the cushions and stretched out his long legs in front of him and Sam looked at him and thought

Desert.

He turned to her then and saw the look and smiled again. His eyes were dancing.

Sam said crossly

"God damn it! You know you're irresistible. I don't know if I –"

He leaned over and took the glass from her hand and placed it carefully on the table next to her, putting down his own next to it and then turned back and leaned down and kissed her and Sam thought

Why not...

He pulled back momentarily and looked at her face.

"Thinking again? What this time?"

"Oh, just that I'm making love with a guy who I remind of his lost lover; his male lost lover- did I mention that?"

"It's a compliment you know" said Kaamal and kissed her again.

The plan was to visit the Alambagh first. This was where Henrietta and Gerald had begun to cement their relationship, which started on the night flight from the Residency and Sam's memory was full of her words and the sound of her quiet voice as she had described the discomfort mixed with pleasure of those weeks. Kaamal had warned her it had changed and was now famous for being a wholesale marketplace for the farmers from surrounding villages to display and sell on their produce to local retailers.

When they arrived it was a bit of a shock. To say it was densely populated, both residentially and commercially was an understatement and Sam felt her head spinning struggling to overlay the impressions given her by Henrietta sufficiently to create a hint of the past. She wasn't sure why but it seemed important for her to do so. Kaamal helped by telling her that it had originally contained a palace, a mosque, as well as other buildings and a beautiful garden but was converted into a fort in the mutiny, where General Outram and his forces were repeatedly if unsuccessfully bombarded.

Now there was still the ruins of the old gateway and remnants, surrounding all, of the wall which had originally enclosed the bagh. There was also a dilapidated two story house, very badly maintained. But Havelock's memorial, an unpretentious thirty five foot high square pillar, was still there, marking his remains, protected by a fence. The sprawling market encroached upon it all like carnivorous plant life.

"Havelock died at the Dilkhusha Khoti but his body was brought here. And there is a .plaque to his son who died far from here but whose name at least rests with his father's" said Kaamal pointing to the small tablet.

Sam looked around. The place was extensive and you could buy absolutely anything. Anything! Including food- so they did.

As they walked and Kaamal went back through the historical events Sam heard Henrietta's voice and saw the place as it had been, the many stalls becoming the stores of the baggage train that was left there when Outram and Havelock fought their way onward to the Residency. She saw the ground rutted and covered with slime and mud as the rains deluged those left there. She saw Henrietta's calm face quite clearly and Gerald, black hair plastered to his forehead, narrow face begrimed, as he sought out her tent to bring her supplies and news. But not Vivian...

"Lucknow; the city of the Nawabs; the Constantnople of India!" said Kaamal with a grin. "Maybe not so much right here."

"I like vegetables" said Sam, "and the colours are amazing."

"Moving on?" said Kaamal. "I thought we'd go to the Dilkhusha Khoti next, another beloved haunt of mine, and leave The Residency until tomorrow. Then if you like I can show you some of the other places which are- my favourites-"

He paused and Sam was aware that he'd almost said 'our'.

The Dilkhusha Khoti; beauty in ruins Kaamal had described it and that's what it was. An enormous, classically built, baroque hunting lodge, from around 1800 Kaamal said, built by a European, a friend of the Nawab. A mosaic of past and present, of green and rainbow colour. Vast and well maintained but not highly populated with visitors and part of the residency complex, it was peaceful and relaxing. There was no way to explore the interior of the ruins because all entrances were barred. But it was beautifully well kept. It must have made a wonderful summer residence.

"It has changed in the last 20 years" said Kaamal. "When I was a boy it was just barren. But I liked it even then." Desolate or peaceful, it depended upon your state of mind thought Sam, looking at Kaamal's pensive expression. The ruins themselves had majesty and magic and Sam wandered around and around, quietly enchanted. It had witnessed the horror of men killing men but had shed it like an old skin and preserved a forlorn, dignified diffidence.

"It has a smaller footprint than most Indian buildings because there is no inner courtyard" said Kaamal. "I believe it was designed the like of something in England, Northumberland? That river is the Gomti and further along is the Martinere College and the Residency. All major sites for the British defence and the insurgent's defiance as I'm sure you know."

He seemed preoccupied and Sam was suddenly certain that he and Ata had come here too. He looked across at her and laughed.

"Reading my mind? Yes we came here too. It was usually quiet and even then, even distracted as I was by Ata, its atmosphere arrested me. Do you know what Dilkhusha Khoti means?"

Sam shook her head.

"The palace of heart's delight."

Sam sighed with pleasure. If one had a home built to house things of beauty with grounds for those who lived and loved there that would be the name to choose. That would be a real fairy tale.

"We all have fairy-tales" said Kaamal watching her face. "I think we must try not to become attached to their outcomes."

Sam, who had struggled with this concept all her life, sighed and Kaamal took her hand.

"Come" he said. "There is somewhere else I wish to show you. It is not far."

They walked barely fifty metres from Dilkhusha Khoti

"This is the Villayati Bagh" Kaamal said, waving his arm expansively across an area of overgrown plants and trees with ruins among them. "It is said to have been established by King Ghazi-ud-din-Haider of Oudh for his European wife and was the most beautiful of all gardens. It suffered tremendous damage during the mutiny but now there is talk of it being restored to its former glory, both architecturally and botanically."

Sam absorbed this while Kaamal went on,

"It has two entrances; the principal on the west and the other on the east, leading to the Gomti river. That building on the north west", he pointed, "has a few cells and the usual central courtyard embellished with arched entrances. There is also a Qadam Rasul, the impression of the footprints of Mohammed, in black stone...The remains of all this were largely covered with shrubs and mould but you can see they've begun to dig it out and it will, I believe , challenge even the best of Lucknow."

Kaamal sighed.

"It must have been beautiful. Rare plants and trees; the soothing breeze from the Gomti. Now it's just a place for the graves of British officers...but maybe soon..."

"It still has, even as it is now, great natural beauty" said Sam, feeling the need to console. The peaceful grace of the trees and the high walls which must have once screened the zenana still added enough magic to allow the spirit to go back in time.

She said as much to Kaamal and added

"I guess it's long, slow work."

He looked down at her and then away across the still embedded ruins. He said

"It keeps the pleasure and the beauty of the place from the masses."

It seemed very personal to him, Sam thought. Perhaps that is how he feels about his relationship with Ata. Perhaps he feels that his neglegence has allowed the moss to grow...

Kaamal said

"I am not a very devout Muslim; I do not very often bow my head in worship; sometimes I wish I had been born Hindu. Sometimes I wish I had not chosen to study history..."

Sam looked at him with great compassion. How well she knew and understood such thoughts. She took his arm and said

"But as an Indian, of whatever creed, and an historian you are perfectly placed to know and understand your country's amazingly complex, erudite and dramatic, beautiful past which still remains as an anchor despite the 20th century's efforts to persuade us all that technological advancement, entertainment and communication is the new God. You must not forget that. Don't change."

Kaamal smiled then, rueful and then charming.

"Enough" he said, walking away from the ruined tableau. "We eat, we sleep, we rest. And tomorrow, again the sun rises. Come, let me tempt you with more Lucknow delights!"

They went to the chowk and bought food and strolled and ate. Kaamal seemed pensive. Eventually Sam said

"Did no one query where you went or how much time you spent together?"

Kaamal had obviously been thinking about the same thing because his answer was pertinent and immediate.

"I was nuts about history and Ata crazy about any living thing. We were good friends. No one thought anything of it."

"No one noticed the yearning looks you were giving each other?"

"No."

"People are blind. I'm sure I'd have noticed."

"Ata's sister did."

"Until he invited you to the house when no one was in."

"Yes. That's right." He looked at her sharply. "Are you making a point?"

Sam hesitated. What was the point? It was history. But then- so was Vivian...

"Do you think, subconsciously- I'm sure it wasn't a conscious thought- it was a risk- right? Do you think he might have wanted you both to get caught?"

"Why in the name of Allah would he want that!" Kaamal was angry.

"So you could own up to it- so you'd both be free to do as you pleased?"

Kaamal stared at her, his eyes flashing, his mouth a forbidding line. He looked, thought Sam objectively, very fierce. And then his face changed and his eyes went blank, like a cloth wiped over a whiteboard.

"And I failed him" he said quietly.

"Maybe he believed in the fairy tale?"

"And I just calculated the outcome." His voice was so flat it was unrecognisable.

"Come on" said Sam. "Let's go back to the hotel."

Kaamal was quiet all evening and they went to bed early and separately. And Sam wished fervently that she could take back her words.

The Residency was in the centre of Lucknow. The buildings and their surrounds were a huge complex. Sam knew the history of course, through reading and Vivian's account of his experiences. There was still the evidence of the conflict in the walls.

"After the war the British abandoned it" said Kaamal. "It was built in the 18th century and was quite beautiful. Since about 1920 it is being maintained as a heritage centre."

"Did you and Ata come here?" asked Sam.

"No. Too much competition." He waved a negligent arm around him and Sam could see in various corners couples indulging in not too covert activities. There were also numerous scrawlings on some of the walls.

The buildings themselves were majestic, left as they had been all those years ago and it was not difficult to take yourself back and imagine the struggles of the conflict, the despair and defeat on both sides. The gardens were vast and beautiful and their maintenance back then must have involved armies of gardeners and hours of work. Willing workers? Some, possibly. Henry Lawrence had been known for his benign and fair attitude to all. Ali and Mohammed had been devoted to Vivian. But nevertheless they were servants of a conquering race, a race in which some of them considered themselves superior in every way. How did that feel? How would she feel if someone, anyone, tried to dominate her?

The museum, on two floors, held lithographs, paintings, photographs and sketches of the time, including those of the people involved. There were also the weapons of war;

cannonballs, revolvers and swords. For Sam it was a bit too much and Kaamal, seeing her expression, cut the visit short. He said

"Sometimes it is better to put the leaves of a book between ourselves and reality, even if the reality is historic fact, no?"

The cemetery at the ruined church had the graves of 2000 men women and children including that of Sir Henry Lawrence who, his epitaph read "tried to do his duty" and another which said "do not weep my children for I am not dead but am sleeping here". Sam stood for a long time in front of this one. She was thinking of Henrietta and how blessed she must have felt, not only to have survived when so many didn't but to have met Gerald. No wonder she dispensed with her Victorian feminine misgivings. No wonder she put aside propriety of the day and asked him to accompany her to Lahore.

Kaamal was watching her. He said

"India; a land of contrasts. Even more exaggerated then than now. Paradoxes and extremes. The Himalaya, 1500 miles long and thousands of feet high and as cold as the Arctic. The Deccan plain, flat as the desert, hot as a furnace. The plain of the Ganges, fertile as a market garden. Burning sun, monsoon rain, so much rain! The people; some rich beyond belief, some still impoverished beyond acceptance; the ascetic, a lover of Gandhi; the begging hungry India. The pale skinned northerner, with his straight black hair and blue or grey or brown eyes; and the more negroid southerners with their curly hair and blunter features. And then the religions; the Muslims with their belief in one god and a paradise overflowing with milk and honey. The Hindus, with more gods than you could fit on any Greek mountain, who believe in salvation for all and life purified through reincarnation. And eons of history where Aryans made slaves of Dravadinians who went south and enslaved Aborigines. Light brown, darker brown, darker still. The source of the caste system. Saints and sinners; high priests and emperors; hit and run conquerors. The British Raj and

Independents. Ancient and modern standing side by side, even now. That's the tabloid India that you can read about. I'm still hoping to find the real India."

He stopped suddenly and looked apologetically at Sam.

"Forgive the soapbox."

Sam said

"I like that you love your country; I like that you care."

It was still early. Sam gazed up at the almost cloudless blue sky and reflected how utterly impartial and unmoved the universe was by the trials of men. Just like the birds...

"Are we going anywhere else "she said.

"To the Begum Hazrat Mahal park" said Kaamal. "It used to be the Victoria Park but the memorial was built to the Begum in 1962 to celebrate her support in the First War of Independence- the Mutiny to you."

"Is it stuffed full of history as well?"

"Not so much. It is large and although it does attract visitors and families it is quite easy to find many secluded spots."

Sam's lasting impression of the Begum Hazrat Mahal was trees, marble walkways, fountains and steps.

It had a serenity which seemed to cascade from the domed memorial and get caught up by the water in the fountains, and if you were very centred you could feel in its fine spray, a spiritual rain of absolution, falling down on you, washing out the past.

An auspicious day, there were only a few walkers. Standing back from the memorial and gazing up at it with beautiful trees framing your vision, Sam found it very easy to go back, way back, before the mutiny, when the Nawabs of Oudh held power and cherished beauty. Their signature was not especially in this place and yet as you turned about and about the whole of Lucknow reached up and proclaimed- we were once cultured and beautiful and celebrated and we still are! She was not very good when it came to going up long flights of narrow steps in tall buildings to see the view from the top but right now, to do that, and to look out over the minarets and towers and domes of Lucknow…that would answer a need.

There were lots of benches and they sat down on one.

"She took over for a while didn't she, when they shipped her husband off to Calcutta?"

"Yes that's right. Hence the memorial. It is a beautiful building is it not?"

"Yes. I love all the steps and the tall trees and the fountains. I'm guessing you and Ata came here?"

"Yes. It was very quiet in the early mornings and late evenings; even more so a decade ago. Ata liked it. Not so much history to distract me he said. For such a shy and ingenuous boy, he was very-physical."

He sounded very sad.

Sam decided.

"I think it's time to leave Lucknow. I think it's time for us to get in a car and head for Cawnpore and then the Himalaya. What do you think?"

"I think yes" said Kaamal.

"Just one last place I'd like to go before we leave" said Sam.

"Yes?"

"The Kaiserbagh Palace. Can we?"

Assuredly. The beautiful Kaiserbagh, the Begum's last stronghold and destroyed… First thing tomorrow?"

"Yes."

"Shall we go back to the hotel and plan a route then, for after Cawnpore? After food of course."

"Of course!"

Kaamal took her to a quiet family run restaurant nearby and ordered a small but adventurous range of dishes which delighted Sam and pleased the owner who was more than happy to explain what each dish comprised and how it was made. After that they strolled about for a bit and then went back to the hotel. When they'd finished the planning Kaamal at first seemed intent on going back to his room but Sam forestalled him and persuaded him to stay in hers. He was almost his usual self but she was sure that a part of him was still brooding on her comments of the day before and she was furious with herself for not recognising that understanding what had happened in your past did not change it. But maybe it could alter the future...

"I am so sorry Kaamal" she said to him.

He knew exactly what she was talking about.

"For speaking the truth? For reminding me that I had a choice and I didn't take it? For making me realise that you and Ata are braver than I? That he would have given up everything, gone anywhere, to be with me? Please don't apologise for that. I'll get over it. Apparently I am quite good at that!"

"Sometimes we just need to forget" said Sam and took his hand and led him into the bedroom. She stripped and climbed into the bed and for a moment she thought he was going to walk away and then he changed his mind and did the same and climbed in next to her.

That night, gone was the experienced, solicitous lover; that night Sam was loved by an 18 year old boy, tentative, quite shy, very affectionate. The young man who had fallen in love at 17 and was still trying to find his way... Afterwards Sam lay awake and made herself a promise. If the opportunity presented itself, if the universe gave her the chance, some way of making this right, she would take it. And when she looked back, when what was to happen, had happened, she remembered that moment...

She woke up alone to see tea on the table in the window alcove and shower noises from the bathroom. Five minutes later Kaamal came out, towel round his waist, rubbing wet hair with another.

"Awake at last!" he said, his arms above his head and the towel fell. Sam blinked. Kaamal grinned, completely unabashed. The 18 year old was back in the box.

Kaiserbagh Palace. Vivian had spoken of it. The beautiful palace that the British had ordered destroyed after the mutiny. What a pitiful, vengeful act. Did no one on planet earth ever acknowledge that vengeance never brought back the dead or peace to the living?

Sam thought, it must have been breath taking. It still was.

Kaamal said

"They demolished residential sections, courts, tombs and other important parts. Initiatives have been taken to renovate and restore and the gardens help but we will never see it in its glory..."

"A mixture of styles yes?"

"I think it may have been frowned on as a bit of a hybrid in its day; part Mughal, part European, part Persian; everything is reflected."

"Wajid Ali Shah must have had an eye for beautiful architecture" said Sam.

"Oho! You have put in the time to study haven't you?. Oh yes. Columns, minarets, laid out pathways, Persian gardens –it has it all."

He took her to the Lakhi doors, gateways, which were decorated with outstanding images of fishes and mermaids, to greet the visitors.

"Fish?" Sam queried.

"The Nawab, Saardit Ali, had a fish jump into his boat when he was out on the river and as it was considered an auspicious event he subsequently had fish incorporated into his insignia. The custom was continued. Wajid Ali Shah added the mermaids. He was I think more suited, temperamentally and idealistically to the artistic life, rather than that of administration and governance."

And there was a white stone structure, placed centrally, which Kaamal called Baradari, about which the women's quarters had been built and which had once been covered in silver.

"Baradari; it means brotherhood. Twelve doors; four sides, three on each side" said Kaamal.

"Interesting name for a structure placed near the women's quarters" said Sam.

"They were in Purdah, behind screens or curtains."

"I bet some of the young ones peeked!" said Sam. "I would."

"Of course you would!"

The northern terrace of the courtyard was the resting place for the tombs of the Nawab Saardat Ali, the man of auspicious fish fame, and his wife.

Sam took Kaamal's arm and said

"I know it's not as it was but it retains its beauty and…and its magic; its mystic charm…"

Kaamal looked down at her.

"What a little closet romantic you are."

Am I? thought Sam.

Cawnpore. Kanpur now. Kaamal had asked her if she was sure she wanted to go, before they set out, and during the hour it took to get there Sam asked herself the same question. It was not as if Vivian had dwelt on his time there but what little he had said and the circumstances of the telling were so vivid in her mind's eye she might have been watching a screen. Kaamal seemed his old self and was very attentive, telling her what she could expect and by omission, what she could not.

"The British dismantled the bibighar after the mutiny, covered in the grave-well, put a fence around it and a cross over it. The angel of the resurrection, a statue, was commissioned and placed over it. In its time it attracted more visitors than the Taj Mahal. The British also built a church, the All Souls memorial church, and after Independence the statue was moved there and another memorial placed over the site of the well. Tantia Topi." Kaamal was watching her face. "So you see it is no longer as Vivian described."

"No, I see" said Sam.

"We can see both if you like" said Kaamal.

They went to the church first. It could have been a church anywhere in England. Gothic style, with bell tower in red sandstone, quaintly attractive. Through two gateways there was a small garden, separated from the church by a beautiful gothic screen. The angel, the statue, was very understated with lowered eyes, possibly a hint of rebuke, to all who gazed upon it and held two branches of palm leaves across her chest. She was indeed a mournful seraph. Pity, sorrow, remonstrance, victory over death- who could tell?

The Nana Rao Park now took the place of the gardens Vivian had described outside the bibighar and there was a very small ridge around a wide, concreted area where had once been the well and was now peered over by the bust of Tantia Topi. It was a grass oasis in a largely commercial city. The statue looked new, the park much older. Surrounded by four marble frogs, Tantra Topi overlooked the unremarkable sandstone circle and without prior knowledge, the whole scene was commonplace.

"For almost a hundred years an iconic site of Imperial remembrance" said Kaamal. "It still attracted so many visitors I think it was considered politic to put something nationalistic in its place."

"Not one of the UK's better moments" said Sam reflectively, "pulling out the way they did, at that speed. If they had taken their time could it not have been so much better for the administration, for the princely states, for the people on the ground?"

"Many believe so" said Kaamal calmly. "I will not even pretend to understand the minds of politicians, of any race, although I suspect that at root level you would probably find money; or lack of it. The Second World War was a drain on capital. The administration of India was also a drain. Something had to go."

He looked grim. He said

"That's just my historical perception and what do I know?"

Perception and interpretation thought Sam. My perception is governed by what Vivian told me of his, and that was subject to his interpretation. The statues do not speak for themselves. Perhaps we would all have a clearer view if they did. Selectivity, manipulation and purpose all transposed what had once been fact. How long did fact survive before it was coerced and corrupted by outside agents?

"It is a pity, is it not, that the statues do not speak for themselves?" said Kaamal, echoing her thoughts.

Sam smiled at him.

"Yes. I prefer the angel. She does not look like a warrior of God. She looks like a counsellor of men. Is that my closet, romantic soul pontificating again?"

"Yes but I agree. And she is care worn with the task." said Kaamal grimly. He pointed to the trees a short way from the memorial.

"Are those bats?" said Sam.

"Bats, yes. But some believe they are the unquiet spirits of the dead. More food for your romantic soul."

He looked at her for a moment as if deciding whether or not to speak. Then he said

"I'm guessing Vivian's description was of a site of delinquency, with trees and grass festooned with blood."

Sam nodded.

"For a long time it took from him his ability to be anything more than a soldier and almost that as well. He had a friend, for whom he felt responsibility as well as love and that kept him from the edge of the pit for a while."

"Someone he loved died here?"

"More than one. They both had family killed here and blamed themselves for not being there-"

Kaamal said nothing. They walked away from Tantia Topi and his frogs, across the open grass.

"Did you hope to see him here?" Kaamal asked.

"No. Yes. Maybe-I thought he might go back to the places he'd been when-"

Kaamal said slowly

"If I'd been in 19th century India at that time and experienced what he experienced I think I would choose places to visit that reminded me of peace and the beauty of life and not its agony and destruction."

He paused, watching her face.

"I'd choose what is now Uttarakhand and Himachal Pradesh and the lakes and mountains and valleys, where the gods teach us that divinity and nature walk hand in hand."

Sam said thoughtfully

"I remember him mentioning the Terai- I'm not sure if that's where we were or adjacent to or where he took his troop-a lot on my mind you see. Is that a place?"

"It's quite a big place" said Kaamal. "Grasslands, savannah, rivers, swamps even and forests at the foot of the Himalaya. It spreads across Himachal Pradesh and Uttarakhand, amongst others, or it does now. Literally tarai, means foothill in Hindi; in Urdu the translation mentions water. There are a lot of perennial, Himalayan rivers and seasonal rivers as well and there has been much deforestation. In Vivian's time there would have been a lot more forest than there is now. There are established wildlife parks and sanctuaries now."

Sam smiled reminiscently.

"Why the smile?" Kaamal asked.

"Oh, he took me on a shooting trip, towards the end of- well anyway, I gave him a lecture on his dereliction of duty towards fauna and flora. Fauna in particular..."

"Did you still go?"

"Yes. But we only shot for the pot."

Kaamal laughed out loud. "So he knew you rough and smooth?"

"Yeah. He called me a 20th century wildcat."

"So?"

"Yes" said Sam, answering his first statement. " I would choose the places where divinity and nature walk hand in hand too."

So, as Kaamal had originally said they could, they changed the plan and set out for Uttarakhand. They headed for Haldwani.

Kaamal said the drive was not a long one and when they got there they could decide what places to visit or move on.

"Haldwani means forests of Haldu and it is literally surrounded by forests" said Kaamal. "The accommodation is all reasonably good and you'll love some of the local dishes. We can visit lakes and temples and walk or drive – anything you like. How about horse riding? Nainital is only about 25 kilometres and there is a beautiful lake there, the most amazing colour and of course we will only be about 50 kilometres from the Jim Corbett tiger reserve if you want to go back."

"I think you'd better sit me down with a map and show me where we are and where you're planning on taking me" said Sam.

"I know we talked about the Valley of the Flowers. That's north from Nainital so when we travel on we can see it then, as well as the other places we mentioned."

"I'm exhausted just thinking about it" said Sam.

Sam fell in love with Uttarakhand. She had been in love with a few places in her life; the plains of East Africa, the rolling hills and space of her chalet lodge in South Dakota, the Greek Islands; she remembered the wild sparse magnificence of Ngorongoro in Tanzania; she remembered the stark abandoned beauty of the island of Delos; the ancient mystery of Thera,, Santorini, with irs blue roofs and sapphire sea; she remembered a moon like an alien craft, so big it took up the whole sky, at Zakinthos; but she had seen nothing to compare with this...

Adjacent to Tibet and Nepal, it was indeed, as Kaamal had said, a place of myth, magic and mountains; Dev Bhumi- the Land of the Gods. Sam felt, breathing in its purified air, as if her body and mind had been renewed; as if her limbs were more mobile and her sensibilities sharper; that she was 37 years old and looked and felt 20. Maybe this magical perception was the door through which one atttained a state of grace; not god given at all but locked within awaiting the right circumstances to be set free. Finding the personal nirvana that awaits you in the space behind your little self. And Kaamal, who had travelled here before, saw it through eyes renewed and was in awe.

When she looked back on it all it seemed like a dream, some parts and places very clear, pure and unblemished like glacial water; some hazy, misty and out of focus, some just beyond recall, just as in a dream. And just as in dreamscape, the images were not sequential and afterwards she could never quite visualise the exact route they had taken. Kaamal was in the dream; more than a companion; almost an alter ego, with shared thoughts and emotions, as if the land itself opened possibilities unknown to them both, making them feel microscopic in the magnificence of creation and yet an enduring, intrinsic part. Kaamal did not talk of Ata and Sam did not speak of Vivian, but as he took her hand in his, the fingers gently caressing hers, as they went up the steps of the temples, or along a steep track up a hillside or through forests and meadows of the wildlife sanctuaries, it was as if Ata was on his other side and Vivian on hers.

She was well aware that the Buddhist doctrine said that all attachment, even personal love and devotion, even the feeling one got from the spiritual quintessence of these mountain overlords, all attachment was but illusion and bound you to the wheel of life and therefore kept you from the ultimate enlightenment. But sometimes... She gazed around her... She looked at Kaamal... She thought about Vivian and Ata... Sometimes some things seemed worth going round the circle again a few times... Sometimes when one had to choose between love and pain and benign surety, one chose love and pain...Sometimes one felt enlightenment could wait...

Har Ki Pauri ghat, the steps of Lord Shiva, in Haridwar, where Lord Shiva and Lord Vishnu were said to have visited and Vishnu was said to have dropped divine nectar /and left a footprint). A holy place near the source of the Ganges, where thousands of pilgrims visit for a variety of festivals and hold worship ceremonies and float baskets overflowing with rainbow flowers. Teeming, though they went very early, but nevertheless with a spiritual overtone which allowed the mind to wander away from the swarming humanity to the contemplation of legend.

Kaamal told Sam that bathing in the waters was considered auspicious and raised his eyebrows in question and by common consent they stepped in, fully clothed and hand in hand. Sam found it impossible to say what she felt, only to feel it, only to say it was a good feeling and she carried that mood for the rest of that day and through the night.

Nainital: known as the Lake District of India, Kaamal had insisted on taking her there. He said it would be busy, though less so than in the peak tourist season. It had some oddly horrific legends and the town itself some very distinctive colonial vestiges. There was the lake itself. One legend held, that after Sati, consort of Lord Shiva had consigned herself to sacrificial burning, (after her father had insulted her lord), Shiva danced with her body until Vishnu, (who had presumably had enough of this undignified spectacle), cut her into bits and scattered them all over the land. In the process one of her eyes had fallen out and created the lake Nain, eye. The rest of the bits created the other lakes. (Apparently the gods liked their money's worth.)

Some of the many lakes had now disappeared but it was still easy to see why the plains drained British had gravitated to Nainital in the hopes of recreating their beloved wet Lakes.

Kaamal said that the lake was thought to still demand a human sacrifice each year and apparently there were suicides and misadventures to support this. The original temple of Naini Devi was covered by the dramatic landslide of 1879 but the area was still considered a sacred place and some believed that the temple maintained its routine of prayer and ritual at the bottom of the lake, (it was very deep), with giant fish guarding the entrance and water snakes and mermen propitiating the goddess in her new underwater abode.

And then there was Tiffin Top, or Dorothy's seat, (named by the beloved husband of said Dorothy), where lovers and newlyweds had thrown themselves off and created a whole mythology around the spot.

But if one let go the melodramatic death toll, with mountains on three sides, beautiful meadows, deciduous forests and leafy lanes, the place had a spirituality all of its own.

They drove a lot, they walked a lot. They enjoyed and dodged what seemed to Sam an unpredictable array of northern British weather, the sky continually prewarning them of its intent to change and then following through with unremitting precision. You could, in the course of one day, experience mist, fog, low banked cloud, thunder, torrential rain and then a sunset fit to sacrifice to and a night sky embedded with the jewels of the Orient. They hired horses and rode along the banks of isolated lakes, Kaamal pointing out and naming mountain peaks and Sam's attention divided between the attendance of those overlords and how good he looked on the back of a horse.

Whilst Shiva and Parvarti's presence seemed to dominate, there was also much evidence of the British Raj, in the hill stations that they had left behind.

Ranikhet, in Almora was such an imprint. Lush green, forests and mountains, the exotic surroundings where legend had Queen Padmini giving her heart to King Sudhardev and chosing the area for her home and giving it its name, Queen's meadow. Pine, oak, cedar and deodar provided a lofty canopy. Sam remembered the river Kosi flowing through the valleys where they rode and Kaamal pointing out the peaks of Nandadevi and Nandaghunti. It was cool and unhurried and the legend embraced you like a warm shawl. She had bought a beautiful woollen sweater there and they had eaten some truly amazing sweets. One in particular was a favourite. It was called bal mitai and was apparently was made by cooking evaporated milk cream with cane sugar until it became dark brown, allowing it to cool and set, cutting it into cubes and plastering it with white sugar balls. Or so Kaamal said. 'Licious!

She remembered the Swarg Niwas temple with its 13 stories and multitude of shrines dedicated to a variety of Hindu gods and goddesses. Impressively dramatic with its orange yellow and white architecture, it tapered towards the top to small turrets. It was surrounded by dense forest and mountain ranges which gave it an air of Tolkein fantasy. It was a very strange experience to meet the gods and goddesses almost face to face; a kind of spiritual presentation of the uninitiated to the divine. It made Sam wish that she knew them all personally and their backgrounds and how they were interconnected. At Kaamal's insistence she had with some reluctance gone right up to the 13th floor and was rewarded with a wonderful view out over Rishikesh and Kaamal's very secure and comforting embrace. Despite the overwhelming presence of the gods, or perhaps because of it, the place was a peaceful and contemplative haven and whilst Sam forgot the many elaborate faces of the individuals, she long remembered the quality of the peace and the positive energy which seemed to emanate from every stone.

The Shri Tryambakeshwar Temple, the temple of the three eyed god, Lord Shiva, was also in Rishikesh. It was a three storied shrine ornamented with sculptures of Hindu gods and goddesses, and was arresting in both atmosphere and architecture. Sam had read that all wishes of a person coming to the shrine and paying homage to Lord Shiva would be granted and found herself wondering whether or not Kaamal was influenced by such things. As a Muslim he should not be of course. As an historian and literary enthusiast and a man of the 20th century – well maybe he adopted the view, 'there are more things in heaven and earth'...

It was another snapshot that she would hold in her memory album.

Maybe it was that the veneration of thousands of devotees over hundreds of years had seeped into its magnificent walls and eeked out onto any new seekers as they passed, helping them blend the ambience with the visual memory. Or maybe it was simply because it was one of the twelve Jyotirlingas, a radiant sign of the almighty, a pillar of light. Maybe it was that it just spoke to her in a language she could understand...

She made her wish. Later Kaamal told her he had too.

She remembered the long drive to Uttarkashi and her first wildlife sanctuary. She let Kaamal choose, there were so many, and he chose Govind Pashu Vihar National Park and Sanctuary, surrounded by the majestic, snow capped mountains of Black Peak, Bandar Punch and Swarg Rohini.

Govind Wildlife Sanctuary, criss crossed by pristine streams, surrounded by primeval forests and mountain peaks, with its protected wildlife and more than a hundred species of birds, was one of the sharpest of the dreamscapes. Standing next to Kaamal, watching an eagle whose variety she did not know, as it soared and dived, she knew he was watching it with Ata, hearing his voice, seeing his face, creating his presence, thought made manifest.

That evening, in their room, they had given up hiring two separate rooms; there seemed no point, that evening Kaamal had said quietly and very seriously, much too seriously, with a completely different note in his voice from that first time,

"We are very good together are we not?"

"Yes" said Sam hesitantly.

"It would be very easy for us to live together – it would be very natural."

"Are you suggesting an easy way of gaining respectability?" It came out harsher than she had intended.

"You think I'm that self-interested? Really!" Kaamal was angry and hurt.

Sam thought about the proposition and the companionship and comfort and enjoyment it would bring. She thought about it much more carefully than she had that first time when they were driving, when he had said he liked her a lot. It was more than that now. There was already love between them and it will grow, she thought. But I would always know where his heart lay and that would be fine until the day I saw him looking at a beautiful young man – a man with black hair and soulful brown eyes - then what would I do? It would be nice to think that that would be OK too but I don't think I'm that evolved. And it hadn't worked with Steve, who had been her best friend and companion for years and with whom she had shared almost everything that was possible for a man and woman to share. It hadn't stopped her walking out. And it hadn't worked with Luc either and it should have; Oh yes by rights it should have... She turned back to Kaamal who was still scowling at her.

"I'm clearly worth consideration!" he said, his voice cold and brittle and challenging. He undoubtedly cared a lot.

"I think you have spent most of today thinking about Ata. I think you visualised him there with you at the wildlife sanctuary, watching the birds, and I think you thought that if you couldn't have Ata you could have a happy existence with me. I am flattered but I have actually been in this position before and in the end it didn't work out. Even then I knew there was someone out there... Someone that I 'loved with a love that was greater than love'; greater than the sum of its parts... And right at this moment it would be a mistake. I just know" she added when he was going to argue and he shrugged his shoulders in an imitation of the charming, arrogant man he showed the world and said

"Edgar Allan Poe!" He blinked rather rapidly and bit his bottom lip and then went on "Then we will continue as we are" and his smile, Sam reflected, was enough to melt stone. He said

"'Whoso loves believes in the impossible'."

"I know that quote. Elizabeth Barrett Browning?"

Kaamal smiled. The tension eased. He said

"We should both remember that."

He made to get up, thought better of it and turned to her again.

"Did you ever have a past life regression in India before? Before Vivian I mean. Surely something must have driven you to return?"

Sam was startled. The question was unexpected and she didn't respond immediately. The wide, gray eyes were studying her. She looked away. It wasn't the first time she had seen eyes like those; compassionate, troubled eyes...Siva...it seemed so very long ago, almost beyond recall now. And she didn't want to remember; the memory was dim but the pain was sharp.

So she said simply

"Yes I did.".

Kaamal was watching her.

"Did you meet anyone?"

She looked up at him then.

"Yes I did. Two people of whom I became very fond. They died..."

Kaamal looked at her for a few minutes more and then got up and went into the kitchen and began making tea.

It was after all this that Sam made her decision. If the opportunity presented itself she would find a way of contacting Ata. Vivian? Well Vivian might be lost to her. But Ata? He was very real and just a hop-on-a-plane away.

After a very pleasurable night, Kaamal even more solicitous than usual, which did nothing to convince her that her decision was the right one, with perfect timing, the opportunity did present itself, as opportunities do, if they are meant to.

The next morning, while Kaamal was writing reports and Sam was reading a book Kaamal had bought her on Hindu gods and goddesses, their origins and traditions, there was a tap on the door and the polite young man from the reception desk confronted Kaamal with a small speech in a dialect Sam did not recognise until he ended it with "very urgent; truly!"

Kaamal sighed. Sam raised her eyebrows.

"Problem?"

"No, not really. My tour company have just rung to speak to me. Apparently they are ringing back in 10. Why in God's name didn't-" he wenr to his briefcase as he spoke and looked into it accusingly.

"You forgot to send our itinerary ."

"Yeah. A subconscious neglect I think."

Sam smiled at him, her heart quickened. Kaamal said

"I'll have to go. They probably think I've abducted you! Dammit, I've been sending updates." He waved a hand at the new laptop computer open on the desk where he had been working. The tour company had acquired it for him, to make the paperwork easier they said. Kaamal was very disparaging about it. "I'll print off some of this stuff and fax it to them. It'll take me a half hour or so, if I'm lucky."

They were lodged in one of the separate chalets away from the main buildings and it was a five minute walk to reception. Sam thought quickly.

"When you've finished with them, go down to that small stall that sells those squidgy honey cake things, whose name completely escapes me and bring some back- please?"

"Your wish etc, etc- I guess the time will depend upon the length and detail of the interrogation. See what you do to me!" He flashed a dazzling smile and was gone. Sam thought, was he doing it deliberately? To make her regret what she'd turned down?

She waited until she heard his footfall on the veranda steps, stood up and took a deep breath.

The screen was still on the page where he had left it. Was he a man to create address files with phone and fax numbers? Probably.

She typed Ata into the search box and his details appeared. Well if this wasn't the hand of the universe –

There were two addresses and two fax numbers, one personal, one for the main hospital. She made a note of both. And his second name.

What was she going to say?

She closed her eyes.

Then, without thinking she typed:

I will be in Himachal Pradesh in 10 days' time. Can you meet me there?

Fly to Chandigarh. I'll meet you at the airport

With love

Kaamal

Was it too brief?

Was it too didactic?

Was it right to put love?

Was it right to send it at all?

Her finger on the mouse over the print button, she paused and then stopped. She couldn't have him reply, there was no fixed address. What about a phone number? But where? What about having him reply on the lodge's fax number? If he got it before they moved on. She typed, reply to this fax number, checked it twice out of anxiety and then hit the print button and leaned back. Done. For better or worse. Then she took the printed sheet from the printer, folded it carefully, put it in her back pack and returned the screen to the one Kaamal had left.

She sat on the sofa and picked up her book. Hell! Is this what criminals felt like? How did they ever get beyond the guilt?

Fifteen minutes later she heard his footsteps and then thirty seconds and the door banged open and Kaamal walked in. He dropped a couple of packages on the table and flung himself down beside her.

"They want you to ring them! Can you believe it? How long have they known me? Seriously!"

He turned to her and raised his eyebrows. Did she look guilty? But he just said

"Do you mind? It's ridiculous but-"

"I don't mind. I'll do it now. Don't eat all the squidgy things."

She went down to the office and sent the fax first, telling the reception clerk she might get a reply and if she did would he keep it for her. Just for her. He made a smiling promise and then she made the required phone call to the tour company, extolling Kaamal's virtues and confirming what a good time she was having.

For the rest of the day they investigated Uttarkashi, also known as the town of temples, Kaamal said and a major pilgrimage centre. He reeled off a list of them all but the only ones whose names remained with Sam were the Shani Dev and the Annapurna, because of the beautiful eloquence of their names and of course Kali.

With so many temples, so much emphasis on religion it should have been overpowering or oppressive and yet it was not. Quite the reverse. It was almost as if the temples and the surroundings combined in an act of purification akin to an out of body experience. Sam floated next to Kaamal, her anxieties over her earlier actions transmuted by a sense of wellbeing which she had not experienced to any degree since Vivian had gone from her life. Kaamal was quiet, companionable and seemed at peace.

They ate out at a delightful restaurant where the menu was in Hindi and Kaamal had to translate and explain each dish and then meandered back to their chalet. They went to the reception to collect their keys and the young man gave Sam a very conspiratorial smile and as Kaamal turned away slid an envelope across the desk.

"What was the cute look for?" Kaamal asked as they walked away.

"Oh I just gave him a bit of sisterly advice earlier" said Sam, marvelling at how easily the lie came to her lips.

So far so good. She hoped it was an auspicious sign and not an indication of burgeoning criminal tendencies.

Kaamal made them coffee and Sam sat on her sofa with hers and Kaamal came and sat on a heap of cushions at her feet and they watched the moon rise and cast her light like a spiritual veil over the surrounding hills and mountains.

And suddenly and without warning Sam was overwhelmed with a sense of loss. All the earlier composure vanished. Sitting there, Kaamal's head resting against her knees, her fingers playing with the shiny black strands of his hair, she suddenly felt as if she had given up her very last chance of any kind of happiness. Vivian seemed a world away, literary a world and she felt utterly devoid of hope and ridiculously sorry for herself. Kevin would say she was being self indulgent. She could hear him saying it. She could *see* him saying it!

"You can only do what each individual can do; choose the contents of your own mind, govern your own thoughts. Every thought comes back at you like a boomerang. So work at making thoughts good; honest, questioning attitudes, and good feelings. If you do that you will radiate good outwards and draw good to you. And you will be changing the only thing that you have the power to change, controlling the only thing you have the right to control and you will be changing *your* world."

I know Kevin! *I know.* But it's not working. And does my world include Vivian?

By the time Kaamal realised that her fingers were no longer playing with his hair, tears were coursing down her cheeks like an early monsoon rain.

He looked at her in astonishment.

"What is this? What has happened?"

Sam shook her head.

He studied her for some moments and then took her hand and pulled her down on to the cushions beside him.

She closed her eyes and made an effort to stop the tears but failed so she opened them again. And Kaamal looked straight into them.

"I can't bear this" he murmured and bent his head and gently kissed each of her eyes in turn and said quietly

"It has been a very long time since I cared enough about someone to stop their tears with kisses."

She gazed at him and he said in Urdu

"My dear Samanthar how you do knot my heart strings."

And she remembered Vivian's words of love in the same fluid tongue.

He held her close. Thus confined it was difficult to cry and the tears dried. He looked down at her and said

"'Tears at times have the weight of speech'."

Sam rubbed her nose and said

"Who?"

"Ovid if I remember rightly."

"You are very well read."

"I've had a long time to become well read."

Sam gazed at him, her own tragedy forgotten temporarily.

"Are they finished then? Shall we try this, just to be sure?"

The kiss was slow, intense yet tender and he took a long time over it. Afterwards she stayed in his arms with his cheek resting on the top of her head, her knees pulled up and resting against him. If you were going to fall in love again this would be the moment to do it.

They must have stayed like that for an hour or more and when they finally went to bed Kaamal did not make love to her. She didn't ask why. She didn't need to.

In the middle of the night she went to the bathroom and read the return fax. It was even briefer than hers.

I'll be there. On the 26th. The 2pm connecting out of Delhi to Chandigarh.

All my love

Ata

Sam thought with amusement, exactly 10 days from the date of her fax. A man of action and few words. I can live with that. Well, she had her confirmation.

The next morning they drove to Govindghat with a view to staying a day and then moving on to Ghangaria to start the trek to the Valley of Flowers. They did not discuss the events of the evening before. Sam had awoken with a greater sense of equanimity then she would have believed possible and had decided to let the universe make the choices. One way or another she would know...

Govindghat was nestled on the banks of the river Alaknanda and surrounded by alpine hills covered in mist. Trekkers and devotees, Kaamal said, of nature and spiritual peace were frequent visitors. A starting point for Hemkund Sahib, the lake and sacred destination for Hindus and Sikhs, as well as the Valley of Flowers.

"It's surrounded by seven wonderous snow capped mountains and it is idyllic" he said of Hemkund Sahib. "The trek is about 15 kilometres and is pretty strenuous. What do you think?"

"Have you ever been?"

"Yes. Once. I came up here about six months after I said goodbye to Ata."

"And?"

"It was a bit punishing. The weather changed quite dramatically while I was there and I think I got a bit of altitude sickness, because of the height. Anyway being there was cathartic; getting there was uncomfortable."

"Altitude sickness! Will I get it?"

"Who knows. Quite a large percentage do."

"It's pretty non-discriminatory isn't it?"

"Oh yes. The young and fit suffer when the older and not so fit do not. It can be very humiliating to be vomiting by the side of the path while a smiling granny ambles past unconcerned."

"A salutary experience."

"Oh yes, very. I was suitably humbled." He paused, remembering. Then he added

"I seem to remember I cried a lot as well. I think that was the altitude sickness also -maybe-"

"You would risk going again for me?"

"Of course!"

Sam, who abhorred even nausea, thought this beyond the call of duty.

"What if we both get sick?"

"That would be- interesting."

"Did you make it all the way?"

"Oh yes."

"Did the nausea get any better?"

"Not appreciably."

Sam looked at him thoughtfully. She said

"Only six months after saying goodbye to Ata. You must have been hoping for some kind of solace."

"Yes." He smiled wryly. "I did not find it there. But the tears brought some release. And there is nothing like nausea to take one's mind off one;s troubles."

No wonder he had not scorned her search. No wonder he understood. He was looking at her consideringly. Sam said hastily

"Ok. Decision made. Let's go to The Valley of the Flowers."

Kaamal was still looking at her but all the laughter had gone from his eyes. He said

"You have brought Ata back to me. I had never spoken of him to anyone until you. I have returned to our time together through you. What will I do when you leave?"

At that moment Sam wanted to tell him what she'd done. He was breaking her heart. But it was too soon; too many what-ifs...

Instead she said quietly

"You will have Ata" and as she had hoped, he took it as a consoling reference to his renewed memories.

They hired mules and rode to Ghangaria, to a pleasant comfortable lodge as a base for the trek to The Valley of Flowers.

What she remembered most looking back was the extraordinary setting. The frame of huge, snow capped mountains seemingly at the head of the river valley, the unexpected, more pink than blue, colour of the water and the yellow and white carpet of flowers. Yes there were flowers, so many flowers, some she recognised, many she didn't, of every kind and hue, but it was the yellow, as always, which impressed itself on her memory. Yes the flowers would have been more profuse during and after the monsoon but it was still ridiculously beautiful and the more so to Sam without the rain.

There were waterfalls, green meadows and white clouds; a dream landscape, pristine and mystnical, it reminded Sam of the movies of Miyazaki whose enchanting landscapes and stories had influenced her when she was younger; it reminded her of the travels with Kevin and the wild bunch when she had been Jennie and had gone looking for citadels and knights.

Kaamal was very quiet for most of the time. He held her hand as they crossed the streams and climbed the slopes, he smiled a lot and Sam knew he was only seeing one knight.

And Sam sifted through her own stored memories and picked out individual ones and embraced them, seeing and hearing Vivian in the small snapshots and interacting with him. Maybe, she reasoned, maybe if I can materialise him so clearly in my mind I can actualise him into my life and past memories will create a current reality…

And if she had any doubts about her interference in Kaamal's life, they were assuaged if not obliterated. Only a successful outcome would do that now. And that was in the lap of the gods, with the added help of British Airways.

When they got back to the lodge Kaamal went to take a shower and while he was in the bathroom Sam planned her next move.

When Kaamal came out of the bathroom she told him she had someone to meet at Chandigarh airport in about 10 days' time. He made little of it, just asked

"Anyone special?"

And she had replied

"No. No one special" and had nearly choked on the lie.

He told her they would be driving to Shoghi, near Shimla in Himachal Pradesh and would have time to visit some of the attractive hill stations before her friend was due to land at Chandigarh. He seemed about to ask her more searching questions but then changed his mind and , running a hand through his wet hair, asked instead if she had enjoyed their sojourn in Uttarakhand.

Sam smiled at him radiantly.

"What do you think?"

He smiled back.

"Me too." He looked away from her, out of the large window to the hills and mountains beyond, his eyes becoming lost and unfocused. He said, almost to himself

"A land of magic. A land of myth and mountains. Indeed, the land of the gods."

And then he looked back down at her and said

"And chilly. I had better find clothes." And walked away to do that leaving Sam watching him with her own thoughts.

Shoghi with its fresh mountain air and its spectacular views of the Himalaya and its open air dining, was a delight. Their accommodation, set in forest surroundings on a ridge, with panoramic views, seemed a setting for honeymooners Sam thought wryly but held her thoughts. One could only hope. Kaamal said it was a business retreat as well. Really?

Quieter, more peaceful than Shimla, it was also nearer to Tara Devi and the temple. It was their first excursion in Himachal Ptadesh and for Sam the experience left a lasting impression. Maybe it was the setting, surrounded by fragrant pine forests and lush meadows and with views to the mountains one way and to the plains the other. The air was sparkling, as if the gaze of the goddess cast a discernible spell over all she could see. Its history, which Kaamal provided, told the legend of the locket belonging to the Raja of the Sen dynasty, which contained an idol of the goddess, who apparently spoke to him in a dream and expressed her wish to be revealed before the people and then have a shrine established on the hill top. This he did and then later generations replaced the wooden effigy with one created from eight rare metals. The serenity of the shrine seemed to cascade from the walls, tumbling down the hillsides into the forests. It was all of this and more. Sam could not explain to herself let alone Kaamal but she knew Vivian had been there, had breathed the same air, had watched the same sunlit strands bringing to life far snow capped mountain peaks and near blades of grass; had listened to the wind which rang with a frequency only the heart could hear. She didn't know if he'd been there in the last month or a century before, but she knew.

And when Kaamal turned to her and said

The Goddess of Stars speaks, no?",

she knew he felt it too.

She remembered the garlanded offering that Vivian had made at the shrine near the ruined hunting lodge and wondered if he'd done the same here. She wondered about the many nationalities and creeds that must have visited this place, stood where she was standing now. She wondered if peace and serenity felt the same in all languages, in all religions. She thought it must.

She asked Kaamal about all the boundaries and frontiers that had arisen since 1947. How did the ordinary people feel?

"Like anything else; some hate it, some prefer it; most live with it as best they can" he said.

"Surely lines only accentuate division?" said Sam.

"I think some would prefer no lines" Kaamal said carefully.

"And some must have history with the English?"

"Oh yes, myself included, if you go far enough back, as I told you."

"Ah yes" said Sam remembering. "And Ata?"

"His grandmother, his father's mother, was very convinced there was a northern prince in her ancestry amongst others."

"And what did you think?"

"I thought his grandmother was very beautiful. She was light skinned and unusually slender. Ata had, has her eyes. "

He looked down at Sam and smiled his irresistible smile.

"So maybe he has European blood too."

Now it appeared that Ata would be coming, although she had no way of having any further communication from him, Sam considered whether or not she should change their behavioural practices. In the end she allowed things to continue as they had for the past weeks. To suddenly announce a reluctance to share a bed with Kaamal or to try and avoid close physical contact was not only going to invite unwelcome interrogation but it was also something she really, really did not want to do.

For the next week they visited a captivating and intriguing range of hill stations, embroidered by rivers, gem studded with lakes and embraced by mountains.

With the Punjab on its west and Kashmir to the north it seemed more than likely that Vivian had been here in the past, certainly on his way to Kashmir. With interlocking mountain ranges, every pass crossed into a new valley with its own culture and deities and people, as Kaamal had described. Villages on slopes with fairy-tale architecture, hill forts, temples, monasteries and glacial lakes, snow topped peaks and river valleys, it seemed like an illustration from Tolkein's imaginary world of The Lord of the Rings.

They went to Chail; Kasauli; the beautiful lake Renuka, regarded as the embodiment of the goddess Renuka and shaped like a reclining woman, and Naldehra.

Chail; small, so small; small is beautiful; if only words could convey the meaning of beauty… It covered three hilltops, with deodar and pine and lush green meadow. The Maharaja of Patiala had an eye for beauty. He had built his summer palace there after being ejected from Shimla, apparently, it was said, owing to some 'ignoble behaviour' of the Prince towards the Commander in Chief's daughter. Disappointingly, Kaamal did not know any details but there had been anger on both sides. The palace, built in 75 acres of forest and lawns, orchards and quaint log cottages, had a fabulous view over Shimla especially at night. So there! thought Sam. Did 'ignoble' mean just bad mannered or something more exciting? It could mean shameful, immoral or despicable, and more. Wouldn't it be wonderful to ask the Commander's daughter how she'd interpreted it.

It was now a heritage hotel but at least you could experience a bit of the Maharaja's creation.

And then there was Kali ka Tibba, the temple to the goddess Kali, with a bit of a sticky climb rewarded by spectacular views of the mountains and a 360 degree platform for sunrises and sunsets. They opted for easy and walked the rounding roads and paths but not visiting the cricket ground. Or the golf course. Sam said she was more interested in polo but declined to see the polo ground. She had a clear mental image of Vivian on the back of a polo pony at a match that she was reluctant to pursue.

She found herself wondering if she was going about it all the wrong way. Maybe by seeking, with an intense, frontal focus, she was only seeing what related to the search. Maybe the seeking was in some way impeding the finding. Maybe her obsession with the search was preventing her absorbing many things that were just as important. And beyond all else, beyond her obsessive goal she wanted the journey, the exploration, to change her; she wanted to metamorphose. Nothing was permanent; she only needed to look about to see that. And in order to be part of it you have to embrace the elemental change.

She glanced at Kaamal. He wanted it too. He wanted to be part of something that allowed him to rise above whatever life threw at him, whatever life took from him. She knew, without asking him, that this was a shared understanding and whatever happened it was a permanent bridge between them. They could cross it, one going to the other's side, or meet on it and always be able to share. If nothing else came from this pilgrimage, she would always have that...

Kasauli, created when Lord Hanuman placed his feet on a hill there; quiet and unfound, they walked, accompanied only by the voices of the birds and the leaves.

Naldehra; another little paradise; another golf course. Lord Curzon this time. The place was picturesque, a delight. But it was the apples that captured Sam's heart; so many different kinds of apples, just hanging there, fragrant and shining with a savoury untouched sweetness. Sam, a lover of American red delicious, had never tasted anything like them before. With the meandering peaceful lanes, the tall magnificence of the deodor trees, capped with light mist, the many and varied lush green carpets and the outstanding views of the Himalaya, somehow reality stepped aside, or at the very least moved behind a closed door. They ate a curd based curry which Kaamal called kadhi chawal, and then they went back to the chalet they'd rented for the night, with calm hearts and a bottle of wine.

Sitting side by side, in companionable peace Sam turned to Kaamal and asked

"I understand why you did what you did, especially in the early years, but why, when you had established yourself, when you had your own career and your own interests, why didn't you ask him to come and visit?"

Kaamal looked at her in surprise.

"Well I know you were thinking about him; you think about him a lot" said Sam.

Kaamal frowned.

"You mean why didn't I invite him over for a dirty weekend?"

"There's no need to put it like that. But yes, fundamentally. Was it so much of a risk? Did you really doubt his feelings for you, or maybe yours for him?"

Kaamal sighed.

"Things change. People change. I suppose I must have known on some level, although I've only just admitted it to myself, thanks to you, that I had screwed up and I didn't want to get him over here and screw up again. It was easier, it was safer, to leave things as they were. I was not unhappy; he was not unhappy."

"How do you know that? He wouldn't write it in a letter and you couldn't see his eyes."

Kaamal looked miserable. He said

"I am a coward."

Sam said thoughtfully

"When I was younger I read a lot of Herman Hesse. I loved the way his mind worked and how he presented it and his thoughts. If I remember rightly I think Steppenwolf was my favourite but Siddhartha held a special place in my heart. At the end of the book when he's talking to his old best friend, who is desperate to get some atoms of wisdom from him, he tells him that knowledge can be learned and passed on but not wisdom. Wisdom can only be experienced. He tries to explain that there are no divisions, no rights and wrongs, no saints and sinners, just circles. That we are all part of everything and everything is part of us. We only see divisions because we believe time is real. But he says time is not real, only an illusion and if time is not real then the dividing lines that we perceive, between this world and eternity, between happiness and suffering, between good and evil, they are all illusions as well. And I want to believe that, because if there are no dividing lines and time is an illusion, I, we..." she stopped.

Kaamal was watching her. Then he leaned back on the cushions and pulled her against him. He said quietly

"Then in common parlance it's never too late, because there is no never and there is no late. I have not read Herman Hesse. What did he believe was the most important?"

"I think he believed that was love" said Sam.

The next morning they hired horses and trekked through the forests. God but the man looked good on a horse! Kaamal caught her eye and grinned. He said

"Your thoughts fan across your face like the wind through a beautiful field of corn."

And Sam scowled at him and kicked her horse into a gallop that left him laughing behind her.

They rode to Chabba, to the Mahakali Lake with its temple of the same name where they tethered the horses and walked round the lake. Sam knew that there was white water rafting available at Chabba. Kaamal didn't even ask, just took her hand and walked with her. They didn't talk much. Words seemed to have become obsolete. Then they rode back to Naldehra, returned the horses and went back to the chalet to change and watch the sunset before going out for dinner. Like two lovers thought Sam.

Kaamal had wanted to take her to the Moon lake.

" Not so high as Hemkund Sahib. But still high, and cold. It will take us a day to get there but the drive is beautiful, empty, just fields of yellow flowers, some sheep and tricksy rivers after Kaza and then a stopover in tents at the lake, then a hike around it and then back again."

"Did you get sick?"

"No. I paced myself better and the lake," he paused, looking away from her as if he was seeing the lake, as if the memory had taken him right back to the shoreline,

"the lake, the lake was turquoise and still, like a goblet of nectar; I don't remember the hike up to it; it was as if it captured my mind and my heart and I was only aware of it and not my body; the clouds moved across the mountain peaks and the water changed colour with the shadows; I hadn't planned to do the circumference but something drove me; there were piles of stones along the way, Ovoos they are called and you place your chosen stone on top as you pass; the walking was effortless, like I was absorbing and not using energy…It is supposed to be the place where Indra Dev's chariot picked up Yuddhistra when he was on his way to heaven; I remember thinking – but this is heaven! There is also a fairy-tale legend about a shepherd who met the love of his life at the lake and foolishly lost her… I stayed the night in one of the tents and I looked out in the middle of the night and it was as if the galaxy had fallen and you could reach out a hand and touch the stars…"

He stopped and looked back at Sam and smiled.

"I am sorry, I got carried away. It's just that it stays with me as some things are meant to I suppose."

"You do know that it's the passion of the dialogue and not the subject matter that certifies the listening don't you? And you describe the scene and I walk beside you."

She had been watching his face as he had spoken. That was the place where he and Ata should go. Legends and dreams and otherworld energy and heart stopping beauty. That was the place. She said

"In England we call them cairns and I think the Moon Lake would be the place to go when-after my friend comes."

"Friend? Oh the one arriving at the airport in a week? OK, sure. Will I like him or her?"

Sam swallowed.

"Yes. Without a doubt."

This was getting difficult.

"Is it male or female?"

Tricky.

"Just wait and see."

"Are you plotting?" Kaamal looked and sounded suspicious.

"Who, me?"

"You're not trying to fix me up are you?"

"Don't be ridiculous!"

I vow, thought Sam, I vow never to get myself into this situation ever again.

After one last considering look Kaamal let it drop. Sam went over to him and took his hand.

"Let's go eat" and smiled at him persuasively.

He looked down at her for a moment and then bent his head and kissed her. It was a very nice kiss but she was sure his thoughts were elsewhere.

They visited the Habban Valley, another paradise. Sam felt intellectually challenged. There were not enough words in the English language to describe these places or her feelings for them, in their presence.

Kaamal said

"Just breathe in the wonder of the air and the sky, see how the peaks reach up to touch the heavens, smell the pines and the deodars, as if you were meditating on a higher plain and think in Urdu."

He spoke in Urdu.

So she did.

And what remained was the stillness and silence of the dawn of time.

Though the valley was not far from Shimla Kaamal had said it was worth a stopover and had booked a forest log hut.

And there were apple and peach orchards again and aside from the amazing bird life there were peacocks.

Kaamal was deeply affected. He had not visited before despite or because of its nearness to Shimla.

He said

"It's like everything that has gone before and everything in the present moment have met in harmony and made the future irrelevant."

"What if all our yesterdays came suddenly into view, our future, past and present as one composite hue…" murmured Sam.

"Just so" said Kaamal in English.

Sam sighed. If you could bottle it…

The morning they left they got up and hiked to the top of the nearest incline and watched the dawn paint the peaks with crimson which turned to a circlet of gold as if the sun had wedded the mountain.

Sam thought, some say god's paradise is a garden; I think it's up there, in the heights… where only he sees the snow fall.

Kaamal said

"God's home, no? The top of the wprld."

From there they went to Rajgarh known as peach valley and once ruled by Maharajas.

They hiked to Shiya village to see the stone and wood temple of Lord Shirgul there, who, according to legend, had visited the village and then settled in Churdhar mountain and which, Kaamal said, had an enormous following.

Then Kaamal proposed they went further to Nahan before returning to Shoghi.

Nahan in the Shiwalik mountain range and overlooking lush green meadows, was picturesque and very clean, as if the roads and walks were regularly swept. Princes and saints were linked with its origin, Kaamal said, depending on which legend you espoused. In the saint version he was supposed to live with a companionable nahar, which means lion and probably gave the town its name. In another version, the prince was going to kill a lion and a saint exclaimed "Nahar!", meaning, "don't kill!" and the town's name came from that. Either way it involved lions. Sam liked the companionable lion version best. There was a manmade lake called a tank, (did they really know what kind of mental image was conjured up by the word 'tank' to the average English or American, Sam wondered) and a surfeit of gardens and temples.

Everywhere in Himachal Pradesh the bazaar vendors, the authentic cafes and the restaurants poured their heart and soul into the dishes they served. The Pahari revelled in spices, ghee , buttermilk and yogurt and it was foodie heaven so long as you weren't on the fat free wagon.

Bhey, spicy lotus stems, thinly sliced and cooked in ginger, garlic, onions and flour; bahru, a crisp and scrumptious flatbread; sadu, another bread kneaded, pan fried and steamed; khatta, made with pumpkin, special gravy, raw mango powder and spices; chha gosht, marinaded lamb, yogurt and spices; patande, indian breakfast pancakes; and dhalls of course and rices and grains of every kind made in to breads and cake, and of course fruit.

The walks were pleasant and amazingly flat, evocative of its colonial past, and the evenings were soft and romantic. Walking and mixing with friends and relatives along the roads and in the bazaar in the evenings was obviously a main pastime for the young and old alike in Nahan and Sam and Kaamal just fitted in. The Ranital Lake and gardens in the middle of the town evoked the era of the rulers of this once princely state and Sam allowed her imagination to run through all the stories and histories she had ever read about the princely states and their rulers and their dynasties and their struggles and romantic escapades.

She said to Kaamal

"I read a lot of historical romances when I was young. The ones based in India, in the 19th century were always my favourites. Later I read histories. I remember thinking the princes spent a lot of time in conflict with each other."

"Yes" said Kaamal, "Indian history is somewhat violent. Right back to Alexander."

Sam nodded. " I read this one series and just fell in love with main character in the first book. He was tall, with black hair and grey eyes," she grinned at him, "and also several of the minor charaters. There was a couple of gay boys in the 2nd in the series. In the 3rd book one of the main characters was a southern prince, gay and gorgeous and very young; trying to be brave and a better man than his father. He saves several members of the northern ruling family, with whom his father had been in conflict. But hey, we get to book 4 and the families are still at loggerheads with each other- the young southerner has a tenuous claim to their throne. I find out in the 5th book that another main character, half English, half Indian, who I never liked, has taken the northern army into battle against the southern and defeated them. Ok it happens. But he *kills* the prince. I was appalled. I didn't like the English one anyway."

"You get very involved" said Kaamal. "Was there another book after that one?"

"Fortunately yes. And the new northern maharaja, the great-grandson of my original favourite from book one, is the main player and very cute."

Kaamal laughed. "But not gay?"

"Sadly no."

Kaamal said lazily

"I am flattered, I think."

The Pakka lake, Sam refused to call it a tank, had a beautiful fountain and there were a number of park benches and she and Kaamal bought food to go and sat side by side and watched the ducks and cranes and Sam thought, how very English.

How she was going to miss this. Kaamal was leaning forward watching a pair of very elegant cranes as they bent their necks into the reeds at the side of the lake. She looked at his strong profile, the determined lines of his chin and jaw, the beautifully shaped mouth and the luxuriant black eyelashes- straight out of that damn book- my god – he had a double row, top and bottom! He suddenly turned and caught her studying him.

"What are you looking at with such concentration?"

"Your eyelashes! You have a double set of eyelashes!"

"I have the body of an Adonis, or an Indian prince, and you look at my eye lashes?" Kaamal said lightly.

"Do they stick together when you close your eyes?"

"Only if I've applied too much mascara the night before" said Kaamal with a completely straight face. "Your eyelashes are long too and very beautiful."

"Yes, but they're brown not black and I have to paint them, as you well know, and they're not double!"

Kaamal sighed theatrically.

"What can I say? I am beauty incarnate."

Sam threw the remains of her chapatti at him which he deftly caught and tossed into the lake for the ducks.

"That was very juvenile" he remonstrated.

"I know" said Sam, "but it made me feel better and alleviated the consuming urge I have to slap you, in public."

Kaamal laughed at her and took her hand and kissed the palm.

"Don't go" he said and his smile was teasing but not his eyes.

Sam held his gaze. For several minutes they just looked at each other and then Sam said

"You do know what happened to Adonis don't you?"

"For being the beloved of a goddess? Alas, only too well" Kaamal said soberly. "Are you my Aphrodite then?"

"No" said Sam. "But I do a really good line in ruined relationships."

On the way back Kaamal stepped into a small shop in the bazaar whose surrounds were draped in beautiful scarves and came out again with a parcel. When they reached their lodge he handed it to her and she opened it carefully. Inside was a shawl, deep colours of blue and green, lightly fringed, fine and soft and warm to the touch. Sam gasped. Then she handed it back to him and rushed into her room. She opened the wardrobe and took out the green robes she had worn on her wedding night, stripped swiftly and dropped them over her head and went back into the room where Kaamal still stood holding the shawl. She smiled at him and reached out and then she saw his face.

He was staring at her as if he'd seen a ghost.

"Ya Ali" he whispered. "A Pahareen."

Sam whirled on him.

"You didn't fucking believe me!" she spat, instantly shattering any hint of 19th century femininity.

Kaamal stared at her in astonishment.

"What did you think? That I was just a poor deluded aging single woman, with a predilection for fantasy? And a very active imagination! Did you humour me as a challenge to see if you could get me to sleep with you and exorcize some of your own masculine eccentricities?"

Kaamal blinked several times; then he became very calm and very angry.

"Yes I did" he said quietly.

"Did what?"

"I did believe you. Completely."

"Really!"

"I believe in God. That doesn't mean to say that if he popped up in front of me next to a burning bloody bush I wouldn't be shocked!"

Sam's fury fizzled out. She had the grace to look ashamed. She said softly

"There's a lot of mixed references in what you've just said."

"Yes. Well. Like I've said, I've read a lot!"

Sam said appeasingly

"I picked a fight with Vivian the day before he married me."

"Of course you did!"

They looked at each other and then smiled.

"I would have liked to buy you earings but-"

Sam nodded.

OK?" said Kaamal.

"Yes."

"Believe me?"

"Yes. Sorry."

"How come you still have the robes?" said Kaamal.

"I had them on when I-when I came back into the present" said Sam, remembering her surprise when she'd finally opened her eyes and found she was wearing kashmir robes and not denim jeans. "I had meant to change but clearly I didn't."

She paused, the images so sharp.

"I had a shawl just like this one. But it got left behind-"

"Along with the jeans?" said Kaamal.

"Yeah."

He was still gazing at her but the expression in his eyes had changed. The challenge had gone; and the anger. Now they spoke of longing and something else. He said

"He must have loved you so much. Beyond life-"

Sam looked at him sharply but his eyes had become unfocussed.

She said

"All I ever wanted was to find the other bits of me. The other pieces of the jigsaw. I saw them as a friend, an alter ego, a soul mate, a partner. I met all of them over the years. In the end I took what they mirrored for me and incorporated it. And moved on. I know that sounds very callous but it was never intended to be. It was something that I had to do. You see, if I am whole I am complete. And from my completeness comes my balance. I thought I'd have everything I need and I always would. Up until then I had been searching and gradually unravelling the knots and breaking the bonds and cutting the wires that I had tied around myself. Trussed more like. Mentally, with attitudes and fears; emotionally, what I could and could not love. I had the help of kindly spirits, guides who always surrounded me. If I could walk this path, with all its wrong turns, congestion and delays, anyone can."

She looked steadily at Kaamal.

"I discovered there is no prescriptive path. You just have to choose to walk."

She paused, watching him closely to see if he was following.

"My guide, my very special Kevin, taught me that every word I said, every thought I'd ever had, I'd given a shape to in my mind; and every seed he'd ever sewn was still there, is still there, forever echoing, forming and reforming, fruiting, stimulating, supporting, comforting, feeding and guiding, for all time. He taught me that I wasn't looking for someone to save my life, to complete me; just working on my own jigsaw. He also taught me that the important thoughts, the ones worth preserving, are those that pierce the heart like a silver arrow. The unimportant, but manipulative, disruptive thoughts are the ones that go round and round like a hamster on the wheel of trivia and we need to let them go."

Kaamal said

"Did you tell Vivian all this?"

Sam said

"I didn't need to; he knew. Before him I wasn't ready but when I met Vivian I was. When I met Vivian he was the most beautiful thing on two legs that I had ever seen. His passion was beyond anything I had ever imagined. My response made me whole as a physical being, not a race, or a gender, just a being. He was educated, well read, a linguist with an extraordinary way with words. He combined the capability for action with a predisposition for thought, for self examination, which made him irresistible to me but caused him to challenge both his own and the beliefs of others. But that wasn't why I fell in love with him. When we married he made the ceremonial words a patchwork of beliefs. He taught me them in Urdu and translated them for me. They express much better than I can what I felt for him and he for me.

"You have become mine forever. Yes, we have become partners. I have become yours. Hereafter, I cannot live

without you. Do not live without me. Let us share the joys. We are word and meaning, united. You are thought and I am sound...."

She watched Kaamal's face, his grey eyes steady with understanding. She went on

"When you were seventeen, before the world had a chance to colour or distort your vision, you met someone about whom you felt the same and fell in love. It was irrelevant what that someone's gender was. You gave your heart and received one in return."

"If I had met you at seventeen I would have felt the same about you" Kaamal said gruffly.

"If I had met you then, I would too" Sam said. " and you would not have considered yourself a gay man and I would not have found it necessary to search the planet for love and fulfilment –and we would have lived happily ever after –maybe –and we wouldn't be having this conversation."

"Give or take the occasional blazing row?"

"Probably. In my experience falling in love has not changed the fundamentals of my personality."

"Do you think I would still have found men more attractive than women then?" said Kaamal.

"Probably. I'd have been 23 when you were seventeen. But like I said. Fundamentals. I hate large breasts and bulging muscles and thighs. What does that make me? I like what I like. Slender and flat is beautiful. I don't see that you're any different. I might have been sufficiently androgynous to fit the bill!"

"To see it that way makes it very acceptable doesn't it? It's just that –"

"The world sets its standards and leans on us all to conform? Yeah well. Each century seems to have its own pet foible, pet hate. In 100 years, maybe less as communication channels expand, it will all have changed again so who knows? I think it's important to remember that even religion, like history, is filtered through the mind of man."

They were still standing in the middle of the lounge. It was now dark outside, the moon had climbed to her zenith and the evening sounds had died away. Kaamal took her hand and they sat down on the couch. He let it rest palm upwards in his two hands for a moment.

Sam said randomly

"Have you read Interview with a Vampire?"

"Yes I have actually" said Kaamal.

"I loved that book although I hated what Louis did to Armand."

"You got that involved again?"

Sam thought for a moment. There was some kind of threshold here.

"Yes. I felt for Armand, his power and his loss –when he thought he had found the perfect companion, the perfect antidote to his loss of the will to live and then Louis didn't let him in."

"No repulsion? No shock?"

"No. Quite the reverse. It was my idea of the perfect relationship –play to my strengths and I'll play to yours – and we both grow in a loving way. At that time I had grown plenty in a destructive way –no regrets –but that seemed to me to be a better way –"

Kaamal continued holding her hand, tracing patterns on the palm with one finger. Sam went on.

"I think you need to know yourself before that can ever happen. If it's just a mirror reflection and you don't like what you see –"

"You try to change each other?"

"Yes. But even when we think we may have reached a stage where we can make equable decisions, doubt jumps in. Doubt is a log the ego throws on the path for you to trip over. Step over it. If what we do in the world comes from the heart, the spirit world rejoices. If what we do comes from the ego the spirit world pulls back. That would be the time to question."

"The ego" Kaamal said thoughtfully.

"Yeah. The eyes, the ears and mouth can act independently of one another. If we force the three senses to act together, on the basis of, two ears, two eyes, one mouth, the ego is curtailed, although not banished. It can still creep in but has less corners in which to hide. We can still behave in ego ways but without the comfort of ego justification."

"I think I may have lost some of my ability to curtail the ego when I lost Ata" said Kaamal.

Sam said

"If you have a mind like mine, which accepts on one hand the wisdom of the right brain, intuitive path, guidance through contemplation and meditation, but also on its left logical side, pursues the rational; very critical, keeps harping on about what if, then I find the best thing to do to shut it up is to work it through with it, examine the facts, allow it to reclaim for itself acceptable hypotheses. When it has that, and I hasten to add, it doesn't need to be a proven truth, whatever that is!, it will leave off the hassle and you are free to pursue your higher path and actually feel more comfortable, more complete, both sides reconciled, win win. Sometimes one's first thoughts and feelings are the accurate ones. But they can often be overwhelmed by the second thoughts, the ones that say, yeah, you're unworthy, you've got it wrong; and they're the ones that gain supportive evidence. They are the ones that we focus on and the reality data mounts up, because our minds are selective, and the accurate first thoughts get lost. The key is to get back to *them*, negative or positive, because in them lies the clue to your truth."

Kaamal was very quiet, still holding her hand, still tracing the patterns.

Sam said

"Look. Most of my life I've been paddling the conventional stream in the opposite direction to everyone else; following my own inner current. More times than I care to remember I have lost the bloody paddle, got into rapids and sometimes been overturned and left clinging to an upside down canoe.

And survived. If they'd never told me –you can't! -I'd never have discovered that I can."

"You are very enlightened" said Kaamal.

"Enlightenment is just a huge flowerbud with you in the centre. All you have to do is open its petals."

He didn't speak. Suddenly Sam said

"I've rattled on about change; I think there are points in a bi-ped's life when the idea of change is more receptive to them. They are predisposed to change at different stages of their lives. When they are making a transition of any kind; from child to young adult; dependency to independence; security to insecurity; death, ones own or that of a loved one; facing up to a threshold and looking for hand holds. That is change forced upon them but change nevertheless; and opportunity. In your insecurity you have a chance now to embrace an opportunity; take it."

He still had not looked up. His finger traced the patterns for a little longer and then he said

"And what threshold do you think I stand at right now?"

"The bridge to the rest of your life" said Sam.

Now he was looking at her but his mind was elsewhere. He looked, Sam thought, very young; just a boy. Then the man reasserted himself and he said

"I must go to him mustn't I?"

"Yes."

"I must find out?"

"Yes… Have you read The Persian Boy by Mary Renault?"

"A long time ago."

" Near the end of the book The Boy apologises to his dead father that he is not a warrior; that he has accepted being a eunuch. Embraced it and fallen in love. And goes back to his Lord, Alexander…I believe there are only two things that the world can't take away from us; the capacity for love and our right to choose. You don't need to be a monk, a philosopher or a saint, recycle your rubbish or drink camomile tea to be a seeker of stars. You can just choose; it is your right."

Anxious eyes gazed straight at her now.

"Will you come with me?"

"Yes."

It was an easy commitment to make. All things being equal she would be there with him when Ata got off the plane.

PLATO

They stood at the arrivals barrier in Chandigarh airport, Kaamal bemused, Sam anxious. She had committed a venal sin. She had invaded someone's privacy, accessed *their* private address book and sent a fax to one of *their* friends in *their* name.

And lied!

Then another thought winged in like an evil bat.

I sent the fax in English. What's he going to think? Would two Indians communicate in English? I don't even know what language Kaamal would write in- he has so many! Well I guess it's too late now.

Kaamal said impatiently

"Who are we waiting for again? Will you recognise them?"

Admittedly she'd been very vague. She'd said she had to meet someone who was flying in from Delhi. When she sent the fax she'd had the presence of mind to request a response via the same fax number and had received date and time of arrival in Delhi and approximate transfer from Delhi to Chandghar. But that was more than a week ago and of course there'd been nothing since. And her heart failed her when she thought about how many things could go wrong.

Back in 350 BC this is when you'd be making a sacrificial offering...

So she stood next to Kaamal, her heart thudding. If he didn't show, what was she going to say? If he didn't show and contacted Kaamal by some other means instead, what was she going to say?

The only thing to do was to come clean. Confess. She had, after all, done the wrong thing for absolutely the right reasons. And Kaamal was a very understanding man; mostly. She took a deep breath...

The young man striding through the barrier was tall and slender, with untidy black hair falling over his eyes and a small frown between his brows as he cast about for a familiar face. He looked somewhere between twenty and twenty five, and his stance and bearing might have made him seem arrogant but the puzzled frown gainsaid that and made him appear younger and vulnerable. He had a pale brown beauty and an aura of innocence and he seemed to light up the claustrophobic dimness of the Airport surroundings like a candle in a monastery. He stopped, his attention caught, and for a moment time stood still, frozen in a tableau of shape and form and colour like a Miro, or as if someone had pressed the pause button controlling a screen. Sam gazed at him. Kaamal was right; it was a compliment.

The young man came closer, now hesitant, shy, the wide, soft brown eyes under the straight black brows seeming to grow larger. Sam watched his face change, the eyes, hazel brown with flecks of colour, *her* eyes, now expressing recognition and then joy, the mouth curving in a beatific smile; and reality was restored.

Beside her Kaamal, who had been restlessly pacing, turned and gasped. It wasn't a very large sound and whilst he was looking directly at the young man a few paces away, he seemed incapable of movement. She reached out and touched his arm. For a moment he still didn't move and then he looked down at her, bewildered.

"It cannot be..."

Sam smiled and nodded, flicking her eyebrows.

"Oh I think it is!"

He stood for a second longer, and then walked forward, hesitantly. Ata dropped his bag on the floor at his feet and in two strides was there. They met with a clash and wrapped their arms about each other. Sam, alarmed, looked around her and then laughed at her own foolishness. Everyone was embracing; everyone in the same way. Men with men; women with women; men with women; children with both; young and old.

Like a universal embrace, thought Sam, tears standing in her eyes.

"Kaamal" murmured Ata. "Kaamal…"

Minutes passed. The world steadied and came back into focus.

The two men were standing in front of her. Ata was weepng, silent tears flowing unheeded down his cheeks.

Kaamal cleared his throat and said

"Ata, this is my good friend, my very special friend, Samanthar." His voice was squeaky as if unshed tears had made the mechanism damp.

He turned to the young man standing shoulder to shoulder with him. They were similar in looks, except for the eyes, thought Sam, and the fine outline of black around Ata's jaw and upper lip.

"And this, my dear Samanthar, is Ata, who I've talked to you about so much and who appears to have flown in on a wing and a prayer."

She met his questioning gaze and then turned to Ata.

"I am so pleased to meet you. I am so glad you came. I feel I know you but it is wonderful to see your picture made flesh." She said the last in Urdu and Ata smiled, wiping the tears away with an impatient hand and said, also in Urdu, glancing at Kaamal

"It is good to have a friend who is prepared to undertake such perils for our happiness." His voice, like Kaamal's, had the undertones of melody. She wondered if they could sing; she must ask.

Ata said

"I am sorry-I am not usually so- I did not know what…it has been such a very long time…"

He stopped, shy again and Sam took his hand.

"Blame me" she said and they all smiled at each other conspiratorially and Sam said

"Let's go. You have been travelling for ever, yes?"

"For ever!" Ata rubbed his hand along his jawline and grimaced. "And I am so tired. But not too tired- I do not need sleep-I can sleep when I'm dead."

And Sam and Kaamal looked at each other and laughed out loud.

They went out to the car park and piled into Kaamal's car. Sam insisted on sitting behind and so they drove back to their chalet in Shoghi and Sam watched two men, with 12 years absence between them, start to build the bridge which they must cross to their reunion. It was tentative at first, a shyness gilding everything after that first embrace, but by the time the drive was over the news updates and the memories had all been mixed with laughter and love, and the bridge had been built. Sam watched, spellbound. It was like seeing a flower unfold in the light from the sun. They kept turning to include her and Sam knew she had not lost a companion but gained another.

They reached their lodgings where the young man at the reception told them they had no spare chalets until the day after tomorrow.

"Never mind" said Sam. "We've got two bedrooms and acres of space. You two guys share my room, which is bigger than your's Kaamal and I'll take yours." She looked at the reception clerk who gave her a grateful smile.

"Is that good" she asked him in Urdu.

"That is very good!"

Seemingly sleeping arrangements in these multi purpose lodgings were no concern of his. And he'd probably read the faxes.

As they crossed the tree shaded lawns to the chalet Kaamal said quietly in her ear

"Have you planned the wedding ceremony as well?" He frowned. "You do know that in India to be gay is not –of course you do."

"You can just exchange rings and I'll officiate. But no, I haven't. Just the honeymoon."

He smiled then and turned to Ata.

"We have planned to go to Chandratal. What do you think?"

"Ah yes, Chandratal, the Moon Lake. That sounds wonderful" Ata said. "Does anyone mind if I take a shower and then perhaps we could all sit and talk? It has been so long..." He looked at Kaamal and then said to Sam "you must know him better than I."

"I have come to know the man you know" said Sam quietly. "I think you will find in essence he is unchanged."

He looked back at Kaamal and they gazed at each other. Then he nodded.

Ata went to take his shower and Sam and Kaamal switched their stuff to each other's rooms. As they finished Ata came out of the bathroom, wrapped in a towel and rubbing his hair with another. They both stared at him. Sam ran her eyes over his body. He was fractionally shorter than Kaamal and on the thin side of Kaamal's slender, but his frame and its muscles were taut and his skin was an all over wheat brown, with the glow of youth. He reminded her of the Greek boys in the murals from Akrotiri or Knossos. Sam thought wryly, if you were that good looking it ought to be mandatory that you were heterosexual. Ata became aware of their joint scrutiny and suddenly blushed like a shy schoolboy.

Sam glanced at Kaamal who was transfixed. She didn't think there was going to be much talking done.

She excused herself.

"I'll see you boys in a couple of hours. I'm going to take a walk down into the town.."

She looked at them both. Ata had stopped towelling his hair and was standing dripping in the middle of the floor gazing at Kaamal; Kaamal was by the bedroom door, his arms full of clothes, gazing back. Apparently neither had heard what she said. Sam smiled and walked to the door and opened it. Best to make a tactful exit before that precarious towel fell to the floor. As she quietly closed it she looked across at them. They were still standing looking at each other. Would two hours be enough?

As the door closed Ata walked over to Kaamal and said "Hold me" and unwrapped the towel.

Kaamal dropped the clothes on the floor and took him in his arms.

Ata put his arms around his neck, lifted his face and kissed him.

It had been a long time but Kaamal remembered that kiss...

Sam walked across the lawns, past the reception hut and took the lane down into the town. There were few people about.

She knew what she had done was right. Gandhi had said "Happiness is when what you think, what you say and what you do are in harmony."

Was she happy? What was this raw edge then? Was this how Vivian had felt when he saw Gerald and Henrietta united and he still alone? Completely uplifted; utterly bereft. She went into one of the small tea shops and ordered chai. A boy with the face of an angel brought it to her, warning her in careful English that it was very hot. Sam smiled at him and thanked him fot his concern in Urdu. He grinned at her and said if she wanted anything else she must call out; his name was Tomas.

She gazed out of the window seeing nothing; only Kaamal and Ata, and the looks on their faces. That was joy and joy could be shared...

Three hours later Ata came to fetch her. Kaamal had told him where to find her. They walked back to the cabin in companionable silence and went into the big windowed lounge and Ata told her Kaamal had gone for a shower. The bedroom door was ajar and the bed was in chaos. He brought her a glass of lemon tea and sat down beside her. He looked completely relaxed but ignited with an inner vitality as if a flame within was burning brightly.

He was not, she reflected, good looking in the accepted way for a man. He was too thin to be entirely masculine, fine boned, almost elfin. But those deep set eyes, the colour of hazelnuts, the narrow nose, with just a touch of hawk and lips almost a perfect cupid's bow and the untidy, black hair... God he was beautiful! She realised she was staring and that he was shyly aware of her scrutiny. In confusion she spoke the last words that had been in her mind

"You are beautiful!"

The corners of the perfect mouth twitched and then broke into a wide smile, and he laughed. It was a pleasant sound, unaffected, full of real mirth, but maybe, thought Sam, not something he has done often for a while. He was looking at her calmly, his eyes absorbing data like a scanner. She hardly knew him at all, except through Kaamal, but of some things she was certain; he was kind, old fashioned, unambiguous kind and good. Finally she said

"Please forgive the scrutiny. My only excuse is I finally have the frame on which to hang the knowledge. And seriously, you are beautiful!"

"It is understood. Although I have never been called beautiful before. Not in words," he added, flushing. "An incidence of this sort is not uncommon in a country like India, even now. I believe some of the princes still have prearranged marriages to girls they have only seen once and I expect when they finally arrive at the end of the ceremony, many of them will feel the same."

They smiled at each other and then he said

"Kaamal has told me everything about you."

"Everything?"

"Of course. He feels shamefaced."

"*He* does?" said Sam.

"He told me about your search and his- offer- and your response. And then when he was ready to come and see me, finds that you have done it all for him; for us."

"It was the right thing to do" said Sam emphatically. "Although I had some uncomfortable moments."

"You thought I might not come?"

"No. But I thought you might ask questions."

"My heart would not listen to reason!"

"That's what I hoped."

He looked at her calmly and asked

"Is your search so hopeless?"

"He told you the details?" Had they really had that much time to talk?

"Of course." He grinned at her surprise. "In between..." He blushed again.

"And you don't think I'm insane?"

"This is India" said Ata complacently. "Real magic, if it is magic you seek, takes place on the inside. When there is real magic, there are miracles. Have we not just proved this. I repeat- is it so hopeless?"

"Pretty much." It was a relief to admit it.

"You know what they say about love don't you?"

"It shines like a light within? It does in you. It opens all the doors? There is no bridge it cannot cross? No door through which it cannot pass?"

Ata said

"It out lives the living" and then, "you should never give up hope."

"Did you?"

"I think not. When I got the fax I booked the first flight I could get to match your dates."

"You are very evolved" said Sam.

Ata looked at her quizzically, his fine eyes crinkling.

"You do not need to have reached the highest level of spiritual consciousness to live in harmony with your own truths."

"And your truth?"

He smiled then.

"You need ask?"

"And work?"

"I told them I had urgent family business."

"Good man! Well, you did. Will you go back?"

"I am under obligation I think."

"Don't! Lie! Tell them your family needs you. That's not a lie."

Ata said nothing. The small frown had returned.

Sam said

"Do you love this country as Kaamal does?"

"Oh yes."

"And you love Kaamal?"

His eyes were as clear as mountain pools.

"Beyond life" he said quietly.

The shock of those words again almost made her drop the tea glass.

"Then stay. Stay together. Here." She suddenly felt quite desperate. "Stay! Don't give it up! Please, don't go back. Don't do what -"

Then Kaamal walked in from the bathroom, with the ubiquitous towel around his waist and towelling his hair. He raised his eyebrows at them.

"I feel like a gooseberry" said Sam.

"A gooseberry?" said Ata, puzzled.

"You are not very idiomatic for one who has lived so long in England" said Sam.

"The English language seems very inexpressive to me unless you wish to swear. Then it becomes quite inventive!"

"What about Shakespeare? Milton? Keats?"

"I did not find many of my colleagues conversant with such celebrated authors. Although I am being unjust; many

Indian dialects have very expressive swear words too. And gooseberry?"

"Never mind." She flung her arm out to encompass the semi naked Kaamal standing in front of them. "Look! You can't walk away from that."

The lady who ran the small eating house that she and Kaamal had been frequenting made them a wonderful dinner. Ata ate his way through so many dishes that Sam was forced to comment.

"Have you been starved? Don't they give you time to eat in British hospitals?"

Ata looked up from his plate and flushed.

"Since I got Kaamal's message, your message I..." He stopped, and shot a look of appeal at Kaamal who grinned.

"I remember" he said. He turned to Sam.

"He was always the same. In the early days if we'd planned to meet, he didn't sleep and he didn't eat until we did. Allah alone knows what his mother thought!"

Ata coloured again.

"She thought I was studying too hard" he said remorsefully.

"Just so" said Kaamal, gently fondling the untidy, glossy hair. Ata bent his head to his plate again and Sam smirked.

The lady of the house expressed her delight at the appetites she was serving.

She said in accented English

"Some pick like hens; especially women."

"Yeah" said Sam to her two companions. "Not me. Love me love my eating habits."

Kaamal said as if it was the most natural topic of conversation in the world,

"Did Vivian?"

Sam was suddenly back to that first night, with Vivian and Ali watching while she devoured chapattis and dhal. She remembered his voice, his words; 'you eat like a starving boy'.

And then in the old hunting lodge: 'you should be a small elephant but you are a gazelle!'.

"Oh yes" she said with a smile that was a little crooked.

They had coffee sitting out in the garden watching the moon rise over the mountains. It lasted until Ata had dropped asleep twice and then Sam stood up and said

"Bed?"

She turned to leave but Kaamal caught her arm and said

"I haven't thanked you for what you did."

Sam looked over at the weary Ata and said

"He is thanks enough and your face when you saw him. Sleep well both of you- or something!"

The next morning Sam climbed out of bed and went into the lounge with the intention of making herself lemon tea in the small kitchenette. The door to the larger bedroom was standing open and Kaamal, dressed only in a pair of diverting black boxer shorts covered in yellow smiley faces, and holding a coffee mug, was lounging against the doorway.

Sam blinked. Kaamal glanced down and then grinned.

"Apparently the latest design in London."

"Where's Ata?"

"Still asleep." Kaamal stepped away from the door and Sam peered in. Ata was laying on his back, with the abandon of a happy child, one arm above his tousled black hair and the other resting just above his groin, palm open, fingers lightly curled as if holding something precious. His lips were curved in a small, secret smile.

Sam thought, we never really know how we look when we are asleep; one could quite easily look like a prune with indigestion. It would probably depend on what you'd eaten the night before... or were dreaming about. She moved closer and looked down at him. The black lashes, fanning out, formed perfect half moons in the hollow above his cheekbones; the black brows shaped flawless arches above the closed eyes;

there was no frown. The dreams pleased the dreamer. And he was beautiful; not masculine, or feminine; just beautiful, in the way a landscape is beautiful, created by the hand no artistry could ever match. The kind of beauty that made you recognize the wonder of creation...

"Adorable, no?"

"His beauty bypasses the eyes and embraces the soul" murmured Sam.

Kaamal looked at her and then back at the sleeping Ata.

"That is just how it was for me, the first time I saw him" he said. "As if he had cast a silver web over my heart and I would never be free again, nor would ever want to be."

"'I have spread my dreams under your feet; tread softly because you tread on my dreams'" Sam whispered.

"Just so. He never..." He bit his lip.

They both were still watching him and as if their warm glances had entered his consciousness Ata moved his arm, and stretched to the space beside him and murmured in Urdu.

"Oh, don't move, lovely one."

Sam hid a smile and glanced at Kaamal. The sadness had gone. There was a faint colouration to his cheeks but he just grinned and gave a careless shrug.

Registering the empty place, the small frown appeared between Ata's brows and he opened his eyes and looked at them. The frown cleared.

"Not a dream" he said as if to himself. And then he sat up, pushed the bedcovers away from him and swung his legs out of the bed. Sam blinked.

"I thought he was shy" she muttered.

"He's got over it-with me" Kaamal muttered back. "Apparently with you also!"

Ata smiled engagingly, reached for a pair of white baggy trousers which were hanging on the end of the bed, stood up, completely naked, pulled them on, stretched and then turned his back on them and walked with a negligent swagger to the bathroom.

'There's a boy across the river with a bottom like a peach, but alas! I cannot swim...' thought Sam. Where have I read that?

"Kushal Khan Khattak" said Kaamal. "'There's a boy across the river...but alas! I cannot swim...' one of my favourite poems."

"Sometimes" said Sam, staring at him, "sometimes you are quite scary."

"You forget, I know your literary and- erotic preferences now."

They both went back to watching Ata, who was washing his hands at the bathroom sink, and sighed in joint appreciation and then laughed.

"Adorable, no?" Kaamal said for the second time. " How did I get through these last twelve years?"

"I have no idea" said Sam. "I'd go back to bed if I were you."

Kaamal went back.

Sam on her way again to the kitchen, passed a smiling Ata who caught her hand, put it to his lips and then followed Kaamal back into the bedroom, gently closing the door. Sam moved on, her spine tingling in a delight she hadn't felt since Vivian...

They spent the next few days trekking in places that she and Kaamal had not yet visited and some they had.

On the second morning Kaamal said he'd heard that there was a cricket match at Chail and that they were short of players.

"You mean that small hill station we visited, where the Maharaja built his palace after being thrown out of Shimla? It's not far is it? I liked it there" said Sam.

"That's the place. We didn't visit the cricket ground but Ata is an excellent cricketer and so I thought you might be persuaded to break your no sport rule? He's just changing" said Kaamal.

"What about whites? Don't they have to be decked out in white?"

"He's got a shirt and he's borrowing my white pants" said Kaamal as Ata came out of the bedroom looking like she'd always imagined Milton's Lucifer looked, as an angel, before he fell from grace.

"I haven't played for ages so I probably won't be able to hit the ball –are you sure you're OK with it?"

Sam nodded. A picnic in sunshine with nice scenery; who was going to argue with that?

"I liked the place" she said, "although I was disappointed that Kaamal didn't know more about the incident involving the Maharaja and the Commander in Chief's daughter."

"Bhupinder Singh had a reputation with the ladies. He developed an association with one of the Viceroy's daughters. She eloped with him" said Ata matter of factly.

"Really! How do you know that?" said Kaamal in surprise.

Ata shrugged his elegant shoulders negligently.

"I heard of it somewhere I think. The Maharaja is supposed to have eloped with her and then built his palace in Chail after he was thrown out of Shimla; but the dates don't match up. The Maharaja in question was known to be a bit of a womaniser but the identity of the lady is not verified. There probably was the seduction but it may have been an officers wife. I think it depends which guide or taxi driver or coffee shop owner you've talked to. You'd probably have to get it from one of the princely families themselves for complete accuracy."

Kaamal was gazing at him.

"The wonderful, fluid interpretation of history. I didn't think you ever paid attention to things like that. You never cease to amaze me!"

Ata smiled radiantly.

"That's good isn't it?"

Sam thought, I must see if I can get a book. Someone will have written about the lives of the Indian princes.

Kaamal said

"What time does cricket start? Hadn't we better go?"

The Shivalik snow capped peaks and the verdant orchards welcomed them back. There was quite a crowd turned out, on this, probably the world's highest cricket ground. It was multi national, it appeared, but the majority of the players were Indian, casually well turned out, youthful, some just teenagers.

"I thought you weren't interested in sport" said Kaamal watching Sam's face.

"I'm not" said Sam, pushing escaping crumbs of samosa into her mouth. "This isn't sport. This is visual masturbation."

Kaamal's eyebrows shot into his hair line and he choked.

"True" he said after a moment.

She took his hand.

"I like it here" she said. "Do you remember Chail the last time we came and then Naldehra and I told you about Siddhartha?"

Kaamal smiled.

"No dividing lines; no time. Wisdom cannot be taught, only experienced. Yes I remember."

"Well" she extended her arm to embrace the surrounding peaks, the endless sky, the forests and the twenty two plus men in white dotted over the pleasant green expanse, "that's what we're doing now."

"Experiencing wisdom?"

"Livivg."

They finished the samosas.

Kaamal said,

"I believe the Maharaja used to have his invited guests get up in fancy dress for the matches. Women's clothes on one occasion I think!"

"That must have been worth seeing" said Sam. "Didn't the pads and things get in the way?"

"I believe so" said Kaamal consideringly.

They watched the game in silence for a while and then Sam said

"He is very good isn't he? What I know about cricket is postage stamp size but I'm guessing that if he keeps clobbering it like that and nobody catches it he's going to be making a lot of runs?"

"You bet!" Kaamal was riveted.

Sam studied Ata closely. His focus was intent, as if nothing in the world existed beyond the ball he was facing. He didn't even seem to notice the bowler and certainly not any of the other players either to his front or to his side. There was only him and the ball. She commented on this to Kaamal. He said

"That's what makes him a great batsman; that ability to hold just the one thing in his mind. He won't be hearing anything, not even the applause when he strikes a good shot; he won't see anything; he won't feel anything."

"And you?"

"Me? No, I'm not nearly as good. I can hit the ball, I could catch the ball but I –"

"You start thinking about it" Sam finished for him.

"Yes!"

"I would probably be the same. Do you think he's like that when he's working?"

"I expect so. The nurse probably has to poke him to get his attention."

"Is he like that in everything?" said Sam."So focussed?"

"Yes" said Kaamal. "Everything." His smile was pensive and, Sam thought, just a bit secretive.

"Did he just learn to play at school?"

"Yes I expect so. But he told me once that he showed promise and his father got him a tutor. High hopes, you know, having a son as an international cricket player. It was never going to happen. Ata was as single minded about his chosen profession as he was when playing cricket."

"There are a lot of famous Indian cricket players aren't there? Even I know that!"

"The best in the world" Kaamal said. "You seem to know a bit about the game. How did you manage that?"

"No idea. Probably something to do with a good looking guy and a half decent day of sunshine and nothing better to do when I was at university."

"Of course!" Kaamal took his eyes off Ata for a moment and smiled at her. "I suppose it would never have worked if the game was played by women?"

"Of course not. Silly you!"

They carried on watching. The sun was quietly sloping down the sky and whilst his partner batsman had twice been caught out, Ata was still there, still concentrating and looking very much as if he was going to make a century. Sam could see that the players and the spectators were checking the scoring board. Ata wasn't. Reading her mind Kaamal said

"He'll have no idea how many he's scored until someone tells him."

Well! If that wasn't the most appealing quality a man could have.

Sam said, glancing at the board

"I think the team he is playing for is winning –am I right?"

"If he hits another four they will have won, with him not out."

He glanced at the sun and then at the umpires.

"He'll have to hurry up. I think they'll be calling an end very soon."

Sam looked about. The grass of the pitch was turning to deep emerald and the shadows were extending and the crowd was exhibiting a certain amount of tension.

Ata was facing the bowler. Sam watched closely. She recognised he had bowled but it seemed so fast and she lost sight of it until she saw Ata lift his bat and hit it. Thwack. It sailed up in a long, graceful arc with various fielders teetering backwards to try and be beneath its fall. But they were wasting their time for it cruised over their heads and into trees beyond the boundary line. There was a unanimous shout from the crowd, both sides jumping to their feet and clapping tumultuously. And then someone, she wasn't sure who, called time and it was over.

The players began to walk off the pitch, some towards the little clubhouse, some to greet members of the crowd. Ata was being cheered as he made his way purposefully towards them, touching the peak of his cap in acknowledgement as he passed. Sam noticed there was a small group of young women at the side of the pitch taking a particular interest in him. He didn't notice. He came straight towards them and Sam rushed at him and flung her arms around him knocking the cap onto the back of his head. The girls watched for a moment and then dispersed.

"You were magnificent!" she squeaked. "Mesmeric! And I don't even like cricket!"

Ata smiled and looked at Kaamal.

"Good game?" he asked quietly.

"The best. What do you want to do?"

"Do? Sit down; wash; eat; sleep."

"In that order?"

"Yes. Maybe wash first."

"But you smell wonderful!" said Sam.

He smelt of linseed oil, clean wood, fresh air, warm sweaty maleness and a faint aroma of something that might be musk.

Ata laughed.

"You are being very polite. I'm hot and sweaty and I probably stink."

"I've booked one of those little cabins that Sam and I had when we were last here" said Kaamal.

"That is good. So I can take a shower? And maybe we could eat in?" He looked around at the crowds and added

"I've been playing cricket all day. I don't want to talk about it all evening."

"There'll be some disappointed female fans" Sam said speculatively.

"Possibly some male as well" said Kaamal, glancing round.

Ata smiled vaguely and linked his arms with them both and they strolled away.

Sometimes he reminded her so much of Vivian it hurt.

The morning after they had returned to the lodge Kaamal had announced that they should all go and stay at Manali. Sam, who was by now almost competent at map reading, knew that Manali was an approach point to Chandratal Lake. As neither she nor Ata had tested themselves against altitude sickness it seemed like a smart idea although she hadn't planned on being part of the honeymoon. It was over 200 kilometres to Manali but Kaamal said that the journey would be picturesque and Ata, well Ata was happy to do anything and go anywhere, so long as it was with Kaamal.

Manali was at about 2000 metres above sea level, around the height altitude sickness could start to kick in. Sam had looked up Chandratal and it was about 4000 metres so the longer they spent acclimatising and exploring in the area, the better. But nothing had been said about the lake as yet. Kaamal seemed to be playing a very odd game. Sometimes when they were out and about she would catch a strange look passing across his features when he looked at Ata, but then it would be gone and she thought she'd imagined it.

Manali was set in a beautiful green valley of the river Beas and surrounded by snow capped mountain peaks. It was, as Kaamal had said, an adventure junky's paradise but they were out of season and the numbers of tourists were modest. There were back packers and climbers and in the small surrounding villages what seemed to Sam a plethora of what once would have been called hippies. There were Indian families and couples who had a definite air of honeymoon about them. There were a few who were obviously set to do rafting or skiing but not so many of them. Ata went around with a kind of captivated delight on his face, as if he'd ended up in Narnia and couldn't work out at what point he had walked through the wardrobe.

There were a number of Buddhist monasteries and temples and some Hindu sites connected with ancient legends. Ata seemed particularly taken with the Von Ngari Monastery and its prayer room brimming to the eaves with what Kaamal said were Bodhissvatas, or enlightened beings, and its lamas. Ata spent a long time there, staying inside after Sam and Kaamal had gone back out into the sunshine, and it occurred to her that he might have had a vocation for a monastic, celibate life if he hadn't become a doctor. Maybe it still had appeal... The thought had obviously occurred to Kaamal and he looked troubled. Maybe that was in part responsible for what subsequently happened.

On the third night in Manali Sam woke suddenly. It was early for the moon was still up and she couldn't work out what had disturbed her. She lay listening for a few moments and then, sleep refusing to return, got up to make tea. The first thing she noticed was that the boys' bedroom door was open. The second thing she noticed was Ata.

He was standing by the window clad only in his loose white pants and staring out into the night. It was immediately obvious from his stance that this was not a post coital contemplative moment. His shoulders were hunched and rigid and his arms were clamped tightly across his chest, as though he was in pain. Sam went straight across to him and slipped her arm round his waist. He flinched and then looked down and relaxed a little.

Sam glanced at the empty bedroom.

"Where's Kaamal?"

Ata lifted his shoulders despondently.

"I don't know." Then, as if the statement needed further clarification. "I thought he was out here." Then he looked away from her and back out of the window. "He's taken the car."

"Car! Where the hell has he gone at this time of night?"

"I don't know."

But Sam did.

The room was chill and Ata was shivering. Sam fetched a quilt, steered him to the sofa and wrapped it round him. Then she went to make tea. She made two cups of chai, sweet and strong, wrapped Ata's hands around one and sat down next to him with hers.

"What happened? Everything seemed good last night."

Ata didn't speak.

"Well?"

"It was-good I mean. We talked for a while and then I stripped and got into bed and just laid there watching him. He was half smiling. He said that I was such a sexy little beast I could have been a hooker. Then he said 'you could have made a fortune at that cricket match.' We both laughed. Then he got a strange look on his face. I guess he was still thinking about the cricket match..."

Or you at the monastery thought Sam.

"Then he started asking me what I did in my days off. I said, not a lot. Studied; played cricket. He said, Ah, cricket players- good looking boys, yeah... I said I thought we were going to make love and he just looked at me. Then suddenly he said that he couldn't believe he was the only one who had ever meant anything to me. So I said 'why did I fly all this way to be wth you then?' and he said 'I've no idea.'

I was tired so I turned over with my back to him and he walked out."

The moon had slipped down and the sky was ablaze with a myriad stars. It was too dark for Sam to see his face but she didn't need to. His light had gone out.

"Where has he gone?" he whispered as if the spoken word might elicit the answer or dispel the dream.

"He's gone to Chandratal" said Sam.

Her first thought was to hire a jeep immediately and set off. Ata pointed out that they would need to wait until dawn to stand a chance of that and also that they must get a permit for

Rohtang Pass. That could take days. They sat together and did some investigating.

"It says it can take up to 8 hours to get there" said Sam, flicking through the guidebook. "What time did Kaamal leave?"

"I suppose it must have been about 1 am " said Ata.

"And he probably already had the permit for the pass."

Ata looked at her in surprise.

"Oh yes, I think he's been planning this little trip to Chandratal –just not alone!"

Ata looked at her desperately. This really wasn't fair on him. He'd done nothing to deserve it.

Ata said

"That means he'll be well on his way by now. Why…"

His eyes were shining with tears.

"Because he's an idiot. Yes. So here's what you have to do. You go down into the town and find us a jeep to hire. Then you must find someone who can get you a permit. You'll have to be be your most seductive; a sexy little beast- and persuade someone, somehow, to get you a permit immediately. Smile and use those beautiful eyes to promise a night's passion; it doesn't matter whether it's male or female. You can do it!"

Ata looked at her sceptically.

"How do you know it will work?"

"It will work. Trust me, it will work."

Just after dawn Ata left. In his absence Sam pulled together extra sweaters, socks, jackets and blankets and all the portable food and drink that they had in the kitchen. The temperatures in Manali had been between 10 and 20° but the nights in Chandratal could be below freezing, possibly -2. As she had experienced much lower temperatures in cold winter spells in South Dakota, -2° did not seem any big deal. But both Kaamal and Ata seemed to feel the cold and she did not expect that Kaamal had done anything more sensible as he left than pick up the car keys and permit. By the time Ata returned everything was ready.

"Did you get it?"

"Yes" he answered perfunctorily.

"What did you promise?"

Ata blushed and Sam didn't pursue it.

"I picked up a can filled with diesel as well" he added.

"Have I told you that I think you're wonderful?" She smiled at him.

He grimaced.

"It is a pity others do not share your opinion."

They drove out of Manali; traffic was light and conditions good. When they reached the Rohtang Pass post conditions became good and bad. They showed the permit to the guard at the pass. He scowled. Ata smiled. They drove on. At Grampoo they came to a signposted right turn down a dirt road, 'Welcome to the Spiti valley'. Sam had Ata drive to start with. There were several reasons for this. First she thought from the point of view of getting on the right track, she was less distracted. Second, investigation led her to believe that road conditions down the Spiti Valley to Batal were challenging. She felt she was in a better frame of mind to be challenged than Ata and she should take over at that point. Thirdly, how much driving experience could one get based in a London hospital?

Rohtang apparently meant 'corpse plain' due to the number of deaths it had claimed over the years. She said a silent prayer to the mountain gods; no avalanches please! Let us tame mortals pass. They had nothing to sacrifice.

It was a switchback climb but the view from the top was spectacular though the wind was hurling sharpened swords at them, penetrating every crevice of vehicle and body. She could see a river but also glaciers.and a range of mountain peaks that defied description. Ata's mouth was a grim line; the light had not returned even with the unfolding action plan and he took little interest in his surroundings. And Kaamal? Kaamal would have been seeing inside his head. She wondered if he would ever really understand how much Ata loved him? Or how much *she* missed him at times like this...

They were climbing all the time. The air felt thinner somehow but so clean and sharp it was like inhaling life. She ran through her body parts. No signs of altitude sickness yet.

The road to Batal was on the high side of challenging. She and Ata swopped places and she took over the drive. She remembered trips with Steve in the Peloponese and the Greek Islands and in the Lake District and South Scotland. They had been challenging; this was something else. Steve would have been proud of her.

The entire stretch was filled with potholes, waterfalls which apparently had no qualms about spilling across the narrow road; streams pouring down from the mountains like undisciplined children and loose stones everywhere. The potholes had potholes and the boulders had offspring, but she could handle them; she felt the water ways were taking unfair advantage although she'd driven through Cumbrian floods in her time. She drove slowly and with intense concentration. The hours ticked slowly by. Her shoulders ached with gripping the wheel. When they finally reached Batal she pulled over and dragged out bread and cheese and water from the rear. Ata shook his head but she forced him; blackmailed him actually by telling him they had no idea what state Kaamal would be in when they found him. He ate. He got out for a pee. He got back in. They didn't speak.

From Batal they continued, Sam hoping she hadn't missed a turn. Shortly before the Kunzum pass top there was a narrow dirt road to the left and a board announcing it as Chandratal road.

"Fourteen kilometres from here" said Sam.

It was difficult to believe and she had to fight the urge to cry.

She turned to Ata who was looking tense and said

" He gets altitude sickness you know. Have you brought anything with you if we find him suffering?"

"I have my emergency medical bag with me, but really the best and safest remedies are slow accustomisation and plenty of water."

Sam said her second silent prayer of the day.

They drove on. The road conditions were getting worse, if that was possible, and Sam started conjuring a range of fates Kaamal might have met. Then just up ahead they saw Kaamal's four x four.

"Pull over!" Ata shouted and jumped out .

He was back before she'd turned off the engine.

"He's not there! He's run out of fuel."

"How do you know?"

Ata held up the car keys and jangled them at her.

"I turned the ignition. The gauge is below zero."

"Don't you just love him" said Sam between her teeth. "Was he always like this?"

"He could be," said Ata, "if he was upset and stressed. But we never rowed... I don't think he's thinking clearly..."

"I don't think he's thinking at all!" Sam snapped.

"The good news is the engine still has warmth. He may not have got much further" said Ata.

He hadn't. Sam measured the distance. About 7 kilometres down the winding, single track road they saw a hunched shape by the roadside. Ata recognised it immediately.

As they drew closer Sam said

"What's he doing? Is he praying?"

"I think he's being sick" said Ata and jumped out of the car, while it was moving, for the second time.

Sam followed on behind. When she reached them, Ata was squatting on the stony ground with his arms round Kaamal who was alternately weeping, coughing and vomiting. Ata was alternately gently rocking him and wiping his face with something that looked like a prayer scarf.

Sam sighed, reached into the back of the vehicle and pulled out the medical bag. She climbed out and handed it to Ata who smiled radiantly and Kaamal looked up and peered blearily at her through sticky black hair. Under his usual shade of pale tan he was greenish-grey. She'd read about this in books but always taken it as a descriptive metaphor for sickness rather than a visual reality. He took her scrutiny for criticism and mumbled

"I am sorry for all the trouble I have put you t-" and then leaned over and was promptly sick on Ata's right boot.

Ata smiled fondly and Sam sat down beside them on the road, not too near, and waited while Ata wiped vomit off his boot and conducted his examination.

"Is he OK?"

"He's fine; nothing that water and a little TLC won't cure" said Ata. "Lets get him into the car and drive to the camp site. Hopefully we can hire a tent and walk to the lake tomorrow."

"He doesn't deserve you" Sam muttered, taking Kaamal's left arm and wrapping it around her.

"I know I don't" said Kaamal, piteously. "I tried to phone you" he said to Ata, "but there aren't any-"

"I know" said Ata and smiled.

Ata climbed into the back of the vehicle and Sam pushed Kaamal in after him. Ata settled him against one shoulder and plied him with water. Kaamal drank thirstily and then passed out.

Ata met Sam's gaze in the rear view mirror and smiled again.

"Ar sixteen I was a hopeless case. I couldn't interact with anyone; at seventeen I wasn't much better; women petrified me and alcohol made me sick. Kaamal made it right for me."

The light had come back.

Sam drove very carefully and was inordinately grateful that they met no outcoming traffic. The road to Chandratal was like a ledge carved into a mountainside. She kept her eyes fixed on it and tried to blank out how much it reminded her of the tortuous track which she had once hiked, to camp down in the Grand Canyon…When they finally got to the campsite, she turned around to find them both asleep.

A mother's work is never done! She climbed quietly out and went to see if she could organise sleeping accommodation. The sky was a piercing blue and the sun still had warmth. She sighed with pleasure. Twenty minutes later, after a very pleasant though pigeoned conversation with the dark skinned, laughing eyed young man in charge, she had rented the largest tent available and put in food orders for later.

She went back to the car. They were both still asleep, like nestling puppies. Ata opened his eyes. Sam said

"I think we ought to wash *that* before we put it in a clean tent." She pointed at Kaamal. " I'll get some water and a bowl." She grabbed a bowl from the back of the jeep and went to the washrooms which were pleasant and clean, though basic.

It was a faintly farcical performance; would have been more so if Sam had been doing the washing but Ata took the lead and Kaamal submitted with boyish grace, holding out his arms, lifting his knees, all the time gazing up at Ata. When he'd finished sponging his face Kaamal took Ata's hand and pressed it to his forehead and said "Nice. Cool."

Sam unloaded the blankets and quilts and food from the vehicle into the spacious and good quality tent. There were beds and blankets already in it but Sam reckoned that the boys might prefer a different arrangement; the beds erred on the narrow side. Ata had stripped Kaamal to his boxer shorts for the washing; now he made him drink more water, then took his temperature and his blood pressure. Finally, and much to Sam's surprise, he plucked an odd looking object from his bag and handed it to Kaamal, who looked at it suspiciously and Sam said

"What's that?"

"Ginger root. Chew it!" This last to Kaamal.

Kaamal looked at him defiantly, was about to refuse, saw the look in Ata's eyes and complied. Finally he dabbed something on Kaamal's forehead and checked his pulse. This Sam recognised; lavender oil, a very efficacious relaxing remedy and one she used herself. Then Ata made Kaamal lie down. This time Kaamal protested but Ata took his hand and laid down next to him and Sam left them to it. It was now 4pm.

She wandered about the camp and its environs. The track to the lake was clearly marked. It was about 3km and motor vehicles were not allowed but swimming apparently was. For such high altitude the setting was startlingly verdant; green meadows and blankets of many coloured wild flowers. The perfect place for shepherd romance. The birthplace for legends, as Kaamal had said. She had read of another. The legend of the celestial marriage of the daughter of the Moon God and the son of the Sun God, who, contested in their love by their parents, stole away to Chandratal and made their celestial vows in this very place. She liked that one. That was a perfect one for Ata and Kaamal; a love match in defiance of parents and the world. Then you looked up and there, beyond the meadows and the shale scree slopes, were the snow covered mountain peaks, plucked from somewhere and carefully positioned there because someone wanted a romantic backdrop. Perhaps they did; perhaps that's how it had worked…The enchantment was physical…and the harmony… was this the peace that passes all understanding?

For Sam, peace and therefore serenity, had always been an illusionary target; or at least transitory; glimpsed, touched, even embraced briefly, but never quite attained. She suspected that Kaamal was the same. But Ata? Ata *was* peace…

She went back to the tent. Kaamal was fast asleep; Ata was laying on his side, his head propped up by one hand, watching him.

He glanced up at Sam, smiling wearily.

"I won't wake him" he said quietly. "Did you order food?"

"Yes. For three."

"That is good. I'll eat his."

It was plain but delicious; rice, bread, mixed vegetables, chai. Berween them they polished off the lot and were rewarded with winning smiles from the cooks. Then the proprietor asked if they would like him to light a bonfire to sit around and watch the shooting stars.

Sam and Ata looked at each other. They were both wilting.

Ata explained about their companion, said they would stay two nights and could they postpone the bonfire until tomorrow? He seemed to speak in a mixture of Urdu and Hindi, with something else tossed in but whatever it was, was understood and agreed. They walked back to the tent hand in hand. It was almost full dark and Sam, with Ata's hand to guide her steps, was gazing up at the sky, now beginning to sparkle with fairy lights. Suddenly she stopped.

"What is it?"

She didn't answer him. He peered into her face.

There was magic all around.

"You have understood something? The stars have passed a message to you?"

She looked at him blankly and then smiled.

"Yes" she whispered, "a message."

She knew in that instant that Vivian had been to this place and he too had gazed at these same stars and wondered...

Ata squeezed her hand tightly and they walked on.

Kaamal was still asleep.

Ata stripped to his boxers and Tshirt and laid down next to Kaamal and indicated Sam should lie on Kaamal's other side.

She raised her eyebrows.

He chuckled.

"I don't think you will be getting in the way of anythingn tonight. You are cold; sleep with us; we will all keep each other warm."

So she did.

She woke very briefly in the night. The air was chill but she was warm. She was lying on her back. Kaamal had turned slightly towards her and had stretched his arm across her. Ata was facing him on the other side and his arm too was stretched across Kaamal . Their hands were very lightly clasped.

"Ahhh" she thought and fell back to sleep.

They all awoke more or less simultaneously. Kaamal stretched, sat up and looked down, saw Sam, blinked twice and smiled. Almost his old self. His colour was back to normal and his eyes were bright and questioning.

Ata struggled his way out of the quilt layers and jumped to his feet.

"I need a pee" he announced and pulled on his clothes with an extra sweater and left the tent. Sunlight poured through the open flap.

Sam turned to Kaamal who had been watching him with hungry eyes. She said

"He is light. Pure white light. Don't fuck it up."

He looked at her consideringly.

"Are we both in love with him?"

"Perhaps. Just a little. Sometimes. Don't f-"

"Fuck it up. I know. But why does he want me?"

"Because you are his compass Kaamal. Without you he is just adrift; on automatic pilot."

She thought he was going to say something else but changed his mind.

Instead he said

"Breakfast? I feel as if I haven't eaten for a week."

"Three days actually" said Sam with asperity.

He gave her a boyish grin. He was back on form.

After breakfast they set out.

"Are we walking right around the lake?" Ata asked.

"Of course" said Kaamal, "clockwise."

Sam recalled Kaamal's words when he had spoken of his first visit. How the place had captured his mind and his heart and made the walking effortless; as if he was absorbing and not expending energy... The colour of the lake, changing as cloud shadows passed across its surface; a goblet of nectar...

And there it was. She could feel legends in the making and they were part of it.

It was not a long route and they took their time. And there were the cairns, the Oudos, and they each carefully chose and added their stones to the piles. Ata seemed to be in his own enchanted world; his face had the same absorbed expression Sam had noticed on it when they had visited the monastery. As if he was considering a life, or lives, way beyond the one he had known for the last 12 years. As if he sensed change was imminent and he embraced it. Kaamal watched him.

Two thirds of the way round Kaamal stopped abruptly and said

"How about a swim?"

Sam had been prepared for this. She had known beyond shadow of a doubt that Kaamal would want to go into the water; she handed him the sun protection.

Ata stripped and Kaamal proceeded to cover him in cream. Or at least he tried but Ata proved to be excessively ticklish and in order to succeed Kaamal had to hold him while Sam applied the cream. Sam then insisted that Kaamal applied his own cream; otherwise, judging by the look on Ata's face, the proceeding was going to take until dark. She helped with his back regions. Kaamal proffered her the sun screen but she gracefully declined. She had tested the water temperature and it seemed definitely sub zero. Two minutes in it and she would pass out with cold.

So she propped herself up against a rock and watched them.

It was a curiously tantalising spectacle; part farce, part romcom, part sexual drama. They couldn't keep their hands off each other but the cold had shrunk their parts to infant size. It was seriously funny.

Finally they succumbed to cold and ran out to throw themselves down next to her and let the sun, now surprisingly hot, dry them and restore circulation. Sam had brought the remains of their food supply and they spent the next hour eating and talking and sharing individual anecdores about challenging escapades. And Sam hugged her private message from the stars and was content.

That night they had their bonfire, a convivial affair with wine as well as food. And the galaxy had fallen to the ground. Kaamal had been right when he said the heavens were within touching distance; a million stars... You gazed and you gazed and you weren't a mortal on a planet, with crowds of others; you were alone in a galaxy of wonder and you were *immortal*...

They went to bed intoxicated and slightly drunk as well.

Sam insisted on sleeping on one of the camp beds and the boys wriggled under the pile of quilts and wrapped their arms around each other. Everyone slept.

They rose early, said their goodbyes and drove away. There was a long drive ahead and an abandoned vehicle to deal with. Kaamal drove, Ata beside him, one hand on his knee. Sam gazed out of the back window and wondered if she had left Vivian behind at Chandratal...

They topped up Kaamal's jeep with the spare fuel that Ata had bought. Kaamal drove his own vehicle back to Batal and Sam and Ata followed behind in the hired truck, Sam driving. Ata gazed straight ahead and smiled. Dear boy. Clearly contemplating his new world. How difficult was Kaamal going to make it?

Arriving at Batal they had a short discussion and decided to spend the night there and rented a couple of rooms in one of the guesthouses. It seemed the smart thing to do in more ways than one.

They all retired early, the boys to one room and Sam to the other. She undressed and climbed into bed and was asleep in moments and knew nothing until Kaamal awakened her the next morning with very sweet tea and an even sweeter smile. Clearly he had had a pleasant night.

They set off for Manali almost straight away. Kaamal drove his own vehicle again, with Ata, and Sam drove the hire car; she felt they had developed an understanding. The relationship saw her safely down the Spiti valley, across the watercourses, safely through the Rohtang Pass and back to its home in Manali. She wondered if it was as tired as she was.

Back at their accommodation she found that Kaamal had taken the initiative and gone out to get food. Ata was sitting on the sofa, wilting. She sat down and wilted next to him. It had been a long few days.

"How is Kaamal?" she asked him.

"Tired; happy; questioning."

"In that order?"

"No."

"Ah. Does he give you reason to doubt?"

Ata turned his lambent eyes on her.

"No."

They drove back to their rented honeymoon lodge in Shogi and spent some days doing very little except eating and sleeping. Sam reckoned that Kaamal would feel the need to explain himself; she was fairly sure Ata would have listened, smiling benignly and then taken him to bed.

After some discussion they decided to go to Amb, the once princely state of the Tanoli rulers, the Khans, in the area known as Tanawal and now incorporated into the North West Fronteer Province since 1969. It was a long drive but Sam wanted to go because the surrounding areas were supposed to be on the invasion route of Alexander the Great on his way to India. His supply base was theoretically to be located on the right bank of the Indus. The history of the Tanoli rulers went back centuries before the Mughul Empire, Kaamal said, and its ruling dynasty had largely remained free of the outside challenge of various invading powers. It had a reputation for strong and fair leadership. Jehandad Khan of the 19th century,was reputedly of a 'sincere and gentle temperament', tall, slim and good-looking with wide fine eyes (or so Kaamal said, with a good deal more relish than was necessary , thought Sam, looking at Ata, who grinned) and ruled well and fairly in an area of many settlements and tribes.

Sherghar – tiger den- was an interesting place, instilled with history. Kaamal said that before independence Muslims and Hindus lived there quite happily together until the partition, when Hindus were forced to migrate to India. There was still evidence of Hindu tradition. Much of the original state area had been given over to the construction of a dam in the 1970s and its inhabitants given land in the Abbottabad area by the Khan.

The region had its own special beauty; lakes, rivers, mountains, the Karakoram range. Cool not cold, green; lots of small villages; in the past communication must have been difficult. Scarce any wonder that the British left it to its own devices. Sherghar also had Sherghar Fort, the summer residence of the Nawab of Amb, and a lot of private schools. Kaamal said the literacy rate for the area was a hundred percent. Sam felt quite inadequate in its very presence and Kaamal laughed at her.

"Nothing wrong with your literacy. Your vocabulary on the other hand…"

And Ata looked at them with raised eyebrows and Kaamal said

"Oho! You have that pleasure to come."

It was largely an agricultural area. Like Cumbria, thought Sam; precipitation and indecipherable dialect. But you couldn't deny its beauty.

It was an easy place to get to know each other. They became close and companionable, collectively, and in pairs. The empty spaces and time defying landscapes encouraged it. Natural beauty and solitude, with land to the north that challenged belief, even for a well travelled 20th century woman. Sam felt more and more that the places on the earth the farthest away from what passed for civilization, were the places where all the answers lay…

She felt she was not tough enough to live in one of those places. It wasn't the spiritual challenge of the emptiness, or the solitude, or the deficient communication channels. It was the sheer enormity of actual survival, living and staying alive in conditions and temperatures which made her human soul quaver. The places where the snow fell and there were only the Gods to see... to hear its soft flump...

She glanced at Kaamal and Ata, who were sitting close together, heads touching, bent over a map of the area. But they were! She said suddenly

"You could live somewhere like this. Even the remotest areas need doctors and teachers."

They both looked up and stared at her, then at each other.

"We could" said Ata. "And I would like to study entomology and anthropology. The Indian past, pre caste, has always fascinated me."

Kaamal said nothing.

So Ata continued.

"I would like to go and visit the lake at Saif-Ul-Maluk near Naran in the Kaghan Valley. It is said to be very beautiful and the people very hospitable... I believe that the facilities there are somewhat basic in terms of education and medicine."

He glanced at Kaamal.

"That's Pakistan isn't it?" Sam said.

"Hazara, yes. Cold but beautiful. I have read that the lake is icy and clear, fed by the glaciers and green blue in colour and surrounded by snow capped mountains. And there is a legend there. The story of a Persian prince, who heard of a fairy queen who lived in the great Naked Mountains, and was inspired by tales of her beauty to set off to find her. After much travel he finally reached the lake and there was told in a dream that he would have to wait twelve years to see her. Twelve years!" He looked at Kaamal who didn't respond.

Sam said

"Did he wait?"

"Yes! Yes he did. Twelve years."

"A man after your own heart. Go on."

Ata went on,

"So he waited and was rewarded." Again the look at Kaamal. The subtext was flagrant.

"He fell in love with her and stole her clothes and made her promise to marry him before he'd give them back. So she agreed. The impact of the lake's beauty is such that people still believe fairies come down at full moon to bathe there."

Kaamal spoke for the first time.

"She had a demon giant for a guardian who did not wish to lose her; adventure, danger, betrayal, magic, faith and love. What more could any man ask for."

Sam thought the comment was slightly sardonic.

"What happened to them?"

"There are several versions. The betrayed demon causes a great water rising and they both drown in the lake: that's one. Another says that they hide in a cave as the water rises and when they come out the land is stilled and calm, the demon vanished and they live happily ever after."

Sam walked across to Ata and took his arm. She said

"We'll take the happily ever after version won't we?"

Ata smiled radiantly and Kaamal scowled.

Then he said, still looking at Ata

"It's a bit different from a well ordered life in a centrally heated hospital."

"Yes, isn't it" said Ata, beaming.

"And there'll be poverty and in some places very crude sanitation" said Kaamal.

"There will be, yes. But it will not destroy any beauty" said Ata.

"We might find that the local population don't welcome gay lovers with open arms and report us to the authorities."

"So we won't tell them we are lovers" said Ata. He said 'lovers' as savouring the word for the first time. It brought him pleasure..

Kaamal sighed.

"When I first went to Greece" said Sam," I saw only beauty, the blue and white beauty of the architecture, the warmth, the openness, the welcome of the people, the timeless historical imprint... Later I went with a companion who saw only dirt and shabbiness and poor service. Then I went with a good friend. He saw both, judged neither, embraced the whole." And would have stayed, wouldn't you Steve?

Kaamal turned to look at her.

"And you? Will you be coming? Will we have the smallest, mixed gender, multi racial, multi cultural commune on the planet?"

"You just never know" Sam said lightly, and thought, if I can't find Vivian I can at least look for answers. Pre caste anthropology sounds like a good place to start. She glanced at Ata, who was gazing out over the surrounding cornucopia, a wistful smile on his lips.

Bugs and bi-peds! Kevin would love him.

They went to Tara Devi, The Goddess of the Stars, hiking through the pine and larch forest with its crazy array of birds, ducking and diving and shouting like a multi-coloured football crowd, and Sam looked at Ata's eyes, alight with pleasure, and remembered the bulbul.

Walking through the trees with the light cascading over the mountains, spangling the green with silver that changed to gold as it touched their feet, Sam watched Kaamal who watched Ata, a boy again, in faded blue denims and a white T-shirt, who watched the birds. Then Ata turned and smiled and the smile passed down the line, tracing itself on each face.

Was this happiness? thought Sam. Was this 'man's fitfully splendid soul' at play?

Was this life?

Was this love?

Wasn't God love in all religions?

Was this God?

She didn't know. But she did know that this was what the world was looking for, despite what the governors of the world and their cohorts would have everyone believe.

They visited the small temple and this time Sam offered up her own prayer to the goddess, for joy for Kaamal and Ata in their chosen life, and for herself? She asked for hope. Not for hope for anything specific; just Hope... the twined, golden thread that the gods lend to man, for his dreams...

And she stopped at the top and gazed out over the endless mountain ranges remembering the hope she had built for Vivian and wondering whether it had served him well...

She shared six weeks with them.

Part way through the second week, after visiting another hill station, Sam stopped off on the way back to their rented chalet to check out some of the beautiful cashmere sweaters in the bazaar. The evenings were getting quite chill and anyway she wanted a reminder, something she could cuddle that would cuddle her back. As she approached the chalet she could hear raised voices. She opened the door in time to hear Ata say

"They are my parents and I love them and they paid for my education and I want them to know I am back in India. It is important to me."

And Kaamal's snapped response

"And I'm not?"

Ata was sitting cross legged on the sofa, wearing his loose white trousers and nothing else. Sam sighed. He was like a sixteen year old, sometimes shy, sometimes aggressive, sometimes saintly aesthetic. Sometimes- what had Kaamal called him? Sexy little beast. Dear God you couldn't have a row dressed like that!

She had noticed that her language had undergone a marked change fot the better since her time with Vivian and then Kaamal, but in exasperation it suddenly reverted quite dramatically and she said

"What the fuck is-"

Kaamal interrupted.

"He wants to visit his parents in Lucknow and tell them he might be moving back to India! Presumably so we can visit! How do you think that's going to go?"

"That's not what I said" said Ata trying to hold onto his temper and swinging his legs off the sofa.

Kaamal threw his hands in the air.

"I cannot do this. They told my parents about us, who sent me away! They sent you to another country! They destroyed our lives. They branded us as mentally ill, as criminals, unworthy to be part of our families and cut us loose. Your father couldn't even look at you! I have not your capacity for forgiveness.. I am a changed man. You cannot possibly love me" He spoke fast, in Urdu and with the self assurance of anger.

Sam rolled her eyes in frustration and said

"Oh, *please!*"

She usually reserved the worst of her venom for the infuriating habits of inanimate objects but right at this moment she had to suppress a desire to smack Kaamal across the head.

Kaamal turned towards the door.

Ata had risen to his feet, the trousers now barely covering his groin. Sam had closed the door behind her and now stood in front of it, barring Kaamal's way.

Ata said quietly

"You are not a changed man. You are an angry man. You were always an angry man."

Kaamal turned back and spat

"Always? We were together for 18 months and you are telling me I was *always –*"

He turned on his heel and made to leave.

"I did not mean it like that!"

Kaamal did not turn his head. Sam blocked his way and he met her eyes reluctantly.

She said

"You remember our conversation about Siddhartha? No such thing as time...'it's all the same fucking day, man...'"

Kaamal frowned at her and then turned back to Ata.

"So, I am an angry man."

Ata, calmer now, said

"It is part of you, but just a part. There are many parts and I love the whole."

Sam lifted her hands, palms upward, and sang

"'You don't know what it's like...to love somebody...the way I love you...'"

Kaamal scowled.

She'd brought wine back with her so she went and got three glasses and handed Kaamal the corkscrew.

"And really it's not that big a deal is it?"

Kaamal shot her a glance that could have cut granite and she hurried on.

"Ata goes to see his parents, tells them he's thinking of returning to India to employ his talents doing good in the nether regions of the north, that he'll visit from time to time, if they wish, and keep in touch. No need to mention Kaamal or anything else. If Kaamal doesn't want to be in touch with his own parents, that's his choice. That's the thing about choice! I really, really don't see what the problem is here. No one needs to lie or thrust anything down anyone else's throat. Just choose your place and live your lives."

Ata laughed.

"So simple!"

Kaamal said

"You should have been a fucking diplomat."

"It always is for someone else" said Sam, ignoring him. "On your own you're up against fear and doubt and sometimes guilt. I trained as a counsellor. Most people I saw were stuck in some kind of struggle between what *they* wanted from life and what they thought was expected of them or what they deserved. If they asked what I thought I told them; I wasn't supposed to, it's not in the rule book, but I did. I told them what others said was right for their moral, physical or spiritual health was not important. All that mattered was that they had the courage, the conviction, to choose and follow their own path. Choice being the operative word."

They both looked at her, Kaamal still battling with the cork, Ata playing with the waistband of his pants.

Kaamal said

"That can be really tough if you're one of the ones in a marginalised sector. Like gays."

"Yes I know" Sam said.

Kaamal had won the fight with the cork and was ladling wine into three glasses. He handed one each to Sam and Ata, picked up his own and emptied it in one.

Ata looked at Sam and raised his eyebrows.

"All men are boys" she said dryly, watching Ata's tussle with the baggy pants. "It's part of their charm. If they're not, they're old men."

"And some of them are so loved!" said Ata, blushing, giving up on the pants and moving up to Kaamal. "And you are so loved. Is he not?"

He turned from Kaamal to Sam.

"Oh yes" she said quietly. "So loved."

Halfway through the third week Kaamal announced that he was going to Delhi, to see the university principals and deal with the selling of his flat. He had decided to go alone feeling that it would speed up the whole process if, as he put it, there were no distractions. Ata apparently agreed to this, saying he'd had enough of cities to last him a lifetime and he'd much rather stay here where they were. He suggested that he and Sam could do preliminary investigations about areas with work opportunities for he and Kaamal and Sam was enthusiastic. Ata drove Kaamal to the airport and returned mid-afternoon. He looked tired and deflated. He sat down on the sofa with both legs and arms crossed, in opposite directions. He was gazing out of the window but his eyes were unfocused. The small frown was in evidence. Sam made lemon tea and sat down beside him.

"I know a troubled soul when I see one" she said lightly.

Ata did not respond immediately. Whatever it was he was having some difficulty putting it into words. Finally he said

"Kaamal thinks" he stopped. He tried again. "He thinks that I do not have enough experience in relationships to make a decision about spending the rest of my life with him."

Sam stared at him. Even for Kaamal this was paranoid.

"He drives me insane!" she said furiously.

Ata smiled wanly.

""You love him too" he said.

"He says I feel the same about you" said Sam.

"That's because you see in me the child you will have" said Ata.

Sam laughed.

"Vivian has probably been dead for eighty years...Anyone can see –*anyone* can see how you feel about him."

"He says he has had more involvement, with both sexes, and he knows."

"He's just worried about trapping you in something that's not right for you. Especially with the difficulties you might face... as a couple."

"Yes I know. He thinks I might not be gay, just repressed."

"A repressed heterosexual. Oh please!"

"He thinks you could help me –" Ata stopped.

"What! What does he expect me to do about it?" Sam snapped. "Am I supposed to seduce you? Or you me? Does he have a preference!"

Ata lifted his hands in a very small, very eloquent, very Indian gesture.

"I presume you had a row about it?" Sam expostulated.

Ata sighed.

"Things became a little strained" he said sadly.

"Do you want to have a sexual relationship with me?"

"No" said Ata miserably. "No offence intended."

"None taken" said Sam. "I like things the way they are."

"Me too."

"We could lie" said Sam.

Ata gazed at her.

"OK. We couldn't lie."

"Is he afraid *he* prefers women?" said Ata.

Sam gave it some thought. Finally she said

"No. We got close because I reminded him of you- in all respects."

"But I'm not the same. I have not found anyone or looked for anyone like him."

"No. But he sees the way women look at you." And men, she thought.

"Women look at him like that!"

"Yes I know but he doesn't really notice them."

They both fell silent.

"You probably wouldn't be having this problem if you were both ugly" said Sam.

Ata grimaced.

"I have told him I love him. I have shown him. What more can I do?"

Sam said

"He has lived alone with his self doubt and recriminations for a long time. He has not lived with you at all. He sees you as a gift and he doesn't think he deserves it. And he's afraid."

"Of me?"

"No. Of you finding out that you cannot accept the man he is."

"Because he can't."

"That's right. He's been looking for someone who he can make a life with. Who can love him. Transform him even. You do know don't you that he's never had a physical relationship with any man other than you?"

"But I do! I have told him I love him. You have heard me tell him." His eyes were full of tears. Then he reflected on what she'd said. "Hasn't he? He has not told me this."

"He tried a few times but his feelings for you just got in the way. He would get so far and then make excuses and walk away. In the end he stuck to women, but he found they got demanding and so there weren't many of those either."

"I did not know" said Ata. "He always seemed so confident, so self assured- with everyone."

"That's just one of his masks" said Sam. "The ones he uses to get through life. The Kaamal who looks back at him from the mirror every morning, that one is a bit critical ."

"Self acceptance..." Ata mumbled.

"Yes. And forgiveness. For what he failed to do. How he failed you."

Ata sighed and looked even more miserable, if that was possible.

"I do not think I have a mask, or masks" he said.

"I know dear boy. But most of us put one on from time to time."

"Do you?"

Sam thought about this.

"I used to. But not so much these days."

"Why is that?"

Sam laughed.

"Oh, maybe self acceptance; caring less what people think; being loved..."

"So there is hope?"

Sam said

"Oh most definitely! But you heard him the other night. Part of him believes that if your joint parents had loved you enough they could have accepted you as you were, in spite of the social taboos. They didn't make it easy. India does not make it easy. You're still criminalised by a colonial law from the mid 19th century. He externalises the blame...the blame he carries for making the wrong decision twelve years ago. I think you'll have to accept that this could be a problem for a while."

"I am not a complicated man" said Ata. "I think a lot but not in complicated ways. Before Kaamal I wanted to be a doctor. After I met him, I just wanted a life with him. You know; 'married'. I know Kaamal is complicated and I find it easy to accept. But surely he wouldn't want me to change, to be like him?"

"Hell no! He thinks you're wonderful just as you are. That's part of the problem."

"I didn't realise I was gay until I met Kaamal and then loving him didn't seem to be a problem. It was just a fact. Then it became a problem…"

"Things are improving for the gay communiities, internationally. But if you want social acceptance and equality, it's still a problem."

"Especially in the East… here."

"Yes."

Ata brooded a while and then said sadly,

"He was prepared to marry you."

"The risks weren't so great and by that time we had already lived together longer than you two ever had. And you were not even 18 when you left. And since you have apparently lived a blameless not to mention celibate life for the last decade —well let's just say it doesn't surprise me that he is struggling to convince himself that he's right for you."

"Oh" said Ata. Then he said "so there's nothing I can do is there?"

"There may be. In small ways. For you it is simple. Nothing has changed in the way you felt all those years ago and how you feel now. You love each other; you like each other; you appreciate each other's skills. So you live together. Somewhere quiet where no one bothers. Simple. With Kaamal you need to lead him gently through all the complexities of his worries and doubts. Through to the simple again. I think then there may be a chance for him to believe what you had still exists. That might be a slow process. I might see if I can remind him of the value of his memories and the love demonstrated therein."

"What will you do?"

"How long did he say he'd be away?"

"He said he'd be about five or six days" said Ata unhappily.

"Really? Well he is obviously planning on tying up all the loose ends in his Delhi life."

"That's a good thing, yes?"

"Definitely. He probably just needs a mental hug" said Sam. And privately thought, and a sharp reminder of how fortunate he is to have you.

"When he lets you know his arrival time I'll go and get him."

She looked at Ata. He looked depressed.

"Will they be playing any more cricket up at Chail?"

"Probably." He sounded about as enthusiastic as a foreign tourist who has suddenly discovered what lays behind the many lagoons and beautiful green backdrop of the English Lake District and how much of it there is. She said

"Well let's find out. I'm sure you'll be welcomed back in some role or other, yes?"

"OK."

"What did you do in your leisure time in England anyway? Did you play cricket there?"

"Yes."

"But you're not really interested in sport are you?"

"No."

"So why cricket?"

Ata thought about the question.

"I like the formality of movement and its grace. It is very self contained; almost remote."

"Not messy like football or rugby-yeah?"

"Just so."

This was hard going.

"Did you do anything else-besides cricket?"

"I did a lot of horseriding as well."

He looked and sounded, Sam thought, vaguely uncomfortable. Did she remember Vivian saying something about horse-riding being an encouraged pastime for unattached subalterns? Really! Ah well, whatever it takes.

She said

"So we could go horse-riding too?"

"OK" said Ata.

"One day at a time?"

"OK" said Ata.

"I try and take one day at a time, but sometimes they gang up on me."

"It is understood" said Ata.

Ata went to bed early although Sam couldn't imagine him sleeping much. It was only then that she reflected upon the earlier part of their discussion. She realised that when he had said she saw in him a child of her own she had seen Vivian as its father. Her conscious mind had responded with derision. But her heart...

The cricket day went reasonably well, if you discounted the fact that before the match and after it Ata slumped. There was no other word for it. He just caved in; an anonymous seclusion that enveloped him like a blanket. He still played well; he still attracred attention. He got invited for drinks by two young women, with slender shapely bodies and elliptical dancing eyes and one exceptionally good looking young man, who had bowled at him during the match and was on holiday from Delhi. Ata smiled at them all and politely refused. The young man looked particularly disappointed Sam thought.

So she took him back to their chalet. That night she plied him with wine. She thought it might loosen him up. It did. He drank most of the bottle and fell asleep on the sofa. She covered him with a quilt and went to bed.

She half expected to be woken in the night by the bathroom noises that accompany an excess of alcohol. But all was quiet. Perhaps he'd grown out of those kind of responses.

The next morning, in the absence of any word from Kaamal, she decided to take positive action and after some research chose Rampur to visit. It was about 130 kilometres away, on the banks of the river Sutlej and had a lot to recommend it. It was the seat of the former princely state of Bushair, whose ruling family, legend had it, traced their ancestry back to the son of Lord Krishna, and was situate on the old trade route from Hindustan to Tibet. It was apparently still a melting pot of cultural and historical interest. Once a bustling centre of trade and diversity, it apparently still bustled.

It had temples, a palace and monasteries. Surely these would be enough to divert Ata. And as a fall back there was horse riding.

When she fronted him with the proposal he checked the phone answer machine, gazed at it for a moment, the way one looks at a puppy whose training plan is proving ineffectual, and then nodded his compliance. The nodding brought a grimace of pain to his features and he accepted Sam's offer of coffee and paracetamol.

An hour later they set off, with overnight luggage. If she achieved any success at all they could stay over.

On entering Rampur they were greeted by the roaring river Sutlej and an enormous statue of Hanuman, the Hindu monkey god and ardent devotee of Lord Rama. This kind of set the stage and Sam's spirits rose. So apparently did Ata's for she witnessed his first smile in days. The city seemed to operate on both sides of the river with fragile, precarious looking bridges linking the two.

And bustling it was! They found a small café selling chai and fresh from the pan samosas and perched there for a while, watching.

Palaces and monasteries; Sam and Ata shared a common interest, both delighting in the architecture and the embedded history. For Sam the palace echoed a bygone age of romance, intrigue, fierce loyalty and treachery; life and death in a world she had once very briefly touched. She looked at Ata. Had he been born into that time he was unlikely to have been persecuted for his preferences. Not those ones anyway.

The Padam Palace was beautiful and reflected the documentation of its time. Dark brown and turquoise blue were the predominant colours; a lawn sprawling and a magnificent central fountain and looming hills beyond. With its red roof, stone pillared columns and wooden fretwork, it was an architectural history. Peering through stained glass portals it was possible to see wide rooms and hallways with more stained glass splintering the light into rainbow fragments. Though clearly sound in its structure, its curves predominated, and conjured the magic of fairy tales and one half expected it to bow or to join its buttresses together in obeisance.

Though less than 100 years old the local people seemed to consider it much older. Maybe it's spirit was older. It really didn't matter. The enchantment was real.

In one corner there was a smaller structure called Sheesh Mahal, the Glass Palace; it too was blue and had an air of being older than Padam.

They breathed it in and wandered on.

There was a small stone temple on the bank of the river, old to judge by its worn walls, which was clasped by a stone lotus flower. This, Ata was intoxicated by. He spoke to the attendant priest for a little while and then stood and gazed at it. He said

"the more you look, the greater the lotus blossoms!" He looked at Sam.

"Can you feel the energy of the river? Can you feel the thousand prayers that have been spoken here?"

He turned away. He did not seem to need an answer.

Dungyur, a Buddhist Temple, with its beautiful, carved wooden main door also appeared to hold Ata in sway. It seemed to be the essence of these places rather than their history which enraptured him. As if they were speaking their own language and he understood them. What Sam liked was that they all seemed to live and breathe now, in the present; that they had been created for people to use and meet in; to talk and share and think. And that was how they were still being used. People sat within the Palace compound, outside the temple and on its platforms. So the buildings lived.

Despite everything that had happened in their histories their soul was intact...

After the monastery Ata seemed in a less troubled frame of mind so Sam decided to ask him about the early relationship with Kaamal to which he had eluded when they were at Chandratal. She had considered suggesting he stayed for a few days at the monastery but then reflected this might be on the high side of risk.

Ata's response was so natural and eager she wondered why she hadn't asked before. He talked so willingly Sam realised that he had probably never spoken about this to anyone. He and Kaamal were more focussed on the now and the future and who else had there been to tell? She reflected sadly that there must be many people in the world in this position... always had been; always would be...

"What would you like to know?" He grinned impishly.

"Well, when Kaamal was throwing up all over you, you implied that he had been the long suffering party when the two of you were first together."

"Ah yes" said Ata, his eyes looking back. "The first time we met, when he came to see my sister, I barely recognised myself. I'd always had interests which absorbed me completely. Now I couldn't think about anything but Kaamal. I closed my eyes and I saw him; I went to bed and stayed awake thinking about him. I turned hot then cold. I ached in places I'd never ached before! I lost my appetite. My parents, as I told you, thought I was studying too hard and unbeknown to me invited him to come around. Suggested that he take me places and 'socialise' me! When he just turned up I nearly passed out. I left the room and went out to my aviary at the end of the garden. Kaamal followed me, apparently encouraged by my parents! It's really quite funny isn't it? If they'd known...He came out and found me with my birds and asked me if I'd like to go with him to Delhi the following week. He said he was going to get some information from the university but I could come and we could go into the old city afterwards. I couldn't speak. He came up behind me and put his hands on my shoulders. I started quivering like a jelly! He must have thought me an imbecile. I just nodded. He told me when he'd be there and then he slipped his hands down to my waist and gave me a little squeeze. That touch burned a brand on me for the next five days." He looked at Sam shyly. "Ridiculous, no?"

Sam smiled.

"Not ridiculous. Adorable! Go on."

"You're not bored?"

"Bored? I'm fascinated! A rare glimpse into true love as it unfolds."

"I don't know how I got through those days until he came. We caught the train to Delhi and I sat next to him. It was quite crowded and our legs touched and I quivered the whole time. Yes I think I actually trembled-and I don't think I said a word. Kaamal just talked about where we were going. I don't remember much. He was so... so... capable; so self assured. So handsome! I couldn't understand why he had asked me to go with him."

"Couldn't you?"

"Not then. I thought he must just feel sorry for me. I mean, he could talk to anyone and I was a deaf mute. But by the end of the day..." He looked shy.

"Yes?" Sam prompted.

Ata didn't respond.

"Just go on with the story. I am curious to see cavalier Kaamal in action."

"He took me to the university first. He told me he was planning on studying there in the following year. After that he took me to the centre of old Delhi. We walked around the bazaars and we went in perfume shops and jewellery stores; he dabbed musk oil behind my ears and I blushed and he laughed...I felt very foolish. He asked me if I wanted to eat. I didn't; not at all. My stomach was in knots but I said yes, so he took me to a café; well it was more of a bar really."

"I thought Delhi had drinking laws. Weren't you both under age?"

Ata laughed.

"I told you, Kaamal was very confident and he looked older than his years."

"You didn't I bet."

"No I didn't and I was very nervous. I can remember exactly what he said."

He paused for dramatic effect.

"He said, 'when we're 18 we can vote in elections; when we're 21 we can get married; when we've fucked those two up then at 25 we can have a drink to celebrate! Oh the irony!'"

Sam laughed out loud. Kaamal had been the Kaamal she knew for some years then.

"The bar was very full and I was terrified. He got us both Coca-Cola, or so I thought. It was really hot in there. I drank mine straight down. He'd bought little spicy titbits, samosas and things and I ate some of them. They were very hot and I was very flustered. He chose a small boothe at the back, made me sit down and he sat next to me. Our thighs were touching and my stomach was doing summersaults. Then he saw someone he knew at the serving counter and the girl beckoned him. He said he'd only be a moment and went over to her. I was panic stricken. And hot. So I drank his drink as well. Then this woman came over to me. She was a woman, not a girl. She said, was I alone? I shook my head but she sat down next to me and smiled. Then she put her hand on my leg, really high up next to my groin and gave it a little squeeze! And said 'nice.' She said I looked warm. I was warm; I was boiling! She had a drink in her hand and offered it to me. So I drank that as well. By then I was feeling quite peculiar. I looked around for Kaamal but I couldn't see him. I just had to get out so I said to the woman I was going to get some fresh air. And she said 'good idea' and followed me. By this time I was fairly sure I was going to be sick so I tried to walk away from her but she caught me up and put her arm around my waist and squeezed me into her…"

"And you threw up?" Sam enquired, desperately trying not to laugh.

"Yes" moaned Ata. "All down her dress. She was very upset."

"I bet she was! Then what happened?"

"Kaamal turned up. He apologised to her. Said I was his young brother and not used to alcohol. Gave her some money and told her to go and treat herself to a new dress on him. Got her to give him her number; promised he'd ring her. Smiled like an angel…"

I know that smile thought Sam.

"And then?"

"I was feeling pretty bad by then. He just put his arms around me –and made me sit down next to him. I remember my head was turning in circles and I put it down in his lap. I must have passed out for a few moments because all I can remember is suddenly coming round, sitting up abruptly and being sick again, all over his jeans!"

This time Sam just had to laugh. So history had repeated itself at Chandratal. As history has a habit of doing. The irony of that would not have been lost on Kaamal.

She wiped her eyes.

"You have to finish the story. It's wonderful. Romance at its height!"

"I fear you are mocking me."

"Only a teeny tiny bit" said Sam.

"He was so patient-"

"That was your clue Ata. He was in love."

"Really? Then? With all that disgusting-"

"Precisely!"

"He pulled me up, tugged off my jeans, struggled out of his, pulled mine on, told me to stay where I was under the trees and not move; he'd be back in ten minutes."

"Was he?"

"I don't know. I must have passed out again. When I came round he was back, wearing new jeans, with mine under his arm and a new Tshirt for me. Mine had got- splashed. It was black with a slogan in English on it."

"What was that?"

"Signed, sealed, delivered…"

"That was your second clue. It's a song: Signed, sealed, delivered, I'm yours."

"Oh. I didn't know that."

"And then?"

"He asked me if I thought I could manage the train ride home. I wanted to say yes but I couldn't lie to him. I said I thought I'd be ill again-and he just smiled! He said, 'you've not had alcohol before?' and I told him, no, never and my head started spinning again. I pulled my jeans back on, sat down and I remember he looked at me for a while with an odd expression on his face, as if he was trying to choose between two options. Then he got me to my feet, gave me a brief hug and we went to find a phone box. There was one in the mall nearby so he sat me down outside it and said he had some calls to make. He made one, and then he made two more. I wasn't really following. Then he came out and told me he'd rung a friend and she'd said we could stay with her for the night. Then he'd rung my parents and told them we were going to see a show and would stay with friends. I think they were thrilled. He rang his own with the same story. He made me promise not to be sick again until we got to the friend's bathroom and got me into a taxi."

"Were you-sick I mean?"

"Almost; the taxi went fast round corners and I only just made it. I opened the door and was sick in the gutter as we pulled up. It was only a short way to the flat. She was very nice."

"So what happened?"

"I don't actually remember. Only fragments. I felt really rough. Kaamal told me what happened, on the way home the next day. Apparently there was only one spare room, with one bed."

"I thought you and Kaamal only slept in a bed together that one fateful time?"

"That's right. He put me to bed and he slept on the rug next to it. That's where he was when I woke up the next morning. He must have taken my clothes off because I woke up naked."

Dear Kaamal, thought Sam.

Ata was watching her expression.

"You think he wanted to sleep with me then?"

"You bet he did!"

"Ahh" said Ata.

He thought about this for quite a long time, while Sam watched him and shadows started to creep over the walls behind them with reptilian grace.

Finally he said,

"I had forgotten it all until Chandratal. I'm not sure how he got me home. I don't remember much of the train journey; only leaning against him and dozing. I remember how safe it felt. I remember my mother looking at me a bit sharply and whisking me off to bed. I remember being quite unwell for nearly a week. I don't know why."

"Alcohol, shock, anxiety, sexual awareness," said Sam, "not necessarily in that order."

"Hmm. I was very young...I stayed in bed and Kaamal came every day and sat with me; read to me. Fed me soup. Massaged my feet...he said I had beautiful feet... Then at the end of the week when I had just about recovered he said 'I'll see you around' and left. He didn't come the next day. Nor the one after..."

"What did you do?"

"Moped. Remembered his arms around me and imagined him touching me... Then he rang me and said why didn't we meet at Sikunder Bagh the next day... So we did."

"The bulbul."

Ata smiled angelically.

"Yes. That's when it started..."

It started much earlier than that, thought Sam. It started the moment you met.

She watched him for a while. The shadows were now slithering past their feet. The clouds were shuffling across the sky like nomads searching for a place to rest.

She said

"I have to ask. You were so, so close, so completely in love and committed - how did you cope when you were stopped from seeing each other?"

Ata stared in front of him. He didn't say anything.

Sam waited.

"I thought about him all the time. I revisited everywhere nearby we had been together; everything we had done together. But within the month I was sent away. It did not get better when I got to London; worse in some ways; the lack of familiar places; the isolation. I used to lie in bed and imagine Kaamal beside me... I weaved little dreamscapes where we were together and happy...Then one morning my uncle made a comment; I don't remember what he said but I do remember I went and looked at myself in the mirror. And I knew if I didn't do something people would begin to notice...and I couldn't bear the thought of that; the interference; the questions...the reports back to my mother... so I gathered up all the memories and I put them in a locked box in my heart and I promised myself that I would only open the box when Kaamal got in touch with me. I promised myself that when I'd spoken to him or read his words, afterwards I would choose a quiet time and open the box, look at all the memories and then put them back and close it up."

"Oh Ata!" Sam's eyes filled with tears. She said

"Did it work?"

"It was a struggle at first. I had to force myself to eat. I took stuff to help me sleep. But it got easier after I was in college; there was less time to think...less time to dream...So, yes it did."

"Does Kaamal know any of this?"

"No."

Sam took his hand and pulled him towards her.

"You are breaking my heart" she murmured.

Ata turned to her, his cheek close to hers.

"It is not a matter for sadness now" he said.

Sam said

"I think if you had told Kaamal what you were going through nothing would have kept him away."

Ata looked down across the river, pursuing its inexorable course.

It was almost dark.

They found some pleasant lodgings, with one bedroom furnished with two single beds; sleeping with men, not sleeping with men was becoming a pastime Sam thought wryly. They'd eaten out but Ata only ordered a dish of dhal and didn't finish that, so they did some people watching at the chai café and retired early. Ata said goodnight and seemed to fall asleep immediately. Sam lay without sleep and watched him. How had he functioned for twelve years? What would he do if Kaamal thought it better for them to stay apart? No; no! Kaamal was down in Delhi finalising his life- wasn't he? She looked across at the sleeping Ata. She whispered "he loves you so much Ata".

Ata's lips curved in a small smile and he went on sleeping.

The next day they hired horses and went riding. They stayed out all day, exploring lanes and the banks of the river. Ata had apparently talked himself out the day before, because he didn't say much. Sam watched him covertly. His narrow hands were gentle on the reins and on the mare's mouth. He controlled her with his knees and calves. She responded to his touch. Who wouldn't thought Sam and blushed inwardly.

Suddenly he turned to her and everything he was feeling was on his face.

"I think I'd like to go back" he said.

So they did.

Five days after Kaamal had left, five fairly downbeat days it had to be said, with the occasional lift, Kaamal left a message at the lodge reception to say he was arriving at Chandigarh Airport at 10.30 a.m the following morning. That evening they sat together, Ata with a book on his knee that he wasn't reading and a vague expression on his face ; Sam, trying to extend her Urdu vocabulary and plotting and occasionally glancing at Ata and wondering why she'd turned down the opportunity of seduction.

In the end he put the book aside and leaned against her. Then he put his legs up on the couch and his head in her lap and closed his eyes. Sam played with the silky hair.

He murmured

"Kaamal used to play with my hair…"

The next morning she left Ata drinking tea outside the lodge, sitting on the steps and watching the birds in the surrounding trees. He looked the same as he always did, quiet and calm, but the enormous black smudges under his eyes spoke testament to the last few sleepless nights. She noticed that there was no breakfast with the tea. She sat down beside him before she left and took the hand that wasn't holding the tea glass in hers. She wasn't prepared to say that it would be fine because she wasn't exactly sure that it would be; eventually yes, but right at this moment, well, not sure.

He understood what she wasn't saying and turned to her and smiled.

"You smell nice. Like fresh air."

"Kaamal said that to me once" said Sam.

"It shows how much he loves you" said Ata.

"It does? Why do you say that?"

"What could be more important to a mammal than the air he breathes?"

"I'd never thought of it like that."

Then he put down the tea glass and took her hand between his two palms and pressed it to his lips, then to his forehead. The gesture was both simple and eloquent and Sam accepted it gracefully. She leaned over and kissed his cheek and got up and left. Ata returned to watching the birds.

The flight was on time and Sam was grateful. She was not in the mood for hanging about in airport lounges. Kaamal came striding out of the gate, paused momentarily in surprise at seeing her alone and then came forward. His first words were for Ata.

"Where's Ata? Is he all right?"

He too had dark circles under his eyes. Ya Ali! thought Sam, if they just read what was written all over their faces.

"He's fine. Sleepless like you."

Kaamal frownwd.

When he got to the car he said

"Do you want me to drive?"

"No. I drive, you listen."

She'd thought a lot over the past couple of days about what she was going to say but in the end decided she would just let it happen. They drove in silence for a while and then the verse that Vivian had spoken to her out of the blue, a couple of lines that he seemed to have plucked right out of her past existence, came to her.

'If our eyes were mirrors we could see our souls; but they are windows so only other souls can see who we really are.'

She and Vivian had had a small, explosive scene over the words. Well, she had; Vivian as usual had remained calm.

She spoke them out loud now.

There was silence. She glanced at Kaamal. He was gazing straight in front of him and there were tears on his cheeks. She looked around for somewhere to pull off and took the first exit and then the first opportunity to pull over.

She looked at him again. Had he understood?

Without looking at her he spoke the words but this time in Urdu. In her head she translated back literally. The meaning was beautifully explained and enhanced. He understood.

Kaamal said quietly

"He knows who I am just as I know who he is. It is enough."

Sam breathed out.

"And as you can receive and understand his thoughts, so can he receive and understand yours."

"It is understood."

Sam said

"I watched a movie once; ages ago; can't remember what it was called or anything about the plot, if there was one. I just remember the ending. I can still see it. A group of people, men and women, old and young. They're on some kind of journey; a quest I think –in search of their Shangri La I expect. Lots of bad things happen along the way and they lose some of the group and they lose hope and belief in what they're doing but they've gone past the point of no return. And they're climbing up this steep hillside; that's all you can see, a barren hillside, a few rocks, the strip of sky above; they're all spread out in a straggly line. And then suddenly those at the front reach the crest of the hill and stop. They look out and down. The camera is behind them. So you don't see what they see, only it's effect upon them. And all the stragglers catch up and they all stand there... No one speaks; there is just this haunting music playing; like it's the earth herself singing to them right from her centre. Then they look at each other and then, as one, walk on and over the crest.

I can remember how it made me feel: as if it was my present, my past and my future. Looking down into where I was going but also where I had already been and that moment, on the top of the hill, that was the now and how it all came together..."

She stopped. Kaamal nodded.

"It is understood" he said again.

"You are one of the lucky ones. You have found a love where romantic, spiritual and physical love are combined. You've asked questions. You feel you've made mistakes. Sometimes you felt that life had no meaning but you kept looking. Someone once said, Carl Jung I think, that the separation of spirituality from life leaves us homeless. We cannot tolerate the lack of meaning. You are no longer homeless. The golden thread that joined you both twelve years ago binds you now. Grab it with both hands and hold onto it. Shoot for the moon. Fall in the stars."

Kaamal nodded.

"Did I upset him? You?"

"Yes."

"I am sorry."

"I know you are. Shall we go?" Sam said.

"Yes. Can we stop off for food?"

Sam scrutinised him then. He looked thinner.

She sighed

"Ata hasn't been eating either. Misery and anxiety never stopped me eating."

Kaamal grinned at her.

"That's because you are very special."

Sam said

"I had a good teacher." Dear Kevin. Nothing came between the Rat Boy and his food.

When they reached the chalet Kaamal got out and Sam parked the car. She found him standing at the corner of the building watching Ata who, to all appearances, had not moved since she had left him that morning. He suddenly became aware and stood up, turning towards Kaamal, anxious eyes searching.

For a moment an unwavering shaft of golden light seemed to span the distance between them.

Kaamal nodded and like the bowled ball went toward the locked gaze.

Just like in cricket Sam thought.

He dropped his bag and took Ata in his arms. Ata was weeping quietly.

Sam thought,

The moon *and* the stars...

Eventually Sam made her decision and announced to the two men at breakfast that she would be returning home; that she had booked a flight from Chandigarh to Delhi the following day and would they mind delivering her to the airport. They looked at each other and then Ata said he had some calls to make before they went out and slipped away.

Sam went to her room and Kaamal followed her in.

"He's phoning London to-"

Sam burst into tears. She had not intended to cry. She had not felt like crying but once she started she couldn't stop. Kaamal came and put his arms around her, holding her close.

"My dear Samanthar. It cannot be so bad."

Sam cried harder. This was the second time she'd cried like this in recent days; before that it was when Vivian- she cried more.

Kaamal said very quietly

"You're getting very wet. I'm getting very wet. You do not have to leave. Come and live with us."

Though not intentional it had the desired effect. Sam pulled her head back and gazed up at him.

"Come and live with you? Are you insane?"

"Why not? We're in love not joined at the hip."

"Maybe now is the time to acquaint you with the meaning of the word gooseberry!"

"I'm guessing it means some kind of intruder or intrusion or maybe even chaperone? But you wouldn't be."

Sam stared at him and then suddenly realised what he'd been saying.

"Ata is phoning London? He's phoning to tell them he's leaving?"

"Yes."

Sam burst into tears once more and Kaamal pulled her close again.

"This is not good news?"

"Yes" said Sam between sobs. "It's probably the best news I'll ever have in my life again, ever."

He stroked her head for a few moments and then said

"You must not give up hope."

"That's what Ata said" Sam sniffled.

"It helps if there is more than one in the equation" said Kaamal thoughtfully.

"You mean Ata and me?"

"Yes. Would Vivian give up hope?"

Sam thought.

"No. Never."

"Do you remember what I told you after Cawnpore?"

Sam nodded.

"When you get back to Delhi visit Gandhi's memorial again, early, before you leave. Promise me."

"I promise" Sam said.

"And whatever happens I want to know. We both want to know and I will tell you where we have decided to live and what we are doing and I will invite you, singular or plural, to come and stay with us for as long as you like."

He looked down at her then.

"Amazing. No puffy eyes."

"It has been remarked upon before" said Sam. "But I suspect I might be a panda?"

"Very becoming. While you repair I will go and see how far Ata has got with his disengagement. And then we can all go out into this wonderful morning."

Sam walked towards the bathroom and then turned and said

"Did you ask Ata about me staying with you?"

"It was his idea."

At that moment Ata came through the door.

"It is done" he announced.

Sam came back from the bathroom and flung her arms about him.

He laughed and then looked down at her.

"What's all this?" he said pointing to the black smudges all about her eyes.

Kaamal explained and Ata nodded in agreement over the open invitation and the visit to the Gandhi memorial.

He turned to Kaamal.

"You have told her where we met for that last time?"
Kaamal looked defensive.
"No. I haven't."
Ata said furiously,
"Why? Why would you not tell her that?"
"I didn't want to- to create any false-"
"False hope?" said Ata, his eyes flashing . "There is no such thing as false hope. There is just hope."
"For God's sakes" said Sam, "tell me where you met before you have your second break-up. Or is it the third? I'm losing track!"
"Gandhi's memorial" they both said together.
"Gandhi's memorial!" said Sam, parrot fashion, thinking obscurely of Kevin. "Really!"
"Yes really" said Ata. He glared at Kaamal and Kaamal glared back.
"So you obviously did not tell her what we did." Ata was furious.
"No I did not."
"What you did?" said Sam faintly, trying to imagine what two teenage boys would do on parting in a public place. "What *did* you do?"
Kaamal looked miserable. It was Ata who answered.
"We made a vow: 'where there is love there is life... and hope'. We vowed it would not be an ending."
Neither of them moved or said anything for what seemed like an hour but was probably only a few minutes and then Ata went across and flung his arms about Kaamal and kissed him with so much passion Sam thought she felt the earth move.
Should she leave?
She ventured,
" I understand, really I do. Kaamal didn't want to set me up for a fall."
They broke apart and Ata said
"I am so sorry. My nerves are still like bare electrical wires, sparking at everything. I have not long flown home to my

country, resigned from a job I have held for some years and found again –"

Kaamal was looking at him like a starving man looks at his first meal and Sam said

"Look, I'll go. I can go and amuse myself for a couple of hours, no problem."

"No!" They both said.

Sam went across and stood in front of them both.

"OK. So now I'm going to go and wash my face and then perhaps we could go for coffee somewhere and decide on the rest of the day. I want it to be good. I want to walk and drink in these glorious surroundings so their patterns are indelibly printed on my mind. And I understand where both of you were coming from and I appreciate both... so thank you."

She made for the bathroom and said over her shoulder

"And a thinking man once said 'all truly great thoughts are conceived while walking'. Let's go out and see if he's right. And I have one especially for you. Those who bring passion to love, will take it into hate when they fight. You will fight. But nothing needs to get broken."

They drove, they walked, they picnicked, they climbed; they sat in silence gazing at views that were designed for the soul to consider its immortality, like watching a panorama of rebirth. As Kaamal said

"If God was anywhere he was here."

"'Earth is crammed with heaven'" said Sam.

"Elizabeth Barrat Browning" Ata said.

Sam and Kaamal just stared, as if doctors, like lawyers, could not be credited with literary sensibilities.

They walked back to the car, Sam between the two men, arm in arm and she plied them with questions about their youth, their life together and apart and stored it all away; a Golden Treasury...like Ata's box...

They ate dinner and sprawled with wine in the large, windowed lounge and as if by mutual consent, no one suggested bed. So they talked and laughed and watched TV and listened to music and stretched out the hours. Sam didn't know if they were doing it for her or to avoid the separation of sleep, but accepted the gift. While they were together, while it was still dark with only the moon and the stars as sentinels, she need not think about the tomorrows...

Part way through the evening Kaamal, who was lounging against the sofa with Ata's head in his lap, gently playing with his hair, said easily

"I know you've been told about my early exploits with the deliciously young and nubile Ata in Delhi; has he told you about Goa?"

Sam looked at Ata. He was blushing ferociously, turning his pale brown skin a rather entrancing shade of peach.

"No. Nothing. What happened?"

Kaamal looked at Ata.

"Oh come on! It was very trying at the time but surely only amusing now?"

"In some small way" said Ata sadly, "I feel it characterises the struggles of my early years."

"That's what makes you so adorable" said Sam.

"What? The fact that I was a social pariah?"

"No" said Sam, leaning over to kiss him from the sofa.

"Because you made it through despite it. Didn't he?" She looked at Kaamal who as usual was looking at Ata.

"Yes" he said quietly.

"Go on then" said Ata in a voice he might use to the dentist who has just suggested the filling of a tooth.

"Well, as you know we were struggling to *be* alone together anywhere that didn't involve grass and pestilential bushes and possible discovery. It had been about eight months and he was about to turn 17 and I thought it would be a great idea to go somewhere; a proper trip; away from family. I suggested Goa, you remember? You were thrilled; wild life sanctuary; turtles!"

"And lots of history for you" said Ata smiling.

"Yes. That too. I suggested it to his parents and they thought it was a great idea. Such an improvement in their son since I took him in hand!" He giggled.

Ata blushed again.

"So we fixed a date, as close to his birthday as possible and I told my parents. I can remember my father giving me an odd look. I didn't think anything of it at the time but looking back... I wonder if he was suspicious. I mean I was almost 18... according to my mother, when he'd been 18 there had been dozens of girls hanging around him; so she said. Anyway I ignored it but unbeknown to me he'd asked a friend who lived in Panaji, the capital of Goa, to meet us at the railway station there and put us up for a couple of nights while we looked for somewhere to stay; we were flying to Mumbai and then catching the train. It started on the plane-"

"What did?" said Sam.

"The air hostesses-"

"You don't need to tell her about the air hostesses!" cried Ata in despair.

"They were all over you! Moths to a flame."

"They were all over you too!"

"Not in the same way. They flirted with me; they practically-"

"Kaamal!"

"Moving on" said Sam.

"OK. So we get picked up at the railway station and taken to this friend's house. A beautiful building; sort of Portugese/colonial; a huge rambling place, near the Mandovi river with its own ballroom and chapel, set in luscious green with rainbow trees. A bit faded but still quite beautiful... and there, lying in wait, there were two daughters... very un faded; red lipped maneaters and bristling with adolescent lust!"

Sam leaned forward. This was getting interesting."Did your father know?"

"I suspect he did. OK, I thought; we'll just stay a couple of nights; be polite and be on our way. We got shown to separate bedrooms and after dinner and an exhaustive tour of the more secluded parts of the gardens by the two sisters, we all went to bed. I strpped off and then went down the corridor to Ata's room. The elder of the sisters had shown a very special interest in him at dinner and I went to check if he was OK."

"Did they have names?" Sam inquired.

"No idea" said Kaamal.

"I think the elder one was called Safa" said Ata.

"Pure? Not so much!"

Ata blushed again.

"I went into the room and all I could see was two bodies, one on top of the other. I switched on the light and found Safa, as she was apparently called, stretched out over Ata... poor boy was twisting his head back and forth, trying to avoid her kisses and looked terrified. He always sleeps in the nude! So I hauled her off, pulled her out of his room and took her to mine."

"What did you do there?" asked Sam.

"What do you think I did? I made love to her."

"You made love to her?" squeaked Ata faintly. "You never told me that."

"You were in no state to hear it. Anyway what was I supposed to do? She was on you like a bloody praying mantis! I thought she was going to eat you."

"Did you really make love to her?" whispered Ata.

"Only enough to persuade her away from you. Not full conjugal rights! Not sure I could have managed that. She really wasn't my type. Then I told her if she tried it on with you again or said anything to any one I'd tell her father she'd tried to seduce me; and then I sent her back to bed."

Sam looked at him consideringly.

"You are really quite something!"

Kaamal dipped his head in acknowledgement.

"I'll take that as a compliment" he said.

Ata lifted his head from Kaamal's lap.

"You don't have to tell her about the other- incidents- do you?" he murmured persuasively. "You could just tell her about the birds and flowers and the beach; and the turtles; and what we did on my birthday night..."

Kaamal twisted his fingers in Ata's hair, smiling.

The smile turned inward; pictures curled up and out, like wreaths of mist, and took form...He remembered Old Goa, a magnificently preserved Portugese city rising out of a jungle; relics and churches, impressing Goan history so indelibly on the mind ...the remains of St Francis Xaviour in his solid silver casket; the still apparent wealth; the ferry trips, with carts and beasts and colourful friendly natives...very friendly...Ata beside him, clutching at his hand; trying to hide...

And then the beach; they chose a southerly one, hoping for easy accommodation but finding everywhere fully booked. So they'd slept together on the fawn sand tucked into the palm trees and pines...two robinson crusoes...the cocktails they'd had on Ata's birthday; a very Goan Pina Colada made from local coconut sap spirit hugely diluted in Ata's case with pineapple juice and topped with whipped cream...and he saw the birth day, with the turquoise Arabian Sea lapping the soft seductive sand; the walk along the empty miles to hidden coves; the sun setting and laying comatose on the tranquilly sentient water; and the moon rising and taking her place; and Ata, carved from beauty...a graven image...

Behind his eyes Ata was also seeing...the wildlife sanctuary, with its leopards and cobras, whose feline and reptilian grace had entranced and excited him in strange ways...the tiny turtles whose enthusiastic and rapid, awkward perambulation to the sea he had watched, laying in the sand beside them so he could follow their purposeful flight over what to them must have been a thousand miles of desert...the birds; so many varieties; so many hues... each one a miniature, perfect paintbox of colour... and walking into the water on his birthday night, hand in hand with Kaamal, looking up at the moon and then turning to him and pressing his water slicked, naked body against Kaamal's and breathing in his aroma, his passion, his strength, seeing the love in his eyes which reflected his own and laying down in the shallows, flesh upon flesh, becoming one and wondering...wondering if anything could ever feel or be greater than this moment...

Kaamal's fingers played with the dark strands of his hair...

Ata opened his locked box and took out the memories, one by one...

Sam watched them; she could see the green and gold, the rainbow colours, the blue, turquoise sea... the naked sand... the firm, young bodies clasped in passion... the memories... She could feel the love... She closed her eyes...

Sometime around 7 am Kaamal got up, stretched and announced he was going to phone the travel company office and bring them up to date and then the university and arrange for time off and then he would go and collect some breakfast and bring it back. Ata rang down for tea to be brought to the room and he and Sam sat in the window seat , which had a view of the hills and the snow capped peaks beyond and drank lemon tea.

Ata looked very tired and very happy.

Sam plied him with questions.

"Why did you not arrange to come back to be with Kaamal? It is obvious from your response to his/my fax how badly you wanted to."

Ata did not answer at once. He seemed to be examining his reasons in some detail, the small frown in evidence. Finally he said

"When we first came together I was 16 and, as you are now fully aware, socially inadequate. Kaamal was 17 and though we shared everything I think I saw him as the leader and I would have followed him anywhere. To hell and back! I was a boy and a child in many ways. I had no experience of love other than filial love and I was much more comfortable with birds and animals than I was with people. Kaamal came into my life like a hero from an old Persian tale and embraced me, body and soul. Whatever he had decided I would have been his disciple. And because he seemed to accept the severance of our relationship, so did I."

"So you've spent the last 12 years waiting for him to beckon?" said Sam, incredulously.

"Stupid, yes? I think that's what happened. And I didn't have a lot of time to think about it after the first couple of years; I had been brought up to believe that as an Indian in England I would have to study and work twice as hard to achieve the same results and so I did. When I was brave enough to think about Kaamal I thought maybe he had changed. I did not think he did not love me only that perhaps life had presented him with alternatives that he thought would be better- for both of us."

"I think it did. I think he tried. By the time I met him, well, let's just say I think he had decided that there was only one man for him and he too had been celibate for a while..." She paused and then added "From what you've told me I have assumed you have been celibate too. Is that right, because-"

"AIDS?" said Ata quietly. "I am aware of the tempest that is sweeping across the USA, particularly San Francisco and New York. As yet the cases in London are few...and here also... but a disease that destroys the immune system...at present its effects are incalculable and drugs to arrest its progress, still in their infancy... I have had no sexual relations with anyone other than Kaamal." He paused and looked at her, his soft brown eyes troubled. " Life has odd ways of compensating us, does it not? The storm is only just beginning..."

They were both silent.

Then Ata said,

"But despite his decision he still hadn't contacted me."

"No."

"Maybe it needed a catalyst" said Ata thoughtfully.

"Maybe it did. But when he stayed in touch, was it not obvious what he felt?"

"Oh yes."

"And so you waited" said Sam thoughtfully. "Waited for him to lead."

"Yes. Foolish, no?"

"Foolish yes! Ata, all that is understandable between two young boys of those ages. But now you are men with different personalities and there is no need for a hierarchy. Yesterday, when you got so angry with Kaamal not telling me about your last meeting place, and when you stuck to your guns on the parent issue, you levelled the playing field. There is no leader and follower any more. There is just understanding and negotiation and love in an equal relationship."

"So simple" said Ata smiling.

"And Ata, he needs your simplicity. Really he does! I love him to bits but he has a mind like a Mandala."

He grinned at her. Sam shrugged.

"Yeah I know" she said. "It takes one to know one."

They sat for a while and then Sam asked

"You know when you said Kaamal had told you everything, did you mean *everything*?"

"Do you mean did he tell me about making love with you?"

"Yes" said Sam. "That's exactly what I mean."

"Of course. You seem surprised."

"Just a bit" said Sam, thinking about the classic reaction to such a declaration between two newly united lovers. "It didn't bother you?"

"Bother me? Why should it?"

"Oh I don't know" said Sam sardonically, "because he loves you and makes love to me! Maybe I'm just old fashioned."

"Do you think that love is exclusive? Do you not think rather that the more that is shared the stronger it becomes? Love does not run out like petrol or sugar. It multiplies. I hold his heart as he does mine. Love is for sharing."

Sam sat looking at this slender piece of masculine beauty and said

"You are remarkable. Monogamy is almost built into modern DNA. Otherwise you're a cheat or a slut. Maybe it's different in gay relationships?"

"Possibly for some, although I believe many like a committed 'marriage'. But I'm not talking about casual sex here am I?" said Ata. "I'm talking about love."

She leaned up against him and put her head on his shoulder and thought about her relationship with Kaamal.

"Yes. Love. We should clone you! Did you not get girls, women chasing after you when you were training, when you worked in the hospital?"

"Chasing?"

"Yeah. Like the air hostesses or the un faded sisters. Wanting dates. Flirting."

"I don't know. I didn't notice."

Now who does that remind me of, thought Sam.

"What about boys? You must have noticed them?"

Ata looked a little uncomfortable.

"There were some yes. And I did notice but ..." he answered evasively.

"Kaamal?"

"Yes...there was one boy, training like me...we became friends but he wanted more...he came round one night and brought wine. I drank too much...dutch courage I suppose and it made me very sick. He spent the evening cleaning me up and bathing my forehead. It brought back memories and I told him about Kaamal...he was Indian too and had left a lover behind in Delhi who had been committed to a prearranged marriage...so we shared stories and remained friends...in the end he went home to India... and I never tried again..." He paused and then said "He would have made you happy you know. Kaamal."

Sam said

"Yes I think he would. But I would not have made him happy. I would just have reminded him-"

"Of me?"

"*Yes*. We should clone you!" she said again, pondering, as the door opened and breakfast arrived.

"You're wearing the frown" said Kaamal handing her several parcels of delicious smelling breads and dumplings and a dish of scrambled eggs.

"Your lover makes me think."

" My lover! That's right. Yes I know this to my cost." said Kaamal. "Sometimes I do not want to think" he murmered gazing at Ata, the look sensuous, covetous and pure gold.

Sam said

"Have either of you read Plato?"

Ata looked evasive. Kaamal said

"Not since college."

"'And when one of them meets with his other half, the actual half of himself, whether he be a lover of youth or a lover of another sort, the pair are lost in an amazement of love and friendship' or words to that effect. I think its from the Symposium."

They both looked at her expectantly.

"I did Greek studies at college. If I remember rightly The Symposium is a kind of after dinner discussion on Eros, with various presentations from key contributors. Aristophanes puts forward that humankind was originally created with two literal parts, faces, bodies; males were created thus and females and an androgynous model. Then, he claimed Zeus got jealous of their power and split them all in half. So from then on they all search for their other half, men for men; women for women and the androgynous become heterosexual."

"Yes. I remember" said Kaamal and looked at Ata.

"I too" he said.

"Really? Amongst all that biology and science!" said Sam.

Ata looked at Kaamal. He said

"You spoke of it once."

"I did?" Kaamal was astonished. "We discussed Plato?"

"No. You said the Ancient Greeks had a different attitude to sexuality; you were angry at the time I think. When we parted and I was studying in London, I looked it up."

They both stared at him.

"I was interested" he said as if it explained everything. "I was interested to see how attitudes and beliefs and time have altered people's perceptions; from Barbur, who thought it acceptable to fall in love with a young man in his camp and record it and his feelings in his journal, to now. One of the perceptions was that relationships between members of the same sex when they were young dissolved when they grew older. So I waited to see."

Kaamal and Sam were still looking at him. Then Sam said

"I've said this several times. We should clone you!"

Kaamal finally took his eyes from Ata and said

"Only if I can keep the original."

It was a late flight so it was a mutual decision to have one last stroll out through the trees and up onto the nearest vantage point to see the mountain ranges. Kaamal shouldered a rucksack with two flasks of coffee, one with strong, black and the other with hot milk, especially for Sam, he said. Ata announced that he liked it half and half as well and Kaamal raised despairing eyebrows at both of them but complied.

Sam, standing between the two young men and drinking milky coffee, staring out over the footprints of the gods, thought- it doesn't get any better than this. And then Ata looked down at her and said in a quiet voice

"The end is also the beginning."

Kaamal heard his words and smiled.

"For all of us" he said.

Sam looked from one to the other.

"You've made some kind of decision?"

"In part" said Kaamal. "I've handed in my notice at the university and taken all the leave I am owed. I have told the travel company I will continue to offer my services when I can." He looked at Ata who said

"We are going to do some travelling in Himachal Pradesh and Uttarakhand and look for somewhere to live."

Sam was speechless.

Kaamal said

"This is good news, yes?"

Sam nodded.

"So. No need for tears?"

Sam shook her head.

"And you, when you have revisited Gandhi's memorial, you will phone us and let us know your- plans?"

Sam nodded.

"You promise?" said Ata.

Sam found her voice.

"I promise."

She flew from Chandigarh to Delhi and gazed out of the window at the cotton wool clouds that perversely reminded her of snow-capped mountains, and thought about walking back through the doors of the hotel where she had first met Kaamal, running the memories like a slow rewind of a movie. Up here, in an otherworldly vacuum, between the cloud quilt and the timeless forever, anything seemed possible.

She had refused to let Kaamal and Ata come to see her off but left them at the airport doors. Ata had held her very close and then kissed her hands and handed her to Kaamal who had kissed her on the lips with gentle vehemence and said

"I will miss you, but not for long I hope?"

while Ata simply looked on and smiled. She watched them walk away, turn and wave, look at each other, their hands lightly clasped, then walk on and she went through the doors before they were lost to her view...

But as the aircraft began its descent, once again she was forced to admit that she could not coerce fate or the universe into opening the right door. She had followed Kevin's advice and travelled extensively revisiting past explorations and some new ones along the way. They were always outside odds. Maybe the time had come to acknowledge that she had rolled the dice and lost. *And I am nailed to the cross of my own dreams...*

She remembered a piece of writing by Sylvia Plath which had always seemed particularly evocative.

Her tranquil features were set in a slight secret smile of triumph, as if, in some far country unattainable to mortal men, she were, at last, walking with the dark, red caped prince of her early dreams...

Was that how it was going to end for her? A quiet resting place and a secret smile? Would that be so very bad?

She got a taxi and returned to her hotel and asked Rajesh, still stationed behind his desk, most delighted to see her and full of questions, if he would mind booking her a flight out of Delhi tomorrow and then went up to her room to sort out clothes to travel in and documents and pack the rest. There was a knock on the door and it was Rajesh to say that he had booked a flight and she would be leaving at 16.30 on the following afternoon and would she like him to book her a taxi to take her to the Airport? Sam smiled gratefully and accepted the offer. That would give her time for the last visit to the Rajghat, the memorial gardens where Gandhi's ashes lay; the place of farewells and vows...

The fulfilment of her promise to Kaamal and Ata.

Ata had been insistent. He had seemed to see it as a connection between them all. She had told him of her first visit those years ago as well as the recent one with Kaamal. The voices she had heard in the stillness behind the chatter of modern day life. He had quoted Gandhi to her.

"'Truth stands even if there be no public support. It is self-sustained'. You must follow your truth."

Kaamal had not been so sure; clearly outcomes still worried him. Sam got the sense that after what had happened he was prepared to think anything possible but was nevertheless still concerned for her.

Thankfully he had forborne to say *It is as Allah wishes,* but it had been in his eyes. Dear man!

And there in that place, in the early morning, two young boys had made their vow: Two young boys quoting a man of different faith who they honoured for his honesty, who had said,

"Where there is love there is life."

Well there was love...

She arose the next morning and early, just after dawn, so that she might with luck be able to walk through the gardens of the Rajghat before any crowds descended upon them. She had taken a loose leaf pad with her in the hopes that she would hear again the troubled, sorrowing voices that she had heard on that long ago first visit and record her impressions of them. Old style. But all was quiet. But for the awakening song of the many birds and the sounds of a city coming to life in the background, there was only the quiet dead.

She sat down on a low wall with the pad on her knee, gazing out at the small, cone shaped trees on the periphery of the paved walkway. It had all been for nothing. One risk too far. All those experiences, all those fragmentations, all the effort she had put in –to make a whole of me. Perhaps after all she was just destined to be alone...

A small impish dawn breeze sprang up and before she knew it had whipped the pad from her knees, dislodged the sheets and scattered them carelessly all about the grass around her.

"Damn-bloody-nation!"

She jumped to her feet and began chasing them around the area, not so much to prevent the loss of their unprepossessing content but to try and stop them making an unholy mess. But the breeze was negligently mischievous and thwarted her.

She was watching them, cursing the flagrant disobedience of ordinary objects which seemed to be part of everyday life when suddenly she was aware of a shadow falling on her. She gave up on the attempt to capture the remaining sheets and straightened up. And froze.

There was a man standing a little way from her. A tall man, in faded denims and a black T shirt, which had a yellow smiley face on it with the words

I can't keep a straight face'

emblazoned across it. He was wearing a black baseball cap with a strange logo on the front. The rising sun was behind him and the peak of the cap was pulled down so his face was partly hidden but she could see deep set eyes, almost black with their querulous expression.

As she stood, rooted to the spot he reached up and removed the headgear and set it down on the low wall where she had been sitting a few moments before and said

"Good morning; can I be of assistance?"

He was possibly the most beautiful member of the male species that she had ever seen. His hair, freed from the cap, was blonde, streaked with sun scorched gold and silver, mismanaged straight, and gently lifting in the wind and his skin was tanned a deep honey brown. It was impossible to determine his age; there was experience in the well carved features but also a childlike innocence. But his fascinating eyebrows were black and slightly arched, reiterating the question he had just posed.

She simply stared at him, gaping at the T-shirt monogram and unable to think of anything to say that that would not sound bizarre.

He saw her attention fixed on the slogan and smiled.

"I'm not-", he struggled for a moment with the word, "gay? I went to buy a T-shirt and this one just spoke to me." He shrugged. His elegant shoulders were broad but somehow insubstantial giving him a boyish and oddly ephemeral look.

Sam remained mute.

He looked around at the scattered papers and said

"I can see that you are fighting a losing battle with these miscreants but another pair of hands might help? And then perhaps we could go somewhere and-"

It was like taking elocution lessons. His voice was deep, resonant yet soft, like being stroked with warm velvet. She didn't know whether he was inviting her to his hotel, his estate or his bed and she really didn't care. He apparently could also read minds because his perfect lips curved and his eyebrows went a little higher as he said

"Nothing untoward I do assure you. But you seem a little-perturbed... so, a coffee, chai?"

Sam nodded, still dumb, her mind racing. What was happening?

For some unaccountable reason she looked down at his hands. The right was stuck in his jeans pocket; the left, with its long, slender well shaped fingers, was hanging loosely by his side and on the second finger from the left there was a plain, slim band of antique gold.

He caught the look and glanced down and then he looked straight at her left hand which was partly covering her lips as if to avert a betrayal of sound.

He frowned at the slender antique gold band on the second finger from the left. Then he looked at the willowy gold strands, that she always wore threaded through her ears, turned to dazzling light by the rising sun. The frown deepened as if his mind was grappling with a conundrum. His eyes ranged over her hair, escaping from a very unruly clip at the back of her head, and also hued by the sun's rays and then travelled down the contours of her body so that she felt she'd just been stripped. Then his brow cleared and he looked back, into her eyes. He murmured

"There is no bridge that love cannot cross; no door through which love cannot pass" and raised his eyebrows at her. His eyes, under the fierce black brows, were alight. Sam held her breath.

He said carefully

"My name's Vivian. What's yours? I feel as if I know you-"
He paused and then said in Urdu

"My heart tells me I know you." and then in English again
"Have we met before?"

'you will discover that for you the world is transformed!'

Sam nodded. His eyebrows went a little higher and did a small dance. He seemed to want more.

"Samanthar" squeaked Sam, and cleared her throat, "my name is Samanthar, long for Sam. And yes, we have met before."

And then in Urdu
"A long time ago…"

And then in English
"Let us now understand that our journey so far
Was chosen with care, to bring us to here …"

The expression in his eyes changed his whole face. He whispered

"Samanthar."

He said it again as if to test its sound against his understanding.

"Samanthar."

Sam gazed at him solemnly and pulled from her back pocket a small plastic wallet from which she took three folded scraps of yellowed, coarse, Indian paper. He stared at them.

"Beyond life…"

His words echoed between them.

'And time, the 'longest distance between two places', stood still…'

Nothing moved. The breeze was stilled, the birds hushed. They didn't speak. They simply looked.

Finally Sam said quietly

"There are two friends of mine you must meet. They'll love the T-shirt!" In a few years time, after the advent of the mobile phone, she could have rung Ata on the spot and heard his ecstatic squeak of joy and triumph. And then, "they will want to meet you...they will want us to stay with them..."

She was gabbling; Vivian was laughing.

"We must go to my hotel. I have a plane to cancel and a phone call to make."

The phone call that would make this real.

She looked at the man standing in front of her, watchful, intent; incredulity vying with hope...

She said

"Have you been to Himachal Pradesh?"

He did not seem surprised by the seemingly random question.

Instead he smiled and the smile was sunshine through rain, Indra's bow, splashing the world with colour. He said

"Yes. I have seen Tara Devi, the Goddess of the Stars and made my offering... And I have been to Chandra Tal, the Lake of the Moon. And I reached out and touched a million stars... It was bitterly cold in my tent, but then I went alone."

His eyes told her it was all he needed. He closed the distance between them and took her in his arms, his embrace fierce, holding her close to dispel the dream, crushing the breath from her body, and the multiplicity of thoughts that crowded her mind.

Leaving just William Blake.

'But he who kisses the joy as it flies lives in Eternity's sunrise.'

He pulled the clip from her hair and pushed his fingers into the loosened strands. Then as she leaned back to look at him, he took her face between his hands and his kiss ...

'soul meets soul on lover's lips'

brought the past into the present and united them.

* * *

A wise man once wrote 'true love stories never have endings'; and a wise woman,

'Whatever our souls are made out of, his and mine are the same.'

And of course Plato, and the importance of two halves to make a whole.

Where would it all end?

She remembered asking Kevin once, "what am I doing Kevin?"

And Kevin, inscrutable as ever, had said "I think you are exploring alternative realities that other 'yous', in the past and possibly in the future, have considered. Paths that your various choices have taken you down."

And she had asked him plaintively, why?

And he had said

" Mmm...'Why'- the road to self discovery." And then he'd said

"You're a bit of an extremist Sam. The green and gold Knight; the black and silver Knight. Maybe you're trying to align the two."

And she had said, "so I'm looking for khaki am I?"

And she remembered his response very clearly.

"You are looking for balance."

"And when I achieve this magical and estimable balance, if I ever do, what will it bring me?"

And Kevin had sat up on its haunches, with his paws in front of him, like a small furry Buddha and said

"Love."

Was this just another alternative life? Another path? Another Sam, Samanthar?

Just another one of those lives she had been going through for as long as she could remember and if so, how long would this one last? Would she suddenly wake up and bump back into some dreary reality like falling out of bed onto a hard floor?

Was she still on the wheel? Had she stepped off it to enjoy the merit she had earned?

Did it matter?

She looked into the dark eyes of a man called Vivian.

No, it didn't matter...

If I shatter,

let it be,

For from the pieces

We might

make

a whole of

Me.

Go beyond thinking to just being...Where the 'I' is the doorway- the archway- between the inner and the outer worlds.

I remember the archway thought Sam. I remember walking under the archway from the outer to the inner, from the corridors of the citadel to its inner sanctum. I remember-...

While we are fragmentations we feel pain, we feel fear, and we feel alone.

But when we are One we amalgamate with the whole. Then there is no fragmentation, no pain, no fear, only being. We have been the drop of water in the waterfall and now we are the drop of water in the river. Again.

The individual

The world.

The universe.

The drop of water.
    The river.
    The ocean.

A whole of me.

The door.
    Am I close Kevin?

And Kevin, who had seated himself Buddha style on the low wall next to Vivian's hat, sighed with satisfaction and then took an experimental nibble at the peak of the cap. He'd had worse.

Life presents us with doorways and circles.
    Doors – some are locked; bolted; barred; no handles; some have signs on them – Private
    Or
    No Entry
    Or
    At Your Own Peril...

Circles- the medicine wheel, the Mandala, the sun...the serpent eating its own tail...

The western world believes in linear time, thought Sam. So I chose the East, where there are some who believe in circles...

"Where does it all end Kevin?"
    "Well it doesn't end does it? You know that now."
    "Yes and no. Right now it all feels like a weird dream."
    "Dream; illusion; reality; who knows? Who cares? Your choice."
    "My choice" Sam mused.
    "That's all there is Sam-love and your right to choose."

Then she knew. They weren't just doorways, archways... They weren't just circles...they were life. And this? This was just the beginning.

She took a deep breath, and in an amazement of love and friendship, walked through The Door.

You can spend your whole life, a bird in a cage; the door is open but you don't see it, so you keep on fluttering around and around, banging up against the bars...but there are no bars, there are no limitations, boundaries or barriers, except of your making; accept your freedom; the cage door is open; you are the drop of water in the river and the river itself, and you are capable of being anything you desire...

The Little Dancer

She says it all, the little dancer,
With her hands behind her back;
With her little chin stuck forward,
With her beauty, grace, and lack.
She is set towards a future,
While at present in repose;
Too wise to try to shape it;
Enough to know she chose.

*

Be not fooled by her countenance,
Calm bought at a price.
For life has had its turmoil,
And fortune played its dice.
But note the one foot forward,
To step, if step it needs;
The quiet self assurance,
That can follow where it leads.

You may fail to understand her,
For she keeps her counsel well.
Her inner thoughts, her own domain,
And hers to keep or tell.
But the peace you sense surrounds her,
Is balance of all parts;
A completeness without ending,
Where deepest wisdom starts.

Take courage, Oh little dancer,
That you have come this far;
Take pride, *life performer,*
That you are who you are!

To be continued...

Excerpt from THE DOOR
PART TWO
The Big Rock Candy Mountain

Sam and Vivian had gone to live with Kaamal and Ata. After that first phone call from a Delhi hotel telling Ata what had happened in Gandhi's gardens, he had invoked the standing invitation and Vivian and Samanthar had flown to Chandigarh. After that it just fell into place. Sam sold everything she owned in America and never went back. Vivian had family money going back generations. Ata and Kaamal were living together in the north of Himachal Pradesh in a modest home of modest proportions. After some months together it was plain to all that they could share their living arrangements and their lives with one another. So. they all decided on and contributed to the purchase of the large and comfortable house that resided on a hill overlooking the valley, and made it their home.

Samanthar named it The Dilkhusha Khoti...The Palace of Heart's Desire...

And there they stayed.

Sam wrote and researched history and legend with Kaamal. Kaamal taught in three local schools and discussed history and writing and the vagaries of the educational system with Sam.

Vivian explored the history of the state, travelling to its furthest remote corners and debated anthropology and entomology with Ata, and taught local children to ride and the older ones, to play polo. Ata worked in three local hospitals and shared his insect and ethnic passions with Vivian.

They walked, rode and climbed, together, in pairs and sometimes individually.

Children were never part of the equation. Never. But when Samanthar discovered, (how did that happen?) eighteen months in, that she was pregnant all the men were delighted. Sam, not so much. Sam had been thinking about the past; and the future. Sam had been thinking about the mountain where there are no footprints and only God sees where the snow falls...

She had been thinking about doorways in time...and Vivian...

That all had to be postponed.

www.ingramcontent.com/pod-product-compliance
Lightning Source LLC
Chambersburg PA
CBHW020929020726
47495CB00002B/409